I0780882

MADDY

Book Two:

A Woman of Good Standing Trilogy

Cathi Bond

MONTREAL PUBLISHING COMPANY

ISBN: 978-1-998353-06-4
Maddy/Cathi Bond—1st edition.

Any references to historical events, real people, or real places are used fictitiously. Names, characters, and places are products of the author's imagination.

Editors: Christian Fennell and Nathalie Guilbeault
Cover art: Yevhen Verlen
Cover design: Nelligan Design

www.montrealpublishing.com
www.cathibond.com

MADDY

Book Two:

A Woman of Good Standing Trilogy

Cathi Bond

CHAPTER ONE

Our family lived in a three-story white frame house with a deep wooden veranda in a small town called Sterling in southwestern Ontario. Dad's medical practice was on the main floor on one side of the house, and we lived in the other. The day after they moved in, Mom carefully stripped the veranda floor, stained the wood and bought matching his and hers chaises. She loved the two stately horse chestnut trees that stood on either side of the house, certain they'd keep the home cool in the summer. Instead, the trees mercilessly dropped their blossoms and nuts into the eaves with Mom having to spend nearly every autumn weekend up on a ladder. There was no lassoing Dad into doing the job. He always used the same excuse, "I think that sick people are more important, don't you?" Mom, on her way out the back door in her gardening gloves, didn't look so sure.

The house was located on the busiest road in the village, a murderous stretch of Highway 10 that turned into McKenzie Street, as it made its way through Sterling and shot out again at the other end of town. The McKenzie began at a gas station and short-order restaurant at the top of the hill that served truckers mostly burgers, fries, and pies. The hurtling trucks, their drivers jacked up on instant coffee, sped by our house at breakneck speeds and, more than once, an unfortunate family pet was chewed up and cast aside by a thundering eighteen-wheeler. When all that remained of the neighbour's three-year-old apricot poodle who loved to hump children was a smashed jewel-encrusted collar, Mom and Dad sat me down and sternly warned me to never, ever leave the backyard. I was only five at the time, and down the street, within eyeshot if I craned my neck, stood Comfort's Diner, a candy castle of chips, toffee, and creamy chocolate milkshakes poured from frosty stainless-steel blenders. It was also full of older kids doing things that were a lot more fun than what was going on at my house.

The first time they discovered me sneaking across the neighbour's backyard to Comfort's, Mom gave me a "love tap," my mother's version of a spanking. No pants were ripped down. No belt flying around, or dark warnings of the woodshed. I was tapped and sent to my room where I dug out my Chatty Cathy doll from under the bed. I'd begun an operation earlier that day and was trying to remove Cathy's voice box from her chest with a screwdriver.

"I love you, do you love me?" Cathy asked.

"No, I don't," I replied. I was too old for dolls. Mom had just given her to me for my eighth birthday, when I really wanted dungarees and a pellet gun.

Cathy didn't have her top on. While I was digging a screwdriver into her back there was a long, howling screech of tires followed by a horrible, mangled bang, punctuated by a woman's scream. Forgetting my punishment, I ran down the stairs and followed Mom out the door and onto the veranda and across the snow-covered lawn.

Dad was already there, on his hands and knees in a pool of blood, cradling a little girl younger than me in his lap. The blood ran out of the back of her head, seeping onto Dad's trousers. One eye was open, staring at the sky. The other was shut. The driver had both hands clamped over his mouth while the mother screamed for Dad to save her little girl. Mom approached the mother, wrapping her arm around her shoulder, drawing her close. They were a new family who'd moved in down the street last year.

"Why don't you come into the house," Mom said, gently pulling the woman away from the road. "Teddy will do all that he can."

I stood and stared as Dad lifted the child from the road. How could she be alive? Her neck was twisted like Chatty Cathy's when I spun her head around. I followed Dad as he carried the girl across the snow, her head lolling in the crook of his arm, face tilting toward the sky. The sidewalks were filling with grim-faced spectators, some in coats, most not, while a police siren howled in the distance. Could that ever happen to me? Running ahead of Dad, I threw open the office door. He carried the little girl into an examining room and carefully set her on the examining table. He glanced down at her limp body and started to cry. My fists rolled themselves into hard balls. I didn't like it when my father cried; it made me antsy—my father was a man who cried a lot.

"Can you save her, Dad?"

"She's dead, Maddy."

Gently, he closed her open eye and pulled a white sheet over the little girl's body. Was she a ghost now? Could she fly like Casper or was she just dead and buried like President Kennedy? Everyone was so upset when he died last November. I looked away to the neon sign from Comfort's Diner cutting faint flashes of red into the blue sky of the dwindling day, and thought, death can come so fast with no warning at all.

It took more than a month, but I couldn't resist the diner any longer. Peering into Mom's study, where she worked on her project to help African children, I put on my coat, slid open the patio door, and sprinted across the neighbour's backyard, ducking behind trees and hiding behind the bushy cedar hedge, looking to see if anyone was coming. All clear. Standing up, I kicked my way through the drifts, dreaming about gumballs and toffee, when there was a bellow. Dad, wielding a yardstick, roared across the neighbour's yard, legs pumping up and down while his striped tie bannered out behind him. There was no way I could make it to Comfort's. I had to make a break for the gully.

The gully was deep, a natural home for tobogganing and sledding. Beyond it stretched a mile of scrubby field, dotted with only a line of telephone poles, where it was eventually severed by the railway track.

Glancing over my shoulder, I saw Dad was getting closer. Mom having joined in the chase, her red and white polka dot dress spreading out behind her, was calling, "Stop, Teddy! Stop!"

Dad wasn't listening. He was all red, huffing and puffing. Running toward a thick line of bramble where I knew there was a hole, I dove in. Scratching and digging, I heard a rip as my coat tore. A black freight train picked up speed in the distance. I tasted mud and ice. My body was nearly through when a big, meaty hand grabbed me by the ankle, and with a hard yank, my father pulled me out of the bramble, back to the civilized side of the lawn.

Dad dropped to one knee and threw me over the other. The yardstick came crashing down. Once, twice, three times. Mom pulled on Dad's arm, begging him to stop. I knew it was wrong, but I couldn't help it. I started to laugh. Dad's face flamed like fire.

"Don't you remember that child?" he shouted. "That child is dead!"

Up went the coat and down came the stick on bare skin. Real pain came this time, followed by tears. Mom pulled on Dad's arm.

"Teddy, stop it!"

The yardstick fell into the snow as Dad grabbed me, holding me tight, kissing me, asking repeatedly, "Why did you do that?" he asked, starting to cry.

"I just wanted some candies."

Mom pulled a handkerchief out of her skirt pocket and wiped away my tears. "Oh Maddy, why are you so willful?"

Why was willful bad? Now that the show was over, the neighbours who had assembled on their back stoops slowly filed back into their houses. The three of us walked hand in hand through the snow. Dad felt terrible about spanking me. He was still crying when the workmen installed a chain-link fence the next day. They said the ground was too hard and it could wait until spring, but Dad didn't care what it cost. Mom stood on the back patio as sledgehammers finally broke through the frozen earth, sadly watching "the blight" go up. The neighbours tried to convince her that it wasn't all that bad, but Mom knew it was ugly. She went back into her study to work.

Watching her work so hard to help others, I felt bad for ruining Mom's backyard, but I was equally upset I'd lost my last chance for a sneak solo run to Comfort's.

The fence never came down. Not when my younger brother, "Frankly I wish you'd never been born," came into the world, and not even eight years later, when Tedder arrived. Mom and Dad didn't want to risk one of the boys making a break for the diner, but they didn't have to worry. Frank always did what he was told, and Tedder was still too small. Frank got his name after Mom's great-grandfather and Tedder was short for Theodore, a name that had been in the Barnes family since we first arrived from Scotland in the late 1700s. I was named Madeline Anne, Anne after Mom's oldest sister, and Madeline because my mother had always wanted to go to France. She loved to wear French cologne. Eau de Joy was her favourite, and whenever she passed through a room the scent lingered.

I could smell her Joy in the backseat as we passed through an old mill town on the way to Granddad's farm. Frank was counting hockey cards while Tedder played with Kanga and Roo, two stuffed animals Mom made for him that he took everywhere. Mom and Dad were singing their song.

"Never thought my heart could be so yearning. Why did I decide to roam? I gotta take this sentimental journey. Sentimental journey home."

"No more," I moaned, clapping my hands over my ears. Since I'd turned twelve, I'd decided to hate all old-time music.

Mom just sang louder. Tedder started dancing Kanga and Roo on my head as the Oldsmobile clattered over a rickety bridge that spanned a churning river below. A group of kids played hockey on a ridge of ice that shot out from the shore. Blue water rushed past them, racing down the centre of the river. Frank said it was risky playing near open water like that, but I thought it looked exciting.

"How long can a person survive in freezing water before they die?" I asked, leaning over the front seat of the car.

"Not long. First you sink, then your body starts to fill up with gases and eventually you'd float back up," Dad replied.

A sheet of ice slid off the top of a truck in front of us, smashing onto the road. Dad veered.

"Like that dead cat in Granddad's pond?"

Dad nodded. Ick. The cat's eyeballs were gone and the rest of it was green and foamy with bones poking out. Granddad had seen the coons chewing at the corpse.

"Morbid," Mom said, opening her compact.

A deep red spear rolled up out of the silver lipstick tube and Mom's face flashed in the mirror. Her eyes were green, and her auburn hair was flecked with strands of gold. My hair was much darker than hers, with no gold. Plain old black hair with big blue eyes. The kids at school called me

Bug Eyes Barnes. I reached forward, slowly running the palms of my hands down the sides of her hair. Electricity made the soft strands cling to my skin.

"You don't need any makeup," Dad said, his hand reaching for hers.

"Dad's right," I said, throwing my arms around her, nuzzling my face into her hair. "You're perfect just the way you are."

Nothing else smelled like Mom. It was home and something I couldn't quite name—something dark and mysterious and sweeter than chocolate. Mom's hand touched mine.

"Don't muss my hair, honey."

Reluctantly, I pulled away as she dropped her head onto Dad's shoulder. That was going to mess up her hair more than I would. I rolled down the window.

"Mom, it's cold," Frank complained.

"Too bad," I snapped.

"Maddy, shut the window," Mom said, lifting her head from Dad's shoulder and turning to look at me. I pretended not to notice.

"We don't want to get those ear infections going again," Dad added.

Ignoring them all, I put my arm out, and cupping the wind in my hand, let it arc and dive with the gulls that soared over the river. The sting of the cold, sharp wind felt good.

An old car was parked at a restaurant across the road.

"Say, doesn't that look like Dad's old Dodge?" Dad asked, with a sad smile.

Mom nodded. Normally Dad didn't talk too much about his parents since they had both passed. I didn't even get to go to Grampa's funeral. My father believed it was better to remember people the way they were when they were still alive, not stuffed in a box on display.

"Where's Aunt Bette?" I asked. Dad's younger sister was what my other aunts called a "real firecracker." When I was little, I thought it was because her hair was even redder than Aunt Anne's, but now that I was much more mature, I understood it was likely due to her temperament. Aunt Bette wasn't all proper manners like the Gillespie women. She was a stout-hearted nurse who always spoke her mind and wore dungarees on the weekends. I knew that Mom didn't approve of those pants, but they made me like her even more. Mom was so old fashioned when it came to clothing.

"She's busy with her patients," Dad replied, glancing quickly at Mom, who was still looking out the window.

"You always say that," I complained. "That's an old excuse."

"And here we are!" Mom said, as we arrived at Granddad's farm.

Giant spruces with snowy branches like greatcoats lined the drive as we approached Granddad's enormous two-story, red-brick house. The shutters stood open, and a wraparound veranda hugged the house like a clean, white apron.

"I want to see Aunt Bette!" I repeated. I always knew when my parents were keeping secrets from me.

"The lower branches need trimming," Mom said to nobody, and then turned to me. "And Maddy, Bette will be over as soon as she's got the time, so please settle down."

Granny Gillespie had planted the line of trees when she was a newlywed. She wanted shade in the summer and a place for her children to play. Granny had died three years ago and now the trees were huge, with thick branches like ladders that my cousins and I loved to climb. We hooted like Robin Hood and his Merry Men when we poked our heads out at the top, gazing over the acres of farmland for miles around. As the Oldsmobile made its way toward Granddad's house, I wondered what it would be like to climb the trees in the winter and look out over the snow.

As Dad pulled onto the parking pad, I could see Cousin Hugh and the other boy cousins playing hockey on the pond out past the cattle pens.

The pad was full of cars. The relatives were already there. Frank grabbed his stick and skates from the floor of the car and reached for the handle.

"Can I go?" he asked.

Mom nodded her head as Dad turned off the car.

"Me too," I said, snatching my skates.

"Where do you think you're going?" Mom asked.

"To play hockey."

Frank grinned. I wanted to punch him.

"You know you have to help in the house," she said.

Throwing the skates back on the floor with a bang, I kicked the car door open. Frank was already past the pens, running toward the pond while the other boys called hello.

"It's not fair," I grumbled.

Dad said that kitchen skills were important for the manhunt.

"She's too young for that," Mom said, reaching for the door handle. "And I don't believe in the manhunt."

Dad smiled at her. "Neither do I, but it is part of life."

"Not my Maddy," she replied. "If she finds a man she loves, that's wonderful, but that's not her purpose in life. She's going to get an education. I want her always to be able to find her way."

Since I was old enough to understand, Mom was always telling me how vitally important it was not to end up a slave chained to a stove. I smiled to myself, thinking about how Mom was no wizard in the kitchen.

Dad turned around and squeezed my thigh. "Can't Maddy play with the boys?" he asked. My parents always encouraged me to have fun, since they had to work so hard when they were little.

"Just this once?" he asked, again.

Mom pulled on her ear and looked toward the house. I knew she was thinking about her sisters, who always said that I was spoiled and didn't know how to pull my own weight.

"I'll help," I said, changing my mind.

"Are you sure?" Mom asked.

When I nodded my head, my mother smiled at me.

A shop where the men sat, smoked, and spat while tinkering with tractor engines stood to the west, and there was an open cattle pen to the south. A hundred or more head shifted and mooed as we crossed the yard, staring at us through the wooden slats. Frank was already at the pond pulling on his skates. Even though Frank was younger than the cousins, he had the best slap shot in the family.

"Is that you, Laura?" Granddad bellowed, as he swung out onto the back porch.

Granddad was a tall, strong man with a stand of white hair and a sharp, bristly white beard. He wore his pants high, held there by a thick black leather belt, and a white dress shirt rolled up just beneath his elbows.

Since Granny died it, fell to Mom and her sisters to take care of Granddad's needs, and he sure had a lot of them. He was a busy cattleman who couldn't boil water, so every weekend, one of "the girls," as Mom and her sisters were known, had to come and take care of the house. Once I overheard Aunt Anne talking to Mom in the kitchen.

"Dad hasn't bounced back since Mother's death. If he had, he'd be able to manage the place better."

"You worry too much," Mom said.

"You don't worry enough," Aunt Anne replied.

Granddad seemed just fine to me.

While Granddad was walking toward Mom, the screen door exploded and a scruffy, brownish dog tore down the stairs and across the yard, leaping at Tedder knocking him flat on his back, fangs snarling and snapping in his face. Tedder screamed. A zipper of terror ran up my neck. Granddad always had mean dogs, but this one, Buster, was the worst. Dad shoved Buster off with his foot, sweeping Tedder up in his arms.

"Dad!" Mom exclaimed. "Why isn't Buster tied up?"

"What good's a tied dog if you've got thieves and weasels?" Granddad growled at Dad. Then he gave Mom a light kiss on the cheek. "How are you, Laura?"

"Honestly," she replied, returning the kiss, along with a stern look. "You should get rid of that dog."

Granddad ignored her while Dad asked Tedder if he was okay. Tedder buried his head in Dad's shoulder and held on even tighter.

"Of course, the boy's okay," Granddad said. "If you can't face down a dog, you're not good for much, are you?" he asked. Then he turned to me.

"How's my girl?" Granddad asked, giving me a good hard pinch on the cheek.

"Fine, sir," I replied with a smile, even though the pinch really hurt.

"And how's Tedder?" he asked, reaching out to give Tedder his pinch.

But Granddad missed, because Dad turned away with Tedder still in his arms. Granddad started pinching us when we were old enough to walk. Sometimes they were hard enough to turn into welts, but being able to take them was part of being a Gillespie. Granddad always said you had to be tough to rise in God's world, and only the strong survived. Tedder hid his face in Dad's neck. He sure didn't look like much of a Gillespie right now.

"Come and get your pinch, son," Granddad said, a bit louder than he needed to.

"We should get lunch on," Mom said, looking toward the house, but Granddad didn't answer. He and Dad were staring at each other.

"He's just a little boy," Dad said quietly.

"There's no boy too young to start being a man," Granddad replied. "Go!" he said, and Buster lunged. Granddad laughed as the dog leapt and snapped. Dad turned away. Mom hesitated a moment, then followed him, trying to keep the peace.

"So Maddy, are you going to help your mother make me a pie?" he asked, giving Buster a sharp whistle. The dog immediately returned.

"I'd rather play hockey, sir," I replied, watching the boys on the ice.

"Women shouldn't play hockey. You need skills," he said, following my gaze. "How's Frank's team doing?" he asked. All anyone seemed to care about was Frank and his sports. "Do you think he's going to win another trophy?" Granddad asked, his eyes moving between the pond and the conversation Mom and Dad were having over by the car.

Buster sat at Granddad's feet, and I reached out my hand to pet him. Maybe that would get Granddad's attention. The hair on the back of Buster's neck bristled. My heart jumped, but as Granddad was still watching Frank, I put my hand on the dog's head. "Hello, boy."

Buster's tail dropped as my hand touched his coarse fur. It was gritty, and his eyes were as yellow as his teeth. He let out a low growl. Wanting to step back, instead I gave him a scratch. Buster's head whipped up and he gave me a sharp nip. I yelped but didn't cry. Now Granddad looked.

"Why did you go and do that?" he asked. "You don't have the good sense that God gave a billygoat."

Mom and Dad were still talking by the car and didn't notice. The skin on my hand was raised and bruised but there was no blood.

"Go into the kitchen and get Anne to put some ice on it," Granddad said, walking away without another look.

My hand hurt. He wasn't proud of me; instead, he was mad, and I was only trying to show him how brave I was.

The kitchen was the land of Mom and her sisters and it always smelled like something good was cooking. Wide planks of golden pine with grooves from years of wear covered the floor. The white enameled sink was large enough to wash babies in, and deep wooden countertops that had to be scrubbed down weekly with salted water stood on either side. Tall pine cupboards were full of dishes and glasses, pots, and pans, and two stoves stood against another wall. One was an old wood-burning job, made of cast iron with a round steel plate on top. Granny Gillespie had done all of her cooking here. She got up early in the morning, popped up the steel plate and chucked wood into the stove's round belly. Then every few hours it was up with the plate and in with the wood. The stove was always at the ready. After she died, Mom and the aunts decided the stove was a fire hazard and made Granddad buy a new one. A dazzling white General Electric model stood beside it now, but the only time it was ever used was when the family came to visit. Granddad preferred the old one.

Granny had given Granddad four girls and one son. Uncle Jack was the eldest. He was a thin and serious man with horn-rimmed glasses, and he had been a medic in the Second World War. Granddad had always wanted Uncle Jack to take over the family business, but Uncle Jack had no interest in farming. However, his son Hugh sure did. Hugh was our oldest cousin. He was tough and dreamt up scary dares to test our nerve. When I was ten, I had to climb into the pen with a boar. When I was eleven, I had to jump into a silo full of oats. I didn't know what would come next, but there would be something. Every weekend Hugh arrived on the train to learn the business. Mom always said Uncle Jack couldn't be far enough away from Granddad, and Hugh couldn't be close enough. I think the aunts secretly resented the fact Uncle Jack didn't do much to help at home, but they never said it out loud, as that wouldn't be polite.

Aunt Anne was the oldest girl. She was short and wiry with curly red hair, the silliest giggle you ever heard, and always wore crisp white shirts and slacks. Aunt Anne was a registered nurse living in Toronto. She wasn't big on hugging and claimed it was a good way to swap germs. Aunt Anne and Dad were practically best friends, always talking about new medicines and advances in surgical technique. Aunt Anne said she couldn't marry because her patients were her family, but Dad told me that most men wouldn't want a woman who worked and wore the pants.

Aunt Augusta was a teacher who never taught. The day she left teacher's college she married Uncle Leon, a spic and span air force lieutenant, and ever since then they'd been gadding around bases across Ontario. They had three children: two boys, and my best friend, Peg. Aunt Augusta wore her hair up in a bouffant and loved wearing costumes and jangly jewelry from foreign ports. Dad claimed Aunt Augusta had been bounced around so much that she had a screw loose. I liked her.

Aunt Janet waved a dirty plate in the air. "I found this one in the tub." She plunged her hands back into the soapy water as she methodically made her way through the impressive stack of dishes Granddad had created the week before. Her fingers were red and raw from the hot water. Aunt Janet was tall and blonde with broad shoulders and a serious disposition. She studied agriculture, fell in love with a burly, fun-loving Scot, and moved to his sprawling farm. They had two children: twin girls, fourteen, and dressed in matching tartan jumpers with bright red socks and black patent leather shoes.

"Hi," I said, dropping my coat on the captain's chair by the door. Everyone turned to say hello, but no one stopped working. Peg had potato detail, and she looked miserable. The coils of peel reminded me of summer snakes waiting to spring as I told Aunt Anne what happened.

"Oh, Madeline Anne," Aunt Anne sighed, walking to the ice box to pull out an aluminum tray. "You know better than to play with Buster."

"But he tried to bite Tedder," I protested.

"All the more reason you shouldn't be petting him," Aunt Anne said, setting my hand in a bowl full of ice and water. "No wonder you worry your parents sick."

Mom and Dad didn't have anything to worry about. I was as tough as Granddad who I could see through the big bay window standing at the edge of the pond and watching the hockey game. It was freezing cold, and Granddad was only wearing a shirt. His pants rippled in the wind and his hands were cupped around his mouth, creating a megaphone to cheer the boys on. Buster sat in the snow beside him. My fingers were going numb from the ice.

"Dad shouldn't keep that beast around the house," Aunt Augusta said. She was attacking a bowl of whipping cream, madly beating the cream into a fluffy white frenzy. She was strangely focused, too, which was odd for Aunt Augusta. "How are those potatoes coming?" she asked.

Peg shrugged. She wasn't acting like herself either.

"Why are you being such a sourpuss?" Aunt Janet asked.

Peg burst into tears. Aunt Augusta set the bowl of whipping cream down on the table.

"Leon's got a new posting."

Everyone stopped working and I could hear the air.

"That's exciting," Aunt Anne finally said.

Aunt Janet didn't say a word.

"What's exciting?" Mom asked, just arriving in the kitchen, her coat still on.

"They're off again," Aunt Janet said with a sniff that might have been a little cry, but I couldn't tell because she'd turned her attention back to the dishes, sloshing plates around.

"Where are you going?" Mom asked.

She was trying to sound happy and light, but I knew how much she hated it when Aunt Augusta left. The last time they'd moved I caught Mom crying in a roomful of packed boxes. When I asked her what was wrong, she said it was allergies, but I knew that wasn't the truth. My mother never cried—Aunt Augusta leaving must have really hurt.

"Colorado Springs," Aunt Augusta replied.

Suds frothed over the side of the sink, splashing onto the floor as Aunt Janet spun around. Aunt Anne's mouth dropped open, and Mom sat down in the chair with a thud. For once the twins were quiet, rapidly drying the plates their mother set in the rack.

"Colorado? Like the Grand Canyon?" I asked.

Mom rested her hands on top of the table. Nobody answered my question.

"I'll still come home," Aunt Augusta said, trying to brighten things up. "And you can come and visit."

Dad would never pay for plane tickets and besides, it was much too far to drive, especially with Tedder's car sickness. Peg let out another sob and it hit me that my best friend was leaving. I started to cry, too. The twins looked ready to join in and even Aunt Janet's lower lip trembled. Mom hung up her coat, strode across the kitchen and put on an apron, tying it tightly around her waist. "There'll be a lot of work getting you packed up, but first we've got to get lunch on. Dad will be wanting his meal," she said.

Aunt Janet and the twins silently went back to the dishes, as Aunt Augusta began anxiously applying spoonfuls of whipped cream to the top of the aspic. Aunt Anne put a pot of water on the stove. Peg resumed peeling potatoes.

"Maddy," Mom said. "Crying doesn't help. Now please go and get me the eggs." She noticed my hand in the bowl of ice. "What have you done to your hand?"

"Buster bit me."

"Oh, for heaven's sake," Mom said, walking toward the back door. "You're going to be the death of me." She opened the door, sending a gust of frigid air through the kitchen. "Teddy!" Mom called. "Bring your bag."

While Dad was cleaning the wound, Tedder sat in the chair silently watching. One of the twins insisted that boys shouldn't be in the kitchen.

"Why not?" Tedder asked, as Dad squirted a dab of clear salve onto the end of a wooden tongue dispenser.

"Because they shouldn't," the other twin replied. "My Dad only comes to the kitchen to eat."

Mom said she didn't mind, but Aunt Augusta, Aunt Janet, and even Aunt Anne were clearly put out. They'd just gotten the terrible news that Aunt Augusta was going to be moving and now they couldn't speak freely. It was a rule—a dumb rule—that had been in place for as long as I could remember. The men talked in the shop and the women visited in the kitchen. Mom said that the men talked about matters that weren't fit for female consumption and the women talked about matters of no interest to men. That only made me want to go outside even more.

The moment Dad finished with my bandage, Mom pulled him to his feet. "You move along," she said. "Tedder needs some fresh air."

"It's too cold, Mommy," Tedder replied. "Can I stay here with you?"

The back door opened, another shot of icy air, and Granddad entered.

"Dad, shut that door!" the women cried out in unison.

Granddad ignored them. He turned to Dad and Tedder. "What are you two doing in here?"

Dad didn't answer. Tedder hugged Dad's leg. Mom and the aunts were silent. I stuck out my bandaged hand. "Dad was fixing the bite."

"What a lot of fuss for a little nip," Granddad said, turning toward his daughters. "Isn't the food ready yet?" he asked. "We've got hungry boys out there."

"It'll be ready when you men get out of the kitchen, and that means every last one of you!" Aunt Janet said, waving a wooden spoon.

Granddad laughed, but he knew the rules and pushed Dad and Tedder out ahead of him. The boy cousins were sitting on top of the snowbanks taking off their skates. The aunts were the ones who'd done all the work. Maybe they were hungry too. That was another good reason to be like a boy. You got to be a hero instead of a slave.

We all sat around the table while Granddad said grace.

"For what we are about to receive, may the Lord make us truly thankful."

Opening my eyes, I wanted to see who else was peeking. A couple of the boys were stealing a couple of Mom's devilled eggs while everyone was praying. Frank's eyes were shut tight.

"And please remember those who aren't with us today," Granddad said. Peg's eyes opened and met mine. Soon we were going to be separated.

Hugh was down at the end, sitting next to Granddad—the spitting image: tall and broad, with strong arms and clear blue eyes. He looked up near the end of grace, caught my gaze and held it. The twins giggled until Aunt Janet cleared her throat.

After Granddad said, "Amen," we all dove into the meal. Dishes clattered and everyone chattered, even the kids, until we were told to "be seen and not heard." We sat quietly for a moment, but then we started up again. Family lunches were riotous events. Aunt Janet congratulated the twins on their magic in the kitchen. They smiled modestly, said it was nothing and to please pass the peas. Taking a spoonful for Tedder, I dumped them on his plate, laughing as he stuck one up his nose. I looked up to see if Granddad was laughing, too, but only saw Hugh staring at me again with a funny smile. I wanted him to like me, so I smiled back.

Peg and I were snuggling in our bed, telling secrets under the blankets when the door cracked open. A flashlight beam squiggled across the ceiling as footsteps softly padded across the floor toward the bed. We lay perfectly still.

"Maddy."

The twins stood at the end of the bed in identical housecoats, holding flashlights under their chins. Matching demons.

"You have to come with us," they whispered.

Hugh, I thought, and I sat up. It was time to face another one of his dares.

"You don't have to," Peg hissed.

"Yes, I do," I whispered back, putting on my housecoat and slippers. There was no way I'd be deemed a sissy. "Go back to sleep."

Following the twins, I silently crept down the staircase, through the darkened house and out the back door. Moonlight lit the path that led to the barn. Granddad always locked Buster up with the cattle, so nobody knew we were out of the house. We ran over the snow and ice, staying close to the ground, then up the graveled rise to the barn. Panting, I placed my palms on the big barn doors, hearing voices inside. The twins stood on either side of me. We pushed open the heavy doors and the voices stopped. I was terrified.

The twins' flashlight beams danced around the barn. An old cutter rested at the back, covered in dust and feed bags. Building blocks of hay bales filled the area. One of the boy cousins sat on a bale near the top. Another was perched on one near the bottom. They were smoking cigarettes. It was dangerous to smoke in a barn, but the boys didn't care. It wasn't as dangerous as if Granddad caught us in there. The twins tittered, shining their lights in one another's faces. They were having fun, but they looked scared, too. Then, a spooky laugh echoed down, followed by a flap of wings as birds struck the rafters. Crows, angry at being disturbed, began to caw and swoop.

I looked up through the gloom to the oak beams that supported the mows. Something large shifted in the centre of the middle one. It was too big to be a cat. My stomach jumped. What was it? A flashlight shone a circle of light, getting wider and wider until it struck Hugh. He was sitting in the centre of the beam, a rifle across his lap, smoking a cigarette. Twenty feet high in the air, with nothing but the bare boards below to break his fall. Another crow cawed, a black shape flying high into the rafters and swooping down toward the ground.

"Are you ready?" Hugh asked. 'Or are you chicken?"

The boys made clucking noises, and the twins giggled like mad.

"I'm not afraid of anything."

A cold draft cut through my housecoat, making me shiver.

"You're twelve now," Hugh said, flicking the cigarette down onto the floor. The ember glowed. "Get up here." His voice echoed, reminding me of the man in *The Twilight Zone.*

It was a hard climb in slippers. When one of the boys behind me pulled at the hem of my housecoat, I let out a kick. I'd always been afraid of heights, but climbing into the pitch black, watching the twins getting smaller and smaller, was only making things worse. Shaking, I forced my eyes to focus on the rung in front of me until I reached the top stepping out into the hard, spiky straw. Hugh's giant shadow spread across the ceiling. He stood, the rifle loose in one hand, the other beckoning me to step out on the beam. He didn't waver, just as steady and sure as if he was standing on the ground.

"Come here," he ordered.

I started across the hay. The boys kept clucking, "Chicken, chicken!" The twins joined the chorus down below. More crows sat in the rafters, shifting black shapes cawing into the night.

The beam didn't look so wide and sturdy from up here in the mow, it was more of a rigid tightrope. Shaking, I looked down. The twins stared up, their mouths gaping as wide as the chickens they fed every day. A hired man had fallen from here once and broken his back, never to walk again, and suddenly I didn't want to go out on the beam. Hugh rammed his free hand in his pocket. I looked into his eyes and stopped thinking about the floor. This was about courage. This was about being a Gillespie.

My legs wobbled. Even my feet were shaking. Maybe I could get down on my hands and knees and belly across like a snake, but that wouldn't do. They'd all brand me a coward. Opening my arms wide for balance, I willed myself onto the beam and began to walk. Ahead of me, Hugh set the rifle down on the rafter then slowly walked backward toward the safety of the other side. His eyes never left me. A few steps later, I stood over the gun, out in the centre, all alone.

"Pick it up," Hugh said.

I was shaking so hard I was sure he could feel my trembling through the beam. I reached down, feeling the cool metal of the muzzle, and grabbed the rifle, clasping it to my chest and I stood up. Hugh grinned. I grinned back. I'd done it. I'd shown him. Then his hand shot out and he released a handful of corn up into the air. Golden kernels struck my legs and head and suddenly the crows, dozens of them, swooped hungrily down from the rafters, rushing at me, searching for food. Hugh threw another shower of corn. An enormous black shape flew past, so close I could see the red in the centre of its eye. My free hand rushed instinctively to protect my face. A bird flapped against my housecoat. The boys yelled for me to shoot. I brought the rifle to my shoulder—we'd all learned how to fire a gun. The rifle cracked. There was a bang down below, followed by a series of angry shouts, but nothing registered. I just stood in the middle of the beam firing shot after shot into the black, hearing nothing, feeling nothing but the rush of pure adrenaline.

"Maddy!"

It was Mom. I stopped and looked down, disoriented. Her face was white. Everyone else was there, too, all the adults, dressed in their pajamas, shaking off sleep. Aunt Anne was rigid. Aunt Janet clutched the twins. Aunt Augusta had a firm hold of her boys by their ears. Hugh was nearly at the bottom of the ladder. Dad shoved him out of the way and started climbing. Granddad yelled something about there being hell to pay. My foot slipped. The rifle fell, and with a bang it hit the floor. A round went off. Everyone scattered.

"Stay steady!" Granddad ordered. The crows cawed.

"Drop to your knees," Dad said. "Straddle the beam, I'll come and get you."

Kneeling, I put my hands in front of me, dropped one leg and then the other. Safe.

Hugh stared at me. The other cousins did too. I could see it in their faces. I'd gotten them all in trouble. Slowly I stood back up.

"Maddy!" Dad yelled. "Stay down."

A crow swept by, catching my housecoat with the tip of its wing. Swaying, one foot shot out as my arms wheeled wildly.

Granddad opened his arms. "Jump!" he called.

"Stay put!" Dad yelled.

"Jump!" Granddad called again, moving right beneath me, his arms held wide and high. "I'll catch you."

Of course he would. I leapt. Granddad scooped me out of the air seconds before I hit the ground as easily as a bag of seed or a bale of hay. The roughness of his white bristle scratched my cheek.

"Were you scared?" he asked, setting me down.

"No, sir."

"That's a good girl."

Mom swept me up in her arms and held me tight. Her hand gently stroked my hair. All the adults' faces looked tight and stricken. All except Granddad, who smiled and gave me a hard pinch.

"I'm sorry," I said, glancing around.

Aunt Janet snorted.

"You should be sorry," Aunt Anne said, her hands clasping and unclasping. "If you were mine, I'd spank you within an inch of your life."

Aunt Augusta dragged the boys out the door. The twins weren't spared any humiliation either; they were spanked right there on the spot. There was a thump behind me. It was Dad. He was so upset I thought I was going to get it, but instead he pulled me to him and held me fast. Then he stared at Granddad, who glared right back.

"Nobody's hurt," Granddad said.

"This time," Dad replied. He turned to Mom.

"Get the boys."

"Oh, Teddy," she implored.

"We're going home."

"You don't need to do that," Aunt Anne said.

"Get the boys," Dad repeated.

My father had never been so angry. Mom and Aunt Anne ran ahead while Dad grabbed my hand and pulled me out of the barn. When I looked back, Granddad was shaking his fist at Hugh. Was Hugh going to get the belt?

We crossed the yard toward the Oldsmobile as Mom and Aunt Anne ran up the stairs and into the house. The lights flicked on, light spilling out into the yard.

"Are you sure you're all right?" Dad asked, as I got into the car.

"I'm sorry," I said, nodding my head. After he closed the door, I rolled down the window.

Aunt Janet's family was standing by the car. Aunt Augusta appeared from the dark side of the barn. Both the boys were crying. So were the twins. Granddad and Hugh walked out of the barn. Hugh's face was red, and he was trembling. Whatever Granddad had said to him was obviously worse than the belt. Everyone approached the car, but nobody looked at us.

"Teddy, please don't leave," Aunt Augusta said.

The bottoms of Dad's pajamas were dirty with mud and snow while the wind clipped through his hair.

"You know I'd never drop her," Granddad said.

"She could have been killed," Dad replied. His voice was cool and firm, but his hands shook.

Mom emerged on the veranda holding a sleeping Tedder. Frank was behind, rubbing his eyes, looking confused. Aunt Anne followed with blankets and pillows, clothes, boots, and coats. Dad and Granddad just stood there glaring at one another, not saying a word.

"Are you sure you won't stay?" Aunt Anne asked, making sleeping nests in the back of the car. Dad shook his head. "Theodore, you know he'd never hurt the kids," she added.

Aunt Anne was always the voice of reason and she and Dad were the best of friends, but tonight her words weren't enough.

"Dad, say something," she said, turning to her father. Granddad just spat.

"It was an accident, Teddy," Mom said, Tedder in her arms. "Let's stay."

Dad got into the car and the engine fired to life. Mom looked to her sisters for support, but there was nothing they could do. What could they say? You didn't interfere with other people's squabbles. Mom got in, closed the door, and waved goodbye. As the Oldsmobile carefully made its way down the lane, I turned to look at my cousins. They were all standing there, watching as if frozen in time. All except Granddad. He was halfway up the stairs, already on his way back into the house.

The car was quiet. We didn't even see another car on the road that night. Where were all the people? The world was empty except for us. Tedder was asleep in Mom's lap, her head leaning against the glass, their combined breath fogging the window. Frank leaned into my ear. "This is all your fault," he quietly said.

"You don't know anything," I replied. Dad's eyes shifted to the rear-view mirror, settling on me.

"It's always your fault. You ruin everything," Frank repeated, more loudly this time.

"Quiet back there," Dad said.

Mom didn't speak and Tedder stirred but didn't wake. We passed a silent abandoned barn by the side of the road, fallow fields growing wild around it. Dad would never understand what had happened. He'd seen too many farm boys dead and maimed. But the Gillespie dares, well, you couldn't say no. Granddad would never let us fall. Smiling to myself, I thought about how Granddad finally knew that I was as good as any boy. Frank pulled a blanket over his head. Mom and Dad would get over being mad. They always did. The lights of the car swept the road as we passed by the Sterling village limits. Drapes were drawn and everything was dark as if we silently flew into a mysterious night town.

When we got home, Mom and Dad tucked us into bed, but I was too excited to sleep. Sneaking out of my room, I crept down the hall, settling into my special spot at the top of the stairs. Every night I secretly watched Mom and Dad sitting on the sofa in the living room. Usually they hugged and held hands, talking about their day, but there was no hugging that night. Their voices were raised and hushed at the same time, as if they were trying to keep the words muzzled, but sometimes they slipped out with a power of their own.

"In my family, we talk," Mom said.

"He never listens," Dad replied. His voice shook and I couldn't make out the rest of the sentence. Dad drove his fist down on the coffee table. The magazines jumped.

This had never happened before. My parents were fighting. Mom always said that decent people didn't shout any more than they drank. That was as much a part of me as the fact that my hair was black and my eyes were blue. What was going on? Should I go down and stop them or would I get spanked? Would it make things better or turn them even worse? What could I do to help?

"I've never run!" Mom said, her voice volleying around the room. She caught herself, glancing quickly up the staircase.

Holding my breath, I ducked out of sight. Dad's fists were clenched, pounding steadily on his kneecaps.

"The next time, it's going to be Frank," Dad said, jumping to his feet, pacing back and forth out of my sightline and then back in.

"No, it won't," Mom replied. "Those two are very different."

"This is no good," Dad said.

They sat in silence for a moment until Dad stood and left. I couldn't see him. Where did he go? Something clattered in the kitchen. Then I heard the cellar door open and footsteps pad down the stairs.

Shaking, Mom tried to pour herself a cup of coffee but gave up after some of it splashed on the rug and she didn't even bother to clean it. Instead, she rubbed her neck and began nervously shifting things around on the coffee table. My toes dug into the broadloom. Dad had been gone a long time. The house was quiet. Then, steps coming back up from the cellar. There was a clatter of glasses as he rummaged around in the kitchen. Dad wasn't getting a snack, or I would have heard the refrigerator door. Then I heard a tinkle and a ping. Mom looked up. "What are you doing?"

Dad appeared carrying two cut-crystal glasses and a bottle of liquor. I stood up as he set the glasses down. We didn't drink liquor. It was more than wrong—it was practically evil. Granny Gillespie said she'd turn anyone out of her house who took a drink, and the Barneses never touched the stuff either. Shaking, Dad's fingers twisted off the cap. The bottle was full of something yellow.

"Teddy," Mom said so quietly I could barely hear her.

His hand tipped and golden liquid poured into the cut glass. Then he filled the other.

"We don't drink."

He handed her a glass.

"We don't fight either," he said.

The shadow from the church spire crawled down the carpet as Mom and Dad took a drink. The taste must have been really bad, because the second Mom swallowed it, it shot back up as she spewed vomit across the lovely white rug. Dad took the glass and touched Mom's forehead.

"You're burning up."

She pulled away.

"I'm fine. I'm just not used to liquor."

Mom was in the reception area of the office, pinning pieces of a dress pattern onto Dad's receptionist. It was a large open space, broken up by a glass wall where there was a counter to pay bills and make appointments. Ruth, twenty-two and recently engaged, stood atop her office chair, offering free entertainment for all the patients waiting to see Doc Barnes. When Mom discovered Ruth couldn't afford a proper engagement outfit, she insisted on making one for her. Ruth said that she felt she was being a burden.

"Every woman needs a little black dress," Mom replied, her mouth full of pins.

"You shouldn't talk with pins in your mouth," I replied, leafing through a copy of *Teenage Confidential*. "You could swallow them, and they'd become lodged in your trachea or bowels."

"How would they get them out?" Ruth nervously asked.

I was too busy staring at a pinup of The Monkees to answer. I'd begged for their new record, any new record, but Mom wouldn't let rock and roll in the house. It was old people music or nothing.

Florence burst into the waiting room. She was a farmer's wife who came in every week or so complaining of an imaginary gut ache. Florence staggered up to the reception, seized the counter, and asked for Dad. He was busy giving a local farmer a pain shot. I walked over to the counter.

"Hello, Florence. Is there anything I can do to help?"

I'd been working in Dad's office almost since I was born. Mom was usually busy in her study, so Dad parked me on top of the filing cabinet in my bassinet while he treated the patients. I'd grown up there and never gotten into the habit of playing with other kids after school. I was either driving around with Mom, handing out flyers to help the starving Africans, or helping Dad.

"I'm feeling poorly."

"Your skin does look a little grey. Why don't I take your temperature?"

Florence sat on the edge of the examining table while I removed a thermometer from a sterilized glass jar.

"Open your mouth."

Florence did as she was told, but when Dad walked in, she leapt off the examining table.

"I need my medicine!"

"Let's check you out first."

While Dad and Florence chatted, he looked into her eyes, took her pulse, and tested her reflexes. Mom said that Florence was in love with Dad, but Dad and I knew better. Florence was in love with the attention.

"You just wait here while I get you some tablets."

Florence's eyes went wide as I followed Dad into the dispensary. The walls were covered in shelves brimming with brown glass bottles of all shapes and sizes, filled with tablets, capsules, and liquids. Dad removed a bottle of red pills from the top shelf and poured a handful into a white paper pack as I hopped up onto the stainless-steel stool.

"What are you giving her?"

"Sugar pills," he said. "There's nothing like the power of the placebo."

There was every kind of medicine in Dad's dispensary. If the drugstore was closed, he had to be able to give his patients any medication they required. Opening one of the big bottles, I stuck my hand in. Tiny pills, white grains of magic, fell through my fingers.

Dad handed me a bottle of clear liquid and asked me to give it to Ruth.

"What's this?" I asked.

"Demerol."

While Dad left to give Florence her magic pills, I opened the Canadian Pharmaceutical Compendium to see what Demerol did. There was the entry: "Demerol: fifty milligrams every three hours for pain." I closed the Compendium and took the medicine out to reception.

"I wish your father wouldn't keep this stuff on site," Ruth said in a low voice, hiding the liquid in a drawer with the other restricted drugs. "Some dope fiend could rob the place." The pieces of dress pattern made her look like a scarecrow.

Ruth crinkled her nose as Florence walked out and Dad walked in. "You should bill her."

"It's only a few minutes of my time," Dad replied, grabbing another file and walking out.

Ruth got back up on the office chair as Mom began to remove the pieces of pattern.

"Can you talk some sense into this husband of yours?" Ruth asked.

"About what?"

"He's treating people for free again."

Florence wasn't the only patient Dad treated for free, or almost free. Some of them were poor farmers who could only pay in chickens or produce.

"Oh, I think that's all right now and again," Mom replied. "You never know when you might need some help."

Slumping down in the chair, I listlessly flipped through the pages of an old medical journal I'd already read twice.

"What's wrong with you?" Mom asked. "You've been sulky for weeks."

"I don't have any friends."

Mom and I always said we were best friends, but since Peg had moved to Colorado Springs, I wanted friends my own age. Frank appeared in the doorway in his baseball jersey. He was lead pitcher for the Sterling Squirts.

"You have to be nice to have friends," Frank said.

"Shut up."

"We don't say shut up in this house," Mom said.

"Every now and again we do," Dad replied, walking back in, rooting around for another file. He asked Mom how her day was going. She said she didn't get around to finishing her charity work.

"I had to take a nap. Can you imagine that? Me, napping."

"You should have asked me to tuck you in," Dad said.

Mom smiled.

"How do you make friends?' I asked.

"Let's see what we can do," Mom replied.

Mom and I were at McDermott's Drug Store that afternoon supposedly buying lye soap. Mr. McDermott handed Mom a big box wrapped with brown kraft paper. He looked at me and smiled. "Are these for Maddy?" he asked, wrinkling his eyes. Mom smiled back and said, "Not quite yet." It was a box of Kotex pads. I could have killed them both.

I was twelve and hadn't had my period yet and, to make matters worse, Mom made me carry them down Main Street.

"Nobody knows what they are," Mom said, stifling a giggle.

"I hate you," I said, holding the Kotex box as a shield, walking quickly, eyes glued to the pavement. Suddenly Mom's hand closed over my arm, signalling me to stop. She wasn't giggling anymore. Laura Barnes, who never stared at anyone because it was rude, stood gape-mouthed, gawking across Main Street at a fat, teenaged girl.

"Who's that?" I asked.

"Stop staring, Maddy," Mom ordered.

"But you're staring," I said. I'd never seen an expression like that on my mother's face. It was a mix of horror, embarrassment, and red-hot panic. When she realized what she was doing, she dropped her eyes.

"You're right, it's rude," Mom murmured, continuing along Main, trying not to look at the fat girl. She was way fatter than I was.

"What a whale," I said, as a black Buick cruised by. The fat girl looked miserable. There was a little line of snot dripping out of her left nostril. She shoved it aside with the palm of her hand.

Mom grabbed my arm, looking straight at me. "That girl is not fat," she said, pointing across the street with her free hand. "That is the very worst thing that can happen to a woman."

Embarrassed that she was pointing, I tried to pull away. This was really unlike her. It was also unlike her to grab me hard enough to hurt. Mom never hurt me. Not once in my whole life. But now she was yanking my arm, stopping me in my tracks. She snatched the box of Kotex and pulled me over to one of the old iron benches in front of the dry goods store, the bench where we normally sat and had our Pepsi. There was no Pepsi this time.

"Sit down," Mom ordered. She sat beside me. Across the street, the fat girl continued her way. "That girl's an unwed mother," she said. I didn't understand. "That girl is pregnant," Mom told me. That wasn't possible. She wasn't old enough. Mom saw my confusion and her tone softened. "I'm sorry, honey. I should have explained it more thoroughly. Remember when we talked about the birds and the bees?" she asked. I nodded. I didn't really, but I didn't want to talk about it, so I picked at a scab. "Once you've had your period, you're old enough to get pregnant," she said. I looked again at the fat girl who wasn't really fat, hauling herself down the road. There was nothing good about the period. I'd suspected it before, but now, I was positive.

"Where's her husband?" I asked. "She can't be pregnant if she doesn't have a husband."

"There is no husband. She had relations with a man and now her life is over." Mom looked so sad and angry; it looked as though her heart was breaking. "You must believe me, Maddy. If you never listen to another thing I tell you, listen to me now. That," she said, looking down the street, "is the absolute worst thing that can happen to a woman."

"Worse than dying?" I asked.

Mom nodded.

How could anything be worse than dying, I wondered. But Mom's expression made it crystal clear. This was the one thing never to doubt. This was the one thing to be avoided at all costs. Never ever end up like that unwed mother. I watched the girl go around the corner and disappear.

"Do you want to share some French fries?" Mom asked. I shook my head. It was the first time I'd ever turned down food. We rose from the bench and headed wordlessly toward home.

It wasn't too long until Mom organized a get-together luncheon with Betsy and Sandy, the two most popular girls in school. Sandy was blonde and had a mole on her chin that she called a beauty mark. Betsy was pretty, with long, straight brown hair and a turned-up nose. Betsy even had a boyfriend, Brad, who was cute and followed her around like a collie.

Their mothers couldn't refuse, because Mom was the doctor's wife, and people didn't want to be in the bad books with the town doc. I don't know if it was me or Mom's influence, but ever since the luncheon, Betsy, Sandy, and I started hanging out all the time.

Sandy was eating an apple, but I couldn't finish my lunch. Betsy and Brad had disappeared into the woodlot behind the school. I was very worried about Betsy becoming an unwed mother and how it would mean a fate worse than death for her. Did that mean it was worse than hell? How could anything be worse than hell? The foliage rustled. What were they doing?

"Have you ever been frenched?" Sandy asked, chewing.

"What's that?"

"A french is when the boy sticks his tongue in your mouth."

"Doesn't it make you gag?"

Sandy opened her mouth, sticking out her tongue for a demonstration. "A good frencher knows just how much tongue to use," she said, giving her tongue a flick. "They've got to slip it in, find your tongue, and then the two tongues dance."

How could tongues dance?

"But you have to be sure you don't get them too worked up," Sandy said.

"Why?"

"Because of their penises. If you get a penis too excited, a boy can't be responsible for what happens. That's why girls have to make sure they don't tease the boy too much. If they do, then the girl gets what she deserves."

"Hi." Kenneth was standing in front of me, spinning his sneaker in the dirt. Kenneth was the shortest boy in school, but he was also the biggest jock, and I'd had a crush on him since grade two when he gave me a red ribbon he'd won in a race. We hadn't really talked much since, but now that I was hanging out with Betsy and Sandy, I was part of the cool clique. Kenneth sat down beside me, his leg jackhammering up and down.

"Are you going to the dance?" he asked.

"I don't know," I replied, trying to act nonchalant. Secretly I was desperate to go, but nobody had asked me.

"So, if you did decide to go, maybe you'd like to come with me?"

"I guess that would be okay."

"Should I pick you up?"

Mom would never allow it. "I'll meet you there."

"Okay," he said and ran back to the ball diamond.

I was stretched across the bed on Mom's green eiderdown while she sat at the vanity table rooting through her cosmetic bag. Her precious bottle of Eau de Joy was displayed against the beveled mirror. I caught my own reflection. Did liars really go to hell? It was probably too late already, because I'd just lied to my mother for the very first time. The thought made my stomach hurt, but Mom would never let me go to the dance if I told her the truth. Maybe lying was an important part of growing up.

Mom patted the floral padded bench. I sat down beside her and looked in the vanity mirror again. It was no wonder Mom told me to watch my weight and stop biting my fingernails. She was the most beautiful woman in the world, and compared to her, I was plain ugly.

"I need rouge."

"No, you don't. Look at me."

When I turned, she smiled and brought her hands up to my cheeks, quickly pinching them. It stung. Then Mom gave me a kiss on the nose.

"There you go."

Turning to the mirror, I saw that her pinches had given me a nice rosy glow.

"What about lipstick?"

Mom twisted a golden tube, and up popped a pretty pink.

"What do you think of this?"

It was beautiful. "Will you show me how to put some on?"

Mom nodded, pursing her lips.

"Put your lips together like you're going to kiss a baby. That's good. Now, you apply just a bit. Roll your lips together to spread it evenly."

Mom pulled out a Kleenex.

"This is to dab off any that's left over. You don't want to look cheap."

Wow. I looked at least five years older. Mom pressed the tube into my palm. "I want you to have this."

My very first tube of lipstick! Throwing my arms around Mom's neck, I was about to kiss her cheek when something made me kiss her on the lips instead.

"Maddy!" she said, pushing me away as if I'd done something awful. When I started to cry, her face softened. "That's something you do with a boy."

"I'm sorry," I snuffled, noticing something on Mom's neck— a bump just beneath her ear that I'd never seen before. I reached out and touched it. The bump was hard.

"What's that?"

Mom turned back to the mirror to freshen her own lipstick. "Mumps, I think."

"That's a childhood disease," I said.

"It's adult mumps. I'm going to have Daddy take a look at it."

A black thought crossed my mind: maybe mumps were contagious. What if I was to take sick before the dance? That would destroy everything. I had lipstick. I had a date.

I didn't get sick. Not unless you count a case of butterflies that nearly caused me to barf three times while I was getting dressed. It was the last Friday night in June. School was over for the year, and I was up in my room standing in front of a full-length mirror wearing the beautiful new dress that Mom had made for me. Carefully applying the lipstick, I pinched my cheeks and stood back. I looked at least fifteen and never felt so grown up. Grabbing my brown purse with the long gold chain, I slung it over my shoulder, galloping down the stairs.

"No later than nine-thirty!" Mom called out as I ran past the dining room.

Mom, Dad, Frank, and Tedder were still finishing their dessert. Mom got up and followed me to the door.

"Let's have a look at you." She pulled me around. "Soon you're going to be all grown up." Her eyes started to moisten.

I hoped she wasn't going to cry. "I've got to go. I'm going to be late."

"You don't have a belt."

There were empty belt loops hanging from the sides of the dress. I panicked.

"Do you think this might work?" She had a belt in her hand, a handmade fabric one that must have taken hours to sew by hand. "Do you like it?" she asked, almost shyly.

"Mom! I love it."

Quickly, I slipped it through the loops as Mom did up the buckle.

"Thanks," I said and kissed her on the cheek.

"Have fun, sweetheart," she called, as I ran down the stone steps.

Halfway down the sidewalk, I looked back. Mom was silhouetted in the doorway, waving goodbye. She fastened the top button on her sweater and turned back toward the house. It wasn't all that cold. For about five seconds I felt guilty about lying about Kenneth, but then I started thinking about the dance.

The gymnasium was packed. A bunch of girls danced together while some of the boys sat on the edge of the auditorium stage. Brad and Betsy were already on the dance floor under a silver ball. Kenneth was leaning against the brick wall by the punch bowl wearing a checkered shirt, blue trousers, a blue tie, black shoes, and white socks. He'd slicked his hair back and I could smell Old Spice. "Crimson and Clover" began to play. Kenneth took my hand and led me onto the dance floor.

His chin pointed into my shoulder as he drew me close, and I could hear his rapid breathing. We were both shaking, first one foot and then the next, until Kenneth stomped on my toes.

He began to apologize, but I didn't care. Kenneth wasn't heavy enough to hurt me since I likely outweighed him by twenty pounds. Pulling him close, I only wanted to sniff him and feel him. That's all I wanted.

Later, the four of us broke the "gymnasium only" rule and went out by the picnic tables. If we were only gone for a bit the teachers wouldn't miss us. The moment we were outside, Betsy and Brad took off. I wanted to follow, but one look from Betsy and I knew enough to get lost. She took the gum out of her mouth and pressed it against the brick wall as they disappeared.

"You want to swing or something?" Kenneth asked.

Following him across the grounds, I looked back at the school, nervous that one of the teachers would see us through the windows.

"You're a good dancer," he said.

"You too," I lied.

We sat there swinging back and forth under the bright full moon. Shadows like witches' fingers beckoned from the trees and the bushes shifted. What were Betsy and Brad doing in there? Kenneth grabbed my swing, stopping it instantly, and leaned over, kissing me so hard I could feel his teeth.

"Do you like it?"

I nodded yes, but the teeth hurt. Then he kissed me again. His lips were tense and tasted like salt, not sweet like Mom's.

"Do you want to get suspended?" Betsy laughed, scaring me so much that I knocked into Kenneth's teeth and cut my lip.

"Very funny," I mumbled, tasting blood in my mouth.

Could Kenneth taste it, too? If he did, he didn't seem to mind. Being a jock, he'd probably tasted a lot of blood.

Betsy took Brad's arm. "We'd better get back. The teachers will notice we're gone."

Mrs. Armstrong dropped me off, but when I walked into the house, nobody was in the living room. That was weird. Mom always waited by the window whenever I went out at night. The flickering television offered the only light. A newscaster talked about the war in Vietnam. I walked across the living room, into the kitchen, and down the narrow corridor. A low yellow light glowed from the dispensary. Hushed voices drifted down the hall. Dad was holding a bottle of pills, telling Mom that she should take one to calm down, but Mom was refusing. She shook her head, saying she didn't want to be all doped up through this thing.

"Through what?" I asked, walking in.

They both jumped as if they'd been caught doing something bad.

"Your mother needs to have some tests done," Dad replied.

"What kind of tests?"

"It's nothing worth fussing about," Mom said.

"The doctors want to check out that lump on Mom's neck."

"I thought it was mumps."

"We're not sure," Dad replied, about to say something else, when Mom cut him off.

"I told you Theodore, it's nothing."

Mom never called him Theodore, unless she was mad. Then she noticed the cut.

"What happened to your lip?"

"One of the kids hit me in the face with the washroom door. It was an accident."

"Teddy, take a look at it."

I weaved out of the way. "It's fine. What are you doing in here?"

Mom slipped her arm around Dad's waist. "We've got a surprise."

"We're going to Colorado Springs," Dad said.

"What?" I asked, stunned. This couldn't be right. Aunt Augusta and the family had just moved, and Dad would never spend the money. "What about your patients?"

"They'll be fine without me."

Colorado Springs was far away. It was halfway down the United States and much too far to drive. Plus, Tedder got car sick.

"That's why we're going to take a plane," Mom said. "You kids will stay with Aunt Anne in Toronto while we're gone." Leaning onto Dad's shoulder, she looked up into his eyes. "Isn't it romantic?"

CHAPTER TWO

Two weeks after they got home, Mom hired an interior decorator. I went into Frank's bedroom to get his opinion. He was lying on his bed reading a book called *Hockey Is a Battle*.

"Don't you think it's strange the way Mom's renovating the living room?" I asked.

"She likes decorating."

"But why hire the lady?"

Mom always made these decisions herself. She took months to pore over colour samples, flip through magazines, and make everyone crazy with swatches of fabric and photos of furniture, but this time she hired a professional. Why the rush? And then there was Dad and money. He was always crying poorhouse. It worried me. Frank put down his book.

"What's going on with you and Kenneth?"

"What do you mean?"

"The kids at school are talking."

"What are they saying?"

"That you're going steady."

"Who said it?"

"Some of the guys."

"Don't you dare tell Mom."

"What are you going to do?" he taunted.

When I made a fist and said to shut up, Frank knew I meant it.

That autumn the whole neighbourhood glowed like the inside of a big, red oven. Nature looked how my body felt, sometimes as red-hot as the changing leaves, but then icy and cold like the wind. Kenneth kept asking me to go into the bushes. So far, I'd said no, but I couldn't say no forever. The workmen's truck was parked in the drive. They were finishing the broadloom installation.

The side door banged open, and Mom appeared in a blue housedress, carrying a spade. I followed her around the back toward her garden. Everything else was fire and light, red and yellow, as the leaves of Mom's oak trees fluttered down. Like Granny Gillespie, she'd planted a line of trees along the side of the property when she got married, but they weren't nearly as tall as Granny's giant spruces. Mom sat down in the garden. There was dirt under her nails. I'd never seen dirt on my mother's hands before. I asked her where her gloves were.

"They're too bulky. Help me."

"What about my good clothes? Shouldn't I change first?"

Mom patted the earth. "Don't bother. The light will be gone soon."

I knelt beside her.

"I want to separate the plants and spread the roots. Oh dear. The irises have really multiplied, haven't they?"

"I guess so."

"You don't like gardening, do you?"

"Not really."

"You will one day," she said.

"I don't think so."

"My girl. Always got to have the last say."

"So do you."

Mom laughed. She had a smudge of dirt on her cheek. She looked pale. I reached out to wipe the dirt away. "Are you feeling okay?"

"Just a bit tired. I've been out here all afternoon."

The plants had been cut back, rotting leaves and stalks piled neatly in the corner. Mud spattered the front of Mom's housedress. The dirt made me uneasy.

"What can I do to help?"

"Dig me some holes near the back of the fence."

The spade mouthed into the earth, the ground already a bit harder from the cooler nights. Mom shook the dirt from the plants, carefully separating the roots as we quietly transplanted the flowers. When she brushed her auburn hair away with the back of her hand, a ray of golden light illuminated her face. "Did I ever tell you about where your father proposed?"

"No."

"He drove me up to the top of a high hill near Granddad's farm. The earth fell away in all directions. It reminded me of heaven."

That sounded boring. I liked noise and excitement.

Something in the garden caught her eye. She leaned over. "Look at that," she said, yanking a withered beet out of the ground. "I missed some of the vegetables. Mother would have said, 'Laura Gillespie, you wasteful child.' We grew up in the Depression, you know."

I knew. I didn't like beets and was happy if some of them were dead.

"I should have taught you how to can."

"What?"

"Preserve. My mother taught all of us how to do that."

"You can buy that stuff now."

"It was something nice to do together."

A train hooted in the distance. Mom glanced up, looking into it.

"Those were the only times I really got to know her—your Granny. We were always so busy working. Do you understand?"

I didn't, but I nodded anyway.

"There was never any time for anything else. You fed the hired hands breakfast, did the dishes, milked, and then gathered eggs. Once you'd done that, you'd have to cook a big supper for the men, and then you went to bed and then it started all over again. When I was about your age, I decided my life was going to be better than that. I wasn't going to spend it chained to a stove." Mom shivered. "Your grandfather thought it was shameful."

"Really?"

"It was the only real argument we ever had. He said I was trying to rise above my station."

"I can't see Dad out in the cattle pens," I said.

Mom laughed. "I'm being silly." She carefully tapped the earth down with her trowel. "How do you like your friends?"

"They're okay."

"Just remember, Maddy. A person is judged by the company they keep."

"Betsy and Sandy are nice."

She nodded. "Are there any boys?" she asked tentatively.

"No." I prayed that she couldn't tell I was lying again, and that Frank hadn't talked.

"Good. You've got plenty of time for that." She finished burying the bulb. "And if you're going to smoke, promise me you won't do it on the street."

"I don't smoke," I protested. Could she smell the tobacco from Frenchy's on my coat? Frenchy's was a hamburger joint where the older kids hung out, and I'd started going there with my friends after school.

"I know you're not smoking, honey. It's just that if you ever do, please don't do it in public."

She reached for my hand. "And promise me, please promise me that you will guard your virtue."

What was that? "Okay," I replied. This was scary. What was going on? Mom brushed some hair out of my eyes.

"I'm awfully proud of you."

I knew I wasn't supposed to, but I couldn't stop myself. I hugged her. I hugged her harder than I had in years. I hugged her the way I did on the first day of school when I didn't want to leave home. I hugged her the way I did the first time I got sent to church camp. The way I hugged her whenever I felt scared, only this time she didn't push me away and tell me I was too big for that now. This time, she hugged me back.

Mom knew exactly what she wanted and, while it must have cost a fortune, the renovation was beautiful. The wallpaper was off-white with a faintly raised moiré stripe, and the green broadloom reminded me of the sea. When the movers finally left and the last vase was positioned, Mom sank into her new pale-green sofa, tossed her right leg over the left and proudly looked around. The main floor was perfect.

Several nights later, there was a flurry of activity outside my bedroom door.

"Teddy! Get up!"

It was Mom. Peering out my door, I saw her bolting down the hall in her mauve dressing gown. Dad stumbled out of their bedroom in groggy pursuit. Frank appeared. There was a sound of rushing water. Tedder stood in his doorway rubbing his eyes as Mom flew down the stairs.

"Did somebody leave a tap on?" she cried.

Mom stopped at the bottom of the stairs, her hand clamped over the newel post, madder than I'd ever seen her, including the time I said "holy cow" in church. Water poured out of the ceiling onto the sea-green broadloom. A pipe had cracked. The rug squished between our toes. Something Mom couldn't control was boiling up inside her when suddenly out rolled the biggest "GOD DAMN!" I'd ever heard and I wondered if the house would split in two.

The broadloom eventually dried out, and we didn't even need to change the under-padding. The carpet man said we were extraordinarily lucky. Of course, Mom kept sniffing for mould.

Kenneth was walking me home from school. "Do you want to go to the fairgrounds?" he asked.

A series of dark clouds was gathering in the west and creeping across the sky, beginning to blot out the sun. Winter was nearly here.

"I'm cold."

Kenneth pulled my hand. "Come on, it'll be fun."

I followed him up the dirt road toward the ball diamond. We climbed the boards and sat at the top, where Brad had carved "Brad and Betsy forever" into the seat. Kenneth pulled out his penknife and started scratching K + M into the wood. Nobody had ever carved my initials into anything before.

"We've been going steady for a long time," he said, giving me a sly look.

It hadn't been that long. The sky was turning black and a drop of heavy rain struck my forehead.

"I don't want to get wet," I said.

We bounded down the boards and jumped to the ground. The sky opened and the thunder clapped as the rain turned to hail. Taking off across the horse track that circled the ball diamond, we ran into one of the animal sheds for the Sterling Fall Fair. There wasn't much inside, just some old bales of hay, an empty cigarette pack, and a couple of crushed 7Up cans. Kenneth guided me toward the bales, pulling me down beside him. "We'll go as soon as the storm passes."

Hail drummed on the metal roof and the shed smelled of manure. Kenneth leaned over and kissed me on the cheek. We'd made out before with Brad and Betsy, but this was the first time we'd been all alone. When I turned, he kissed me on the lips. Kenneth wasn't as shy as he used to be. "Do you like it?"

I wasn't sure, but I couldn't say that, so I said I liked it, and he kissed me again. The thunder was getting louder, and the hail sounded like rocky ice fists pounding on the roof. Kenneth put my hand in his lap, and something moved in his pants. When I tried to pull my hand away, he held it fast. Something was wiggling.

"Do you want to touch it?"

Leaping to my feet, I ran for the door and out into the battering hail, through the slippery mud and onto McKenzie Street, running home to my mother as fast as I could.

She wasn't there, Ruth told me and the boys that Dad had to take Mom into Toronto for a while.

"Why?" Frank asked.

"You'll have to ask your father." Ruth looked uncomfortable. "Why don't you kids watch some TV? I'll get your supper on."

We watched everything we wanted that night. Mom would never allow us to watch that much television. By ten, Ruth had tucked the boys into bed, but I wanted to wait up for Dad. Ruth went into the office to catch up on paperwork. Sometime near eleven, I heard the car door slam and Dad walked in.

He looked at me and sighed. "What are you still doing up?"

"Where's Mom?"

"She's going to spend a bit of time at Aunt Anne's. A couple of doctors at the hospital want to examine her, and it's easier if she's there."

"Doctors?" I asked, suddenly concerned. "What's wrong with her?"

"There's nothing to be worried about. She's going to be fine."

Dad, still in his overcoat, turned on the TV and sat down beside me.

"I'll be going now, Dr. Barnes," Ruth said, sticking her head through the door. "Come on, Maddy, let your Dad alone. It's time you go to sleep," she added, putting on her gloves.

"Ruth's right. You get up to bed. It'll be morning before you know it."

He gave me an absentminded kiss, and reluctantly I left the room and climbed the stairs. The front door closed behind Ruth as Irv Weinstein asked, "Do you know where your children are?" I wondered what Mom was doing. Normally people didn't need to be near a hospital unless they were really sick.

"We get to eat Sloppy Joes every night," I said, "and watch all the TV we want."

Sandy said I was lucky. Her mother would never go for that. Betsy, Sandy, and I were crammed into our booth at Frenchy's. Kenneth and Brad sat at the counter. When Kenneth turned and flashed his sly dog look, I turned away. Worried about his uncontrollable urges, I didn't want to be alone with him. Brad glanced at Betsy with a secret smile that made her beam. She stuck her left hand out, placing it on the table. There was a silver signet ring on the wedding band finger, which officially meant going steady.

"It's beautiful," I said. Secretly, I was jealous and wanted one, too. The signet was engraved with B&B. That meant undying love and you'd be together forever.

A thought came: A ring like that would likely make it acceptable to touch a penis.

Mom had been gone for weeks and we rarely saw Dad. When he wasn't seeing patients, he spent all his time in Toronto and got home late. One night, I decided to wait up. The boys were always asking me about Mom, and I wanted to know, too. Christmas was coming, and the television announcer said *Rudolph the Red-Nosed Reindeer* would be on the following week. When the door opened, I got up and flicked off the set. "Hi, Dad," I said, walking into the foyer.

"Hello, honeybunch," he replied, automatically placing his fedora on the hat rack. Mom had trained him to be neat in the house.

"How's Mom?"

"She's in the hospital."

"I thought she was staying with Aunt Anne. What's wrong?"

"She's going to be fine."

"We should go and see her."

Dad just shook his head. "It's not going to help if you get yourself all worked up."

"I'm not worked up. I just want to see her."

"Mommy just needs plenty of rest." He looked at his watch. "Isn't it time for you to get to bed?"

"Okay," I said, trudging up the stairs.

Something didn't feel right, but I knew my parents wouldn't lie to me, and I was probably worrying for nothing. Sometimes people simply needed a hospital stay to get things straightened out—Dad said it was occasionally part of the cycle of life.

"Look who's here!" Aunt Anne called, opening the front door. It was the night before Christmas.

Dad helped Mom over the threshold. She stood in the hallway in her good tweed coat while Tedder and Frank jumped all over her, making her promise she wouldn't go away again. She was very thin, with skin paler than the new walls.

"How's my Maddy?" she asked, smiling tiredly.

"We've set up the tree just so. Come and look," I said, pulling on her hand.

Frank, Tedder, and I had carefully selected the tree from the lot downtown and dragged it all the way home ourselves. It was a tall, bushy pine with warm, welcoming branches. The scent filled the entire downstairs and made the whole house feel jolly. We'd spent the day decorating the tree so that it was perfect.

"Tedder made the angel for the top," Frank said.

Tedder wrapped his arms around her legs. "I knew you'd really like it, Mommy. I made it just for you."

"I need to lie down for a bit," Mom said, putting her hand on Dad's arm, signaling it was time to go up to bed. "I'll look at it tomorrow."

Dad helped her up the stairs.

"Santa's coming," Tedder sang. "You better be up in time."

The next morning, Frank and I tore down the stairs to see what was under the tree. Tedder was speeding around the living room on a new red tricycle with a big bow on the bars. All the other presents were wrapped, and Frank and I were both desperate to see what we were getting. Aunt Anne arrived in her housecoat carrying mugs of steaming hot chocolate.

"Where are they?" Frank asked, his curiosity getting the better of him.

We weren't allowed to open our gifts until Mom and Dad came down.

Tedder swooped around the room on his new tricycle in accelerating circles. "It's time they come down!" he squealed.

Aunt Anne grabbed a broom from the hall closet and turned it upside down, striking the ceiling. "It's time to get up!" she yelled.

"Get up, get up, get up!" we all called, as Aunt Anne kept banging the broom.

Finally, we heard Mom and Dad coming down the stairs, but when we saw her, all the joy blew out of the day. She collapsed on the sofa, put her feet up on the new coffee table and tried to smile, but all she could do was wince. Poor Mom, she must have been feeling really bad. Tedder gave her a gift to open, but Dad had to do it instead. After we'd finished quietly unwrapping our gifts, Mom went back to bed. She said she'd be down for Christmas dinner, but she never returned. All day she just lay beneath the green satin eiderdown, and every time I poked my head in to say hello, her eyes were closed.

Kenneth came over the day after New Year's. Frank answered the door since I was in the living room. Kenneth was wearing a new coat and looked spiffy.

"Maddy?" Frank called sweetly. Then he yelled, "It's your boyfriend!" Rushing out of the living room, I scowled at Frank.

"Would you please leave?" I hissed.

Frank slowly sauntered by, returning to paint a model boat.

"Hi," I said leaning up against the newel post, trying to look nonchalant.

"Hi," Kenneth replied, staring at the floor, shifting his boots back and forth as bits of wet snow and mud flecked onto the new broadloom. I wanted to tell him to stay on the rubber mat but didn't dare.

"It's nice outside," he said nervously.

"Yeah," I agreed, looking through the window. The sky was leaden and it was miserable.

"Do you want to go for a walk?" he asked.

"Where?"

"How about the bottom of the gully?"

We were sitting on the big rock at the bottom, banging our boots against the stone. Clods of white snow fell off. Kenneth had his hand in his pocket. What was in there?

"What have you got there?" I asked, praying it wasn't the penis.

Kenneth pulled out a little white box with a red ribbon and handed it to me. Carefully, I opened it. Inside, on a bed of white tissue, rested a silver signet ring just like the one Brad had given Betsy. I couldn't believe it. Somebody was giving me a ring. I pulled off my mitten.

"Will you put it on?"

Kenneth slipped it on the ring finger of my left hand. It was a bit too big and wasn't engraved, but I didn't care. I had a ring. Glancing at me for a split second, he darted in for a kiss. His tongue probed around in my mouth, striking enamel. Kenneth was trying to french me! I unclenched my teeth, closed my eyes and was letting his tongue slide in when I heard her—my mother, standing at the top of the hill, screaming my name. Her mauve dressing gown, now much too big for her, was clutched around her body, and her skin, white as chalk, stood out against the flat grey sky. She wasn't wearing a coat. She hadn't taken the time. Mom must have heard us downstairs and followed us across the field. She wasn't even wearing boots.

She called again as the wind tore open her housecoat. I didn't know whether to run up the hill or head toward the horizon running as far and fast as I could. Kenneth jumped off the rock. We both shook with cold and fear. My mother looked terrifying up there, so skinny, like a mauve scarecrow that might take flight, swooping down to pluck out our eyes. She raised her arm and pointed her finger down at me, the mark of ultimate damnation.

"Laura!" Dad's voice cried.

Coatless as well, he swept her up in his arms and glanced down at me, then turned his back and they vanished.

Kenneth pulled his toque down over his ears. "I didn't know your mom was sick."

"She's not sick!"

He tried to take my hand, but I didn't want anyone touching me. I didn't want to talk. I told him to go. Everything was still. Everything except the wind.

I stayed on the rock for a long time. My head was cold since I hadn't worn a hat, but I was too scared to go home. I thought about what Kenneth had said, about Mom being sick. I started to breathe fast. She wasn't sick. She was just having tests.

The Oldsmobile was gone but there were other cars in the driveway. Dad must have left on an emergency house call. Maybe they wouldn't be so mad at me if I entertained the patients.

"Mom?" I called, opening the door and kicking off my boots.

The living room was empty. Tedder's Hot Wheels track roped around the legs of the new coffee table. A bright yellow truck lay on its side. Nobody answered.

"Mom?" I called, even louder this time, walking slowly up the stairs.

The phone in the office rang, breaking the silence. Ruth answered. "Dr. Barnes's office, please hold."

Scared and knowing that I was going to get it, I still had to see my mother. The bedroom door was closed. Without knocking, I quietly turned the knob. The unmade bed was empty, and Mom's eiderdown comforter lay in a pool of green on the floor. Leaning down, I picked it up and buried my face in the satin, but the scent of Joy was gone. Something sweet and earthy had replaced it, the fleeting smell of a garden after all the flowers had died.

"Mom?" I called again.

Frank was in his room doing homework.

"Do you know where Mom is?"

He looked up from the books. His eyes were red and puffy. He'd been crying.

"Dad took her back to the hospital … and it's all because of you and your boyfriend."

"It's not my fault!" I yelled.

It was Mom's fault. She followed me out into the snow. If she'd stayed in bed and drank her fluids, then she'd get better. Dad always said that was the ticket, although sometimes you needed antibiotics. Why did he take her to the hospital? What could they do that he couldn't?

The kiss. I knew it had been because of the French kiss.

Aunt Anne returned that evening. Frank, Tedder, and I were lined up on the sofa, and Aunt Anne sat opposite us. My eyes focused on the design of the moiré wallpaper.

"Ruth is going to stay with you kids," Aunt Anne said. "Where's Dad?" Frank asked.

"He's going to stay with your mother."

"I want Mommy," Tedder whined, clutching Roo to his chest. "She can't be here right now," Aunt Anne replied.

"Why can't you stay?" I asked.

"Because I need to be with your mother."

I couldn't read her face. It was as blank as Granddad's after Granny died. "Will you be all right?" she asked.

We all nodded.

"Can we do something?" Frank asked.

I could see his agitation, fingers wriggling like snakes.

"Behave the way your mother would want," Aunt Anne replied, her eyes shifting to me.

Ten days passed. I barely slept. Every time I closed my eyes, I saw Mom up on the hill. Kenneth had told everyone at school that Mom was sick.

"What's she got?" Betsy asked.

We were down in the rec room, practicing some new dance steps.

"Some kind of flu."

It had to be that, or maybe pneumonia. She was awfully thin. Sandy asked when she was coming home but I didn't know. Every couple of days Aunt Anne arrived to check on us and bring letters from Mom. They were full of the usual stuff: Did I do my homework? Was I being a help to Ruth? But there was never anything about her and the tests, and never once did she mention Kenneth. Trying to read between the lines, looking for clues like Nancy Drew, I found nothing, or maybe I wasn't smart enough to figure it out. I felt so scared, and mad, too. She was punishing me for the french. Did frenching lead to being an unwed mother? I didn't know. And there was nobody to ask.

The phone rang upstairs.

"Maddy," Ruth called down. "It's your aunt."

"Hi," I said, sitting at the dining room table, staring out the window, the green receiver clenched in my hand.

The world outside was white. The chain-link fence was nearly buried in high drifts of snow, and I could see past Mom's garden, beyond the gully, yawning back to the railway tracks. Aunt Anne didn't speak.

"Are you there?" I asked.

I heard her suck in air.

"Yes."

"How's Mom?"

Another long, slow sucking of air, followed by a determined clearing of the throat. "Would you like to come and see her?"

My heart fluttered with hope. If I saw her then I'd know that she was okay, but then a sudden terror clamped itself around my chest, squeezing out the air like a shrinking band of steel, so hard that I could barely breathe. "Why doesn't she just come home?"

Now I was shaking.

"She can't," Aunt Anne replied.

Ruth banged a pot in the kitchen.

"I could come and get you right now," Aunt Anne said.

"Betsy and Sandy are here," I said, staring at Mom's fence. "They're staying overnight," I lied.

"Oh."

"Why doesn't Mom just come home?" I asked again.

The air hung like a blanket—air that still smelled faintly of fresh paint and wallpaper glue. I tried hard to keep that smell fresh in my mind. If I didn't let it go, then Mom would come back and start decorating something else. Maybe we could do my room together.

"I'd better go," Aunt Anne said.

She cleared her throat again, a scary silence hanging between us, and the line went dead. Hearing Betsy yell from the basement, I hung up and raced down to my friends.

There were no more letters or health updates that week. Neither Aunt Anne or Dad came back to the house. Just the odd phone call to Ruth to make sure everything was all right.

"Can I talk to Dad?" I asked, but Ruth just shook her head, placing the phone back in the receiver.

"Maybe next time," she said, picking Tedder up and carrying him into the office. The patients kept arriving, even though Ruth had told them that the office was closed for the time being. Everyone asked the same question: "When's he coming back?"

Mothers bouncing sick children on their hips, old farmers doubled over with rheumatism, and even Florence arrived one afternoon complaining of her gut ache. "I need him. Where is he?"

I tried to talk her through it, but she needed Dad's magic pills. He was gone, and as each day passed, I tried harder and harder to push the scary thoughts out of my mind, but they kept appearing like thought bubbles in the comics: "Batman raced to the cavern. Maybe Robin had been kidnapped by the Joker." "What if Mom isn't ever coming back?"

"Go away!" I told the thought bubbles. But that didn't always work––at night, I never knew what they might say.

The boys and Ruth were asleep, except for me: I was wide awake in the little gabled bedroom that overlooked the church. After Mom left, I started sleeping there. I couldn't bear my own bedroom because the window overlooked her garden and the gully, the gully where she'd seen the French kiss.

Two single beds rested on either side of the window. There wasn't enough room for a dresser, just two tiny bedside tables with driftwood lamps that Mom and I had made. Running my fingers over the driftwood, I noticed they were still smooth. One summer afternoon, we collected the wood down by Lake Erie, sanded the bases, and sealed the wood with shellac. They were as nice as any lamps in the store. There were no slivers. We'd done a good job.

The little room was so cold that I pulled the quilt up under my chin. A sudden blast of wind struck the side of the house, making me jump, the shutters rattling as a cold draft seeped beneath the windowsill. The storm windows were still out in the garage. Mom had forgotten to get the yardman to prepare the house for winter. Another blast hit the house.

Getting up, I looked out the window to see if the shutters had snapped off.

The trees twisted, bare branches swinging like skinny arms. Our metal garbage can had fallen on its side and was rolling across the driveway. A line of red began to peek over the edge of the horizon when suddenly everything went still. The garbage can stopped rolling. The trees relaxed. I opened the window. The wind was gone, and it was peaceful. The air was fresh and brisk when the phone suddenly rang. Shutting the window, I hopped back into bed and could hear Ruth stumble out of the spare room, her body shifting in the dark hall. The band of fear had returned, closing in on my chest, stopping my breath.

"Oh no," Ruth said, letting out the tiniest cry. "Yes," she said. The phone clicked in its cradle, and she quietly walked toward my room.

Ruth paused in the doorway as I pretended to be asleep. Her breath was uneven with jagged gasps catching in the back of her throat. She then turned away, footsteps getting softer and softer as she walked down the hall and descended the stairs. Then the wind resumed its wild dance; the shutters banging, the shingles threatening to rip themselves off the gables.

The wind eventually settled down, but I didn't. Staring straight up, I watched the day begin to spread itself across the ceiling, getting brighter and brighter. The band of steel remained, clamping tighter and tighter. A car pulled into the driveway, the front door opening and closing. Ruth must have been waiting in the foyer. Her voice mixed with Dad's, getting louder as they climbed the stairs. He told Ruth to wake the boys as he entered my room and sat down on the other bed.

"Maddy," he said, his voice trembling. "Wake up."

Dad was still in his hat and coat. His pants were wrinkled, and he hadn't shaved in days. Sitting up, I swung my legs over the side of the bed and put them on the cold maple floor. Somehow, the chill took a bit of the terror away, but it came right back when Dad looked at me. His face wasn't blank. It was full of pain. So deep there was no bottom. I didn't go to him.

Frank and Tedder stood in the doorway. Ruth was behind them. Tedder climbed into Dad's lap, rubbing the sleep out of his eyes. Dad wrapped his arm around him and Frank sat down beside him. The band squeezed.

"How's Mom?" Frank asked.

"She's with the angels," Dad said, one hand stroking Tedder's hair as the other found Frank's hand. His voice shook.

"Where did the angels take her?" Tedder asked.

"What do you mean?" Frank interrupted, his jaw clenching and unclenching.

She was dead—that's what he meant. There was a hangnail on my right thumb. I pulled at it to make it hurt.

"I was with her. She was peaceful. There was no pain."

Then Dad looked straight at me, meeting my gaze, but I turned away. It must have been the french. He turned back to the boys.

"The door opened, and an angel came in, and the angel took her to heaven."

Frank started to cry.

"I want her back," Tedder said, his little voice shaking, about to cry.

The three men of the family sobbed as Ruth stood out in the hallway, not wanting to intrude. I sat straight-backed, staring at the church and the red dawn. I didn't cry. I wouldn't—no matter what, I wouldn't cry, for fear I'd be swept away by the tears or swallowed up in their terrible bubbles. No. I sat on my bed, pressing my feet into the cold, cold floor. No tears.

Aunt Anne arrived a few minutes later. She burst through the front door, flew up the stairs and into my room, swooping the boys up into her arms, kissing them on their cheeks, telling them their mother loved them and that we'd all get through this together. Her clothing was as wrinkled as Dad's, but her face said, "March on! We're strong."

Dad stayed where he was, in his hat and coat with Tedder in his arms. Standing up, I walked past them all, down the hall and into the bathroom, locking the door behind me.

"Maddy," Aunt Anne called after me.

I turned on the cold water tap so I couldn't hear her.

"Maddy!" she shouted, knocking at the door. "Let me in!"

Silently, I stepped into the shower in my nightgown. Standing under the rushing water, I opened my mouth as wide as I could and thought about all the men who rode barrels over Niagara Falls. They'd all drowned, the barrels smashing into bits by the rocks. The cold prickled my skin and rushed into my ears, shards of liquid ice slicing into my body. I couldn't hear a thing. How did the men feel as they flew along the Niagara River, and what was it like when they struck the rocks?

The doorbell chimed. The boys and I were dressed in our Sunday best. Aunt Anne told us it was our job to answer the door. It felt as if everyone in the world was visiting our house that day. I opened the door. The lady whose little girl had been killed on McKenzie in front of our house stood there, clutching a Corning Ware casserole dish. So did all the women standing beside her. Endless casseroles and tubs packed with precooked food.

"Would you please come in?" I asked, opening the door wide.

When they looked at the three of us, they all burst into tears. "You poor children," said the lady with the dead girl.

The others dabbed their eyes with embroidered handkerchiefs, passing into the kitchen to drop off the casseroles and joining all the other friends and neighbours in the living room. Frank and I started carrying in dining room chairs for the overflow of mourners, while Tedder sat on the fireplace hearth clutching Roo.

One of the women said, "Did you even know she was sick?"

"Nobody did," another replied, glancing at me.

"Where's Dr. Barnes? The children shouldn't be all alone."

Dad had disappeared when I was standing in the shower the morning before. Ruth said he just got in the car and drove away and still hadn't returned.

Aunt Anne arrived, pushing Mom's mahogany tea trolley into the living room. It was covered with an assortment of Mom's favourite brightly painted teacups. "Can I offer you any coffee or tea?"

"Oh, no," a lady said, rising to her feet. The other women did the same. "You'll need your time alone," she added.

They left behind a mountain of food that covered the kitchen counters and spilled onto the dining room table. Aunt Anne couldn't make enough room in the fridge, so she pulled out all of Mom's Tupperware containers.

"There's no point in letting good food go to waste," she said, automatically transferring spoonful after spoonful of scalloped potatoes and macaroni and cheese into the plastic tubs.

Snapping the lids into place, I wanted to ask what had happened to Mom, but I didn't dare, since I was the one who had kissed Kenneth in the gully.

Aunt Anne pushed up the sleeves of Mom's black cashmere sweater. There wasn't enough time for her to go home and change, and Aunt Anne needed something decent to wear. Since Mom's slacks were much too long, Aunt Anne had been forced to borrow a sweater and blouse. Other than church, it was the only time I could ever remember her wearing a skirt. Her pale legs looked exposed in the light. The only sounds in the kitchen were the slap of the spoon and the snap of the lids, coupled with the unnerving sight of Aunt Anne's bare legs.

"I'm sorry."

"What on earth for?"

Then I grabbed her, hugging her as tightly as I could, smelling Mom's perfume on the sweater as her Joy washed over me.

"It's all my fault."

"It's nobody's fault."

The harder I hugged, the more Aunt Anne's body stiffened, and the harder I hung on.

"Maddy!"

"Where's Dad?"

"I don't know. Maddy, please let go."

I clung even tighter.

"This is no time to let emotion get the best of us," she said, wrenching herself free. Seizing me by the shoulders, Aunt Anne held me firmly at arm's length and, like the determined nurse she was, administered the Gillespie family medicine: "Now make yourself useful. Run those tubs down to the freezer and meet me in your parents' room."

It was quiet in the basement. The big, white freezer was full of frozen meat wrapped in brown butcher's wrap. Once a year, Mom asked Granddad for a side of beef. He'd personally select the animal and have it sent to the slaughterhouse. Once the animal was butchered, Granddad would load the meat into the trunk of his Lincoln and drive it over to our place.

"Be darned if it doesn't fill the whole thing," he'd say, marveling at the storage space his big sedan provided. "I could fit all you kids in there," he'd say, running after us, threatening to put us inside and close the lid.

Granddad could make sense of this. He'd know what to do. He'd tell me what happened.

I moved the rib roasts to the side and tossed a couple of rigid chickens into the bottom of the freezer, placed the still faintly warm casseroles on the upper rack, then went upstairs to ask Aunt Anne about Granddad.

Aunt Anne was in Mom and Dad's bedroom in the middle of their enormous walk-in closet. Dad's side was a snarl of socks and shoes, with pants and jackets dangling haphazardly from big wooden hangers. Mom's side was perfectly organized, with clothing ordered according to season and function. Her mauve dressing gown hung on a hook. The one she was wearing at the top of the hill.

Aunt Anne was rifling through Mom's clothes. "What do you think your mother would like?"

"What?" I asked, confused by the question, but comforted by the smell. Standing on the threshold of Mom's closet was like walking into her arms. I wanted to tear every dress and slip from their hangers, roll up the sweaters, throw everything into a heap on the floor and lie there, drifting away in the smell that had surrounded me my whole life.

"What do you think she'd like?" Aunt Anne repeated.

"I don't understand."

"To be buried in."

Neither of us spoke. The doorbell rang and I heard Ruth answer it.

Aunt Anne looked at me. "Your father isn't up to it, so I thought you'd like to help."

"Where is he?"

"Maybe this," Aunt Anne said, ignoring my question and selected a good navy Sunday suit.

"No." I walked into the closet, toward the formal wear. Reaching out, I selected the gold dress Mom had bought especially for a New Year's Eve party that she never attended. We'd driven into Toronto in the early fall, and I'd helped her pick it out. The sales lady said that Mom was just as pretty as a model. Mom said she didn't think so.

"And just as slim," the sales lady added.

Why hadn't I noticed how much weight she'd lost? If I'd noticed, maybe I could have done something to stop it.

"Do you have any shoes?" Mom asked. While the sales lady rushed out, Mom asked me if I thought it was too showy.

"I think you look beautiful." And she did. The golden satin shimmered as Mom slowly turned on top of a round pedestal that rested in front of the dressing room mirror. The sales lady returned with a pair of golden shoes and a matching evening bag. Mom put them on, walking down the corridor of mirrors, turning to examine her silhouette from afar.

"I'll take it," she said. When the sales lady turned away, Mom took a look at the price tag and grimaced, giving me one of our secret smiles, and adding, "Your father will kill me."

"She liked this," I said, thrusting the gold dress at Aunt Anne.

"It's much too good to be buried in," she said. "It's still got the price tag. No, we'll give this to charity. Help me pick out something else."

"No," I said firmly. "This is what she wanted. This is what she would have chosen."

Aunt Anne was about to give me a lecture about sassing back, but for some reason she stopped. The gold shoes sparkled on the floor. I snatched them up, handing them to her.

"And these," I added. "I want her buried in her new shoes."

The funeral clothes were ready and we were all packed to go to Granddad's, but Dad still hadn't returned.

Aunt Anne told Ruth she was going to take us up to the farm. "When you hear from him, tell him where we've gone." Ruth and Aunt Anne had been whispering in the kitchen about how arrangements needed to be made, but Dad was missing.

"Where's Daddy?" Tedder asked, pulling me by the sleeve.

"I don't know," I replied, yanking my arm away. "Stop asking."

Frank and Tedder had been pestering me about Dad all day, and the longer he was gone, the more irritated I became. Tedder turned away and wandered off. I felt awful. He was only a little boy.

"I'm sorry, Tedder," I said, going after him. "Dad just needs a little time on his own. You know how you feel after you cut your knee."

Tedder nodded. "You need time to cry. And then a Band-Aid."

"That's right," I said. "We're going to go to Granddad's house."

"Will Buster be there?"

"I'll make sure Granddad ties him up nice and tight."

Tedder took my hand as Aunt Anne picked up Mom's new white Samsonite suitcase, the one she'd bought to go to Colorado. "Have you kids got your good clothes?"

We all nodded.

"We better leave Dad a note," Frank said. "In case he wonders where we are."

"I already did," Aunt Anne replied. Of course she did. "Now let's get going."

We walked into the farmhouse foyer, but everything was still. "Where's Granddad?" Tedder asked, undoubtedly worried about getting his pinch.

The living and dining rooms were empty, but we finally found the whole family sitting in the kitchen, even the men. The only ones missing were Dad and Granddad. The women silently prepared salads and sandwiches for fellowship after the funeral. When we entered, they all rose.

One of the twins said she was sorry and suddenly burst into tears. Her mother passed her a handkerchief and told her that crying didn't help. I was afraid to start in case I never stopped.

Hugh swept Tedder up in his arms and onto his shoulders. "Do you want to go for a ride?" He turned to the other boys. "Let's go check on the cattle."

Happy to escape the death house, the boys nearly ran out of the kitchen.

Aunt Anne sat down, turning to the adults. "They did everything they could."

Who were "they," and what did they do?

"It was just beyond their control," she added.

What was beyond their control? How did a case of the mumps turn into something like this? I looked around the kitchen. "Where's Granddad?" I asked.

"He's busy in his office," Aunt Anne replied. "It's best you leave him alone."

I didn't pay any attention and just walked out.

Granddad's office was at the end of a long, oak-paneled hall. The walls were covered with family photographs and framed photos of him and his prize-winning cattle with their red ribbons, winners of the Carcass Class at the Royal Winter Fair.

His heavy oak door was shut, but a line of yellow light shone out from beneath, and I could hear the radio. The evening cattle futures were on. We were never to bother Granddad when the door was closed, but I had to see him.

He was sitting in his black leather desk chair, the one that spun around while he picked up one of the three black phones, barking out orders to ranchers in the west, making deals with meatpackers in the east, and talking to the railway men about schedules. Always on the go, my Granddad, never still. Not tonight. Tonight, he was collapsed in the chair, head in his hands, staring at something in his lap. When I crossed the room, he didn't hear me. Mom's university graduation photo rested in his lap. Granddad's moaning reminded me of an animal in deep pain. When I reached out and touched him, his shoulders flew back, and the photo fell.

"What are you doing in here?" he asked, furiously swiping the back of his hand across his eyes.

"I'm sorry," I replied, backing up in fear.

"Where are the boys?" he asked, picking up the photo and placing it on the desk, face down.

"They're out with the cattle."

"Did your father bring you?"

I shook my head.

"Where is he?"

"I don't know, sir."

"Sit."

Granddad's fingers drummed the back of Mom's photograph.

"We've got to be strong."

His fingers stopped. I thought my ears would pop. "Do you understand?"

"Yes." But I didn't. "Granddad?"

"What is it, Maddy?"

"What happened to Mom?"

He didn't say a word. The cattle futures had given way to the crop report. Spring wheat was going to fetch a good price.

"There's no point dwelling on that," he said. "Now go and help," he started, "your mo—" He paused. "Go and help your aunts."

The house was black. Everyone had gone to bed. Aunt Anne put me in Mom's old room. The clock ticked. I couldn't sleep. The thoughts in my stomach scared me. I'd never had a nightmare this bad. There was nothing to compare it to. The feelings in my stomach were hot and prickly and they'd started to grow. I could feel them rolling through my body and into my bones. What if the heat got into my head? I opened the window wide and lay down on the floor in my nightgown until I was so cold it hurt. The door opened. It was Aunt Anne. She'd come in to check on me. "What are you doing?"

She stepped forward. "Let me get you back into bed." Aunt Anne shut the window and buried me in a pile of blankets, their weight feeling like earth. Tears hung on her lower eyelashes, defying gravity, but she wouldn't let them fall. She wouldn't let the emotion take hold. This was what Granddad meant by being strong. We didn't hug because it would have been too hard. It was best to push the pain aside. That horrible, hot, endless ache would sweep you away and make you crazy. There could be no talking about it and no thinking about it. Mom was dead, and she wasn't coming back.

The moment Aunt Anne closed the door, I pulled off all the blankets and opened the window again. Lying back down on the floor, I let the frigid air do its work, numbing me, preparing me to be strong for the funeral the next day.

I had just finished putting on the last dress Mom had made for me when someone knocked at the door. When I opened it, I saw Dad standing there, shaking in a black suit.

"Where have you been?" I asked.

"Driving."

"Where?"

He took my hand and only said, "It's time to go."

We walked down the hall, and I looked over the banister. Frank stood at the bottom of the stairs with the rest of the relatives milling around the foyer, a slow-moving sea of black. Aunt Anne was knotting Frank's tie while Granddad stared out the window—his white hair a stark contrast to the darkness of the day. Dad stumbled. Heads turned as the relatives looked up at us, curious eyes darting like the crows in the barn.

It was just as drab outside. The world shrank as clouds of fog floated down, engulfing the fields, then the silo, and finally everything beyond the cars. The boys and I waited beside the Oldsmobile. Granddad and Dad stood next to the long black hearse, having a serious conversation. Uncles and aunts were already loaded in the first hearse, with the cousins sitting in matching black Lincolns. Granddad kept gesturing toward the hearse, but Dad shook his head, no. Finally, he placed his hand on Dad's shoulder, but Dad shrugged it off and walked back to our car. He opened the back door, and the boys slid in.

I was confused. Aunt Anne had told me we'd be traveling with Mom's body. That was the way things were done. "Aren't we going with Granddad?"

"We're going to take our own car," Dad replied, turning over the engine. "That's the way I want it."

I got in the back beside Tedder. The hearse went first, followed by the line of Lincolns, and finally our Oldsmobile. Staring up at Granny's giant spruces, I wondered if she and Mom were in heaven together looking down. Tedder took my hand as we followed the black cars into the fog.

Even though it was only about twenty yards ahead, the fog made it hard to even see the tail lights of the last Lincoln, just the odd flicker of red let us know we were on track. It didn't really matter—Dad could have found his way to the church blindfolded. That was where he and Mom had been married and where we'd been baptized. He admired the minister and loved debating scripture with him.

The Oldsmobile slowed and Dad switched on the indicator.

"You're going the wrong way," I said, as the car swung into the fog.

Tedder squeezed my fingers. "You should never rush a left turn," he whispered.

"Be quiet," Frank said, never once taking his eyes off the back of Dad's head.

"Where are we going?" I asked.

Dad didn't reply.

The Oldsmobile picked up speed, bouncing along the gravel side road. We were flying blind, but it felt as if we were traveling up, up into the sky. The boys were silent. Dad started to cry. Could he see the road through the tears? We struck a pothole and the Oldsmobile bucked, pulling hard toward the left. Tedder's fingers dug into my wrist, and we both held our breath. Another car could be coming and we'd never see it. We'd be wiped out in a crash. Maybe Mom was waiting. We could go to heaven as a family and maybe Dad was trying to take us there.

The Oldsmobile pulled out of the fog and into the sunlight. We were near the peak of a giant hill. Countryside rolled away on all sides as swells in the ocean. The spire of the church poked through the sea of fog below. I knew where we were. This was the place Mom told me about—her idea of heaven—the place where Dad had proposed.

Dad stopped the car, got out, and sat in the back. We all squeezed together to make room, but he didn't turn to face us. Instead, he left the door wide open, staring at the fields and sky.

"I've got to put my feet on the ground," he said, his good black shoes rooted in the snow. He wasn't wearing galoshes.

The fog crawled up the hill toward the car, but the church spire still stood like a beacon. All our relatives were down there, and we weren't. The funeral must have started. None of us said a word. Frank, Tedder, and I sat there like the three monkeys: See no evil, hear no evil, speak no evil.

"You don't want to go to the funeral, do you," Dad said.

It wasn't a question. Dad was crying. The car was cold. We all shivered but didn't dare ask for heat. My little brothers looked at me. I was the oldest, but I didn't want to make things worse. Tedder didn't understand, but Frank's expression said it all. Everything was my fault, and now I couldn't even get us to the funeral.

"Mom would rather you remember her the way she was," Dad said. "Don't you think so?" he asked, turning to me.

"I guess," I replied.

If Frank had a gun, he would have shot me. "Good," Dad said. "We made a good decision together."

What kind of a decision was that? We hadn't known she was dying and now we didn't get to go to her funeral? Dad got up and walked down the hill into the field. The fog embraced his legs as he slowly disappeared.

"Where's Daddy going?" Tedder asked.

"He'll be back," Frank said. "We just have to wait."

We watched as Dad walked the foggy field, vanishing and then reappearing, while not too far from us, at church, everyone was saying goodbye to our mother. Except for us.

We didn't even go to the burial. Dad drove us back to Granddad's house instead.

I was in the billiard room throwing enamel-coloured balls across the table as hard as I could. Nobody was back yet. The blue ball bounced off the green felt bumper, flew up into the air and rolled across the maple floor and under the sofa. Frank was outside pounding pucks into a net by the side of the barn. Tedder sat on the stoop in his snowsuit with Kanga and Roo sitting beside him. I couldn't tell if he was crying. The fog had finally lifted, but snow was drifting down. It was a dreary day. A lousy day. I couldn't remember the last time it had been sunny. I knew I should be taking care of Tedder, but I couldn't make myself move. My mind would say one thing, but my heart another. Dad was upstairs lying down.

I knew for sure because I kept my eye on the car, and that was why I missed the Lincoln.

"Theodore!" Granddad roared.

I didn't hear him arrive. Just the black car out in the drive after the shout. Frank dropped his hockey stick. Tedder was still sitting on the steps, his head tilted up, mouth open, staring as the aunts ran past him, up the stairs, and across the veranda—black veils shrouding their faces. Hugh swooped Tedder up in his arms, carrying him out toward the barn. An uncle grabbed Frank by the arm, the two of them, as dancers, spinning in a half turn. Tearing down the hall, I ran into the foyer.

"Where the hell are you, you coward?" Granddad yelled.

He stood there, white hair on end, wild, his black overcoat thrown open, red-faced with fury. I'd never seen Granddad so mad, and I'd never heard the word "hell" before. Not in my family. The aunts flew in behind him.

"Dad!" they cried when they noticed me standing in the doorway. Granddad grabbed the banister. "Where is your father?" he asked, his voice a bit softer at the sight of me.

My mouth wouldn't open.

"Where is he?" Granddad asked, a lot louder this time.

"We won't have raised voices!" Aunt Anne shouted.

Too scared to defy him, I pointed upstairs. Granddad was halfway up when Dad appeared at the top—hair a mess, jacket and tie askew.

"She was their mother," Granddad shouted. "She was your wife!" he yelled, his finger pointing at Dad. "What kind of a man are you?"

For a moment it was quiet until Dad replied, "The children didn't want to attend, and I thought it was best."

That was a lie. Frank, Tedder, and I had all desperately wanted to go.

"You thought it was best?" Granddad yelled louder and was about to continue when the radio went on full blast.

An old big band song, the kind Mom and Dad used to dance to, filled the foyer. Aunt Anne was up the staircase by now, pinning Granddad against the oak-paneled walls with her bare hands, telling everyone to settle down. Dad came down the stairs, past Granddad and Aunt Anne, and told me to pack my bag. It was time for us to go home. It was a miracle Granddad didn't punch him.

The house was dark. Opening the front door, I reached in and flicked on the overhead light. Dad carried Frank and Tedder up to bed. They'd fallen asleep in the car. I walked into the living room, dropping my coat on a chair. Ruth had dusted and vacuumed. The green broadloom was perfectly smooth. There was no evidence of the parade of women in pointy high heels tramping across the broadloom, bearing casseroles and sympathy. It was as if they'd never been there, a ghostly visitation.

Mom's oak sewing box sat on the floor beside the sofa. She liked to relax doing embroidery when the old black-and-white movies were on, and always said that she was "simply mad" about Clark Gable.

"But don't tell your father," she'd add with a giggle.

I opened the box and looked inside. A starched, white pillowcase, clamped into a metal hoop, held a cluster of bright-red roses with fine green stems. We'd been working on this together.

"You have to be careful, Maddy," she said, as I forced the red thread up through the starched cotton and drove it back down. "It's a cross stitch. You have to bring the needle back down on the opposite side."

"I'd rather watch Frankenstein."

"You have to follow the pattern."

When she took the hoop out of my hands our fingers brushed. Shimmying across the sofa, I burrowed into her side as she carefully undid my mistake.

"I hate patterns. It's more interesting to invent my own designs," I said.

"If you don't follow the pattern, all you get is a mess," Mom replied, putting the pillowcase into the box and closing the lid.

This was the first time I'd seen the pillowcase since then, and I picked it up, burying my face in the fabric, but Mom's smell was gone. Desperately, I pushed even more deeply into the stiff cloth when something sharp stabbed my cheek and a drop of blood fell. The blood began to spread, seeping into Mom's fine green stems. The stain would never come out. Another thing I ruined.

"Maddy." Dad stood in the doorway.

Quickly replacing the pillowcase into the box, I closed the lid.

"It's time for bed," he said.

"Let's watch the news," I replied, patting the sofa beside me. I wanted—needed - to be with him.

"Brush your teeth," he said, turning away.

I obeyed.

After I hung up my good dress, I slipped into my flannelette nightgown and brushed my teeth. The doors to the boys' rooms were closed, but Dad's was still ajar and the lights were on. Pushing the door open, I walked in. He was doing exactly what I'd wanted to do the day before. He was sitting on the floor of their closet with Mom's clothes all around him, crying so hard he didn't even hear me. He looked like a bomb had gone off inside him.

"Dad?"

He jumped up and stepped back. "Why aren't you in bed?" he asked, shaking his head, trying to find his bearings.

I moved toward him. "I love you, Daddy."

"I love you, too," he replied. Then he turned me around, walking me toward the door.

"Dad," I said, trying to turn around to hug him, but he wouldn't let me close.

"We've got to get some sleep," he said. "Things will look better in the morning."

He kissed me gently on top of the head, pushed me out into the hall, and quietly shut the door behind him. When I reached out for the handle, about to turn it, the lock clicked. I sat on the floor, my back up against the wall, waiting, but my father never came out.

CHAPTER THREE

We were out of school for two weeks. When I came back, somebody new walked through the doors. Somebody who had lost the most important thing in the world and had no idea how to get it back. My brain was a balloon suspended on a long piece of string, floating down the hall, propelled by my rack-of-bones body. Every fragment felt disconnected, like the anatomical skeleton dangling in Dad's office, clickety-clack clickety-clack. Betsy and Brad were talking by her locker. He laughed at something she said. It was so good to see my friends.

"Hi, Betsy."

Betsy stopped smiling. Brad backed up.

"I'm sorry about your mom," Betsy said, and looked at her feet.

"Thanks."

Brad grabbed Betsy's arm, pulling her down the hall. "We've got to go."

I was desperate to do something, anything that would trick reality, even if only for a moment.

"Do you want to go to Frenchy's after school?" I called. "My treat."

"Can't," Betsy replied, and they ran away.

All the other kids acted the same way. Once in the washroom a girl I barely knew saw me come in. She gasped and ran out with soaking wet hands, leaving tiny pools of water behind her.

Betsy and Sandy were supposed to be my best friends and Kenneth had given me a ring. During recess, when I was sitting on the swing by myself, he started toward me, but some kids pulled him back, whispering something in his ear. He gave me a sad look and walked away. That afternoon I went over to his locker and dropped the ring through the metal slots in the door, listening as it bounced and clattered, striking the bottom. I didn't have a boyfriend anymore.

There was no one to talk to. Aunt Anne told me to "soldier on" and Dad retreated to the office. He started seeing patients at eight in the morning, worked straight to midnight, and the next day started all over again. One morning I found him asleep on an examining table with an open bottle of pills on the table beside him. The same pills Mom didn't want to take the night of the dance. They were called Valium. While Dad splashed cold water on his face and brushed his teeth, I straightened his tie. He needed a shave.

"Dad?"

"Hmmm?"

"Nobody at school will talk to me."

"I'm sure you're exaggerating."

He filled a Dixie cup with Listerine and began to gargle.

"They hate me. And I don't know why."

"Give them some time; they'll come around."

No, they wouldn't.

Dad threw the paper cup toward the overflowing wastepaper basket, but it bounced off the top and onto the floor. That was another thing that was slipping away. Mom's beautiful, orderly house was becoming a pigsty.

"And don't forget," Dad said. "We've got church this weekend. There's a guest preacher."

I took a deep breath. "I'm not going."

Now he paid attention. "What do you mean?"

When Mom was alive, the house was clean and we had good food to eat. She kissed us goodnight and told us that she loved us. Now she was gone, and it was as if Dad had followed her, but he wasn't dead, and the boys needed him. No. I needed him. We stood there staring at each other. Eventually, somebody had to blink. "I'm not going to worship a God who killed my mother."

He looked at me for a long time. "If that's what you've decided," he said. "You're a big girl now."

My father had gone.

Ruth was still at the nurse's station doing paperwork, muttering about how her new husband was going to kill her for coming home late again. Tedder slept on her lap while I leafed through a record club catalogue, checking off the boxes for records I wanted.

Ruth's eyebrows shot up. "Does your father know you're ordering those?" She knew Mom didn't want me listening to rock and roll.

"Sure," I replied, slipping the order card into the pile of outgoing mail.

"Are you telling the truth?"

"Yes," I lied. I knew that lying was wrong, but the grown-ups did it, so why couldn't I? Nobody was listening to me anyway.

Tedder woke up, snuggling into Ruth's neck.

"I'm going to tuck Tedder in. Tell your father I've gone home and that I'll finish up in the morning."

A messy stack of magazines rested in the window well. Since nobody would talk to me, I'd spent the last couple of months reading Dad's monthly subscriptions, learning about the real world.

The latest issue of *Newsweek* said there was a youth revolution going on. Young people were fighting with their parents and "the establishment," trying to "make love, not war." They took drugs to "turn on, tune in, drop out." I wasn't really sure what that meant, but it was clear that the adults hated what the hippies were doing and thought that drugs were becoming a serious problem. And then it came to me. I had a dispensary full of them.

Pulling the *Compendium* off the dispensary shelf, I looked up Dad's nerve pills. Valium could be used to treat depression, but it was especially effective in dealing with anxiety. Dad pushed his way through the dispensary door, searching for urine-sample bottles.

I closed the book. "What's LSD?"

"What?" Dad asked, looking at me as if I were speaking Chinese. "Where's Ruth?"

"She had to go home," I answered. "It says here that the hippies are dropping pills called LSD. Do you have any in here?"

"Dropping?" he asked.

"What's LSD?" I insisted.

"It's illegal dope," he replied, looking at his watch. "Have you done your homework?"

"It's all finished." Another lie, but it didn't really count because he didn't really care anyway.

"You'd better get up to bed. It's getting late," he said, finally locating the sample bottles. "I'll come in and kiss you goodnight."

The light was still on in Frank's room was on, so I just walked in.

"Don't you ever knock?" he asked.

"Frankly, don't you ever stop studying?"

Sitting down on his bed, I examined a model of the Santa Maria that he was building from scratch. Frank was fascinated by Columbus. Maybe he wanted to sail away to a new land. I couldn't blame him.

"What do you want?" Frank asked, his nose wedged even deeper into the geography book. "I've still got another chapter to go."

"Why are you working so hard?"

Frank set his pencil down. "Because that's what Mom would expect of me. And maybe it'll make Dad happier."

"You're such a suck."

He jumped up. "You're a selfish jerk!"

"Why are you so mad?"

He paused. "It's *your* fault Mom's dead."

I pushed him. "No, it's not."

He shoved back. "Then why did she die?"

"I don't know."

But I did, didn't I?

"She died because she was out in the snow. She was out in the snow because of you and your boyfriend." He started to cry. "I heard Dad. They were talking when he carried her into the house. He kept saying she had to take care of herself. She said you were her little girl. He said she shouldn't be out in the snow in her condition. Then he took her away in the car and she never came home."

Now, I was the one who was crying. "It's not my fault!"

Frank wiped his eyes, picked up his book, and before starting started to study again, whispered for me to go. Now.

I walked down the hall and into my room, put on my pajamas, and crawled in between the cool sheets. The bedside lamp was on so Dad could find his way. The clock ticked as I watched and waited, but he never came up to kiss me goodnight.

Sometime after one I quietly got up, closed the door, and opened the bedside table. There was only one thing the aunts didn't find when they spirited all of Mom's stuff out of the house, and it was hidden in the drawer behind a bunch of books. Mom's magical bottle of Joy.

I lay down and turned off the light with the Joy resting on my chest. Being oh-so-careful, I gently removed the heavy stopper.

Moonlight struck the crystal as the genie silently rose out of the bottle. My eyes closed and Mom appeared, turning every head on the street; that beautiful, long neck and the deep colour of her hair. I could see her dancing around the living room using the dust mop as a partner, when something started happening. The memories began to degrade, like bits of Dad's home movies that had been overexposed to light, or records that skipped. I replaced the stopper and tucked the bottle away. The Joy was a powerful potion that had to be handled carefully, or I'd lose my way back to Mom.

"Can you please turn that down?" Dad asked.

"In-A-Gadda-Da-Vida" was playing full blast on the stereo. We were having burgers and cherry Kool-Aid in the living room while Dad was trying to watch the evening news. Young American soldiers in Vietnam were encountering a terrible device called the Bouncing Betty. The announcer explained how it worked. It was safe when a soldier stepped on Betty, but the second he removed his foot, Betty shot out from the ground and exploded, blowing the soldier clear out of his boots. The lucky soldiers died—the crippled boys sent home to veterans' hospitals, their lives but a broken dream. Unsurprisingly, many of them had joined the hippies to protest the war.

Tedder was trying to cut into the hamburger bun with his spoon. "Do you want some help with that?" I asked.

"No, thank you," Tedder replied, as the spoon slipped, knocking his glass of Kool-Aid off the tray and onto Mom's sea-green broadloom. Instinctively, we all jumped to our feet, petrified that the red punch would stain, but then we stopped. Only Mom would care. Out of habit, or maybe it was respect, Frank ran into the kitchen and got a damp cloth. He was on his hands and knees, trying to get the stain out, when Aunt Anne unexpectedly walked into the living room.

The boys were promptly tucked into bed, and I was sent to my room to do homework, but instead I perched at my secret spot at the top of the stairs. Dad and Aunt Anne were out of my sightline, but I could hear snippets of conversation.

"This is no way for children to live," followed by, "Laura wouldn't want this," and, "You need some help."

When they came toward the foyer, I had to run back to my bedroom.

"Don't think I can't hear you, Madeline Anne!"

Quietly, I padded off to bed. Aunt Anne must be coming to stay with us, and at least things would be kind of normal again.

Two days later, there was a knock on the door. A girl of about twenty with a brown bowl cut stood there clutching a suitcase.

"Allo? Lookink vor doctor."

"That's around the side of the house. But my dad isn't taking any new patients right now."

The girl shook her head. Her English was terrible. "My name Rika," she said. "I am here vor verk."

Dad was sitting at the head of the table pretending to read the morning paper while Frank and Tedder were staring at slices of white Wonder Bread slathered in suspicious brown goo.

"Vat is matter?"

"It's fine," Dad replied with a gentle smile, as Rika excused herself.

"Dad, she can't cook," I said.

She had just served us another breakfast of chocolate sandwiches. Rika was an even worse cook than me, didn't even know how to operate the washing machine, and never cleaned the dishes properly.

"I can take better care of the family than she can!"

"I don't want you doing the housework, Maddy. You've got school to think of and fun to have."

"But Dad, she's useless!"

"Give her a chance," he said, finishing his chocolate sandwich and getting up to go to work. "Your mother would want you kids to enjoy yourselves," he added, as he disappeared.

Frank, Tedder, and I stared at the sandwiches. There was no way we were eating that.

More new records arrived in the mail. Clutching them under my arm, I approached the smokers' wall. It had taken every bit of nerve I had, but I had to lure my friends back and the records were the best bait I could think of.

Betsy and Brad stood in the middle of a big group of kids. We'd had a good spring rain earlier that day, and pools of muddy water pitted the football field. Betsy lit a cigarette. When did she start smoking? Taking a deep breath, I walked into the centre, holding Janis Joplin out in front of me as a peace offering.

Everyone stopped talking and looked at the album cover. Brad pulled back, but Betsy, intrigued, didn't.

"I've got a whole bunch more," I said, nonchalantly. "You want to come over and listen?" I held up the records one at a time, slowly rotating each album cover so everyone could get a look. The crowd moved closer. Somebody oohed. A couple of kids muttered, "Cool." They'd never seen these records before.

"Betsy!" a voice shouted.

The crowd turned. A scowling girl stood near the back, her fists shoved deeply into her coat pockets. The same girl who had run out of the washroom with soaking wet hands because she was afraid of me. The other kids nervously giggled. The girl darted in and out of the milling crowd, getting closer to me and then abruptly pulling back.

"Stay away from her," the girl said, pointing a finger at me. "Or you'll catch cancer."

Silence fell. My face throbbed, and my heart started to thump with raw anger. The records fell into the mud. Then my heart pumped something up into my throat, something I'd never felt before.

"You'd better shut your mouth," a strange voice said. It was my voice, but a deep, scary me that I'd never heard before.

The girl got closer, putting her hand over her mouth, making a finger mask.

"My mother said your mother died of it and everyone knows you only get cancer if you deserve it," the girl said, looking at the pack of kids surrounding us. "Or," she added, "if you've been around people who've had it."

"You are such a liar!" I screamed, grabbing the girl by the lapels smashing her back into the brick wall.

Mr. Thom, the principal, rushed across the field and arrived just in time to hear the end. He seized the girl by the arm and gave her a good shake.

"That is an ignorant thing to say. You apologize right now."

The girl's face flushed. She hated me, and I hated Sterling. I hated every kid I'd gone to school with for the last eight years. I didn't belong there. I turned and ran.

As I was running across Main Street, past Comfort's Diner and down McKenzie, it started raining again. A neighbour taking out the trash waved at me, barely visible through rain and tears. Dad had just stepped out of the car as I tore up the driveway.

"Everyone's saying that Mom died of cancer. Make them stop, Dad. Please make them stop lying!"

Dad took me by the shoulders. "It's true, honeybunch."

It couldn't be. Only bad people got cancer. People who deserved it. People who smoked. Rain bounced off the car.

"Why didn't you tell me?"

"She didn't want anyone to know."

A car pulled into the driveway with headlights so bright that Dad's glove flew up to shield his eyes. Mr. Thom got out and asked me if I was all right.

"I'm going inside," I replied, upset by the news.

Ruth was gone, and the office was empty. I sat down at the desk, watching Dad and Mr. Thom through the window. They were both getting soaked, probably sharing other secrets I knew nothing about. Picking up the phone books, I smashed them down on the desk with all my strength. Did the relatives know about the cancer? Maybe that's why Granddad didn't come to our house anymore. He had no time for sickly things. I didn't care if I caught it. It would be better to be dead than live through this.

Yanking open the drawer to put the phone books back inside, I noticed random bottles of medicine rolling around. The mess was making me crazy. Everything was out of order, even Dad's restricted substances, dangerous drugs that should be under lock and key. An engine turned over outside. As I was straightening up the drawer, Dad walked in.

"Mr. Thom says you gave that girl quite a push."

"What happened to Mom?"

"She got sick."

"But how? How did she catch cancer?"

"It's not something you catch. It's a disease of the body. It's the cells that turn on themselves, Maddy. They are the killer."

"But you don't get it unless you do bad things."

"That's not true."

"Then why did Mom hide it?"

"Because she didn't want people to know."

"Why?"

"Because they might be afraid."

"Why?"

"Because cancer has a stigma."

A stigma. That's what I got at school. I was stained.

"Was she ashamed?"

He didn't answer. He wasn't telling the truth.

"Was it because of me?"

He gave me an odd look.

"Because of that … that day on the hill. Did that escalate the disease?"

Dad always told me how important it was to keep illness at bay, and that meant staying in bed and keeping warm.

"I don't think so."

If cancer didn't follow the rules, that meant it wasn't my fault. I swallowed.

"But it probably didn't help either," he added.

Oh. So it was my fault. If only I hadn't gone out to the gully with Kenneth. If only I'd stayed home and been good, then maybe Mom wouldn't be dead.

Dad rested his shaky hands on my shoulders. "Don't worry, honeybunch. Eventually, this will all blow over."

I wanted to believe him, but I couldn't. My eyes followed him as he disappeared into the dispensary, a rattle of pills in his wake.

It was clear. Dad's body might have been in the house, but the father I'd known my whole life was gone. He was now in the dispensary taking more Valium. And at that moment, I knew everything had changed. My whole life. My father couldn't take care of me and I had to take care of myself.

Staring out the window at the falling rain, I realized my reality as a child was over—as day into night. I had to become tough and strong. Instantly grow up. I closed my eyes, willing a forcefield to appear. It began to hum. If I was going to survive, I had to become invulnerable and live in a Fortress of Solitude. Like Superman.

Pedaling down Main and up Station Street on my way to Wellington High, I whizzed by a group of little kids trudging up the hill to Sterling Public. A yellow school bus honked hello. Instinctively, my hand shot up, but I immediately dropped it. Only twerps waved. A line of buses was dropping off the farm kids. We hadn't had a lot at Sterling Public, but Wellington High got all the teenagers from the surrounding countryside. Dumping my bike on the ground, I straightened my dress. It was a stretchy blue mini. My black hair had grown long, hanging well past my shoulders. I pulled a compact out of my purse and flipped it open, shaking my hair so the bangs tumbled into my eyes. The blue eyeshadow looked good. Sandy and Betsy were talking to some other kid. I couldn't see her face, but she had honey-blonde hair that nearly touched her waist.

Casually, I strolled over. I'd been working on my walk as well as my hair. The walk was a cross between an easy strut and a bounce. The strut made me look cool and not too anxious to please. The bounce showed I was a lot of fun.

"Do you think high school is going to be hard?" I asked.

Sandy laughed. "Like you ever study anyway."

Betsy, Sandy, and I had spent most of the summer together playing my new records and learning dance steps. Betsy asked me if I'd gotten the new Led Zeppelin yet.

"At home," I replied, with a promising smile.

"Can we come over?" Sandy asked.

"Sure."

My basement was the new hangout because we could do pretty much anything we wanted. Brad and Betsy made out on the sofa, but when Kenneth tried to pull me down, I ran upstairs. Something inside me had changed and I didn't want to be his girlfriend anymore.

Betsy introduced me to the new girl. Her name was Ginnie Hall, and her eyes were cornflower blue. She lived on a dairy farm way past the outskirts of town.

I turned to her. "Do you want to come, too?"

"I can't. I have to do chores."

The bell rang. Time for class.

The four of us were crammed into our booth at Frenchy's. While Comfort's Diner was clean and offered good home cooking at reasonable prices, Frenchy's was dirty and dangerous. The red vinyl in the booths were cracked, and the red lettering on the window was chipped and fading away. Frenchy's was run by a short Québecoise who chain-smoked and looked like a Grape-Nut. Our gang always went there for lunch. Sandy and Betsy ordered a 7Up and two straws. I asked for a Coke, and Ginnie wanted milk.

"You sure you don't want a Coke? My treat." Since I'd started helping myself to the change covering Dad's dresser I didn't have to worry about money.

"No, thank you."

I pulled a pack of Export "A"s out of my jeans. At first, I hated the smell of cigarettes and had to really force myself to inhale them, but once I got used to the taste, I'd become a full-time smoker.

I waved the cigarette under Ginnie's nose and took a long drag. "Want one?"

"I don't smoke."

Ginnie was so innocent.

"Do you have a date yet?" she asked.

The big bonfire, the social event of the fall, was coming up and Aunt Anne was going to take me into Toronto to buy a new outfit. I was going to get brown Lee cords.

"I'm going stag," I said.

Betsy lit a cigarette. "You can't go stag."

Ever since the horrible day in the gully, I'd sort of lost interest in boys, but I couldn't say that out loud.

"Kenneth is dying to take you."

"I don't know." I blew another smoke ring. "What about you, Ginnie?"

"Mom won't let me, and besides, I've got chores."

Right. Her chores.

The doorbell jangled and Kenneth, Mark, and Dale walked in. Dale got bussed in for school with Ginnie, and Mark was Sandy's new boyfriend. He and his sister lived with their father, a trucker who drank too much. Sometimes Mark came to school with a black eye.

"He's so cute," Sandy whispered.

When Mark swaggered by, running a comb through his blond hair, Sandy looked ready to melt. Kenneth leaned against the counter and asked for a coffee, shooting me his sly-dog look. Betsy leaned toward Ginnie.

"Do you have the hots for Dale?"

"No," Ginnie replied, turning to me. "Aren't you going out with Kenneth?" She had a milk moustache.

"Sort of," I replied, wiping the milk from Ginnie's lip. She smiled. It was easier having Kenneth as a sort-of boyfriend, but I didn't want to go parking with him. It was all so complicated.

Betsy glanced at Kenneth. "You don't want to get a reputation as a cock tease."

"I never tease him."

"If you tease a boy then you'll get raped, and you'll deserve it," she said.

"It's true," Sandy added.

"I'm saving myself for when I get married," Ginnie said.

Betsy said that if they got over-excited it was better to jerk them off. What was jerking off? Was that touching it? I wanted to change the topic.

"Do you guys want to come for a sleepover next weekend?" I asked. "I could show you my new outfit."

Sandy had a date, and as usual Ginnie couldn't, but Betsy was game.

"It's back here," I said, taking down a dusty bottle from the top shelf in the root cellar.

Our family didn't drink, but that didn't stop some of Dad's grateful patients from dropping off a bottle in thanks for a baby delivered or a wound stitched.

"I thought your parents, um, sorry, I mean your dad," Betsy said, stumbling. "I didn't think your dad drank."

"He doesn't," I replied, blowing the dust off the label. At least he said he didn't. Who knew what the truth was? "And I bet he doesn't even know what's down here."

Dad had stopped working late and started disappearing in the evenings and on weekends. He never told me where he went. After I made sure the boys had gone to sleep, Betsy set a bottle of Coke, the rye, and two glasses in front of her.

"Do you have a shotglass?" she asked

"As if," I replied, rolling my eyes.

She smiled.

"Okay, well then you pour in the rye, count to seven and then top it up with Coke."

About four inches of rye sloshed into each glass. I took a sip that burned my throat. "That's horrible!"

"Then hold your nose and chug."

Betsy picked up her glass, pinched her nose and swallowed, and I copied her. At first, I thought I was going to vomit, but then I started to feel warm and good. For the first time since Mom died, the sadness drifted away.

"Again!" Betsy called, pouring us each another drink.

Arms out like an airplane, I flew around the room. "How do you know about drinking?"

"Dave taught me."

Betsy was so lucky to have an older brother.

"I love Brad," Betsy cooed, falling back on the sofa. "Don't you still secretly love Kenneth?" she asked, wagging her finger at me, her eyes getting all googly. "He really wants to take you to the fish fry."

I turned on the hi-fi and put on a record.

"Don't you secretly want him back?" she asked.

No, I didn't. I set the needle on the record. "Let's have another one."

Every time Betsy started to talk about boys, I just filled up her glass and before I knew it the bottle was empty, and we were spinning around to "Mama Told Me Not To Come." Turning the volume up full blast, we galloped up the stairs, whooping through the house. Frank came out rubbing his sleepy eyes, complaining that he'd tell Dad that we were making a racket.

"Frankly, I wish you'd shut up!" I yelled, laughing at the top of my lungs.

Betsy and I started singing, stumbling back down the stairs, when suddenly she stopped and put her hand on the wall.

"I feel sick."

The floor started spinning and I felt dizzy. Betsy brought her other hand up to her mouth just as I looked at Mom's sea-green broadloom.

There was a knock at the door. Betsy and I looked at one another. We were lying in my bed, still in our clothes. I felt awful. Another hard rap.

"Oh man, I'm going to be in so much trouble."

Stumbling across the room, I remembered all the barfing and especially the empty bottle of booze. There would be no talking my way out of that. When I nervously opened the door, certain of big trouble, Dad stood there holding a tray with two glasses of pop and some dry toast.

"The ginger ale's flat so it should help settle your stomach."

He handed me the tray, and without another word he turned and walked down the hall. Betsy couldn't believe it.

"Your Dad's so cool. My Mom would have thrown a fit."

I knew better. I could have set the house on fire and Dad wouldn't notice. I could die and he wouldn't give a shit.

Not giving a shit was my new superpower way of looking at the world. I made myself not care what the neighbours thought, which I never would have done before. When Rika threatened to quit because Dad asked her to clean up the vomit, I didn't give a shit. I didn't even care what Aunt Anne thought, which was a definite first, but Aunt Anne lived in a world where emotions weren't allowed, and I was exploding with too many feelings that I couldn't control, no matter how hard I tried.

The power of not giving a shit was amazing. Every time I turned down Kenneth's invitation to the bonfire it made him all the more determined to take me.

Betsy gave me a look, stubbing out her cigarette. "You're supposed to go with a boy."

Kenneth and Brad were talking by the jukebox at Frenchy's, and Kenneth kept staring at me.

"If you don't that means you're either an ugly douche bag or you're weird," she added.

After everything I'd done to make people like me, the last thing I wanted was for anyone to think I was weird.

Betsy, Brad, Kenneth, and I piled into Dave's Chevy and headed down to Lake Erie for the bonfire. Who cared about a fire, I thought. I wanted to know where the party was.

Kenneth and I sat on a log watching Brad and Betsy dig a big hole in the sand for the cooler. Dave and some other guys piled driftwood on the fire, while couples huddled under blankets along the beach. A chilly nip in the air said winter was getting close. One of the boys had a green car, its doors wide open as music blasted out. A girl in a denim jacket emblazoned with a peace sign danced in the sand. It should have been perfect, but it wasn't. Something was missing.

Something always was.

Kenneth put his arm around my shoulder.

"Do you know where we can get liquor?" I asked, since the whiskey had calmed me down.

"Follow me."

Kenneth took me around the back of a dune. "It's over here."

But there was no liquor—only Kenneth and his grabby fingers. The minute we were away from the rest of the group, he started kissing me. I kissed him back because I didn't want anyone to think I was weird, but I didn't like the way he tasted—like sour Juicy Fruit gum.

"I thought you knew where to get some booze," I said, trying to wriggle away.

Kenneth squeezed me so tight in his arms that I could barely breathe. His breath was hot against my face. "You want to touch it?"

His penis pushed against the inside of my thigh as he tried to slip his hand under my jacket to grope my boobs. After Mom died, I'd dumped the bras. I didn't want anything holding me back or holding me in. The boys liked it. My breasts had grown and bounced when I walked, and I could tell they held a mystical power. But now Kenneth was the one with the power, and he was starting to breathe harder and harder. Betsy had warned me not to be a "cock tease." Then Mom, in her mauve dressing gown, appeared on the top of my memory hill. I had to get away. I reached out and touched his thigh. "You want me to?"

Kenneth's eyes flipped open and in a flash his hands dropped as he unzipped his jeans. Fumbling with his underpants, he pulled out what looked like a big, old ugly skin worm. I wanted to laugh, but didn't dare, because Kenneth seemed so proud of it. This hard thing with a hole at the top. Kenneth's eyes flickered. "Just touch it," he groaned.

Kenneth grabbed for my hand, but when I pushed him, he tumbled backwards, tripping over his jeans. I jumped over the dune, back to the party.

The school bell rang. Kids pulled their coats out of their lockers and rushed for the door. Ginnie and a bunch of other kids were standing outside in a perfect circle in front of the yellow school bus, but nobody was getting on. They stood still, staring at the ground. Ginnie glanced over at me with a funny mixture of shock and fascination and then looked back into the centre of the circle. Mark's little sister was lying face down in the dirt with her hands underneath her body. She was pumping up and down on her hands, which were tucked beneath her crotch. I didn't know what she was doing, but it was obviously making her feel good. Everyone stood quietly and watched. Nobody laughed or teased. And then she started to moan. A teacher arrived, breaking through the circle and snatched Mark's sister up with an angry yank. "Disperse!"

Nobody moved. The teacher's face was red. Mark's sister had a strange smile. She didn't apologize. She just turned and wandered down the road. The teacher didn't know what to do, so he started yelling. "Country children, get on the bus! This isn't a show! That girl needs help!"

Ginnie and I looked at one another.

"What was that?" she asked.

"I don't know," I replied, throwing my book bag over my shoulder.

"You want to come out to my place?" she asked.

That was a surprise. Ginnie had been to my place for lunch and stuff, but I'd never been invited to hers before.

"You could stay for supper and my mom could drive you home. That is, if it's okay with your father."

"Oh, it'll be all right. I'll just call from your place."

Following Ginnie up the stairs, I asked the female driver if it was okay to hitch a ride. She smiled and nodded. The bus smelled like old gum and forgotten lunches.

The Hall farm was on two hundred acres of prime land. The tilled earth, dark and loamy, stretched from the concession road to a large stand of trees that marked the end of the property. The barn was freshly painted and sparkling white, a sure sign of a prosperous farm. Everything about the Hall place said good crops and healthy cattle. Both the barn and the house were white with green roofs and green trim. New shutters framed the windows, and a deep-green door welcomed you inside. Ginnie swung open a wide screen door that snapped shut behind us. The kitchen smelled like Mom's cooking. Good food. Not Rika's chocolate sandwiches. This was a happy home. Ginnie called out to let her mother know that she had arrived and asked me if I'd like anything to drink.

"Sure," I replied, slinging my books on a chair by the door.

They'd just struck the wood when Mrs. Hall entered the room. She was an enormous woman with a jet-black beehive and pumps. Her hips were round and her calves strong and shapely. Poured into a skimpy black dress with big jangly earrings, Mrs. Hall was way too fancy to be a farmer's wife. Mom would have said she was overdone.

It wasn't as if she wasn't nice to me, but there was something definitely scary about Ginnie's mom. The moment Ginnie said she'd brought me home for dinner, Mrs. Hall chucked me under the chin and said that she'd put in some extra turnip. Then she jabbed me in the stomach, saying that I could use a bit of fattening up. I flinched, not wanting to be fattened up, but I smiled at Mrs. Hall and thanked her for the invitation.

"What time is your father expecting you home?"

"Oh, jeeps! We haven't called him yet," Ginnie cried, pulling me toward the phone.

I knew there wouldn't be a problem. There never was.

Ginnie and I were inseparable all fall and winter, and she gave me a Monkees record for my birthday. For the first time ever, Dad forgot, but Frank and Tedder didn't. They asked Rika to bake a cake, and we all sang. Mom said birthdays were our own special day and important to celebrate, but Dad wasn't even home. Betsy and Sandy weren't much better. They'd vanished into boyville, and we only saw them in class. Kenneth still asked me out, but after a while, he gave up, just mooning at me with his cow eyes. Ginnie was more fun than I first thought, and it was nice being at her place, even though her mother made me do chores.

"Don't you girls come back unless both baskets are full," Mrs. Hall said, handing us each a wicker basket.

"Yes, Mrs. Hall," I replied, always very careful to be polite.

The henhouse was in a white clapboard shack corralled by a new green fence. A proud orange rooster stood on the gate and crowed. Ginnie and I walked down the path with baskets over our arms. It was late April, but the weather was unseasonably warm.

"Watch your head," Ginnie said, ducking as she entered the coop.

The ceiling was low and so was the light. Ginnie began gathering eggs. It looked easy enough. But when I reached for a bird and touched its feathers, the beak came down with a vicious peck, drawing a tiny bead of blood.

"Hey!" I yelled.

The hens started clucking. I backed up toward the door, but Ginnie told me to follow her and watch closely. When the chickens settled down, she told me to try it again.

My hand still stung. "I don't think so."

"Chicken?" she asked, tickling me.

While my mom had, I had no experience with chickens. "No. I just don't want to get pecked to death."

She tickled me again, making me wriggle and laugh. "I'll protect you. Don't you trust me?"

"I don't know. You've got killer chickens," I replied.

"Give me your hand." Ginnie grabbed my hand and stepped close behind me. She smelled like sunshine and grass. My body went warm, and my head was swimmy. "Let me guide it."

A red hen looked up from her nest.

"You have to be really quick. If they don't know what's happening, they don't miss the egg. Ready?"

"Okay."

Together, our hands thrust forward under the feathers, and then the warm egg rested in my hand.

"Don't break it," Ginnie whispered in my ear. Her whisper made my body feel excited.

In a half-hour, we'd filled both baskets and were walking back up the lane toward the house.

"That was fun," I said.

The sky glowed red with the embers of day.

"This Saturday Dad's going to burn the brush on the back forty and I've got to help. Do you want to come out in the morning and stay over?"

Mrs. Hall emerged from the front door, her big breasts leveled like missiles.

"Get in the car, Maddy. It's late."

Ginnie and I ran toward the shiny new white Buick.

"Is it okay if Maddy stays over next weekend?"

Mrs. Hall paused. "Your father's going to need you."

Oh no.

"That's why Maddy's going to come out. She'll come in the morning and help for the rest of the day." Ginnie turned to me and smiled. "Right? You'll do the eggs."

"If it's okay with you," I added, smiling my warmest, most polite Gillespie smile at Mrs. Hall. Her lip curled as she considered it, assessing me as she did her home and her makeup. Was there a flaw?

"As long as she pulls her weight," Mrs. Hall said, settling into the driver's side. "Now, do as I say and get in the car."

Saturday morning, I galloped in and jumped on the bed. Dad was still asleep.

"Wake up!"

He pulled the covers up and over his face. "The Halls won't mind if you're there after lunch."

Hitting him with a pillow, I shouted, "Come on. Get up!"

Dad got dressed, poured a mug of instant coffee, and we got in the car, heading down the back concession road. I was so excited. Dad took a sip and looked over at me.

"How are things at school?"

Since when did he ask about school?

"How are your friends?"

Like he cared.

"Fine."

"People out here can be a bit backward …"

That didn't sound like my father. He loved country people. Looking at the clock on the dash, I saw it was already a few minutes after nine.

"Can you please hurry, Dad? I don't want to be late." The car picked up speed. He took another sip of coffee.

"I'm going to stay in the city this weekend. There's a dance in Toronto."

"What kind of dance?"

"A doctors' dance," he replied, a smile spreading across his face. It was the first time that he'd smiled like that in a long time, and it was really nice to see.

The Oldsmobile pulled into the drive. Mr. Hall's field truck was out by the barn. They hadn't left yet, which meant I could still burn something. Setting my suitcase on the front porch, I ran down the lane.

Ginnie and I sat on the humming wheel wells in the rear of Mr. Hall's cherry-red pickup. The truck shot across the field so fast I thought we might flip. Mr. Hall was a tall, quiet man with short, grey hair neatly shorn about the ears. He always wore clean overalls and a snappy blue fedora, but the devil got a hold of him when he drove. When Mr. Hall struck a hole, I bounced off the wheel well. Ginnie grabbed me by the waist and pulled me down beside her, holding me tight.

The pickup squealed to a stop. Mr. Hall told us to gather all the loose brush from the edge of the bush and collect the branches that had drifted over the fields. It was crucial to get everything off the ground because a loose stick could damage a harrow or a plough.

Ginnie and I threw armload after armload of brush into the flames, watching the embers fire up into the bright blue sky and float back down to earth. It was a red-hot day and pure hell by the fire. Sweat rolled down my back and I thought I was going to pass out. I'd never worked so hard, but Ginnie was barely winded. She just moved ahead of me, sweeping the branches up into her arms and tossing them back into the fire. She was whistling and teasing me about being a city slicker.

"What?" I yelled over the fire. "My grandfather is one of the biggest cattlemen in the country. I've even helped with the herd."

She poked me in the stomach. "You're soft."

I laughed, pushing back, "We'll see who's soft." When I started tickling her, we dropped our branches and began to wrestle. Ginnie fell, pulling me with her. We were rolling around in the earth when her dad picked us both up by the belt loops, telling us to stop horsing around. He handed Ginnie a picnic basket. "You two amateur wrestlers can have lunch by the pond."

The Hall cow pond was at the far end of the property. A herd of Holsteins grazed under a stand of maples to avoid the midday sun. Ginnie and I finished eating and started tossing rocks into the water, trying to sink a lily pad.

"You want to go for a swim?" she asked.

"It's too cold."

Ginnie stripped down to her underwear. Her bra and panties were white with tiny pink flowers.

"Are you sure you don't want to come in?"

"I am."

"The cows don't use it other than to drink. It's too deep," Ginnie said, stepping in. "Are you afraid?"

"I'm not afraid of anything," I replied, rolling over on my side and pushing the hair off my face. I paused, looking deep into the green, searching for a four-leaf clover. There was a splash and then nothing. When I looked up Ginnie had disappeared, her body gliding beneath the surface. When she came up, her blonde hair was dark and slick. She smiled as I stripped off my clothes.

"Where's your underwear?"

"I don't wear any."

Later we were lying on the blanket, looking up at the clouds talking about boys.

"Are you going to get back with Kenneth?"

She ran her fingers through my hair as I leaned over to pull a tangle out of hers.

"Your hair is black as night," she said, pushing the long strands away from my eyes. "He really likes you," she added.

"He likes sex. That's why he likes me."

She sat up.

"You haven't—"

"I would *never* do that. Not until I was married. And besides, I don't think I'm ever going to get married. I plan on having adventures."

"I bet you will," Ginnie replied quietly, falling back down beside me and looking up at the sky.

I sat up as I had an idea. "You could come with me. We could go to Australia."

She smiled. "I couldn't leave the farm."

I fell back down. It was true. Every bit of Ginnie was tied to this place. She was like Granddad. They'd take her away from the farm in a box one day.

"I'm going to have a life before I die," I remarked to myself more than to Ginnie.

"You're not going anywhere soon, are you?" she asked, her fingers reaching up to tuck another tumble of damp hair behind my ear. Her hand stopped as she rolled over to face me. "You're so pretty."

I rolled into her. "I think you're beautiful," I replied, slowly, gently, taking her face in my hands. When I kissed her, she kissed me back. And we didn't stop.

I became addicted to Ginnie Hall, and for one incredible summer, I think she was hooked on me, too. We never talked about what we did, but the moment the lights went off, we were in one another's arms. Then we'd fall asleep in a happy rumpled heap and wake up staring at each other. I would have been happy if I'd died then. It was like swimming in a cloud or floating in the softest grass. It felt like nothing I could compare it to, and I couldn't get enough.

That Labour Day weekend, Ginnie and I drove to Toronto with her parents to see the CNE. Mr. Hall was showing cattle in the Coliseum, and Mrs. Hall was off to the Better Living Centre. Ginnie and I were on the Alpine Way Sky Ride, a series of tiny primary-coloured two-seater cars that ran along suspension wires crisscrossing the entire exhibition. Our car was canary yellow with matching plastic seats. People lined up beneath us to play a giant wheel.

"There's the Crown and Anchor! When we get down, let's spin it!" I shouted, jumping to my feet. The movement made the car rock. The line-up for the Flyer stretched around to the back of the rollercoaster, the cars slowly rattling their way to the top, plummeting to the sound of riders' screaming in delight and fear as the cars' brakes squealed, ricocheting, and climbing again. Ginnie squeezed my hand.

"Should we go on the Flyer next?" she asked, and plucking a tuft of pink cotton candy from her cone, she looked at me. "You want some?"

"No thanks."

Watching the Flyer plummet again, I felt too nervous to eat. I'd brought a gift for Ginnie, something special that showed her how much I loved her. The most precious thing I owned lay in the bottom of my purse. Could I do it? Could I give it to someone else? Our car stopped, suspending us over the Better Living Centre. Ginnie leaned over, looking down over the milling crowd.

"I wonder if my mom's still out there."

Putting my hand in my purse, I stroked the cool cuts of crystal. "I've got a present for you."

I pulled the bottle out of my bag and handed Ginnie Mom's bottle of Joy.

Her eyes widened. "It's beautiful."

Ginnie quickly kissed my cheek, making my stomach skip. "Thank you," she said.

"I'm glad you like it."

"But it's open."

"Why don't you try some on?"

Ginnie removed the stopper and, just like Mom, she dabbed a bit behind her ears and the tiniest drops on the insides of her wrists. She thrust her wrist toward me. As I closed my eyes and breathed it in, I—what was the word?—swooned. I nearly did. But when I tried to kiss her, she yanked back.

"We can't do *that* in public," she snapped. "Ever!"

That instant the little canary car lurched back to life, and I wondered what was so bad about *that*.

I don't remember the details of the day, just the scent of Joy accompanying us as Ginnie and I rode the Polar Bear Express, lost all our change in the Salt and Pepper, and ate so much peanut brittle we thought we'd get sick. Cramming into a photo booth, we mugged for the camera, laughing at the strip of silly photos that slid out of the machine, and then we got in and did it again. There were times that day I thought Mom was with me. Like a mirage. The sun, the sounds, and the smell. Oh, the smell. I'd see Mom's face, but then it changed into Ginnie's. My beautiful Ginnie, who I loved more than anyone else in the world.

At seven o'clock we met Mrs. Hall in front of the Coliseum. Mr. Hall was in the parking lot getting the car. "Did you girls have fun?"

"The best."

Mrs. Hall sniffed the air. "What's that smell?"

Ginnie thrust her wrist beneath her mother's nostrils. "It's perfume, Mom. Maddy gave it to me."

"Let me see."

Ginnie removed the bottle from her purse. Mrs. Hall's gloved hand snatched it, holding it up to the light.

"This is half empty. Where did you get it?"

Please give it back, Mrs. Hall, please give it back, I thought. "It was my mother's," I replied.

She removed the stopper, took a sniff, and gave me a very strange look. "This is French perfume. Expensive French perfume is something that a man buys a woman. It's not an acceptable gift from a girl."

"But Mom—" Ginnie said, when Mrs. Hall rode right over her words.

"No buts. Maddy, I'm afraid you're going to have to take this back."

"Please, Mrs. Hall, it's just something small."

"No."

"I want Ginnie to have it."

Mrs. Hall thrust the bottle at me, but when I put my palm up to stop her, our hands collided, and the bottle slipped. I tried to catch it. So did

Ginnie. But Mom's prized possession, her bottle of Joy, smashed, shards of crystal shattering across the red brick steps.

"Oh, Maddy," Ginnie said. "I'm so sorry."

Once free from its bottle, the Joy began to evaporate.

"That's a shame," Mrs. Hall said, looking down. "But you shouldn't have put up such a fuss." She took her daughter by the arm. "Come along, Ginnie, we've got to meet your father."

Desperate to get down on my hands and knees and smell the Joy before it disappeared, seeping forever into the stone and air, I stopped myself. I knew it was impossible. Joy was gone. Happiness, too.

After that, things began to change. One night, after we shut the door and crawled into bed and started to kiss, her sister called out, "What's going on in there?"

Ginnie's breath quickened in the dark.

"Nothing," she replied, her lips an inch from mine.

"It sounded funny. What are you doing?"

Ginnie's body stiffened through the bedding. She got up and opened the door. Opened it wide and left it there. "We're not up to anything."

Ginnie hopped back into bed. I whispered to her to shut the door, but she just moved closer to the wall.

"Go to sleep," she whispered.

"I want to kiss you," I whispered back, snuggling in tight beside her.

"Stop it."

"Why?"

"This is supposed to be with a boy."

"Do you want to do it with a boy?" I asked into the black, petrified of the answer.

"I don't know."

She rolled over and pulled the sheet up tight to shut me out.

Betsy and Sandy started asking questions, too. It was late November and Betsy was quizzing Ginnie over by our lockers.

"What's going on with you guys?" Besty asked.

"Nothing," Ginnie replied, way too defensively.

Betsy gave her a funny look. "Dale was wondering if you'd like to double with us. We're going to the drive-in this Saturday."

Ginnie looked over at me, and I violently shook my head. We had planned to have a sleepover that night.

"Sounds like fun," Ginnie said.

Running after her, I finally caught up at the bus line. "Why are you doing this?" I asked, yanking her out of the line.

"Let me go. You're making a scene," she said.

This was bad. She was slipping away. "You don't even like Dale. Why are you going with him?"

Trying not to be pathetic, and trying really, really hard not to cry, I began to realize that I cared about Ginnie way more than she cared about me.

She turned away. "I've got to go."

A bunch of kids watched. I didn't care. I didn't give a damn what anybody thought. But Ginnie did.

Her voice dropped low. "This isn't normal. I don't want people talking about me," she said. "And I don't think you should come out to my place for a while."

I burst into tears in the middle of the schoolyard. "You're my friend. Aren't you my best friend?"

The bus driver honked, and Ginnie ran up the stairs. The yellow school bus kicked up gravel as it pulled out of the lot. Ginnie sat at the back, her beautiful, long blonde hair draping over a seat. Dale sat beside her, sliding his arm around her. It was worse than being kicked in the stomach by the biggest horse in the world.

"Dad?" I poked my head into the waiting room. Nobody was there. The office was closed, and the Oldsmobile was gone. I walked into the kitchen. Rika was finishing up the evening dishes.

"You late vor supper," she said, not looking up from the suds. I wasn't hungry anyway.

"Where are the boys?"

Rika set the frying pan on the dish rack.

"You know this is virst time I hear you ask about them?" She had to be lying.

"You know Vrank is captain of baseball team and Tedder is in Cubs?"

I didn't. Sure, I'd seen Tedder wandering around in a costume, but I hadn't thought to ask. He always wore weird things. Rika pulled a pot out of the hot, soapy water.

"You are bad, selvish girl."

"Leave me alone," I replied, walking out of the kitchen, down the hall and into the office.

The light in the dispensary was still on. Rika was just being mean. None of my friends played with their younger siblings. It wasn't something that you did—yet it had been part of my life. This other life. Frank and I fought, but we also played catch and built rocket ships out of giant cardboard boxes strung with flashing Christmas lights.

The latest copy of *TIME* magazine lay on the metal counter. It was another issue devoted to the youth drug culture. There was a picture of a teenager injecting drugs into the hollow of his arm. The writer talked about how the counterculture had begun with peaceful protests and marijuana, but there had been a nasty shift to hard drugs and riots. Well, there had been a hard shift in my world, too.

The *Compendium* said it would take about fifteen minutes to feel the effects of Valium and recommended taking one. I took two and wandered down to the rec room. At first, I felt floaty and light, but then I just passed out on the sofa with my clothes on. Nobody noticed that I'd slept down there that night, even though the TV was blaring. While the Valium really knocked me out, it didn't help with how sad I felt when I woke up the next morning.

"Hi," Ginnie said, walking toward me.

I turned the other way. It was hard, but I knew the only way to get her back was to ignore her. Nobody wants you if you need them. They only want you if you don't. Kenneth stood by the water fountain. Bending over, I took a few little gulps of water while he stared at my boobs.

"Do you want to come to the drive-in this weekend?" he asked.

Chewing on a strand of hair, I replied, "It depends. Can you get anything to drink?"

Kenneth's head bobbed up and down. "Mark's got his dad's car. We can pick you up at eight."

Ginnie was at her locker, pretending not to watch.

Mark didn't have a driver's license, but I didn't care. Not even if he smashed up the car and we were all killed.

"You want a drink?" Kenneth asked.

Sandy had mixed up a batch of Purple Jesus. That's when you saved all the heels from your parents' liquor bottles and mixed them in with purple Kool-Aid. It tasted horrible but had a real kick, and made the thought of Ginnie being with Dale fade away. Tearing down the middle of a two-lane highway, we chugged the liquor and laughed. About a mile away from the drive-in, Mark pulled over and told Kenneth and me to get out.

"Why?" I asked.

"We're getting in the trunk," Kenneth replied.

Since Kenneth didn't have any money, we were going to be smuggled in.

"But we'll freeze in there."

It was early December, and I didn't bring a coat or cash.

"I'll keep you warm," Kenneth smiled.

"Can I have another drink first?"

"After we get out," Kenneth said.

I followed them to the back of the car. There were a couple of lawn chairs in the trunk already, making it cramped and uncomfortable. Just before Mark shut the lid, I caught Kenneth's glance. He had that horny look on his face and a bulge in his pants.

"No way." I wasn't touching his penis in the dark.

"If you do, you don't have to touch it again all night."

This was gross. Nothing but a close space and bad Juicy Fruit breath. He kept trying to grab my hand and put it on his crotch. "Please?" he whimpered.

I began to wonder if Kenneth and I were so different. I would have begged Ginnie to touch me again. I would have given her anything at all. "You promise you won't tell?" I whispered, reaching into the black, feeling for the cloth of his jeans.

"Never, ever," he gasped, promising over and over, so desperate and pleading.

My fingers traced up toward his crotch. I could feel him fumbling for the zipper, trying to yank it down.

"You can have all the drinks you want," he gasped.

Mark honked to warn us we were near the gate. My fingers closed around Kenneth's penis. It was rock-hard. He tried to grab my hand to pump it, but I wanted to do it myself. Harder and harder, I pumped. Up and down and up and down until he let out a tiny moan. Something felt wet. Then the trunk opened, and for a moment, all I could see were stars.

"Where's the liquor?" I asked, hopping out and pulling a lawn chair with me. I wanted a good seat for the show.

By the time I saw Ginnie, I was totally polluted. The ground rolled when I walked, making me giggle. I threw my arm around Kenneth's neck and slid up against him for support. Ginnie and Betsy were coming back from the girls' washroom by the concession stand.

"How's it going?" I slurred.

Ginnie frowned. She didn't like me being with Kenneth. "Where's your coat?"

"Where's Dale?" I replied, pulling Kenneth even closer.

He didn't mind being used, but then again, he probably didn't know it either.

"He's back at the car," Ginnie said. "I didn't know you were coming."

"We're here with Sandy and Mark. We got a bunch of drinks. You should come over."

Ginnie quickly said, "no thanks," but Betsy thought it sounded like fun.

Brad and Dale arrived.

"Hey, you guys want to party? Sandy's brewed some good Jesus," I added, with a grin at Dale that read pure dare.

Dale slung his arm around Ginnie's shoulder. "Sure."

Dumping the pop on the ground, I filled the concession paper cup with liquor. We were all crammed into Mark's car. He and Sandy were making out in the front seat beside Betsy and Brad. Ginnie and Dale were in the back beside me and Kenneth. Kenneth had his hands all over me, and it was making Ginnie crazy. She kept staring out the window to see if anyone was watching. Betsy took a big drink and handed the cup to Brad, who belted it back. "That burns! What's in it?" he asked.

"You don't want to know," I laughed, handing some to Dale.

"I don't think we should be drinking," Ginnie said.

"Oh, come on, it's Saturday night," I said. Let's have some fun."

"Chug it, Dale!" Betsy yelled. "Chug! Chug! Chug!"

Dale didn't have a choice, but Ginnie refused. I proposed another round. The first round was kicking in and we were all feeling good. The cup passed around again. Betsy and Brad started making out harder. I took another gulp and kissed Kenneth. Dale put his arm around Ginnie and tried to get closer, but she threw open the door and announced that she was going home. Dale tried to follow, but I jumped out first, telling him to wait in the car.

"Hey, wait up!" I called, staggering after Ginnie. "What's wrong?"

She was upset. "When did you start drinking?"

"It's just about having fun. I thought that's what tonight was all about, having fun with boys." I tried to pull her around, then lost my balance and started to fall. Ginnie caught me.

"Are you and Dale having a good time?" I asked.

"No."

"How come?"

"Because I'd rather be with you."

That would have made me happy if Ginnie hadn't looked so sad.

Dad was out. Rika and the boys were asleep. I sat on the metal counter in the dispensary, reading the *Diagnostic and Statistical Manual of Mental Disorders*. The book said that people attracted to the same sex were called homosexuals or lesbians, and their sexual interests were "toward sexual acts not usually associated with coitus, or toward coitus." What was coitus? Then it said, "Homosexuals performed sex under bizarre circumstances such as in necrophilia, pedophilia, sexual sadism, and fetishism." Necrophilia meant having relations with dead people. I threw the book down. Ginnie and I weren't deviants. We were like secret sisters.

The Jesus had worn off, and I needed something more for pain. The *TIME* magazine with the syringe on the cover said the best drug was heroin, but Dad didn't have any of that. The *Compendium* said that heroin was an illegal substance that was derived from the opium family, which was related to morphine. There wasn't any morphine, but I knew where to find synthetic substitutes—Dad's restricted substance drawer.

I went into the nurse's station and dug out a bottle of Dilaudid—little pink pills that Dad prescribed for extreme pain.

"Maddy?"

Footsteps down the hall. I dropped the bottle back into the drawer.

Dad walked in as I stood up, shutting the drawer with my leg. "You're home early," I said.

"You're up late," Dad replied, eyes down, leafing through the day's mail. "Did you have fun tonight?"

"It was okay." I felt myself sway as I crossed the room, leaning into the door jamb for support. "I'm going to bed." I turned and walked out. "See you in the morning."

"Honeybunch?" Dad called, poking his head through the doorway. I leaned against the wall to steady myself. I was way drunker than I thought.

"Are you free next Friday? I want to take you to a recital at Aunt Anne's church in Toronto. A friend of mine is singing."

I was about to complain, but now that I was up and moving around, I was seeing double and knew I might start slurring again. "Okay."

Dad smiled. Waving goodnight, I turned, praying he'd do the same, which thankfully he did, because when I took the first step, I lost my balance and bounced off the opposite wall.

"What was that?" he called out.

"Nothing."

Nothing that he cared about.

Dad parked in the lot at the side of the church. My bare legs stuck to the vinyl of the car seat. Aunt Anne had called earlier that day and asked me to wear my new dress.

"I hate dresses."

"Do this for your father."

"No."

"Then do it for me."

There was no point fighting.

I followed Dad into the church and we took our seats near the front. The church's chancel had been transformed into a forest with wigwams and a fake lake. Aunt Anne slipped into the pew beside me.

She seemed nervous. "Don't you look pretty?"

I shrugged.

"Where are your nylons?"

Pantyhose? No way. "At least I wore the dress."

Aunt Anne nodded and patted my thigh. "Thank you for that."

She leaned over to say hello to Dad.

The program said we were going to see a musical.

"Where's Isabel?" Dad asked.

"Backstage," Aunt Anne replied.

Isabel? The lights dimmed, and a colourful boat carrying a fat man in a stovetop hat sailed across the stage and landed in Indian territory. Placing his hand over his heart, he sang about the brave new world when a tall, handsome woman dressed like an Indian princess stepped out from behind a stand of oak trees. She had an enormous voice, and her presence swamped the stage, dwarfing the Indians, the Puritans, and even the boat. Dad's eyes lit up. I hadn't seen him smile like that since Mom was alive.

"Is that your friend?" I whispered.

He nodded, a smile on his face. "That's Miss McAllister." He turned to me, pausing inside my eyes, and slowly imploded my world. "I've asked her to marry me."

There were platters of sandwiches with the crusts cut off, pickled beets, purple punch, and raspberry tarts. Aunt Anne was talking to some of her friends from choir while Dad and I stood beside the coffee urn. Dad took a sip.

"How can you marry somebody else?" I whispered, numb with shock and fury.

"Miss McAllister is a very fine woman."

He took another sip and smiled at a man pouring himself a cup of coffee. We stopped talking until the man left.

"Have you forgotten Mom already?" I hissed.

"Of course not."

I pulled him toward the wall, my voice rising slightly. "I don't want a new mother."

Aunt Anne glanced over. The Indian lady, Miss McAllister, came out from behind the stage, still in costume.

"Isabel!" Dad called.

She made her way toward us through a crowd of admirers.

Dad turned to me. "I want you to meet her."

"But Dad—"

And she was there, extending her hand. "You must be Maddy. I'm Isabel. Your father does nothing but talk about you kids."

What was I supposed to say? I never heard about you and there's no way you're marrying my father? I shook her hand. It was steady and no nonsense.

"I'm sure this is a bit of a surprise," she said.

Dad stood behind me. Miss McAllister still had me firmly by the hand and wasn't letting go. "I would have preferred we do it privately, but your father thought …"

Dad squeezed my shoulders. "Maddy loves surprises, don't you, honey?"

Aunt Anne arrived. "Isabel, the show was terrific."

"How do you two know each other?" I asked.

Miss McAllister laughed. Aunt Anne slipped her hand through Miss McAllister's arm. "We've been friends for years. We sing together in the choir," Aunt Anne said.

"Yes, if it wasn't for your aunt, I never would have met your father."

I looked at Aunt Anne. Traitor.

Miss McAllister let go of my hand and kissed Dad lightly on the cheek. "Did you and Maddy have time for supper before the show?"

Dad picked up a sandwich from the platter and took a bite. "I thought we'd eat here."

"Honestly, Ted, you need to take better care of yourself."

The man in the stovetop appeared, sweeping Miss McAllister away for cast photos, taking my father with them.

I turned to face Aunt Anne. "How could you?"

I didn't say a word all the way home. The minute we got in, I tore out to the dining room and picked up the phone.

"Who is this?" Mrs. Hall asked, sounding sleepy.

I looked at the wall clock. It was after midnight.

"I'm sorry, Mrs. Hall. Can I speak to Ginnie, please? It's important."

"I don't care how important it is, Madeline. You're not to call here at this hour ever again."

She slammed the phone down as Dad came in, undoing his tie, a desperate look on his face. "Did you like her, honey?"

I couldn't believe he'd even ask. "She's not very pretty."

He ignored me.

"And she sure doesn't have Mom's figure."

"She's got a perfectly nice figure."

"Have you kissed her?"

A look crossed his face, as if he'd been caught cheating. "That isn't your business."

"When are you going to tell the boys?"

"When the time's right." He dropped his tie on the table and walked up the stairs.

When I heard Dad's bedroom door close upstairs, I opened the drawer and fished out the Dilaudid, the little pink pills rolling into the palm of my hand. I looked up the side effects. Nausea. I didn't want to spend the night puking. The *Compendium* recommended Dramamine, Gravol, so I took two of them. Next, the dosage needed to be determined––one two milligram capsules for extreme pain. I decided on four. The *Compendium* noted that Dilaudid could also cause "twilight sleep." That sounded nice. While I waited for it to hit, I thought about Mom and that day in the garden. Her auburn hair and how the golden strands turned white-gold under the summer sun. Miss McAllister's hair was mousey. Dull. Plain.

And just then, as if to spare me from my memories of Mom—I started to dissolve.

My fingers and toes disappeared, followed quickly by my arms and legs. My brain felt as if it was snuggled in cotton batten. For the first time, I forgot to be on guard, waiting to see what horrible surprise would tumble out of the sky. After a while, I stood, wondering if I might fall, but I didn't. Ghost-like, I drifted through the dispensary, trailing my fingers across the brown bottles, stroking the stainless-steel counters, and pushing through the swinging door to lie down on the cool vinyl examining table. I felt nothing. No pain or joy. My worried, always clucking, Henny Penny brain instantly muzzled, now as still as a boat on a calm lake. When the morning came, I knew I'd found my escape hatch.

Every day different pills went in and the pain went out. I didn't tell my brothers about Miss McAllister because I was sure Dad would change his mind, but all my friends felt sorry for me. Mrs. Hall, on the other hand, didn't. We were peeling potatoes for supper.

"It will do you some good to have more supervision."

"But she's not my mother," I replied, "I've only met her once."

"Your father could have handled the whole thing a lot better, but what's done is done. And you three need a mother," she said, as a long twist of potato peel dropped into the bowl.

"I told you: She's not my mother."

It was that loud voice again. The voice that sometimes just escaped. Mrs. Hall set the knife on the counter.

I was mad, and I didn't care.

"And she's not going to tell me what to do!"

Ginnie's face went white. Mrs. Hall was big and bossy, just like Miss McAllister. She quickly removed her apron, hanging it on a hook. "Time to take you home."

I looked at Ginnie. It wasn't time yet, but Ginnie didn't say a word. Head down, she kept peeling. I didn't want to leave. It was horrible at home. "I'm sorry. Please don't send me home."

"Ginnie, get Maddy's coat," Mrs. Hall said, cutting me off.

Ginnie dropped the knife and ran. My peacoat was on the dining room table. Her mother sat me down and took my hands, holding them fast. I started to cry.

"I won't let you drag Ginnie into anything. She's a good girl, and I don't want you influencing her."

"Please," I said. "Please don't make me go."

Mrs. Hall removed her car keys from the hook. Ginnie mutely handed me my coat and opened the door.

It took two months for the secret to finally come out.

At the dinner table, Dad cleared his throat, nobody paying attention. We were waiting for dessert. Tedder was dressed in a goalie mask and red-and-white leg pads. He'd recently taken up goaltending and Frank took shots on him out in the garage. Every night, we heard thwack, thump, whump, or a scream, depending on where the puck hit Tedder.

Dad cleared his throat again, tapping the water glass with his spoon. "I've decided to remarry. You children need a mother."

"Mother?" Tedder asked, as some potatoes fell out of his mouth.

I kicked the table so hard I thought I'd broken my foot. Dad hadn't mentioned Miss McAllister since that night, and I'd hoped—no, I'd prayed, that she'd gone away.

"I thought your sister might have told you."

Frank glanced at me across the table.

"The lady's name is Miss McAllister, and she's coming here tonight with Aunt Anne." He glanced at his watch. "They should be here soon."

Dad shoved his chair back, got up, and left the room.

"Who is she?" Frank asked.

"I don't know," I replied.

Frank could tell I knew something and looked away, disgusted and confused. Feeling terrible about not warning them, I went up to my bedroom and flipped up the mattress. I never believed Dad would actually do it, so I'd pushed the threat away. Clearly, I didn't know my father anymore. A father who was capable of anything. Should I have told my brothers? What good would that have done? Maybe we could have stopped him together. I didn't know. I felt sick. My father was gone. Bottles of pain medication were scattered across the top of the box spring. Washing down a handful of codeine tablets, I lay down on my bed, waiting for the pain and fear to disappear. I looked out. The leaves on the willow began to rustle and twist. They were lovely, like the green fields of tall wheat blowing in Granddad's fields.

The doorbell rang. Dad's heavy feet echoed through the still house as he strode down the hall. A series of voices followed. Aunt Anne rapped on my door. Slowly, I sat up on the side of the bed and got dressed.

A filmy, skintight, black rayon dress barely covered my bum, and the thick streaks of jet-black eyeliner were crooked, but that was on purpose. They went well with the messy smudges of dark blue eyeshadow. My eyes were glossy from the codeine, and I slid into some black slingbacks. Swerving down the hallway, I went over on my ankle twice before reaching the landing. Frank was down below talking to Aunt Anne and Miss McAllister. Aunt Anne beamed at Frank, as if he was one of Granddad's prized steers. Tedder, wearing his mask and goalie pads, stood in the shadow of his bedroom door, silent.

Miss McAllister made a visual sweep of the house. "Hello, Maddy," she called, her voice echoing up the stairwell.

It wasn't a friendly voice like Mom's, it was deeper and threatening. "Hi," I replied, making my way down as she ascended.

The scent of her perfume arrived before she did. It wasn't Joy. She checked me out, looking at my hair, which was hanging in my eyes, my makeup, and especially my dress. Her eyes said she didn't like it. Good. After eyeballing me, she passed by and went over to Tedder. He instinctively pulled back even further into the gloom.

"Is this Theodore?"

"His name's Tedder," I blurted out, but she ignored me, thrusting out her hand and keeping it there until Tedder took it.

"Do you like oatmeal cookies?"

Tedder nodded.

"Good. I made a batch today," she said, pulling him out of his bedroom and into the hall. "Let's have one while we all sit down and talk." Her other hand reached for his mask. "And I think we'll take this off."

We were all in the living room. I tried to balance a teacup on my knee while Miss McAllister passed around a plate of cookies. Tedder, his dark hair standing up on end, looked naked without the mask.

"Your father and I feel that it will be best for you children if we move to Toronto."

"No!" I said, louder than I should have.

"Maddy," Aunt Anne replied in a warning voice. "Hear this out."

"Why do we have to move?" Frank asked.

"Because I've never lived in the country and your father and I have decided that it would be best for everyone if we started with a clean slate."

"There are just too many memories in this house," Aunt Anne said. "It wouldn't be fair to Isabel."

Fair to her. What about us? While Miss McAllister talked about schools, Aunt Anne told Frank and Tedder about the ball diamonds and hockey arenas in Toronto.

"What about the chickens?" Tedder asked.

Miss McAllister laughed, passing him another cookie. "Your aunt and I will make certain you get up to your grandfather's to see the animals."

"But I'm used to seeing them all the time," Tedder replied.

After they left, Dad said it was time for a family talk. He leaned forward on a chair. The three of us were lined up on the sofa with Tedder in the middle, the metal goalie mask back on and clapped tightly over his face. Frank was likely holding his breath. I wanted to disappear into the dispensary and take every pill in the place.

"Why do we have to move?" Frank asked.

"Because we need her," Dad replied.

"No, we don't," I said. "We're doing just fine on our own."

Why had Aunt Anne brought Miss McAllister here? I'd never forgive her.

"You've got to be very, very good, or else Miss McAllister will go away," Dad said, his fingers clamping onto his knees to stop his hands from shaking. Severe shaking often came before a nervous collapse. I remembered that from a book. Frank bit his bottom lip. A Frank way of saying, "be quiet."

"Where would she go?" Tedder asked.

Dad didn't answer. He slumped over, staring at the back of his hands. His wedding ring was gone. "So, do we understand one another?" Dad asked, glancing up.

"Yes," Frank said.

Dad tapped Frank and me gently on the thigh and pinched Tedder's toe.

"I've got some paperwork to finish up," he said, rising to his feet.

The minute Dad was gone, Frank whirled around on the sofa. "This is your fault. If you weren't always getting into trouble, then Dad wouldn't have to go out and find us a new mother," he yelled, shooting across Tedder to give me a hard shove. I was about to push him back when Tedder screamed, "I don't want a new Mommy!"

Frank and I stopped. Tedder never raised his voice.

"It's okay, Tedder," I said, wiping tears off his face.

"Don't worry," Frank added, trying to pull up the hockey mask, but Tedder held it fast.

We both put our arms around Tedder's shoulders. "Do you want me to take shots on you?" Frank asked.

Tedder nodded and waddled out the door in his goalie pads. Frank followed. He always tried to do what was expected of him. Well, I could take my shots, too, and I was going to fight.

A couple of days later, the whole family had an appointment at the dentist's office in Eltonville. Dad asked me to be home by six thirty. He asked me twice. "I've got late patients coming in, and I need to be back."

"Okay," I replied.

But I didn't go home. The moment the yellow buses were gone and all the teachers had left, I started toilet papering the entire school. While I was up on the roof, a horn honked. Walking over to the edge—so close my toes poked out—I looked down. It was Dad. He pushed his hat back. I put my hands on my hips. Frank and Tedder were in the back seat of the car, staring through the window.

"Madeline!" Dad called. "We've got to get going."

I ran to the other side, so he had no choice but to climb up.

Dad stood on the roof, silhouetted against the blue sky, ribbons of white toilet paper rippling in the wind and wrapping around his legs. He glanced at his wristwatch and then at the horrible mess. "We'll have to come back later and clean this up," he said, walking toward me. "Let's go."

"No."

When he tried to snatch my sleeve, I ducked, running to the other side of the roof. "I hate her!"

"You don't even know her." He walked toward me, fists clenched. He was mad, and that was good.

"I don't want to!"

"This isn't your choice."

We'd see about that.

I started to hum. "Does she sing to you the way Mom used to?" Then I began to sing their song. "Gonna take that sentimental journey …"

His mouth went crooked, and then he moved, charging across the roof, kicking up a cloud of gravel and asphalt. My foot stepped back, but the roof was gone, nothing there but the air. My arms spun. The Oldsmobile was right beneath.

Dad grabbed me, pulling me back, holding me fast in his arms. I wanted to hug him and hold him close but spat out the lyrics instead:

"Sentimental journey home. Never knew my heart could be so yearny."

"Stop it!"

I wriggled away, breaking free from his grasp. "Don't you get yearn y for Mom anymore? How could you forget her so soon?"

He was panting so hard his chest heaved up and down.

"Have you forgotten the way she smelled? The way she smiled? The way she laughed?"

Then he slapped me across the face.

We got in the car. My upper lip had started to swell and bleed. It really hurt, but I wanted Dad to hit me again. At least when he did it, he knew I was alive. Instead, he just sank behind the wheel, twisting the key in the ignition.

"Why are you doing this to me?" he asked, his voice beginning to shake.

"Why are you doing this to us?" I replied. "You never tell us anything."

We drove home in silence. I glanced in the rearview mirror, touching my lip. The boys sat silently in the back seat, too scared to ask what happened. And then, Dad started to cry.

Once at home, I sat on the counter in the dispensary while Dad applied ice to my swollen lip. He was still crying, apologizing repeatedly, muttering that he wasn't the kind of man to strike a fifteen-year-old girl. His crying scared me, but his fear made me madder.

"Stop crying," I said.

He didn't. Couldn't.

"I'm sorry, Maddy."

I didn't care he was sorry. I didn't care he was upset. Somebody had to stop this terrible mistake. "Granddad always said you were weak."

That slowed the crying.

"That's why you're marrying that woman. Because you're weak."

He wiped the tears away. "You're going to treat Miss McAllister with respect."

"No, I won't."

"Yes, you will." He slammed his palms on the examining table and left.

I might have to go to the wedding and move to Toronto, but at least Ginnie and I could be together all summer.

Sitting at my desk, I sprayed some of my perfume on a sheet of fancy writing paper, while Ginnie lay on the bed. "They'll never know," I said, waving the paper around.

Ginnie didn't look so sure. "I don't know. My Mom always figures everything out."

The plan was for Aunt Anne to think I was staying at the Halls and for Mrs. Hall to think that Ginnie was staying at our house under Aunt Anne's supervision. Everybody approved of Aunt Anne because she was so strict.

I turned to Ginnie. "Don't you want to spend one last summer together?"

"Yes …"

"This way, we can. And nobody will know."

Using Dad's fancy fountain pen, I began to write:

Dear Miss Gillespie,

Mr. Hall and I would be most pleased if Madeline could stay with us while Dr. Barnes and his new bride will be away in Europe. This will give the girls a chance to enjoy the summer and perhaps help ease the transition for Madeline. Rest assured we'll keep her busy gathering eggs, milking cows, and helping with the housework.

Sincerely,

Mrs. Roger Hall

I handed Aunt Anne the letter later that week.

"You seem awfully preoccupied with that girl," Aunt Anne said, carefully examining the note. There was something about it that intrigued her. She sniffed the edges.

"She's my best friend. Didn't you ever have a best friend?" I asked.

Aunt Anne looked up over the top of the note. "It's important that we have a lot of friends in life. Not just one."

"Betsy and Sandy will come out for hayrides and stuff."

"Will there be boys?"

"There won't be any stupid boys!" I said, starting to get agitated.

"Maybe I should call Ginnie's mother."

Aunt Anne's nurse's instincts were kicking in. I had to calm down. "Just one last summer with my friends," I quietly said. "Is that too much to ask?"

She looked at me, then down at the note. Nothing had been the same between us since she brought that rat into our family. "As long as you call and check in regularly," she finally said.

The wedding happened on a hot day in downtown Toronto. Frank, Tedder, and I sat beside Aunt Anne in the front pew of an enormous church that was as big and fancy as a castle. The floors were made of white marble, and the pews were long and dark. Voices echoed as people talked. Giant stained-glass windows loomed, featuring Jesus at all the different stages of His life. Frank was staring at a man with white hair playing the organ. "Where's Granddad?" he asked.

"He had to stay home and take care of the cattle," Aunt Anne replied.

I coughed. We hadn't seen Granddad since the funeral we never attended. Mom's. When I told Dad the freezer was getting low, he said he'd get the butcher to fill it up. When I told Aunt Anne the meat was nearly gone, she said it would be one less thing to move, and when I called Granddad to tell him we were low, he said he couldn't talk. None of the other relatives had come either.

The white-haired organist began another song. The classical music was beautiful, and Mom would have loved it. I pictured her listening and laughing as Dad covered his ears, claiming he could do a much better job on his ukulele.

The bride's side of the church was loaded with professional women like Aunt Anne and Miss McAllister. Lines of light wool suits and brightly coloured summer dresses filled the pews, every head displaying a grand hat. Men were scarce.

Aunt Anne fanned her face with the program. "Gad, it's heavy in here."

The organ paused.

"There's your father," Aunt Anne whispered, jabbing me in the ribs. "Sit up straight."

Everyone looked up. Dad and his best man, a close friend of Miss McAllister's, entered from beneath a wide marble archway. The wedding march began, and everyone looked down the aisle. Everyone, except me. I was watching my father.

"He looks terrible," Aunt Anne whispered.

She was right. The wedding suit that had fit a month earlier now hung on him like a sack. It was the first time I'd really looked at him since Mom died. He'd aged years and had gone from being a solid guy with a great big grin, to a skinny stick with desperate, hollow eyes. I tried to catch his attention, to smile at him, but he wasn't looking at me. He was smiling at Miss McAllister, who was crossing the threshold to take his arm. He was trying so hard to please her. His legs wobbled, but the shaking stopped when she touched him. She held him up.

Dad needed her, not me.

Aunt Anne drove me and Tedder back to the house. The streets were motionless, as if everyone in Sterling had vanished. Our driveway was empty. The practice was closed, the patients were gone, and Rika had taken a position with another family. Dad and Miss McAllister were staying at a hotel and leaving for Europe in the morning, and Frank had left for camp. Even Ruth had moved her stuff, but she'd sworn she'd be back to say goodbye.

"Are you sure you don't want me to take you out to Ginnie's house?" Aunt Anne asked. "I don't like leaving you here all alone."

"I've still got to pack. Mrs. Hall will pick me up before dinner," I replied. "Besides, you've still got to take Tedder."

Tedder was going to stay with relatives. When I turned to give him a quick hug goodbye, he grabbed me, holding me tight. "Come with me," he said, his little brown suitcase resting on the seat beside him.

"I can't."

"Please."

"You be a good boy," I said, pulling away, trying not to cry. "I'll see you soon."

I stood in the driveway waving goodbye until her car disappeared over the hill. Walking up the sidewalk, I went over all the details for my romantic evening. Fresh flowers, candles, Mom's good china, and silver flatware. Sloppy Joes for dinner, and then we'd go up to my room.

When I opened the front door and stepped in, Ginnie was already there. My Ginnie was sitting on the bottom step of the staircase. She was so excited to see me that she'd forgotten her suitcase.

"Where's your bag, silly?" I laughed.

Ginnie stood up. Nervous. "Mom changed her mind."

No no no. I walked toward her. "Maybe you can come tomorrow?"

"I can't come over at all. I'm only here because Dad was coming into town on business, and I got a ride."

"How does your mother know?" I asked.

"Because I told her."

Ginnie told her mother about our secret plan to spend the summer at my house. That meant we'd never be alone again. I'd move away and never hold her. Never again, for the rest of my life. Everything was ruined. When she opened the door, I started to cry.

"But I love you."

"I'm sorry. No …"

The door shut and my Ginnie was gone.

I was all alone. No patients ringing the doorbell saying how sorry they were to be calling so late, but the baby was quite sick. No Frank flying down the stairs with his baseball mitt. No Tedder racing his Hot Wheels around the living room floor. No Mom—beautiful Mom, kissing me on the end of the nose, saying how proud she was of my straight As. No Dad holding me tight, telling me I was his honeybunch. Nobody left in that great big house where our family used to live. Lost, I ran down the hall and into the dispensary.

The *Compendium* recommended fifty milligrams of Demerol for extreme pain. I'd seen Dad inject enough patients to know how to fill a syringe. I drew back the liquid, tapping the glass lightly whenever an air bubble appeared. They could stop your heart or make your brain explode.

Next, I scrubbed the inside of my arm with an alcohol swab and picked up the syringe. The needle pricked the skin. I shoved the needle into my arm and drove the plunger down and everything tasted of metal.

After three hours, I felt normal enough to call my friends, tell them the house was empty, and that we could party all summer. I couldn't bear to be all alone and was so upset about Ginnie that I couldn't stop crying. But if I opened the dispensary, I could run away from the pain and share the drugs with my friends. Sandy and Betsy came over right away. The moment they arrived, we raided the dispensary and headed down to the rec room.

Sandy took a swig from a bottle of whiskey she'd stolen from her father. She and Betsy had already taken some tranquilizers.

"You're nuts!" Besty squealed.

Waggling the syringe at them, I laughed and asked, "are you sure?

Betsy shook her head. "I'm scared of needles."

"How does it make you feel?" Sandy asked, her eyes glued to the syringe.

"Like heaven."

It was true. I'd spent three hours adrift in the Demerol, but when I came down, I knew I couldn't be in the house all alone.

"When are the pills going to hit?" Betsy asked.

"Any minute," I replied, waggling the syringe again.

Sandy grinned. A clear drop of Demerol clung to the end of the needle.

Betsy closed her eyes, but Sandy couldn't look away. As I raised the syringe to my arm, down went the needle and in came relief. The syringe slipped between the cushions as the Demerol rolled over me. My heart slowed and my vision flickered like a television losing its reception. It was hard to breathe.

"Are you all right?" Sandy asked. "What does it feel like?"

As I sunk into the sofa, all the bad feelings disappeared. "Fantabulous."

"You're crazy," Betsy mumbled, puffing on a cigarette. A thundercloud of smoke hung over her head.

There was a bang upstairs. I ignored it. My neck muscles went slack and my head fell back. Out into the calm I sailed, bobbing far, far away. Ginnie … My head lolled. Ginnie … I tried to sit up. What was Ginnie doing standing at the bottom of the stairs? Was she real? Betsy laughed, offering her a drink while Ginnie yelled something, turned, and ran up the stairs. Coloured pills rolled across the table. I called for her to stop, sliding on some pills scattered across the floor, and wondered if she could tell I was stoned.

"Let her go," Betsy giggled.

I staggered after Ginnie, yanked open the door and out onto the veranda. She was halfway down the drive.

"Come back!" I yelled, tumbling down the stairs, landing on the asphalt, cutting my hand. Ginnie spun around.

"My mother was right. You're damaged!"

I got back up.

"Is this what you do when you're not with me?"

Her lower lip quivered. Was she going to cry? Did she still care somewhere in there? "I rode my bike all the way here to see if you were okay," she said.

When I stood up and reached out to touch her, she slapped me away. "Stay away from me. Just stay away. I never want to see you again!"

With all her strength, she shoved me so hard that I fell back on the sidewalk, striking my head on the concrete. She didn't even stop to see if I'd cracked my skull.

The water woke me up. Sharp, cold, and stinging, it slapped my face. Betsy was passed out on the rec room floor. Sandy was sprawled across a chair. I was on the sofa. Two empty liquor bottles and an ashtray loaded with a mountain of butts covered the coffee table. The sofa was drenched and squishy. As I swiped my hand through my hair, I looked up to find Aunt Anne standing above me with an empty bucket. She was wearing the worst nurse's face I'd ever seen. How much did she know? How did I get down here? Did she find me on the sidewalk? No. I vaguely remembered crawling through dewy grass, up the stairs, and onto the porch.

"Get dressed," she said evenly. Way too evenly for this kind of mess. Betsy moaned. Sandy growled for us to be quiet.

"What time is it?" I asked. The doorbell rang.

"That will be their parents," Aunt Anne said, turning and going back up the stairs.

Oh no. I gave Betsy a kick. Where was the syringe? I stuck my hand between the cushions. Thank God. The tranquilizers were still in my pocket.

"Get up!"

The doorbell rang again—three quick, angry blasts. I gave Betsy another kick.

"Get lost," she mumbled, putting a pillow over her head.

"Your Mom's here."

She sat up. "What?"

"So is Sandy's."

"Oh shit," Betsy said, as their mothers followed Aunt Anne into the rec room.

"Get your shoes," Betsy's mother said, grabbing Betsy by the arm.

Sandy's mother saw the empty liquor bottle and gave her daughter a cuff across the back of the head. "You won't be coming here anymore."

Up the stairs the girls went, rank and file, heads bowed, followed by their furious mothers. Aunt Anne stood at the bottom of the stairs, arms crossed, still wearing the impenetrable nurse's face.

"Change your blouse," she said. "We're going to Toronto."

Aunt Anne gripped the wheel as the Ford bore down on the asphalt. It was like travelling in an ambulance without the sirens. Hard rain battered the cornfields. The windshield wipers threw off the water, only to have it gather again. A horn blared and a well-dressed woman in a hat stared at me as the Ford tore by. Water streamed down the window. Aunt Anne's head turned. The nurse's face was gone. The blood had drained out of it, and instead there was pure fury, Granddad rage.

"I go out to the Hall house to get you, and Mrs. Hall tells me that you're not there. No, it was some kind of ruse you and your friends cooked up so you could drink all summer."

So, Ginnie hadn't told her mother about the drugs. Aunt Anne didn't know.

"I'm sorry."

She picked up speed as the rest of the traffic slowed. "What's wrong with you?" she asked, her palm striking the wheel. "I do everything I can and you just throw it back in my face. And Isabel, I told Isabel that you were a fine girl."

"But Aunt Anne—"

"No buts. You've gone too far this time. You've disgraced yourself. You've disgraced your mother's memory. She'd be so ashamed of you."

I wanted to yell, but I bit down on my tongue instead. How dare she say that? She was the one who disgraced Mom's memory by bringing that woman into our lives.

"Don't you have anything to say for yourself?" she asked.

I didn't reply. If I told her what I really thought I would be disgracing Mom's memory. Mom tried to live life like Granny Gillespie had. "With grace and a quiet dignity." The more I thought about it, the madder I got. But I wasn't going to yell. I stared out the window, watching the trees change to truck stops and then to power towers and then houses until finally we were in the city. At the hospital. The same hospital Mom died in. Toronto General.

Aunt Anne pulled into the lot. The parking attendant gave her a ticket, and as she set it on the dash, she turned to me. "Your father's been in an accident."

What had happened?

Startled, I followed Aunt Anne through the glass doors of the emergency department. We pushed past the gurneys, jostled through the sick and crying, the bloody and the broken, and up to the nurse's station. When we reached the desk, the nurse looked up.

"Anne," she said, rising to her feet and hurrying out from behind the counter. She took Aunt Anne's elbow and began to steer her down the hall. "He's this way."

The two nurses walked in front of me, heads together, softly exchanging information I couldn't hear. The din of the emergency room faded away as we passed through scratched steel doors into a different area of the hospital. My heart started to thump. Was this the morgue?

"Can I see him?" I asked.

"Not right now," Aunt Anne said, pointing me toward a metal chair. "Just sit over there and *wait*."

The nurse and Aunt Anne went into a room, closing the door behind them. There weren't any magazines. The hallway was too quiet. I tapped my jean pocket. At least I still had the tranquilizers. What was this place? My gut pumped up fear and spit. Getting up, I started to pace. Where was Dad? I walked over to the door Aunt Anne had disappeared behind and placed my hands on the cold steel. I could hear voices. Softly, oh so gently, I pushed it open and heard a man's voice.

"His wife told me that Ted disappeared into the bathroom of their hotel room."

Looking through the crack, there was a man sitting on the edge of a desk. Obviously, a doctor who knew Dad. Aunt Anne and the nurse sat in chairs.

"He'd been gone a long time, so Isabel knocked at the door. No answer. Then she opened it. Ted had rigged his belt to the light fixture and stepped off the edge of the tub."

Aunt Anne's hands went up to her mouth. I closed my eyes and swallowed.

"Is he dead?" Aunt Anne asked.

The doctor shook his head. "Isabel grabbed him by the waist and held him up. I don't know how she did it for so long. Security heard her shouting all the way down the hall. If she had let go, he'd be gone."

"How is he now?" Aunt Anne asked.

"He was extremely agitated when they first brought him in, but I've got him sedated. Ted's concerned about the prospect of losing his new wife. If there's anything you can do …"

Aunt Anne nodded. "Can I see him?"

"Of course, but let's keep things positive," the doctor replied. "And we'll need to keep him here for a while."

Hearing the chairs shift, I backed up, right into somebody standing behind me.

"What are you doing here?" Miss McAllister asked.

She was still wearing her blue going-away outfit. She looked exhausted, and I couldn't tell if she'd been crying, but if she had, she was over it. She looked … firm. My back was against the door. Miss McAllister wasn't moving, so neither was I.

"Is it true?" I asked.

"Your father is a very sick man."

My heart was going so fast. "You've got to help him."

"I don't think I can."

She was still wearing her wedding band. This time something in her voice wasn't quite so firm.

"He loves you."

"This isn't about love, Maddy." She looked at me, pausing. "I know what you did. Anne called me and told me how you lied." She shook her head. "I can't do this. It's too much."

She'd held him up. Held him up when he wanted to die. I remembered the things I'd done. Called him weak. Made him cry. This was likely my fault too. "If you stay, I'll be good."

Miss McAllister stared at me—looking clear through. "No, you won't."

If she left, he'd do it again. I knew this was true. I had to do something. Save my dad. She couldn't go or he'd be dead. "I swear I'll be good."

"And if you aren't?"

"I'll go away. But don't *ever* tell Dad you were going to leave. Please."

She paused. "Do you promise?"

"I promise."

The door opened and Aunt Anne appeared. "Do you want to see your father?"

"Miss McAllister should go in. He wants to see her," I said, returning to my seat.

"Maddy," Miss McAllister said.

I looked up. "Yes?"

Aunt Anne was standing right beside her.

"I would never ask you to call me Mom, but I'd like it very much if you'd call me Isabel."

When I nodded, Isabel followed Aunt Anne inside. The stainless-steel door closed behind them. This was the mental ward.

CHAPTER FOUR

My coat landed on the floor as a pot banged. Something fishy was burning. Isabel must have been trying to make her tuna noodle casserole again.

An upright piano stood beneath a colourful oil painting of Algonquin Park that had been in her family for years. Orange and yellow leaves blew from the branches of nearly barren trees. The rest of the landscape was stark. All of Mom's new modern furniture was gone, replaced by McAllister family antiques. Without taking off my shoes, the number one rule in Isabel's house, I walked down the hall. My room was in the basement.

Isabel called from the kitchen, "there's a letter for you on top of the piano."

I ran across the room. Maybe it was from Ginnie. I'd written her every single day since we'd moved and never gotten a word in reply. The envelope was covered in red hearts.

"Madeline."

Isabel stood in the doorway, a glob of mushroom soup stuck to the front of her apron, staring at my shoes. I stomped over to the foyer and kicked them off.

"Who's that from?" Isabel asked.

"It's private."

"Please hang up your coat."

Stuffing the letter into my back pocket, I threw my coat on a hook in the closet and headed for the basement.

"How was school?"

"Horrible." Yeah. Horrible.

Closing the door, I ran down the stairs, tearing open the letter. It was from Betsy. Ginnie had never written me back. Her mother must be intercepting the mail. Sticking my hand under the mattress, I rooted around for pills. Before we'd moved, I'd taken any kind of painkillers or tranquilizers I could find, but now most of the bottles were empty.

I swallowed a couple of Librium and started reading. Betsy said the teachers were a pain and school was a bore, but there was a dance coming up, and she wondered if I could bring some acid. I'd sort of told her that I'd made a ton of friends and that I'd already dropped acid. Both were lies. There'd been no acid, and I had no friends. The kids were spoiled rich snobs, and some of them called me a bumpkin.

My eyes skipped over the words. If I could get to the dance, then I could see Ginnie. If she saw me, she'd remember how much she loved me. There was a knock at the door. Nobody was allowed in my room. It was one of the few laws on my side.

Frank banged at my door. "DINNER!" he yelled.

We all sat around the McAllister oak dining room table. Tedder dropped a knife, and the sound ricocheted off the walls. The room needed a rug. A slightly charred tuna casserole sat in front of Isabel. I took a spoonful of peas and was about to set the bowl down when Isabel told me to use the trivet.

"What's that?"

"It's that square pad. It keeps the bowl from marking the wood."

"The Leafs are going to take the cup," Tedder said, spearing a pea with his fork.

"No way, the Habs have got it," Frank replied.

The boys were completely immersed in hockey and their new public school. They'd both made friends and, as Isabel said, "were blending in nicely."

"How's school going?" Dad asked.

I shrugged.

"Your father asked you a question," Isabel said, stabbing one of Tedder's runaway peas before it rolled off the table.

I looked at Dad. He was just a smear of his former self. He ate meals and drank coffee. Took up space—rarely asked questions.

"It's all right."

"Have you made any friends?" Isabel asked.

"Not really," I replied, wondering what he thought of Leaside, a minor suburb of Toronto where we were now living. I didn't even know if he liked it or not.

"Maybe if you joined the Glee Club," Isabel said, passing the carrots.

Frank burst out laughing. "Can you see Maddy at the Glee Club?"

"What's a Glee Club?" Tedder asked.

"It's a perfectly lovely occasion for young people to get together and sing," Isabel replied. "And Frank, if Maddy wants to go, you shouldn't make fun."

"Oh, come on, Mom," he said. "That's the most ridiculous thing I've ever heard."

And there it was. The first time anyone had called her Mom. Tedder stopped playing with his peas. The oak gleamed and the room stilled. Even the echo fled. Dad caught my eye and held it until I had to look the other way.

"Is it okay to call you that?" Frank asked, knife and fork clenched in either fist.

"I'm very happy that you did," Isabel said. "And there's nothing ridiculous about Glee. I made some of my best friends there."

The conversation bored me. "Can I be excused?" I asked.

"You've barely touched your dinner," Isabel said.

I pushed my chair back. "I'm not hungry."

"Right. Suit yourself."

The boys picked up their conversation about hockey. "Do you think you'd ever buy us season's tickets, Dad?" Frank asked.

Dad chewed, not paying any attention.

"Ted?" Isabel said.

Dad lurched up in his seat. "I think we should wait on that a bit."

"Come on," Tedder cried.

"How much do they cost?" Isabel asked.

I got up and walked over to the basement door. When I looked back, I couldn't help but think how peaceful and normal the scene seemed without me. Even Dad was more relaxed.

Mom wasn't the only ghost.

Her and I—the Leaside ghosts.

The school bell rang, and everyone tore out of the classroom. Keeping my head low, I headed for the girls' washroom.

The school was old, and the halls felt like a tomb, long and narrow with dark wooden wainscoting and ancient grey lockers. I'd already been there more than a month and the kids in the hall still stared at me. It was like being back in Sterling when Mom had to make my friends for me because I didn't know how.

Pushing through the washroom door, I was about to lock the cubicle door when a group of girls walked in, passing by the slit in the door. They were all dressed in pastel skirts: pale-yellow, baby-blue, and pink, with matching knee socks, white blouses, and black penny loafers. There was a flash of red in the centre. I recognized the girl from geography class.

The girl was popular like Betsy, only more like a movie star, and the whole school seemed to be under her spell. When she laughed, everyone laughed. When the boys walked by, they stumbled.

The girl wore a short, pleated red skirt, and a tight white blouse with a button-down collar. Two red barrettes pulled the brown hair out of her eyes. Her teeth were whiter than clouds. Being careful not to be seen or heard, I stared through the crack. The pretty girl made me nervous. She applied a layer of lipstick and smacked her lips. "I'm telling you, she's lez be friends and go homo."

I stopped breathing and leaned forward.

"No way!" squealed the girl in pink.

"Yes way," replied the girl in red.

Astonished laughter as the girls brushed their hair, giggled, and talked about how sick lezzes made them. Someone said that if a lez ever pounced on her she'd call the police. Hugging my stomach, I prayed that they weren't talking about me. I already suspected I might be a lez, but had no idea how anyone else could tell since I didn't even know for sure myself.

The talk in the washroom had scared me. Walking quickly down the hall with my head low, I opened a new pack of cigarettes and didn't see her until I ran into her. The pretty girl in red was standing in the middle of the hall.

"I'm sorry," I said.

"I'm Mary Sharp. Can I please have a cigarette?"

When I gave her one, she smiled at me.

The smokers' wall was near the exit doors, but Mary wanted to go somewhere private, so I followed her across the football field to the back fence. Fresh white lines had just been painted on the field and the grass was perfectly cut. Everything in Leaside was like that, the lawns manicured and maintained by vigilant husbands, out every night raking the leaves or watering the grass. Every house was identical, row upon row of two-storey brick houses with brass knockers on the front door. Isabel said that Leaside was "the ideal place for professional people to live."

I hated it. Hated its perfection.

A group of football players stopped their scrimmage to watch Mary cross the field, pulling their eyes in her direction. She stopped walking and placed her hand on my elbow, moving closer, like we were best friends sharing a secret. "Where are you from?" she asked.

"A village."

"Like in a fairy tale?"

I didn't want to talk about Sterling, and pulled away.

"I know they call you a bumpkin," Mary said, giving my elbow a squeeze. "And I'm going to make them stop."

When we reached the back fence, she slowly leaned into it, placing the cigarette between her lips. "Can you light the match? I'm afraid of fire." The yellow flame licked. Mary took a long draw and a smoky O floated out of her mouth.

"How did you do that?" I asked.

"With my tongue and my lips."

She had the most beautiful mouth, and I wondered what her lips felt like. "Show me."

No matter how many times I tried, only jagged puffs came out. Mary laughed, reminding me of Ginnie, although Mary was a lot more grown up.

"You're funny."

That's what Ginnie used to say.

"Hey Mare!" a boy called. He was a tall, good-looking guy with dark hair and a varsity football jacket. He waved. Mary didn't.

"I've got to go," Mary said, dropping the cigarette. The ember glowed in the dirt. "That's Tim. He's my boyfriend. And you," she pulled her fingers through the ends of her hair, "you're cute. We should double date sometime."

It reminded me of Kenneth and the drive-in. "Or we could just go to a movie, you and me."

A smile. "You *are* funny."

And then she left and all the excitement was gone.

Frank's door was shut. I knocked. "Can I come in?

"I'm studying." Frank was bent over a book at his desk. His bed was made and the room was neat. "What do you want?" he asked without looking up.

I handed him the envelope and a sheet of paper with Ginnie's address. "Can you write this address on the front?"

"Why?"

"Ginnie's mother is intercepting my letters."

"You should make some new friends."

"Don't you miss Pete?"

Frank and Pete had played together since they were little.

"Yeah, but I don't sit down in the basement and write him every day of the week."

"How do you know that?"

"Mom told me. Ginnie's mother called."

Isabel had no right talking about me behind my back.

"Everyone thinks you're fixated."

Closing the door, I walked down the stairs. I wasn't fixated. I missed Ginnie. She was my best friend and that was perfectly normal. Pretending that you didn't care about people or miss them, now that was weird.

Dad was stretched out on the sofa with his feet up on the coffee table, scanning the business section of the newspaper. He used to read the comics. I sat down beside him and put my head on his shoulder. He still smelled the same, like medicine and aftershave.

"How's the new practice?"

He grunted that it was fine.

"Betsy asked me to a dance back home. It's my birthday weekend and that would be the best present ever."

Dad dropped the paper and said we'd have to ask Isabel.

"Please, Dad. She doesn't understand. I miss my friends. I miss everything." I looked up at him. "Don't you?"

He wrapped his arm around my shoulder, rested his head on top of mine, and hugged me tight. "I do."

We sat there for a while, nice and quiet, just me and my dad, and things almost felt normal until Isabel came out of the kitchen, wiping her hands on a tea towel. "What are you two up to?"

Dad pulled his arm away like we were doing something bad. "Maddy wants to go to a dance in Sterling."

I wanted to yank his arm back around me. No, Dad. I thought you were going to let me go. We had an understanding.

"It's time Maddy focuses on the present and not the past," Isabel said.

"Please ... just this once," I begged.

"No," she replied firmly.

"Dad?"

He disappeared behind the newspaper wall. "You must listen to your mother. She makes the decisions around here."

The judge had spoken. I went down to my room and slammed the door so hard the hinges shook.

The classroom was quiet. Everyone was hunched over their desks, frantically answering exam questions. I stared out the window, watching two black squirrels chase each other around a thick tree trunk. The paper in front of me was blank. I hadn't studied, I was going to fail, and I didn't care. The only class I liked was English because I couldn't make myself hate the stories. Mary's white teeth nibbled the pink rubber on the end of her pencil. She must have felt me staring because she looked up. When I couldn't stop the blush, Mary smiled and returned to her exam. A thought bubble appeared. Did Mary like me?

"Did you get the question about the Cabot Trail?" Tim asked me.

The leaves bunched up around our feet as the three of us walked across the lawn in front of the high school.

"Who cares about a stupid trail?" I replied, booting through a large pile of leaves that the school janitor had just finished raking up. Tim slung his arm around Mary's shoulder. She wore it like a sweater that belonged to her. The janitor scowled as coloured leaves fluttered down around him.

We reached Tim's car, a white Triumph Spitfire his father had bought him for his birthday, a two-seater convertible with a jump seat in the back. Mary leaned against the hood and applied a fresh layer of lipstick. Two boys in a coupe drove by and wolf-whistled. Tim gave them the finger, making Mary smile. Tim's pal Ian walked over. Ian was a big blond football player who was always giving me goofy grins.

"Hi," he said.

"Hi," I fake-smiled back.

Mary slipped the lipstick back into her purse and turned toward me. "Want to go out this weekend?"

Mary's mother didn't like Mary being alone with Tim, so she always dragged me along to play chaperone. At first, I did anything to be close to Mary, but sitting in the jump seat watching the two of them neck was getting really hard, and I don't think Tim liked it very much either.

"I don't think so," I said.

"What if we went downtown?"

Isabel was sitting in the living room wing chair reading a book, little silver half-moon glasses resting on the end of her nose, while Dad, stretched out on the sofa, was having a nap. His mouth was open ever so slightly, just enough to make a little whistle. The boys and I were on the floor watching *The Partridge Family*. David Cassidy was singing, "I think I love you so what am I so afraid of/ I'm afraid that I'm not sure of a love there is no cure for." The doorbell rang and Isabel answered. Mary stood there in a pretty white dress and matching shoes. Mary extended her hand to Isabel.

"You must be Maddy's mother. I'm Mary Sharp, and I'm very pleased to meet you."

Before I knew it, Mary was sitting on the edge of a petit point chair, ankles crossed just the way parents liked, telling Isabel how well I was fitting in at school. "Even the teachers like her."

Frank burst out laughing. He knew I never did homework.

"What's so funny, dear?" Isabel asked.

"Nothing, Mom."

Most of the teachers didn't know what to do with me. The math teacher said he'd never had a worse student. I'd already forged Dad's signature on a failed history assignment the teacher sent home, and didn't know what would happen at Christmas when midterms would come back.

Mary smiled at Isabel. "Would it be all right if Maddy came out tonight? Just the two of us going to a movie."

I caught Mary's eye and the look she returned made my heart skip. Isabel tapped Dad on the shoulder. He rubbed his eyes. "What is it?"

"Do you mind if Maddy goes out with her friend?"

Dad blinked, looking over at Mary. Slowly, he swung his big feet down and sat up. "So, you're a friend of Maddy's?"

"Yes, sir."

"What's your name?"

"Mary."

"When I was a boy, we had a horse called Mary."

Oh God.

"Ted!" Isabel exclaimed.

"Can I get you a glass of milk?" he asked.

"We should get going, if that's all right," Mary replied.

Isabel nodded, and the moment the door closed, Mary and I laughed, running across the front lawn. It didn't matter what movie we saw, as long as we shared a giant box of popcorn and sat near the back where it was the darkest.

We reached the sidewalk, and Mary hooked her arm in mine, pulling me down the street, but when we turned the corner, Tim's convertible was idling by the curb. He wasn't alone. Ian was sitting in the jump seat, waving.

"I thought it would be fun if we doubled," Mary said, as the Spitfire raced down Yonge Street.

What could I say? I might be a lez-be-friends and I want to be alone with you more than anything? The overhead sky flew by as Ian's arm crept toward me. My knees jammed into my chin. There was no escape in the jump seat.

"Are you coming to the game next weekend?" Ian asked.

"I hate football," I replied, twisting the knife.

Ian's mouth fell. "Everybody loves football!"

"I *detest* it."

Mary turned and smiled, ruffling Tim's hair while I looked the other way. I'd never been this far south. Isabel said that it was where the "undesirables" lived. There, lights strobed, people clogged the sidewalks, and a neon sign covered in green lights flashed outlines of busty women into the night.

Tim pointed at a place called Le Coq d'Or. The Golden Rooster. "That's where the blacks hang out."

I'd never seen any Negroes, other than in Sunday school books where we learned Jesus loved all the little children of the world.

A huddle of black men in wide-legged pants and afros emerged from the side door of the club. The tallest one had a long rhinestone-encrusted cigarette holder. Another one pulled a pick out of his hair. Only it wasn't a pick. It was a knife.

"A little different than your village, huh?" Tim asked, honking his horn. A car up ahead responded in kind. Soon, all the cars were honking like geese.

I loved it downtown. It was wild and alive with danger and excitement. Men with knives hidden in their hair while neon women danced on signs. I loved the squalor, the noise, the pulsating lights, and the way the music rang out of cars and bars. You could get lost down here. When Tim pulled into a parking lot off Dundas Street, I felt like I'd arrived. The front of the building was covered in twinkling white lights. A lush maroon carpet rolled down the front steps past a couple of big urns with ferns. Two drunken men staggered out as Ian and I struggled out of the jump seat, following Tim and Mary across the lot. When Ian tried to take my hand, I pulled it away. Climbing the stairs, my heart began to pound, mixing with the drumbeat that punched through the brick wall. A tall man in a frilly white tuxedo shirt, black pants, and a red cummerbund held the glass door. He asked the people in front for ID. I didn't have any.

Tim stuffed some bills into the man's hand and the four of us were whisked through the entrance into a long hall filled with mirrors and silver railings. Thick red curtains hung at the end, hiding our ultimate destination. When we reached the curtains, Mary stepped forward, and like a circus ringmaster, with a grand flourish, she pulled them back. A nearly naked girl stood on a smoky stage, all alone in the centre of a rowdy crowd of drunken men shouting, "Take it off!"

Mary turned to me. I couldn't hear what she said, but her lips mouthed, "Surprise!"

The stripper shook her shoulder-length black hair, playing with her black bra, garters, and stockings. Men tossed money on the stage, trying to get her to stick her breasts in their faces. Ian and Tim hooted for the waitress to serve our table as Mary leaned into my ear. "How do you like it?"

Her breath gave me goose pimples.

"It's cool," I replied.

I couldn't bear to look at the girl, but I couldn't take my eyes off her either. A part of her reminded me of the winning cattle Granddad showed at the Royal Winter Fair. The judges clapped enthusiastically for the finest in carcass class. Flashbulbs popped as red ribbons were awarded to slaughtered animals hanging from hooks.

The girl dropped to her haunches, and then I felt the other part of me, the bad part of me that shouldn't be affected by things like this, get hot and excited. Ian ordered a round of something called Tom Collins. The taste reminded me of orange juice and perfume. I flushed it down. The perfume burned but settled the banging in my chest. Ian ordered another round and howled as I chugged the next drink and tried not to look at the stage, but it was impossible. The stripper held every eye in the house. With a slow dip, and a sexy spin, off came the black silk.

Tim howled again. "Gimme some!"

The stripper shimmied a black boa up and over her breasts until her nipples stood like straws. So did mine. I blushed. Could the others tell what I was thinking? Mary looked at me and then giggled something to Tim. Were they laughing at me? The stripper shook her boobs as one bead of sweat chased another down her slick wet chest.

I leaned toward Mary. "I've got to pee." I got up and tried not to run.

While I was slapping my face with cold water, the bathroom door opened, and Mary walked in. As she came up close behind me, I could see the top of her breasts in the mirror—the place where her skin met the white satin brassiere. The sight made me swallow. More slaps of cold water.

"Do you think I could be one?" she asked.

"What?" I gulped.

She turned me around and dropped into a slow grind. "A stripper."

"I guess so." I fumbled, trying to tear paper towels out of the metal holder.

"I think it would be fun. The power to turn guys on like that, you know." I looked at her, knowing Mary didn't need to strip to turn guys on. All she had to do was to stand there.

She placed her hands on my shoulders and pulled my face down so close to hers. "Does it turn you on?" she asked, as her tongue rolled slowly over her lower lip, her hand touching my chest. Fingers splayed so wide they lightly brushed my nipples. "I think it does," she said, her voice a raspy whisper.

Even though I knew I shouldn't, felt it was bad, knew it was trouble, I couldn't stop myself. I kissed Mary Sharp right on the mouth. Suddenly, the door opened, and a stripper walked in. Mary jumped back, shoving me so hard my tailbone struck the counter, the sound of a bat hitting a baseball. "*What* do you think you're doing?" Mary asked, walking across the room, shoving the door open with a bang.

The stripper pulled a tube of lipstick out of her pocket and gave me a funny smile. Sweat dripped through her pink kimono. "I'd watch out for that one if I was you," she said.

Tim's car was parked in front of my house. Mary hadn't said anything, but I was so scared I could barely breathe. She and Tim were necking in the front, and Mary kept wriggling her body into his and glancing back at me. Her dark hair was lightly tousled, and Tim had lipstick all over the edge of his mouth. Ian tried to kiss me, but I dodged him and jumped out of the car, walking up the drive. The car door closed, and Mary's voice came up from behind me. "Wait up."

Mary's silhouette stood against the round headlights. Was she going to tell Dad and Isabel?

"Do you want to go shopping?" she asked. She knew what I wanted to do.

"I don't think so."

"I think you'd better."

There wasn't a choice. If Mary told anybody at school, I'd be as good as dead.

A gust of wind blasted through the tunnel, signalling the arrival of the train. Brilliant light flashed up ahead as we roared into the station platform, brakes tossing up sparks as the train squealed to a stop. Mary and I climbed the stairs at Bloor and St. George, rising from the darkness into the bright light of day.

The University of Toronto area was alive with cars and students hurrying along. Boys with long hair and girls wearing beads moved along the crowded sidewalks wearing frayed, wide-legged jeans, their feet clad in sandals and clogs. Mary bought us pretzels from a street vendor, and we sat in a pair of rusted swings in a park across from a tall concrete building. I asked her what it was.

"That's Rochdale. It was supposed to be co-ed student housing, but it turned into a free love commune." She took a bite out of her pretzel, swinging back and forth. "Do you believe in free love, Maddy? I don't think I do."

Mary wouldn't believe in free love because people would sell their souls for her. Now she had mine, and no matter what the price was, I had to pay. Somebody shouted. A girl was climbing out a second-storey window and out onto the ledge. She was totally naked, big breasts swinging in the air. A pair of hands tried to pull her in, but the girl jumped, making Mary gasp. I laughed, dropping my pretzel. It wasn't a swan dive, more like a cannonball.

The girl bounced off the roof of a little green car, screaming, "What a gas man!" and streaked back into the building.

There wasn't a mark on her. I kept laughing, swinging back and forth.

Mary was confused. "What's so funny?

"That was so cool."

Mary still didn't understand, but I did. I belonged in this place where girls jumped out of buildings.

"Who did you say lives there?" I asked, taking the swing higher.

"Hippies," Mary replied. "And they sell drugs."

"How do you get in?"

"You walk in."

"Where do you go once you get in?" I asked.

Mary shrugged her beautiful shoulders and smiled. "I don't know," she replied, setting her hand on my arm, stopping my swing. Her fingernail slowly, gently traced my skin. "But I want you to find out." The swing chains groaned.

"Aren't you going to come with me?"

"No," she replied, pressing twenty dollars into my palm. "No. You're going to buy me some acid."

Stuffing the money into my pocket, I walked over to the entrance. It was a normal apartment foyer except for a couple of dorky guys sitting behind a wooden table playing chess. There was a phone and a ledger on the table beside them. I pushed the glass doors open, hoping I'd know what to do once I got inside.

One of the dorks asked where I was going. I kept moving toward the elevator.

"You!" he yelled, this time.

Hammering my thumb on the call button, I prayed that the dork would vanish, but he didn't. He grabbed me by the arm, marching me over to the desk.

"Do you live here?"

"I'm going to see a friend."

"What friend?"

"Just a guy I know."

"What apartment?"

"I think it's on the fifth floor."

"No name. No apartment. No entry. Those are the rules."

A guy with long, curly hair came out of the elevator. He had big, round, blue plastic glasses and stopped to listen while I tried to reason with the dorks.

"I just want to see my friend. Can't you give me a break? Please?" I tried flirting. It didn't work.

"Get out."

"Come on, man."

"Get out before we call the cops."

There's nothing worse than a dork on a power trip.

I sat in front of the building, occasionally glancing at Mary waiting on the swing. She didn't look happy. What would Mary do if I didn't get her acid? I lit a cigarette. The guy with the curly hair and the blue plastic glasses walked over.

"Tough break," he said.

"Yeah."

"You really know somebody in there?"

"No."

"Then why are you here?"

Mary was still watching. "I want to buy some acid."

"That's what *they're* here for," the guy replied, motioning toward the dorks. "They're the Greenies. They're supposed to call the cops if anyone comes in looking for dope."

I was about to run when the guy said, "My name's Steve. Maybe I can help you."

Steve signed me in as the Greenies frowned. Smiling back, I followed Steve to the elevator. The doors opened, revealing a naked guy and a dog. The guy shouldn't have been naked because he had an unbelievably ugly body, greasy hair, and a series of volcanic chin zits. The dog was cute. As the elevator doors closed, the dog tilted his head up, and I scratched his ears. The walls were covered in graffiti that read, "Nobody's faster than Jimmy," "Pot on four," and "Beer on eight."

"What does that mean?" I asked.

The naked guy scratched his penis while his dog took a poo. "You want a drink, go to eight. Pot's four, and acid, mesc, and MDA are on six." Steve lived on the acid floor in 602. The elevator shuddered to a stop, and we got out.

The hallway smelled better than the elevator and looked better, too. There were all sorts of posters on the walls: Cream, Creedence Clearwater Revival, and Led Zeppelin. Somebody had sprayed a giant peace sign in yellow dayglo paint. Different strains of music slid beneath the doors as we made our way down the hall to Steve's place. At first, I'd been scared, but now I was getting excited.

Steve's room was painted deep purple, a beaded curtain covered the window, and two car seats acted as chairs. He opened the bottom drawer of a desk covered in candles and removed strange sheets of thick white paper covered in green frogs, each one the size of a postage stamp.

"What do you want?" Steve asked.

"What have you got?"

"Froggy blotter."

What was that? I nodded like I knew.

"How many do you want?" he asked.

"How much?"

"Two bucks a hit, but if you buy more than ten you get them for a buck each," he replied.

An idea formed. "Give me twenty."

If I gave Mary ten, that meant ten for myself. She'd never know the difference, and for once I'd have something on Mary. Steve began cutting frogs out of the heavy paper. There were about a hundred of them, with big glassy eyes and toothy grins.

"The blotter comes from Frisco. This shit is nearly pure. Straight liquid from the lab, where the chemists take a dropper and squirt it on the frog. Cute, huh?"

"Yeah," I replied, as Steve carefully manipulated the scissors.

While he cut out the blotters, Steve told me all about how they made the dope. Its clinical name was lysergic acid diethylamide and had its roots in native plants and mushrooms. Scientists had decided to try it on the brain to cure minor personality disorders and enhance artistic creativity. I couldn't wait to try it on mine.

Isabel and I stood at the kitchen sink finishing the dinner dishes. "Can I go out? I asked.

"Where to, exactly?"

"Mary's house. We're going to study." Sure, we were; we were going to study what happened when you swallowed paper frogs.

Frank and Tedder were out on the driveway playing hockey with some of the neighbourhood boys. A little white vase painted in blue flowers rested on the windowsill. The flowers reminded me of Ginnie's eyes. Isabel touched my shoulder. Her hands were bright red from the hot water. Mom always wore gloves.

"Mary's a nice girl."

I think that's what the English teacher called an irony.

"I'm glad you're making friends," Isabel said. "Just make sure you're home by nine."

"Come on."

"Nine thirty."

"Ten?"

"Nine thirty, and that's final."

"Okay."

"Isabel, you should wear dish gloves. They'll protect your skin."

It was a beautiful evening. Mary was sitting on the bench. "You're late."

I didn't apologize. "Are you ready?"

She nodded. "What do we do?"

"Open your mouth and say ahhhhh."

Her mouth opened and, like a minister giving the Host, I rested a blotter on her pretty pink tongue. The frog faded away the moment it got wet, dissolving in Mary's mouth.

"Now you give me mine." I opened my mouth, and Mary set the paper on my tongue. Chemicals tasted so good.

We were walking down by the river when I started to feel funny. A tingling at the bottom of my spine started to walk, then dance up the back of my neck. A deep, friendly tickle made my whole-body rev like a race car at the starting gate. Drops of delicious salty saliva dripped down the back of my throat, making me swallow like crazy. Then, the river began to hum and sing. I was made of air, and Mary's hair glowed. Her irises were gone, eclipsed by big black bowling ball pupils. She laughed so hard, spinning like a top with her arms out at her sides. Light grew and pulsed, and my voice sounded far away when I talked, like sound flying down a long concrete tunnel, bouncing and binging and turning into something else when it tumbled out the other end. I started to laugh and couldn't stop. Everything was so incredibly funny. Mary took my arm, and we walked toward the river. The sky was still blue.

Sitting by the edge of the water, we took off our jackets and then our shoes, wanting to feel the singing water with our feet. A million years passed while I undid the laces. The eyelets and the laces mystified me. In a millisecond, in a single eyelet, I could see the past and the future, and the lace became a rope that could take me to the centre of the earth. Then I got caught up in the look and feel of the rocks. They were so beautiful. Everything in nature was perfect, and for once I completely understood my place in the order of things.

Mary, who was afraid of fire, lit match after match, mesmerized by the flame. I blew one out before she burned her hand. Her hair blew and flew. Mary was laughing as her teeth flashed white in the twilight. She took my hand, pulling me to my feet, and we walked into the river together. Mary disappeared beneath the surface, her hair spreading out like a Siren's. When I fell to my knees, the water folded over me, baptizing me into chemical wonder. The twilight was gone, the sky was black, and we weren't in the river anymore. We were lying on the grass with our heads together, soaking wet and cold. That's how I knew I was back on earth.

When we reached Mary's house, I pulled the remaining eight hits out of my jacket and handed them to her, but she wouldn't take them.

"I want you to sell them for me," she said.

Then Mary kissed my cheek, a special Mary kiss that could promise unspeakable bliss or the possible detonation of my entire world.

The house was dark as I snuck through the side door into the basement foyer. Everyone was asleep. Good. I was nearly in my room when the hall light flicked on and Isabel's voice rolled down the stairwell.

"Maddy?" She was down the stairs in a shot. "Are you all right?"

"I'm fine."

"Your father finally got to sleep," she said, peering into my face, trying to get a look at me. Her hair was rumpled, and her housecoat had been hastily tied. I kept moving. I had dried off a bit, but if she touched me or got a good look into my eyes, she might figure out something was up. It was so hard not to laugh—her head was starting to turn into a donkey.

"He can't be worrying about you."

Now her body was turning donkey too. Hello, Eeyore. I wanted to yank her tail and see if she brayed. I couldn't help it—I started to laugh, making Isabel mad.

"This isn't funny."

Yes, it was. This whole scene was a joke. Me living in a sideshow in the middle of a city full of snotty kids, being blackmailed by the high school goddess and saddled with a fake mother. It was far too funny for words. While I tried to get the giggling under control, Isabel wanted to know if a girl who broke the rules deserved a nice sixteenth birthday party in a couple of months. Big deal. I didn't want to celebrate with them anyway. The only thing I cared about turning sixteen was that I could leave any time I liked.

"You said that you'd behave," she said.

So, she was going to throw *that* in my face. The thought made me hot.

"You promised to behave for your father."

That wasn't funny. I'd left my hometown, all my friends and given up Ginnie. I'd done everything I'd promised. Isabel wagged her donkey hoof in my face.

"One more time, Madeline Anne! One more time and you're grounded."

I stumbled into my room. Fully dressed, I fell back on the bed, listening to the big blowhard stomp up the stairs. I was furious. How dare she bring that up? I let my little brothers call her Mom even though I wanted to beat them up every time they said it. I'd been good.

I'd kept my end of the bargain.

And lost everything in return.

It was the weekend of the Halloween dance. The Spitfire idled at a stoplight as two hobgoblins with pointy red hats and fake beards crossed the street. Tim, wearing his grass-stained football jersey, revved the engine, trying to act the man. His hand stroked Mary's thigh, lucky boy fingers pressing into her soft skin. There hadn't been even a hint of a possible Mary kiss since that time in the strip club, but there hadn't been any threats either. I passed up a stack of bills that Mary quickly counted and tucked into her purse.

"Did you sell them all?" she asked.

"Fifty at lunch. The rest'll go before the dance."

Mary was so proud of herself, convinced that she was getting rich from blackmailing me into dealing her acid, but little did she know I was secretly ripping her off. Tim shot his hand up Mary's skirt. She playfully slapped his hand and told him to stop it.

"You're stoned," he said.

"So what?" Mary asked.

"You're always stoned."

Mary swallowed all her profits. She took even more acid than me. I watched Tim's hand travelling up her skirt. Then he suddenly stopped, catching my eye in the rearview mirror.

"What are you looking at?"

He'd caught me. "Nothing."

Mary started rubbing his neck, but Tim wouldn't back down. "Why are you always hanging around?" he asked. "Why don't you

get your own boyfriend?"

I tried not to blush. The light changed to green, but the car didn't move.

"Or is it a girl that you want?"

"Maddy's my friend, and if you don't like it, you can find somebody else," Mary snapped.

The Spitfire shot into traffic and the conversation was over, but Tim was right. I was Mary's puppet. Since I'd started dealing, everyone wanted to be my friend, and even if Mary said I was a lez, all I'd have to say is she was lying and the kids would believe me, because if they didn't, I'd cut off their drug supply. I had the kind of power at the school that Mom and Dad had in Sterling, and everyone needed to keep me happy. But Mary, beautiful, mean Mary Sharp held the ultimate power over me. The minute she said, "get in the car," I hopped in like there was an invisible noose around my neck. No matter how badly she treated me, I always came back for more.

I was on my way out when Isabel called me into the dining room. "Where's your costume?" she asked.

"Costumes are stupid."

"They most certainly aren't stupid. You need a costume for Halloween. Isn't that right, Ted?

Dad shoveled in a forkful of meatloaf and nodded. He'd put some weight back on, but still acted like a sad zombie. I wanted to ask him if everything was okay, but I never had the chance because he was never alone. Isabel was always standing guard.

"Why don't you go as a hockey player?" Frank laughed, taking a bite of potatoes.

"Yeah, right." I rolled my eyes and turned to Dad. "What do you think?"

"Why don't you go as a doctor?"

I joined my father in his bedroom, Isabel still busy feeding my brothers in the kitchen. He turned and looked at me, "Try this on," he said, handing me a pair of green hospital scrubs.

The pants were too big, but when Dad got on his hands and knees and safety pinned the pants and sleeves, the clothes fit okay. We looked in the mirror together, first catching and then holding one another's gaze. Dad stood behind me, his hands on my shoulders, giving them a gentle squeeze. Zombie or not, my father did look better. I put my hands on top of his and held them, remembering the touch of those soft, kind, gentle hands. The hands that Mom had loved so much, just like I did. Fingers that had stitched my wounds and dried my tears.

"Dad?"

"Uh-huh?"

"Do you still think about Mom?"

He pulled his hands away from me, walked over to the closet, and started pulling boxes out of the top cupboard. Running over, I tugged on his arm. "I think about her every day. Every single minute, Dad. Almost every second," I added.

"Then you must stop. It's no good for you."

"I don't know how. Will you teach me? I even dream about her. Almost every night. How did you stop?"

"It's a personal journey," he softly replied.

I squeezed his hands. "Dad, please talk to me." I squeezed even harder. "Do you still miss her as much as I do?" I wanted him, needed him, to answer my question, but he turned away, handing me his old black leather bag.

"A doctor isn't a doctor without a medical bag."

Then he draped his stethoscope around my neck, stuffing the breast pocket with tongue depressors.

"Now, don't you look just fine?"

Sitting at a picnic table at the back of the football field, I watched ghosts, witches, firemen, and spacemen discreetly hidden behind trees, waiting to get their acid. When I'd picked it up at Rochdale, Steve told me to be careful, it was the strongest he'd ever taken. I didn't care and took two.

The lights at the back of the school were black. That meant no spying teacher eyes. Slowly, I opened the medical bag, gesturing for my customers to come forward. One by one, they approached as I pressed purple pills into their palms. Half an hour later, we were all inside the gym and starting to get off.

Steve was right. The acid was strong—maybe even bad-trip kind of strong. A girl galloped around the dance floor, gusting and blowing as hard as she could, while two witches sat on the floor staring at their hands. The math teacher was trying to make the witches stand up when a fairy began to laugh. The wind girl was swooping around, blowing on the fairy's wings. I searched the gymnasium. Mary had to be here somewhere. Tim was by the stage talking to some of the other jocks. They'd come dressed as murdered football players, faces painted white, clothing soaked in fake blood, with gun shots through their jerseys.

"What do you want?" Tim asked. His voice slurred. Tim wasn't stoned, he was dead drunk and very loud.

"I'm looking for Mary."

"You're always looking for Mary."

Couples stopped dancing, and heads turned; the floor rolled under my feet, and a crack appeared. The linoleum yawned open as the lion on the school crest snarled at me with yellow fangs.

I needed Mary. "Where is she?"

"She's in the washroom all messed up," he said, in a really pissed-off voice. "And it's because of you!"

He poked me in the chest with his finger, and I poked him back, right in the centre of the gunshot wound.

"Stay away," he said, pushing my shoulder this time, hard enough to make me stagger.

I pushed him back and called him a jerk.

"Stay away from my girlfriend!" he yelled, punching me in the face, hard.

I ran off the dance floor, rushing past a female guidance counselor who tried to stop me, asking what on earth was wrong.

"Mary?" I called, walking into the girls' washroom. My voice bounced around while a million of me stared back from the mirror. Somebody was cooking hamburgers. What was wrong with my face? My eye was turning blue. I wanted to poke at the eyeball with my fingers and try to pull it out. Instead, I pushed open stall doors. "Are you in here?"

A giggle.

"Mary?" I called again, looking under the panels. I found her in the last stall, sitting on a toilet seat, dressed as a princess. Everything was pink: her crinoline, tiara, even her shoes. A cigarette smoldered between Mary's fingers, past the filter, stuck into the flesh, cooking her pink skin, the smell of cooking pink meat.

I ripped the cigarette out and threw it on the floor. "What are you doing?"

Another giggle and then that Mary smile. "I'm not afraid of fire anymore."

Pulling her up, I dragged her out of the cubicle toward a row of sinks. "The water might sting a bit at first, but it'll help."

As I turned on the water, Mary reached out and touched my eye. "You love me," she said, pushing on the bruise.

"How is your hand?" I asked.

"Why don't you kiss me?"

The water was gushing. Mary's fingers were burning. My eye was swelling.

"I know you want to," she said.

"I know I shouldn't."

"But what if I want you to."

Mary's face was in my hands, my lips touching hers, when the female guidance counselor walked in, and the walk of shame began.

The guidance counselor sat me on the front steps of the school, her hand gripping my shoulder. "Do you know what you did is unnatural?" her pink gums asked. The same colour as Mary's dress. I didn't answer, just sat there in my doctor's scrubs, staring at my feet, trying to tune out the words "pervert" and "mentally ill." The Oldsmobile pulled up and Dad and Isabel got out of the car.

"Your daughter," the counselor said, in a disgusted tone, "is seriously disturbed."

Looking down the street, I wondered if I should run. Dad told me to get in the car. I followed him while Isabel spoke to the counselor, who wouldn't stop talking. Dad opened the back door for me to get in, and with his head down, slowly returned to Isabel and the counselor. They were talking so loudly it was impossible to ignore.

"Timothy told me that Maddy's always trying to touch Mary."

I shrunk down.

"Girls are frequently physical with one another," Isabel said.

"Not the way a boy kisses a girl," the counselor said.

Dad looked as if he'd been punched.

"Keep Maddy away from Mary, or the next time—"

"It won't happen again," Isabel said. She took Dad by the arm, and they walked back to the car. Isabel was driving.

The car was silent. I tried to ignore the counselor's words, but they wouldn't stop.

Dad leaned over quietly and said something to Isabel. I pretended not to listen.

"Maybe it's just a phase," he whispered, looking to her for hope.

"Boys never come by," she quietly whispered back.

Dad sighed, long and sad, as Isabel took one hand off the steering wheel and reached out to stroke the back of his neck. There was no blaming Isabel anymore. She wasn't the one wrecking our family. It was me.

Dad trudged up the stairs and disappeared into their bedroom as Isabel took my coat and opened the closet door.

"You must be very confused," she said, a soft look crossing her face.

For a split second, there was a human being standing there. A human being that understood what was going on. She didn't yell and scream and call me a freak. She could have made Dad ship me off to the nuthouse, but she didn't. Maybe I could talk to her about how I felt about Ginnie and Mary. Maybe she could help.

"But I can't have you upsetting your father any further," she said, walking up the stairs. "We'll talk about psychiatric treatment later." And another door slammed shut.

I didn't leave my room the next day until dinner time.

"Surprise!" Tedder yelled.

I'd forgotten about my birthday. The whole family sat around the dining room table singing, "Happy Birthday." A pink cake blazed in the centre of the table and gifts were piled by my placemat.

"What did you do to your eye?" Frank asked.

It was black and blue from Tim's fist. Luckily, I didn't have to answer because the doorbell rang.

"Blow out your candles and make a wish," Isabel said, rising from her seat.

There was nothing I wanted that I could have, so I just blew out the flames. The boys clapped.

"Does it feel any different being sixteen?" Frank asked.

"Not really."

I heard a man talking in the living room and then Isabel's voice shot up an octave. My neck bristled. She was always calm. Dad pushed back his chair. The boys followed him out into the living room with me behind.

Isabel was talking to a man a little younger than Dad, with dark hair and a stocky build. He was wearing a three-piece suit and held a yellow document. There was a uniformed policeman with him.

"This is Detective Bill Read," Isabel said, her voice shaking with fury.

"What?" Dad asked.

"We received a call from your daughter's high school," Detective Read said. "She was selling drugs there last night. We have a warrant to search the house."

He looked at me. "Are you Madeline Anne Barnes?" he asked, crossing the room toward me. I backed up into the piano, making the keys sing.

"She is," Isabel replied.

"Show me your room."

"It's this way," Isabel said.

Isabel opened the door to the basement. The policeman was tearing my room apart while Detective Read interrogated me.

"Where did you buy the LSD?"

"I didn't."

"Two teenagers got sick. Their parents say that they bought it from you."

"They're wrong."

All the drugs I'd sold or taken flipped through my mind as cards in a rapidly shuffling deck. I'd sold all the microdots and was positive everything else was gone, too. But what if I'd forgotten something? Isabel's face got redder and redder as the police flipped the mattress, dumping desk and dresser drawers all over the floor, tearing through the closet, searching my pockets, looking through books and even checking the vents. They found no acid—only bottle after empty bottle of Dad's prescription drugs.

"Where did you get these?" the detective asked.

"From my father's dispensary."

"Does he know you have them?"

"No," Dad replied.

He was standing in the doorway. My brothers stood behind him. Tedder's face said he didn't understand, but Frank did. He wouldn't even look at me. The detective asked Dad if he knew some of the drugs were restricted substances. Isabel looked set to implode.

"Yes, sir," Dad replied.

"You could lose your license."

"Please!" I cried. "He didn't know. This is my fault. I was the one taking them. They were just for me."

"What about the LSD?"

"I don't know anything about that."

The detective stared at me, and I stared back, the two of us, in the middle of the car accident that used to be my room, playing a game of chicken. I wouldn't let him hurt my dad, but I wouldn't confess to the acid either. I'd just turned sixteen and didn't want to go to jail.

"We'll see," the detective said. He paused. "That's all for now." There was nothing more he could do, and he knew it.

"I'll show you out," Dad said, shooing the boys out of the room and up the stairs. The uniformed officer followed. Isabel didn't. She picked up an empty bottle.

"That's it."

"What are you talking about?"

But I knew what she meant. Our deal. The deal I'd smashed into a million pieces.

"It's you or me," she said.

I had to take one last stand. "Then let him decide."

Isabel softly set the bottle on the bureau. "Would you ask him to do that?" Then she left, shutting the door behind her.

Of course not. Dad could never make that decision, and I couldn't ask him to. He was as happy as he was going to be with Isabel. So were Frank and Tedder. It was up to me. I was the one who had to go.

CHAPTER FIVE

The sunlight stung my good eye. The black one was nearly swollen shut. I stood at the corner of Yonge and Dundas holding Mom's white suitcase, stuffed with whatever I could grab before I ran away. A stubby man wearing an old-fashioned derby hat and a sandwich board advertised for a place called Starvin' Marvin's. Huge posters of topless girls with big boobs were plastered on the walls and windows behind them. Some of the girls proudly cupped their breasts in their hands, while another one licked her own nipple. She must have had a long tongue to do that. The man held a megaphone. "Come on in," the man barked, bowing deeply as I passed by. "Don't be shy. We've got more girls than you've got dreams!"

Two burly guys carted cases of beer out of an idling truck and into Le Coq d'Or. As the doors opened, music slipped out, soul music that sounded the way the street felt: smooth and exciting—the way my future was going to be. Granddad started with nothing and made his own fortune. He didn't cry, all alone out on the prairies wrangling cattle. He slept under the stars with yipping coyotes in the hills, built up his herd, and then took the cattle to market. That's what I'd do, too.

I'd spent all my money at Steve's and my pockets were stuffed with little purple pills. Now I needed to find a new customer base and that wouldn't be hard. The sidewalks were full of hippies and heads. I didn't need anybody taking care of me. This was the same as the night I jumped off the beam, which was way scarier than this, plus I was now all grown up and could take care of myself.

The scent of patchouli oil drew me up a wide set of red brick steps into a warren of tiny market stalls selling brightly coloured beads, tie-dye skirts, and boxes of incense that smelled of travel. Strains of sitars mixed with incense and calls of "Girls! Girls! Girls!"

A pretty girl with an oval face and a halo of short white hair stood beside an old man who had a silver brush cut and squatted on his heels. The girl panhandled while the man rolled a homemade cigarette.

"Looky looky, here comes Cookie!"

Was he talking to me? I didn't know what to do, so I kept walking.

"Wine's fine but liquor's quicker."

I turned. The man's fingers trembled as tobacco flakes fell.

"And you know what gin does?" he asked. He was missing a few front teeth.

"What?"

"Gin makes you sin."

I smiled as the old man sucked through the hole where his teeth used to be. "I ain't seen you around here before," he said, looking at my suitcase and then at my eye.

"I'm new," I replied, looking at the girl with the white hair, quickly brushing my bangs over the bruise.

"I'm Gabe and that's Lily," he said, jabbing a yellowed thumb at the girl. "Isn't she as pretty as a flower?" She was. Tall and thin, the white hair ringed her face like a blossom. "We're together," he proudly said.

Was Gabe her father? He couldn't be her boyfriend, because Lily looked about the same age as me. Not wanting to be rude, I didn't ask. Lily asked a mother and a little girl for some change. The lady rooted in her purse, dropping a coin in Lily's hand. Lily turned to me and said hi. I'd never seen white eyelashes before.

"I'm Maddy."

"Where you from?" Gabe asked.

"Out of town." I didn't want to talk about the past.

"Us too," Lily said, sitting down at a place she called the Steps.

While we were hanging out, enjoying conversation, the warm sun on my face and the smell of incense mixing with gasoline, two older boys arrived and asked Lily if she wanted to smoke a joint. Lily said no, but the boys didn't leave. One had a big nose. His friend wore a smiley-face T-shirt and had a squeaky, high-pitched laugh. Smiley Face told Lily that a joint might loosen her up.

Gabe spat on the sidewalk. "The lady doesn't want any."

"Why don't you get lost?" asked Smiley Face.

Lily's ears went pink as she shot to her feet. "Why don't you fuck off?"

It was the first time I'd ever heard a girl say fuck off. Not even Mary said that, and Mary said everything. The boys still didn't move, so Lily and Gabe left. Smiley Face pulled a lumpy looking joint out of his coat pocket and waved it at me.

"Smoke?" he asked.

"Sure," I replied. I'd only smoked pot a couple of times with Mary and Tim and it always made me cough.

Using Mom's suitcase like a coffee table, the three of us passed the joint around. The weed was so strong I couldn't feel my toes. Eventually the talk shifted to getting higher. The guy with the big nose wanted to go buy acid.

"How many do you want?" I asked.

"You carrying?"

I nodded, ready to dicker the way Granddad did. "What'll you pay?"

"Two bucks a hit," Smiley Face said.

"Make it three, and I can help you out."

"Sure."

My hand was already in my pocket when Smiley Face said we should take it into the alley. He was right. It was stupid to deal right out in the open. I was high and not thinking straight. The three of us slipped into the alley behind Sam the Record Man, stepping around flattened cardboard boxes and piles of stinking garbage bags. While I set the suitcase down, I noticed black scuffs on the white leather and wondered if they'd ever come off. A rainbow danced on top of an oil puddle.

"How many you want?" I asked.

"We'll take them all."

"Cool," I replied, pulling the bag of microdots out of my pocket. "That'll be a hundred and twenty."

"I don't think so," the big nosed one said, snatching the acid while I grabbed his arm and started to yell.

Smiley Face had the suitcase and was laughing his high-pitched giggle.

"Give me my acid!" I screamed, kicking Big Nose in the shinbone so hard he yelped. "Give it back!"

He punched me in the stomach, fist blowing out all the air, but I wouldn't let go of his arm. Wouldn't let go until a white box whacked me across the head and I fell, losing my grip. It was Mom's suitcase.

I was back at Steve's door, covered in alley grease.

"What happened?" Steve asked as I walked in and sat down.

"I got ripped off."

"All of it?"

I nodded, rubbing the rising goose egg on my head. It was sore.

"Geez, Maddy. You never keep your whole stash in one place. If you have to travel with it, you hide it on different spots on your body."

I didn't know that, but it was a mistake I'd never make again. "I need you to give me ten hits. I'll pay you later."

Steve frowned. "I don't front."

"Just once?"

"No."

This was bad. I couldn't pay rent if I didn't have money for dope.

My stomach growled. "Can I crash here?"

Steve would help me out. We were friends. "The old lady doesn't allow it."

Since when did Steve have an old lady?

"I'll sleep on the floor. I don't even need a blanket." There was a knock at the door.

"What if I clean the place?"

"Sorry," Steve said, getting up.

It was dark in Allan Gardens and the park didn't feel safe, but I was exhausted. Early winter wind blew leaves across the grass. Shivering, I did up the top button of my shirt, stamping my feet. Smiley Face got my coat when he stole Mom's suitcase. Around midnight I'd walked into a phone booth, nearly calling home, but I stopped myself because Dad would be forced to come and get me, and then Isabel would leave. A golden light glowed in the centre of the park. Maybe it was safe and warm in there.

Pools of light fell from old lampposts that ran along a ropey pathway. I hurried down the path toward the glow, past wrought-iron benches, rushing from lamppost to lamppost, terrified of the rattles and scary hisses that came out of the dark. There was a rustle from a bush to the left and then a girl appeared beneath a tree. Leaves and grass were stuck to the back of her hair and her skirt was hitched up around her hips.

"What are you staring at?" she asked, yanking the skirt down.

"Nothing."

The girl pulled a twenty-dollar bill out of her brassiere and shoved it into her purse. "I never saw you here before."

"I'm new." It was so good to see another person. Maybe she'd like to sit and visit.

But the girl simply said, "Watch out for the cops," and disappeared into the night.

Even if it was weak, and a serious Gillespie sin, for the first time in my life, I was truly afraid.

The beginnings of a glow appeared from an enormous glass observatory that rested in the centre of the park. Fingers of moonlight broke through a roof of palm fronds, stroking a thick grove of exotic plants before they landed on the ground, transforming the dark green moss into a shimmering carpet. The garden felt warm, alive, and breathing, a safe place to spend the night.

But the door was locked. Ducking between a hedge and the glass, I snuck around the side, looking for another way in. Then a sudden rustle and the snapping of a twig, followed by a series of crackles, coming up, racing up fast behind me. I tried to run, but a hand came down, a strong hand clamping onto my shoulder, spinning me around, flashing a beam of blinding light into my eyes.

"What do you think you're doing?"

Squinting, I dodged the glare to see a uniformed policeman.

"I asked you a question. What are you doing out here?"

"Nothing."

"Show me some ID."

It was in Mom's suitcase.

"I don't have any."

The policeman grabbed my arm and marched me through the park, over to a cruiser. He opened the front door and shoved me inside. A truncheon rested on the vinyl seat. He got in the driver's seat and picked up his radio. "What's your name?"

I wanted to lie, but what would I say? "Madeline Anne Barnes."

He looked me over. "What happened to your face?"

"I walked into a door."

"Did somebody do that to you?"

Tim. "No, sir."

"Address."

"I don't have one."

"Date of birth?"

I gave it to him.

"Just sixteen, eh?"

"Yes, sir."

"And you figure you're big enough now to be out on your own?"

"Yes, sir."

"We'll see about that."

While we waited for the background check the policeman lectured me all about the dangers waiting for young girls out on the streets at three in the morning. Did I have any idea of what went on in the park after dark? I thought of that girl with the grass in her hair. So that's what she was doing. I'd never do that. The radio crackled to life. A missing person's report had been lodged for me that morning. That meant Dad cared.

"Your mother reported you as a runaway."

Dad didn't even call. I wanted to scream but then I'd just get locked up. Maybe I was already on some sort of suspect list because of Detective Read. I just clenched my fists and pretended to be Granddad.

"Let me take you home."

"No."

If I went back home, my stepmother would leave, and my father would kill himself.

"Don't you think you should at least call them?"

He could take me to prison for vagrancy if he wanted, but I wouldn't put my dad in that spot, the place where he'd have to pick me. And besides, it hurt less not knowing than to find out for sure that he'd choose her over me.

We sat in silence until the frustrated policeman said, "Okay, get going, and don't let me find you in here again."

The moment the cruiser was out of sight, I started furiously kicking a lamppost. What kind of a father would do this? Not my old father, but that man was gone. Just as dead as Mom was. I kicked the post again. They were bad parents. Kick. Wicked. Kick. Then the kicks slowed as my thoughts shifted, searching for sense. Maybe Dad and Isabel were right. Maybe I was a pervert. I didn't know. I knew I was a drug dealer, but I liked the job. It was noble, cool, and offered a good return to help people escape their troubles. Did that make me bad enough to deserve this? Another kick that really hurt. Maybe I did deserve it. When I almost started to cry, I pinched the skin on my arm, giving it a hard twist. NO! There would be no crying! Ever. All Dad ever did was cry, and I would never be as weak as him. But I also knew that I couldn't do this alone. I needed help. Desperately.

There was nothing else to do, so I walked back to the Steps watching the sleeping city wake up. Before dawn everything was quiet except the distant hum of street sweepers and the odd, lonely cab searching for a fare. Delivery trucks began rumbling by, loaded with fresh produce, and office workers started to stream out of the subway, heading for Bay Street's financial towers, and then around ten, the retail shops opened for business. Nobody noticed me, a sixteen-year-old girl in rumpled clothing and a black eye, tucked into the corner of a doorway.

I heard a cheerful whistling and looked up. Gabe was ambling down the street as Lily loped along beside him. She was nearly a foot taller, but still looked like an innocent little kid. When they saw me, Gabe stopped whistling and they came over, plopping down on either side. Lily asked where my suitcase was. Gabe patted me on the thigh and then gently pulled my face towards his. "Did you get rolled?"

He sounded so kind that I started to cry. "Everything."

"Oh, kiddo," Gabe said. "Those guys with the weed."

"Fuck me," Lily said.

"No, fuck them," I replied, and then started to laugh through the tears. Laughing because I'd said fuck out loud for the first time in my life, but mostly because I wasn't alone anymore.

"Are you hungry?" Lily asked.

I nodded.

"We'll get you some breakfast, and then you're going to learn how to panhandle."

Breakfast consisted of a loaf of bread and a package of bologna. It cost under a dollar, and it fed the three of us. While mustard would have been nice, there was no money for condiments. Lily wiped her hands on her jeans and stood, announcing that it was time for class.

"I'm a rich lady," Lily said, pretend sashaying down the sidewalk as Gabe and I laughed.

"Don't laugh. One day I'm gonna be rich. You just wait and see." Lily kept walking toward me. "So, what do you do?"

I approached her with my hand out, eyes cast down. "Excuse me, ma'am, can you spare any change?"

"You're acting too desperate," Lily said.

"I'm begging for money. Of course I'm desperate." I didn't like begging and was worried that I'd see someone I knew.

"When are we getting a bottle?" Gabe asked.

"We're not getting a bottle. Maddy, try it again."

"Do you have any spare change?" I asked.

"Get a job," she said.

"Even a penny would help," I added.

Lily approved. "That's smart."

"That way, they don't think I'm greedy."

"Okay, try it on somebody real," she said, giving me a shove.

Guilt might work. Lily said nobody wanted to help desperate people, but I'd learned from Dad that most people wanted to do the right thing. All you had to do was give them the proper incentive, and what was more guilt-inducing than refusing to help a girl in trouble? An older woman with several shopping bags approached.

"Excuse me," I said.

She walked on by.

"Please," I said with a little cry. "I got mugged, and I don't have any money for the subway."

She paused. "Why don't you call your parents?"

"They're not home."

"Where do you live?"

"Leaside."

She stopped and looked at me.

"Maybe you can give me a ride?" I asked.

"I'm not going that way."

She opened her purse and carefully counted thirty cents.

"Here you go. Now make sure you get right on the train and don't you spend this on anything else. This is hard-earned money."

"Oh, no, ma'am," I oozed. "You're so kind. I'll be sure to tell my parents that there are still decent people in the world."

The woman left all proud and puffed up while Lily and Gabe split a gut.

"You're good," Lily said.

Guilt worked, but there was something low about using people and lying. Granddad always said there was nothing more despicable than a liar or a thief, and Mom had claimed misrepresenting yourself was the biggest sin of all. Dealing dope had dignity—begging had none. I needed to get enough money together to start a new stash. After a couple of days of panhandling, I planned to go back to Steve's.

We finished at about eight, combined our money and headed for the hotel. It was unbelievable. There'd be nothing left after we paid for a room.

"How are we ever going to get ahead?" I asked.

"Some days are better than others," Lily replied.

Hungry and exhausted, I trailed along behind them. My clothes were dirty and I needed a bath.

"Have we got enough for a bottle?" Gabe asked. "I'm getting the shakes."

Lily scratched her ear. "The doctor said you need a break."

"Please, Lily," Gabe begged.

"Lily, please," I added. I could use something myself.

She gave Gabe a kiss on the cheek. "Maybe tomorrow."

We walked past abandoned storefronts, pawnshops, and shoeshines. Lingerie dangled from the windowsills of crumbling buildings. Alkies were either propped up against brick walls, happily chattering away at one another or flopped over on the sidewalk, passed out cold. Gabe said hello to a couple of guys he knew and asked them if they had any liquor, but they were all empty.

We arrived in front of the hotel, the Warwick, a five-star jewel where big bands once played, which had transformed into a skid row flophouse. A poster outside boasted aging burlesque dancers with saggy boobs, like inflatable dinghies with the air let out. Lily told us to go around back while she got a single room. Apparently, it was cheaper than paying for three. We hid out in an alley until Lily's white head poked through a third-storey window, waving us up.

Gabe and I snuck up the metal fire escape and climbed in through the window. The ripped drapes had once been expensive brocade and the chenille bedspread had luxurious tassels, but the green was fading away and most of the tassels were gone. Wind blew through a transom where the glass was smashed, and the bed had a deep sway. Gabe flicked on the TV. There was an old western playing. The cavalry sounded the charge. Gabe was still negotiating for a bottle when I fell fast asleep on the floor.

It was the banging that woke me up. "Maid!" an impatient woman called.

"I'll be out in a minute," Lily called.

Gabe was in the bathroom taking a shower.

"Check out!" the maid called again.

"Give me five minutes," Lily replied, motioning for me to be quiet.

"If you're not, I'll call the manager. I got cleaning to do."

Lily peered through the peephole as Gabe tiptoed out of the bathroom with a towel wrapped around his skinny waist. Soft patches of white hair curled over a pale-blue tattoo of a warship that sailed across his chest. Had Gabe been in the Navy?

There was no time to shower. The maid banged on the door again, and while Lily yelled back, Gabe and I crept out the window and down the fire escape.

The three of us met up at John's Open Kitchen, a short-order eatery with walls caked in grease and dirty linoleum floors. The short-order cook was a friend of Gabe's from the old days, and he fed us for free.

"He's my buddy," Gabe said, as the cook slapped down plates of French toast. "We were in the merchant marines together."

That made sense. Gabe looked way more like the sailor on the cigarette pack than a Navy man. A gang of skinny kids came in and fell into one of the booths. They were chain smoking and talking loud and fast, yelling for coffee. Lily frowned, saying the diner was losing its class if it was letting speeders in. Speed was on my list of drugs to try, but since Lily didn't approve, I kept my mouth shut and took a bite of toast. It was delicious. I was so hungry I could have eaten all three helpings, but it wouldn't be polite to ask for more. Lily thought that taking drugs was the stupidest thing in the world and, giving Gabe a serious look, went on to say that it was bad enough that people drank liquor. He kissed Lily's cheek and asked her for a bottle.

"We're saving for an apartment," she replied.

I had to ask. "Are you guys related?"

Gabe smiled. I'd never seen such yellow teeth. If I didn't brush my teeth soon, they were going to look like his.

"Lily's my angel," he said, softly rubbing her white fuzz.

"I'm not an angel," Lily replied with a sweet smile, getting up to leave for the washroom.

Lily was wrong. Her white halo of hair glowed, and whenever I felt scared, she magically made me feel safe.

Gabe watched Lily cross the diner with the besotted love of a father. "She's everything I got."

After thanking the cook for the meal, I went into the washroom to clean up. My hair was matted, and my black eye was even worse. Using my fingers, I combed through the knots, holding a cold compress of wet paper towels to my eye to reduce the swelling. My breath was sour, and my clothes were dirty. Where could I wash them? Gabe and Lily went back to the Steps while I decided to try the museum.

A steady stream of yellow school buses transported children from all over the province. Bright banners blew from the top of flag posts as lines of little kids followed teachers into the museum. I wandered up and down the sidewalk, on the lookout for anyone who would listen to a sob story.

"My eye hurts. I need money to get to the hospital."

"Pardon me, ma'am. I've gotten separated from my school trip and need a nickel to call home."

Sitting on the museum's steps crying worked the best of all.

"What's wrong, dear?"

"The bus left without me. I don't know how I'm going to get home!" I wailed.

"Where's home?"

"Oshawa."

"Let me give you a dollar. That should help, now, shouldn't it?"

After three hours, I had four dollars, but once I bought some cotton candy and two Eskimo bars from the street vendor who sold balloons on sticks, more than half of the money was gone. My stomach felt nauseous, and Lily was going to kill me. Another yellow school bus pulled up to the curb, its doors yawning as teenagers spilled out. Most of them looked bored, like they'd been captured alive and dragged onto the bus against their wills.

Pitching the cotton-candy cone in the trash can, I started walking up to Bloor Street when Dad's Oldsmobile pulled up onto the sidewalk and he jumped out.

"Maddy!"

Thoughts of the police, Dad's pill bottles, him maybe losing his license, the counselor shouting and now me dirty and begging on the street, rang in my mind. I ran.

Dad caught me by the statue of a lion, holding me in his arms. He was still faster. "I've been looking for you everywhere. Are you all right?"

So, my dad *had* looked for me. I tried not to cry, but then I saw the look in his eyes, the dark, lost look he'd had after Mom died. He shook it off, but how long would it last? He would try again—he would kill himself if Isabel wasn't there for him, and it would be my fault. Again. I pulled out of his arms and backed away. "I'm not coming home."

His hands fell to his sides. "Where are you staying?'

"With friends."

"Give me the address so I know where you are."

"It's nothing permanent."

He knew what that meant—transient.

"Let me get you a room."

When I started to say no, he rode right over me. "Let me get you a room. Then we'll get you some clean clothes and take things from there."

I wanted to throw my arms around him, but I just said, "Okay."

We drove around the Annex, looking at different rooming houses while I nervously leafed through medical journals that had been tossed on the floor. Eventually, Dad settled on an establishment for young ladies located above a dentist's office. It was an old Victorian with grey shingles and sweeping turrets. The turret rooms were great because they had round windows, but they were already taken.

My room consisted of a single bed, a chest of drawers, a bedside table with a poodle lamp, and a poster of the Eiffel Tower tacked to the wall. The poodle had a pink skirt and matching shade. I put the new clothes Dad had bought me on the bed, along with more medical journals.

The kitchen was communal, and everyone shared the television. A chubby girl with a scowly face hogged the sofa. There were five boarders all together. The dentist's assistant explained the rules of the house: "Rent's every Monday. Don't eat anyone else's food." She glanced at my dirty clothes. "There's a washer and dryer down in the basement, a payphone in the hall, and whoever's first at the TV gets their choice."

The chubby, scowly girl looked like she lived on the sofa.

"Curfew?" Dad asked.

"Eleven o'clock, and we lock the door."

How could I complain? It was better than sleeping in a park with monsters.

Dad and I stood in front of the open refrigerator, stocking my shelf. He glanced at my face. "How's the eye?"

"It's okay." I didn't want to talk about it, and he didn't press.

Dad handed me a carton of eggs. We'd gone out shopping for food and returned with eggs, bacon, bread, chocolate ice cream, and salt and vinegar chips.

"Are you sure this is going to be enough?" he asked, glancing into the empty brown paper bag.

I nodded. It was so nice to have him here with me. He looked different, as if he was clearer or slightly more defined. A white handkerchief peeked out of his breast pocket.

"Is that a new suit?"

He nodded. "Do you like it?"

"Spiffy."

"Isabel picked it out."

I slammed the eggs into the keeper.

"Don't break them."

I didn't want to talk about Isabel. When he said he had to get back to work, my heart hurt.

"When will I see you again?" I asked. "For rent and stuff."

"If you need money, call me at the office. The rent is paid in advance."

That meant he didn't want me calling at home. He just wanted me gone. Coming to find me was only a guilt trip.

"Why don't you leave me some, just in case?" I asked, nudging him into a corner to see what he would do.

Dad frowned. "I'll need to check in and see how you're doing."

"What if you're too busy?"

His hands started to shake as he looked around. "I don't know if this is a good idea."

It's not like I could go home. Isabel wouldn't allow it. "What if you forget?"

"Maddy … I wouldn't forget."

His face looked so hurt I felt sick.

"I might be out looking for a job when you come by. If you leave me money, I can take care of myself."

Silence. I could feel him weighing out what would happen if he brought me home. "I could always call the house."

A part of me had secretly considered going home. Even with Isabel there, at least I'd be safe.

Dad's face went fast into fear as he pulled out his wallet and handed me forty dollars. "Make sure you keep it somewhere safe."

I shoved the cash into my pocket. Forty dollars. That's how much I was worth.

We walked into the foyer, *The Mighty Hercules* cartoon was playing on the television in the living room. A centaur was running around yelling, "Daedalus has got Helena! Daedalus has got Helena!"

Dad looked down the stairs. "Do you want to see me out?"

Not being able to bear a goodbye, I said, "I think I'll stay here to get my room set up."

When he grasped the banister, I saw that fear wasn't alone. Sad darkness was with it. I hugged him as hard as I could. "It's okay, Dad."

Then he started tearing up. Crying was bad. If he cried, he might get sick again, and I had to make him feel better, make him see that he was a good dad and I was the bad one. No wonder he didn't want me calling him at home. He didn't want me infecting the boys.

Pulling a freshly ironed handkerchief out of his breast pocket, I reached up to wipe his tears away. "I'll be fine. This is just what I needed to get me back on my feet."

"Really?" he asked, daring a hopeful smile. "Isabel thinks counseling might be a good idea. Might help you sort things out."

Isabel wanted to put me in a mental ward. That was their plan. They wanted to lock me up. Carefully, I folded the handkerchief back into his breast pocket and gave his chest a soft, loving pat. "By the next time we talk, I bet I've got a job."

"Maybe you could think about school?"

"Maybe … Well, I guess I'd better get my bed ready and stuff."

"I guess so."

We didn't hug, we just stood there for an awkward moment.

"If anything urgent comes up, you call the office. I'll be right down."

And then he was gone.

The chubby girl didn't leave the sofa all week. Maybe it was better being in the park or sleeping on the stinky broadloom in the Warwick than lying all alone in my room staring at the ceiling. I'd tried to talk to the other girls in the kitchen, but they were bank tellers or secretaries, and we had nothing in common. I didn't belong here. I didn't belong anywhere. There was no point in looking for a job because I didn't even have Grade Ten. If Dad's medical journals were right, I had a severe mental disorder, and they'd lock me up and throw away the key. That was me—a throwaway. Granddad always examined newborn animals, saying that you "kept the best and drowned the rest." It wasn't mean. It was practical. You couldn't have deformed animals on a farm because they'd pollute the bloodlines, and soon you'd have two-headed cows and three-legged cats, and that was no good at all. I thought of Hercules's centaur. Everyone loved him. But that was a wonderland. When I thought about what Granddad would do with me, I started to cry. Here I was, all alone, dumped in a rooming house because nobody wanted me.

The next day, I was back at the Steps.

"Look who's here!" Gabe cried. "We got a bottle last night. You missed it, and I woulda shared with you, Maddy, I really would. Lily's no fun. She don't drink."

I gave him a big hug. He smelled of whisky and unfiltered cigarettes. Lily pocketed a dollar bill from a businessman and ran happily back to the Steps. She didn't make me feel like Ginnie or Mary, and whenever I saw Lily and Gabe, it felt like home, and that felt so good.

"What happened to you?" she asked.

"This and that."

Lily lit a cigarette. Thankfully, she never pushed for information.

"Rotten day," she said, counting the money. "We might need to sleep outside."

Gabe negotiated with Lily. "If we got a bottle, we'd be warm."

"No bottle."

"You gotta think of my nerves."

Pulling two dollars out of my pocket, I gave it to Gabe. It was enough for cheap sherry.

Gabe and Lily waited downstairs in the foyer. Other than the chubby girl on the sofa, the coast was clear. We'd gone through half the bottle in the park, but it started getting cold, and since I didn't want to be alone, I invited them back to my place.

"Whaddya doing?" the chubby, scowly girl asked, when I started closing the door to the TV room.

"I can't sleep with the noise."

Gabe hiccupped. The girl grunted but didn't move.

Lily's white head peered up from below, and I signaled for them to tiptoe. Gabe missed a step, but Lily grabbed him before he fell down the stairs.

"What's that?" the chubby, scowly girl called.

"Just dropped a shoe."

"Get in here," I whispered, pulling Gabe and Lily into my room. "You've got to be quiet."

"Aye, aye."

I giggled and locked the door while Lily examined the poodle lamp. "That's nice," she said, adding, "I like stuff from foreign places."

"I been to France," Gabe said, looking at the poster of the Eiffel Tower.

Mom never made it there, but Gabe had. Lily lay down on the floor. Tossing her a blanket, I gave her my pillow. She curled up and closed her eyes. Didn't they ever brush their teeth or wash their faces before they went to bed? Gabe pulled out the bottle, took a slug, and passed it to me. The taste made me gag. We talked and drank for a while.

"What's it like?" I asked.

Gabe took another chug. "What?"

"France."

"They're a bunch of midgets who drink red wine all day."

"Did you see the Eiffel Tower?"

He nodded. "It looked like something on top of a cake. And the people eat giant white asparagus and fancy bacon."

"What about the Louvre?" Mom had always wanted to go there and see the art.

"Ain't never heard of that."

"Where else did you go?"

"Wharf mostly or looking for women."

"How old were you?"

"Long time ago."

"Before Lily?"

Gabe nodded his head, leaning down to gently stroke her hair. "I was young then."

Lily opened her mouth and snorted. We both laughed out loud. "Sleeps like a baby. Always did."

"How long you been together?"

"I forget."

There was a sharp rap at the door. "Madeline?"

The dental assistant. She wasn't supposed to come upstairs.

"Yes," I answered, trying to sound sleepy.

Lily snorted again. Gabe put his hand over her mouth.

"Do you have guests?"

"No."

Thank God the door was locked.

"I heard voices."

"Must be the TV."

"The television is off. Open your door."

"No."

"Open it."

"Get under the bed," I whispered to Gabe, but it was too late. The assistant opened the door with her passkey and found Gabe sitting on my bed and clutching the bottle of sherry, with Lily fast asleep on the floor. She kicked Lily and Gabe out and gave me a warning. If I ever had guests past curfew again, I'd be asked to leave.

Well, I didn't want to stay. I took Dad's money, bought another stash of acid and started my business again. Only this time, I wasn't going to get ripped off. Unless I knew the customer personally, I only sold one hit at a time. Lily kept the money, and Gabe held the stash while the customer and I slipped into the alley to complete the deal. If I didn't come out in five minutes, Gabe would arrive and start jabbing the air.

"You pay up, or I'll beat the crap out of you!" he'd scream.

But it wasn't the threats of Gabe's punches that scared anyone—it was the sight of this ghostly old man with the screech of a hellhound. One time, a girl decided she wasn't going to pay, but when Gabe arrived in the alley and started to howl, she dropped her wallet and ran for her life.

The three of us were sitting on the Steps having our usual lunch. I dug into our loaf of bread, pulled out a couple of slices and slapped bologna in between. "I bought some hash. It's laced with opium," I said.

Gabe got up and did a little jig. "You hear that, Lily? Hear that?"

Lily handed him a sandwich. "You're not taking that. And Maddy, what are you doing offering him stuff like that? You know he's sick." She took a bite. "And you, you're going to get caught," she added.

I ignored her.

"And then you're going to go to jail."

"I'm not going to get caught. I'm too smart."

"You're so stupid dealing dope."

Gabe got up and nervously skittered away.

"At least I'm not a beggar."

That made Lily so mad her ears went pink. "No, you're a mess! Stoned every day of the week."

"Who's paying for our room?" I asked, getting angry, too. Since I'd been dealing, we had a weekly rate with two big beds near the ice machine. The Warwick manager even called me by name.

"Then we'll go," Lily replied, ramming the sandwiches back into the bread bag and standing up.

"No!" I cried, seizing her hand. They were the only family I had. "I'm so sorry. Please don't go. Please."

"I'm just doing the best I can for me and Gabe," she said, and she sat back down, handing back the sandwich bag. "Want another one?"

"Thank you," I said, so relieved they didn't leave. We didn't talk, just silently chewed. My breath came out in icy puffs. Winter was nearly here. Lily shivered.

"We're going to need warm coats soon," I said.

"I can buy them."

I gave Lily a gentle shove. "I never said you couldn't."

For a girl who begged, Lily had a lot of pride. We watched our breath some more, and then she sighed.

"You're right. Begging's horrible. I just don't know what else to do."

Lily applied some orangey lipstick and fixed her white hair. Lately, she'd started applying makeup, trying to look older.

"What did you do before?" I asked.

"We had a place, but then we lost it."

"Me too."

A couple of times, I almost called Dad at the office to tell him that I'd moved, but I couldn't make myself pick up the payphone. It was easier to get high and pretend he never existed. Sure, he gave me forty dollars at the rooming house, which put my worth at about two dollars and fifty cents a year. Even if I was a sick pervert, I had to be worth more than that. I knew I didn't exist for him anymore. I was simply a part of a life he'd lost. A life with my mother. His wife. The damaged, painful remains that he'd rather forget. That made me mad. Two dollars and fifty cents a year. It was so insulting. It was worse than insulting. It was abominable. He was an abominable monster father, and Isabel was the Wicked Witch of the West, making me Dorothy on the run through Oz with killer flying monkeys coming after me.

A young guy arrived looking for five hits of acid, and I asked him to follow me into the alley to show him my stash. Coloured pills rested on my palms like planets strung across the universe.

"So, I've got blotter, sunshine, and microdot. They're all two bucks a hit."

A tiny, clear square sat in the centre. "This is windowpane. It's four dollars."

"Is it worth it?" the guy asked, practically salivating.

"It's the strongest I've ever sold," I said.

He started handing me the money.

"Madeline!"

My father stood at the entrance to the alley. My customer took off, but Dad didn't. He just stood there staring at my hands, my hands stuffed with drugs and money. I shoved them into my pockets, but it was too late. He'd seen everything.

I'd never seen my dad that mad. Not even on the roof of the school. This was different and way worse. He walked toward me. I didn't step back.

"Did you take my money to buy drugs?"

I shook my head.

"Don't lie." His voice shook with fury. "You're not making clear decisions. I'm taking you to the Toronto General for an assessment. Aunt Anne knows a doctor."

A psychiatrist, that's what he meant. A psychiatrist for the "lez be friends." He was going to lock me up. He tried to take my arm, but I backed up. "Get away from me."

"Just somebody to help you sort this through …"

"Through what?" I was going to make him say it. "Through what?"

His voice dropped. "The homosexuality." Then he dove for my arm.

Shoving past him, I ran by Gabe, who'd just arrived in the alleyway and started to scream. Dad was screaming, too, his yells mixing with Gabe's as he called for me to stop. I didn't. He was close behind, keeping up. I ran against the red light at Yonge and Dundas. Right into the traffic, I was thrown up onto the hood of a blue car that screeched to a stop so short that I got tossed right back down onto the asphalt. Something hurt, but I leaped up and kept going, running as if the devil was chasing me. But when I turned around, it wasn't the devil. It was my dad, standing in the centre of the street, his hands high in the air. And then, as giant wings collapsing, his arms fell. He stopped, and I knew right then that he would never run after me again. He was finished. I turned and kept on running. Running from the fact that he hated me and running from the fact that I hated him, too.

CHAPTER SIX

"Whoa!" the huge man yelled, as I ran into him, nearly knocking us both to the ground. "Where's the fire?"

The man was older than me, by at least ten years, and wore a white shirt, wide striped tie, and dress pants, and carried a maroon briefcase with brass hasps.

"Sorry," I said, panting. I couldn't catch my breath.

"Sit down."

He guided me to a stoop. I was shaking. He sat down beside me and put his arm around my shoulder. "Put your head between your legs."

"I'm okay."

I wasn't. I felt sick and dizzy. Dad could still be after me with the police or men with straitjackets from the mental hospital.

"You're hyperventilating. Put your head between your legs."

He grabbed me by the back of the hair, gently pushing my head down.

"Now, just breathe. Breathe," the man repeated. "Concentrate on your breath. One …"

I tried to follow his advice. The big guy's voice was so low it was more like a purr. He softly rubbed my back, and by the time he counted to sixty, I'd stopped panting.

"Thank you."

"What's your name?

"Maddy."

He put out his hand, and I shook it. It was strong. "I'm Vic. Want a drink?"

I glanced around, scared. "I'm underage."

"Don't worry about that," Vic said, as we stood up. "I know every bartender in town."

Nearly naked, yellow-neon girls flashed as we passed through tinted doors into the Zanzibar, a cavern of thick smoke, stale beer, and brassy mirrors. An announcer's voice trumpeted over the loudspeaker, "Gentlemen, give it up for the lovely lady!" as a sexy song began to play.

The black stage curtain parted, and a girl dressed in a white cowboy hat, sparkly bra, and glittery panties strutted into the circling spotlight, shaking her breasts. Clapping was sparse because there weren't a lot of customers at that time of day, only regulars perched on stools in front of the main stage, nursing warm beer. A waiter in black trousers and a crisp white shirt rushed over the moment he saw Vic. "What can I get you?"

"Two Zombies, George," Vic replied, turning to me. "Is that okay with you?"

"Sure." I didn't know what a Zombie was. I only knew about zombie fathers.

Vic waved at a guy sitting at a booth near the back. I couldn't see very well, but I thought I also saw a girl through the smoke.

"You crazy fucker, get your ass over here!" the guy called.

Vic tossed the maroon briefcase down on the vinyl seat. The other guy, only a few years older than me, was leaning back in the banquette with his feet up on the table. My aunts would have pitched fits at that kind of behaviour. The guy had thick, dark, glossy hair that tumbled onto the shoulders of his black leather coat, reminding me of a raven. A sulky girl in a yellow halter top, short jean skirt, and platform sandals sat beside him. She had curly brown hair and lips the colour of raspberries. The guy asked Vic if he had any news.

"Not yet," Vic said, gesturing for me to take a seat.

"This here's Cope and his old lady, Charlene. Meet Maddy." Cope's eyes twinkled like pixies' as Charlene wrinkled her nose.

Vic said he had to make a call and left.

Empty glasses and ashtrays overflowing with brown cigarette butts covered the table. Charlene started peeling the label off her beer bottle. Vic's waiter friend, George, arrived with two tall glasses topped with plastic pink parasols harpooning bright-red cherries. I took a sip. It tasted yummy, like the tropics, and I slurped it all down.

Cope shoved the other Zombie at me. "Vic won't drink it, anyway."

The Zombie made me feel relaxed, and it wasn't gaggy like Gabe's cheap liquor.

"You the new old lady?" he asked.

"We just met."

"I only ask because you'll be disappointed in the cock department," Cope said, rubbing his crotch with that magic pixie smile. Charlene looked down at the bulge and slapped Cope's hand.

"You're a pig. Can't you ever leave it alone?"

"Speed makes me horny," Cope replied, adding, "I'm not like Vic. He can't get it up."

Kenneth's was always up. I glanced at the briefcase. Was speed in there? I'd always wanted to try it. Dad's *TIME* magazine said you didn't get physically hooked on it. There was no physical withdrawal.

"So, what do you do?" Cope asked.

"Acid dealer."

"Never seen you around," Charlene said.

"Street."

"Oh," she said. Like it was lowlife or worse.

"What about you?" I asked.

"Methamphetamine," Cope replied proudly, taking two long puffs and then stubbing the smoke out on the top of butt mountain. "Me and Vic are runners. You want another drink?" he asked, picking up my empty glass.

"I do," Charlene interrupted.

"Does it make you hallucinate?" I asked, as Cope signalled George for another round.

"What?" Cope asked.

"Speed. Does it make you see things?"

"Only if you don't get your sleep. It's a clean drug."

A new dancer came out on the stage.

"Coppers know you?" Cope asked.

I shook my head. "I'm careful."

"You don't look like a dealer," he said, the stripper catching his eye. "Look at that!" Cope yelled, jumping to his feet, thrusting his hips at the stage. "How about me, baby? You think you could take it all?"

Charlene yanked on his arm, telling him to sit down.

"What's wrong with showing a little appreciation for a wonder of the world? What do you think, Maddy?"

The girl's boobs looked bigger than her head. Her eyes swept across the faces in the crowd, and when they lighted on me, she smiled, and before I could stop myself, I smiled back. Cope caught the exchange and jabbed me in the ribs.

"Look at the way they stand up like jelly moulds. I'd mount those babies if they were mine. I'd build them a shrine," Cope said. Then he turned, tweaking Charlene's nipples. "Yours are getting saggy. You better start wearing a bra."

"Fuck off."

"So, what do you think, Maddy?" Cope asked.

"What?"

"The girl."

I glanced the other way.

"Oh, come on, I saw you smiling at her."

I looked back at the stage and then down at the table. "She's okay, I guess."

"She's more than okay." He pulled my chin up. "Look at her. You don't see them that fresh too often."

When I turned tomato red, Cope jumped.

"I think Vic's new *girlfriend* is wet for the dancer!"

"I am not!"

Cope threw his hands up in the air like I had a gun on him. "What's wrong with pussy bumping?" he asked. "That's my favourite kind of action. Right honey?" He kissed Charlene's ear. "It's a whole new scene and I think it's hotter than fuck. What could be better than watching two girls go at it? Or better yet, you ever have a *ménage*, Maddy …?"

I didn't understand and was too scared to ask. He stuck his tongue out and then rubbed his crotch. "Ménage à Trois. Two girls. One guy. Very liquid."

I didn't want to have sex with a guy and didn't want to see any liquid.

"Or it could be two guys, one girl. For the more adventurous man."

"You're a pig," Charlene said.

"I'm a sexual adventurer."

"I'm a free spirit," Charlene replied.

"I don't care about that stuff," I said, as George arrived with two Zombies. "I'm only interested in business."

"Really?" Charlene asked.

"Yes."

Cope stuck his face down Charlene's top, telling her breasts they were the finest specimens in the whole wild world.

Charlene corrected him. "It's *wide* world."

"Not with me, baby. With me, everything's wild."

Then he started talking to her breasts again. Charlene pretended she was mad, but I think she liked it. I liked Cope, too. Sure, he was a pig, but he was the first person who talked about girls being with girls like it wasn't something perverted that belonged in a mental hospital.

Vic walked back into the club while straightening his tie, his eyes scanning the place. Satisfied no one was watching, he squeezed into the seat beside me and with a grin that could split the moon, said Hermann had scored. Cope and Charlene yelped in unison, thrusting their fists into the smoke like triumphant gladiators.

"You want to come along?" Vic asked.

My zombie father might still be looking for me and I could always come back to the Steps later when it was safe. "Sure."

Vic tossed down a twenty and didn't even wait for the change.

A maroon Ford Mercury waited on a side street. Cope strutted toward the car, flicking the long tails of his black leather coat, reminding me of a peacock displaying its plumes. He and Charlene climbed into the back seat, and Vic told me to get in the front. There was a yellow parking ticket under the windshield wiper. Vic snatched it up and tossed it into the messy back seat. There must have been a hundred of them back there, acting as mats. Vic rammed an eight-track into the holder, shoving the silver gear shift into drive as T. Rex's "Bang a Gong" boomed out of the Mercury's windows. He put the pedal down, and we burned rubber up Yonge.

Taking a hard right on Gerrard Street, the car blew over the tall viaduct that spanned the Don River. Shallow and murky, it snaked down to the lake through a gnarled valley of high, wild grasses and the twisted, rusty remains of abandoned grocery carts. Charlene tossed her cigarette butt out the window and asked Vic why I was there.

He looked at me, then stretched his arm across the back of the seat like he was reaching, but it was up to me if I wanted to get caught or not. It reminded me of the sex game with Kenneth in the trunk of the car—a bit of me for a bit of whatever Vic wanted. Cope said Vic couldn't get his penis up, so that meant I could control things. Sliding across the seat, I snuggled up beside Vic. He wrapped his big arm around me, holding me tight. "She's mine," he replied.

And from then on, it was as if we'd always been together.

"Hermann runs speed with the Paradise Riders," Cope said, as we hit the Danforth.

"We're the bag men. We run dope to street dealers," Vic added.

Charlene filed her nails. "Hermann's just tracked down a new chemist in Quebec."

"He cooks the meth and, most importantly," Vic said, handing me a lit cigarette, "the RCMP don't have a lead on him yet."

Cope leaned over the front seat and honked the horn. "As soon as a lab is up, the narcs usually know within a month or two."

"Hermann's smart. He's always ahead of the law," Charlene said, a dreamy look on her face.

"But he's mean," Cope added. "You don't want to get on his bad side."

Vic said that you had to have brains and muscle if you were going to be successful in the dope racket, and Hermann had everything covered. Charlene talked about Hermann like he was a superhero—the Batman of speed. But there was something in Cope's tone that made me wonder if Hermann wasn't more like the Joker.

We cruised around lower Riverdale in the Mercury for a good half-hour, making sure we didn't have a tail. Next, we got out and walked down the streets, checking out cars containing strange men who looked as if they didn't belong there.

"How come we've got to do this?" I asked.

"Undercover narcs," Vic replied.

Uniformed cops had occasionally come by and threatened to arrest me, Lily, and Gabe for vagrancy, but Vic and Cope were being followed by an entire branch of the police force. It was thrilling.

Once Vic decided it was safe, we walked into an alley that led to a long line of garages. Cope banged on a scuffed metal door about a third of the way down. A muffled male voice asked who it was.

"Cope."

The voice said to come in by the side.

It was the strangest garage I'd ever seen. There was no lawn mower, hedge clippers, or toboggans. A checkered sofa was shoved under a narrow window, and a fridge buzzed loudly in the corner. A well-muscled guy with cropped blond hair, jeans, a tight white T-shirt, and polished cowboy boots sat in the centre of the sofa, closely examining a bag of sparkling white rocks.

"That's Hermann," Charlene whispered, a slight catch in her voice.

He reminded me of a snake coiled on a log, tense and ready to spring. Another man, burly with a bald head, kept throwing a knife at a dart board. Then he'd walk over, pull the knife out, and do it over and over again. He never missed the bullseye, and I never got his name.

Hermann opened a cigar box on the coffee table, removed a syringe and spoon and filled the syringe from a glass of water. The needle reminded me of Dad's Demerol. Like a scientist, Hermann dropped several white rocks into the spoon, carefully dousing them with water, and mashed the speed into a paste. Other than the steady thump of the knife, it was as quiet as being in church.

Once the rocks dissolved, Hermann tore a tiny bit of white filter from a cigarette and dropped it into the speed, placing the needle on the filter, and drew up the liquid. He wrapped a thick belt around his bicep, holding it there until the middle vein in the crook of his arm popped up. Once the needle had slid into the skin, Hermann pulled back on the plunger, and a ribbon of red backed into the syringe. I'd never seen Dad do that, and I'd seen him administer lots of shots.

"Why is he doing that with the syringe?" I whispered to Vic.

"Don't call it a syringe," he said quietly. "Makes you sound like a nurse. Are you a nurse?" he asked. When I quickly shook my head, he continued. "It's called a fit and the blood's called flagging. You do it to make sure you're in the main line. Otherwise, you can get an abscess and rot your arm off."

I'd read about mainlining in Dad's magazines. It was the big vein that junkies used. Hermann drew back a bit more blood, let go of the belt, and pushed the plunger down. After a moment, his face flushed, and the odour of chemicals shot out of his nose, with the smell of green apples, too.

"Fuck, yeah," he said, eyes closing. When they opened, they settled on me. "Who's *that*?" he asked, pointing the empty syringe.

"She's with me," Vic replied, wrapping his arm around my shoulder.

Hermann stood, walked over to Charlene and started chewing on her ear lobe. Cope didn't look very happy about it, but Charlene did. I wouldn't like it. I wouldn't like sharing my girlfriend one bit.

"There are a lot of dealers in the joint because they trusted chicks," Hermann said, giving me a nasty look. He started licking Charlene's neck as if it were a popsicle.

"Do you want to fix?" he asked.

It wasn't a question; it was a test.

"Sure," I replied, figuring a fix was a hit.

"Then fill the bowl."

Sitting in a straight-back chair, I carefully placed a couple of white rocks in the spoon and smiled sweetly at Hermann, hoping to make friends. He didn't smile back.

"More," Hermann commanded, as his hand traveled up Charlene's skirt.

There was already more speed than Hermann had taken.

"You got a problem?" Hermann asked.

"No," I replied.

I reached out, dropping two more rocks in. Hermann pulled Charlene down onto the sofa. Cope looked out the window as Vic nervously glanced down at the spoon.

"That's a lot," Cope said.

The knife hit the bullseye. Thump.

"I want to make sure she's no narc," Hermann snarled.

"It's fine," I said, my palms sweating as Hermann mixed the liquid.

Vic wrapped the belt around my bicep, and Hermann filled the syringe. While wondering if it wasn't too much, I focused on the needle tearing through the skin. Hermann flagged, and the moment my blood appeared, Vic let go of the belt. But Hermann didn't take it slowly to see how I'd feel, which I'd read is what you should always do with any kind of drug. Instead, he injected the whole mixture into my bloodstream, pulled the needle out, and threw it on the table.

The rush rumbled up. It started in my toes and blasted up through my body, pounding out of the top of my shoulders, a detonating chemical cannon that threw me off the chair flat on my back on the floor. The smell of fresh green apples forced all the oxygen out of my chest. At first, my heart was beating so fast I couldn't hear it, but then it came back, getting slower and skipping and stopping and starting and skipping. I sucked little shallow gasps, but no air came in. The room was covered in a dewy glow, and everything went white like heaven. Was I dying? If I was, I'd be happy. I'd be with Mom.

Settling into the perfect silence, I floated up and away until suddenly, a giant squall of air pushed me down, kicking me out of heaven to a crash-landing on the garage floor. Vic's mouth was pasted on mine, giving me mouth-to-mouth. Charlene and Cope's faces were ashen. Hermann laughed, saying it was the closest O.D. he'd ever seen. I smiled and asked for more.

"Maddy," Vic said, tapping me lightly on the cheek.

The bald guy with the knife was gone, and Cope and Vic had weighed their buys and were ready to leave. Hermann was expecting other runners. Charlene got up from Hermann's side and walked over to Cope.

Vic rested his hand on mine. "Do you want to come with us?"

He might have been a lot older, but Vic was sweet, and he'd taken care of me. I could make myself kiss him and stuff, but there was no way I was putting out like Charlene. If things got out of hand, I could always just leave. Besides, there was nothing to worry about as long as Vic was stoned, and from all the speed in his briefcase, we were going to be stoned for a long, long time.

The Mercury crawled by a long row of art deco motels clustered at the edge of the lake. Each one was painted white with brightly coloured metal trim. Blue, pink, orange, and green vacancy signs flickered from rooftops. The strip was once a prime tourist attraction, but times had changed, and so had the clientele. Vic pulled in under a red neon seahorse that wore a matching neon saddle. The Seahorse manager didn't care how many of us slept in the room. He just took the money and tossed Vic the key.

Our room was on the second floor, with two double beds covered in orange blankets and drapes that didn't close. The TV hardly got any stations, but that didn't matter. We just shot up again and again, staying up all night endlessly talking, solving the mysteries of life, and then, holding hands, we walked along the stony lakeshore, watching the waves roll over each other as the final star went out and the rim of the horizon revealed a beautiful band of pure pink.

When it was time to sleep, I took off my clothes and lay down in Vic's arms, curling up on his chest. He fell asleep instantly, the soft skin of his penis brushing against my thigh. I didn't want his penis anywhere near me, but I was afraid to move away for fear I'd wake him up. That was something I hadn't considered. Maybe Vic would wake up and have ideas like Kenneth. What if I was the first one up and out of bed? My mind worried and planned while I listened to Charlene and Cope's sex sounds. They sounded like animals, pulling and pushing, groaning and begging. The sheets shifted, and the bed jumped.

Vic tightened his grip and snorted. Pretending he was Ginnie didn't work, and besides, we never slept like that. As soon as we finished rocking back and forth, Ginnie always rolled away, pulling the sheets up under her chin, and went to sleep. That was because our love was sick. I caught myself on the word love. What Ginnie and I had shared wasn't love. It was an affliction. Slowly, I reached my hand out, settling my palm on Vic's chest. It was furry like Dad's.

Vic dropped me off in front of the Steps and I told him I'd meet him at the Zanzibar. I hadn't seen Lily and Gabe in over a month and needed to check in. When I leaned over the back seat to grab Vic's tweed coat, he grabbed my boob and squeezed it.

"Hey!" I said, pushing him away. "That hurt."

"You just need more practice. Give us a kiss."

Cope told me Hermann had been teasing Vic, saying he was a neuter with a frigid old lady who wasn't putting out. He grabbed me by the scruff of the neck, yanking my head back. "Open your mouth."

"People can see."

"You're my old lady. Open your mouth."

I tried not to gag and pretended to like it until he let me go.

Lily was panhandling while Gabe sat on the stoop watching several men install a billboard on top of a building. The sign read "The Green Door" and offered topless body rubs. It was a picture of a tubby, partially naked guy stretched out on a cot while a pretty girl in a bikini rubbed his body. How disgusting. At least I was getting free speed, and all I had to do was kiss Vic and make pretend moan sounds when he grabbed my breasts. Although lately, I worried that Vic wanted a whole lot more.

Gabe was losing weight and had a black eye. "What did you do to your face?"

"Fightin'. And I woulda won if the cops didn't break it up. Looky, looky, Lily. Our Cookie's come home."

I hugged him hard as Lily walked over. Gabe's teeth chattered.

"Where you been?" Lily asked.

"Here and there."

She sat on my other side and gave me a quick squeeze. "You're too skinny."

"Got too much to do. No time to eat."

Lily pushed up the sleeves of Vic's coat. "Your arms look like sticks."

They were white and kind of skinny, but that was because we rarely went out in the day. And besides, I felt great. I didn't need to eat or sleep. My mind burned energy as hot as the sun. When Lily saw the track marks, she slapped me on the side of the head.

"What the hell is this?"

"I'm into something way better now. Way more lucrative."

"Like what?"

"Speed."

"Asshole."

Lily thought speeders were scum, but she was wrong. We were doper royalty. It reminded me of doing house calls with Dad. Every night, Vic, Cope, Charlene, and I drove all over the city delivering bags of whiz to street dealers. When we knocked on the door, speeders fell over themselves ushering us in. They offered us drinks and cigarettes. One of the speeders even called Vic "Sir." When Gabe shivered, I reached out to rub his icy hands.

"So, where are you staying? I asked.

"Hotels," Lily replied.

That wasn't true. They were sleeping outside. It was January, and they didn't even have winter jackets. Wrapping Vic's scarf around Gabe's neck, I pulled ten dollars out of my pocket.

"For a bottle?" Gabe asked, making a grab, but Lily snatched the money first. Gabe wasn't as quick as he used to be.

"For coats. You can get them at the Goodwill."

Lily's pride didn't like it, but I made her take it. "If you're going to stay out here, you've got to stay warm."

"Okay," Lily said. "But I'll pay you back. I mean it. I'll pay you back."

That was the last time I saw them that winter.

Charlene and I were playing dress-up in our latest flat, trying to pass the time. Since the narcs were always after Cope and Vic, we had to move every couple of weeks. The pockets in my pants were deep—1940s pleated dress pants, the kind that Granddad wore, and I liked the feel of the starchy white cotton shirts. Men's clothes belonged on my body and helped hide my curves.

My fingers shook as I tried forcing the buttons through the little holes. It had been nearly a day since our last hit, and Vic was out trying to score. There'd been some big busts lately, and supply was scarce.

"Why do you dress like a guy?" Charlene asked, pulling on a skimpy blue dress.

Charlene and I had gone shopping for spring clothes at the Salvation Army.

"Because Maddy likes girls," Cope replied. He was stretched out on a nubby brown sofa, leafing through a *Playboy* with his hand down his pants.

"No, I don't," I said, when what I wanted to ask was, "How do you know?"

The coffee table was covered in Cope's collection of girlie magazines. Every month, he bought *Hustler* and *Playboy,* and we compared centrefolds. Charlene took off the dress, dropped it onto the floor, and reached for a skirt. Charlene had the most amazing boobs. Her nipples were bright pink, but she had no areolas, and I loved it when the nipples got hard. Cope turned the magazine sideways and looked at the picture.

"Girls are hot. Especially girls who go both ways, right Charlie?"

"I like guys," Charlene replied, pulling up her skirt and turning to me. "Will you zip me up?"

While I tugged the zipper into place, Cope watched. Charlene might have been a slut, but she was a sexy slut, and I loved watching her parade around naked.

"Let her rub your tits," Cope said.

I backed away.

"Don't be scared," he said. "Rub her tits. You want to, don't you?"

I looked at Charlene.

"Go ahead," Charlene said.

"No," I said, but I didn't back up anymore.

"It's okay with me," Cope said.

Was Cope masturbating? I decided not to look. Charlene walked closer. "Give me your hands," she said.

As I raised them in the air, Charlene took them, placing them around her boobs. The skin was so soft to the touch, and when I rubbed the nipples, they sprang up.

"That's enough!" Charlene said.

Pulling my hands back, I asked, "Was that too hard?"

"That was too good," Cope laughed.

Charlene pulled a tight T-shirt over her head and tucked it into the top of the skirt, but that didn't settle down those nipples of hers.

They poked through the fabric like they were waving hello. My fingers remembered how they reacted, and they wanted to say hi right back, but then the door opened, and Vic came in, tossing his maroon briefcase on the sofa.

Cope clicked open the brass hasps, took out a small baggie of speed, and went over to the kitchen table. Charlene ran for the water, fits, and spoons, and I was about to join them when Vic grabbed me by the arm, staring at my pants.

"Make me a drink."

While I poured him a rye and water, Charlene and Cope were already dropping speed into the spoon and starting to fix.

"Aren't we going to do a hit?" I asked, worried that Cope and Charlene would take it all. There wasn't much speed in that bag.

Vic chugged the rye in one gulp, slamming the glass onto the coffee table. "I want to fuck."

He shot a hateful look at my men's shirt and reached out, ripping it open so hard the little white buttons popped off and flew across the room. Hermann must have been teasing Vic about me again.

"Sure," I said, kissing his neck. "But let's fix first."

"Now!" He swept me up in his arms and carried me across the room.

Cope dropped his fit and gasped, "Good shit," as the smell of green apples blew through the room.

Vic caught the scent and froze in the doorway, staring down at me. "Just one and then we fuck."

Kissing his cheek, I murmured, "Yeah, baby."

Cope was right. It was probably the best speed I'd ever had. Charlene and Cope vanished into the bedroom, and Vic opened a bottle of rye and started taking the TV apart. Speeders always get busy with electronics because the drug makes you super smart, like space monkeys in laboratories. There was only one problem. When you came down, you'd forgotten how to put things back together again.

While Vic tinkered, I stood in front of the open window, hands deep in my pockets, watching the streetcars rattle up and down Broadview Avenue. Across the river, the skyscrapers glittered, the CN Tower standing between them like a skeleton sentinel. Newspapers said it was going to be the highest freestanding structure in the world. To me, it looked like a naked Eiffel Tower or the Tower of Babel, a story I heard in Sunday school as my mind drifted away.

Yellow light fell on my face. The night had passed while I was high, speed-dreaming about climbing the Tower of Babel. Was it noon yet? Hot breath settled on my neck, making the hairs prickle. It was Vic. I hadn't gotten up first and snuck out to get our morning coffee. Now Vic was down from his trip and standing behind the chair, his hands clamped hard on my shoulders.

"Why are you always looking at Charlene?" Traffic traveled up and down Broadview. "Hermann says you're queer."

"What do you think?" I asked, thinking of Charlene's naked body.

"I think you need to be taught."

The sofa bed was pulled out.

Something else I'd missed while I was out of it.

He pushed me toward the bed. "Come on."

"I'm too high."

Vic shoved me down on my back and crawled on top. I was only wearing a tee shirt and men's trousers.

"You're always too high."

When I tried to roll away, he pinned me down and started undoing my pants. "I've always been good to you."

"Can't we just cuddle instead?"

"Haven't I always been good to you?"

Vic hadn't shaved, and his beard was scratchy. "This is how you say thank you," he said, yanking down my pants.

"Get off me," I said, starting to fight.

Vic laughed at the kicks and punches, pushing his body down on mine, forcing my legs open with his thighs.

"This is how you pay."

I clamped my legs together, but he just wrenched them open. "Please, Vic," I whimpered, but that didn't work either. He told me to be still, and, with one hand squeezing my breast, he started kissing me. I could barely breathe, his hand was clamped so tightly over my mouth. This is what the other girls did for free drugs. I tried to think about Charlene naked and how it was business, but Mom appeared instead. The time I kissed her—kissed her right on the lips and then felt the bump. The innocent little bump. I pushed her face away.

Vic's hands were tearing down my pants, breathing hard, when Mom returned. Only she was larger and clearer this time, and she wouldn't go away. A giant, like in the movies, standing on the top of the hill with no boots on, in her mauve dressing gown, watching Kenneth french me, screaming my name, pointing down at me, yelling at me to stop.

My hands flailed, punching Vic, slapping him as hard as I could.

Mom kept screaming. The dressing gown flapped in the high wind, her chalky skin and no boots; no boots on in icy snow, and then something popped inro my brain—a baby. This couldn't happen, would *not* happen to me. Not Madeline Anne Barnes. My hand reached for the bottle of rye on the side table and grabbing it by the neck, I brought it down as hard as I could, smashing it into the back of Vic's head, in the place Dad called the occipital lobe.

Vic was out scoring, Charlene was getting dressed, and Cope sat at the kitchen table in his Jockeys. He still had a nice body for a speeder, tight and muscled. Cope had finished washing his hair, and I was trimming the ends. He was like a girl that way. Every day, he washed his hair, conditioned it, and blew it dry. Snip went the scissors as another lock of black hair fell.

"Vic tried to rape me."

After I told them I had bashed his head in, they both laughed. I think Cope almost admired me. There was something in his expression. I didn't mention that I was a virgin.

"What am I going to do?"

Charlene gave me a look. "Sex for drugs is the way it works," she said, turning to Cope. "Like it or not. Isn't that right?"

Cope grunted something about Vic's manly pride as I opened the scissors.

"I won't do that, can't do that," I said, as the blades seemed to snap themselves shut, making Cope jump back. "But Vic said he'd kill me if I hit him again."

What I didn't say is that if Vic ever tried touching me again, I'd be the one doing the killing. He was never going to get his pig hands on me, no matter what the rules were. Cope could tell I was serious because the room got so still that Charlene couldn't stand the quiet anymore.

"What's an occipital?"

Drawing strands of Cope's hair through the comb, I replied, "It's a part of the brain. It's the part that lets you see."

"How do you know about that?"

"Read it."

"You're weird," Charlene said. "You should stay away from Vic. He did time in the pen for assault."

So that's why he was older than us.

"Don't you ever want to quit using and go home and read about occipital shit?" she asked.

Even if I did, that door was closed and locked up tight. Dad wouldn't let me back into the past, and speed controlled the present and future. Charlene smacked her lips. I liked Charlene, even though all she talked about was how badly she wanted to get balled.

"I'm sick of this. But my old man hates me more than my mother loves me," she added, getting up to go to the bathroom. "He'd beat the crap out of her if she stood up for me. So, I'm stuck."

There was a mental hospital waiting for me.

Charlene shut the bathroom door as I set the scissors on the table. The haircut was done.

"Maddy," Cope said. "You know how it works. Chicks put out. Guys take the risks."

Looking directly into Cope's eyes, I said, "I can't, I won't. And I think you know why."

Cope picked up his hand mirror. "You did a good job," he said, admiring the cut. "Let me give you something."

He rummaged through the closet and pulled out a red cowboy shirt. It had white mother-of-pearl snaps and white lassos that roped across the back. He tossed it to me.

"For real?" I asked.

Cope nodded, pulling on a pair of jeans. I buried my face in the cloth. The shirt was so soft and faded, and I loved it. "Thank you."

Cope slipped on a clean shirt, checking out his reflection again. "It's okay to be into girls, you know."

I didn't say anything.

"You ever love anyone?" he asked.

I nodded.

"Some chick?"

I nodded again. "But she didn't love me back."

"I know what that's like."

Was he thinking about what Charlene did with Hermann? Business rules or not, that would hurt so much. Cope ran his fingers through his hair, slipped on the leather coat, and flicked the tails. "Come on, let's go."

Hermann and Gabe both had the same stomping grounds since John's Open Kitchen was home to alkies and speeders, a place for them to eat a cheap meal or nurse a coffee. Cope and I sat in one side of a vinyl booth while Hermann sat in the other, staring at me with his crazy rabies eyes.

"Girls aren't runners."

"That's stupid," I said.

Hermann's eyes narrowed. "You calling me stupid?"

"No. You're the smartest guy I know. It's the rule that's dumb." I said.

Cope broke in. "That's why it's so brilliant. We've had a lot of heat lately." He poured a steady stream of sugar into his coffee. "Not only is she a chick, but the cops don't know her, and she looks like she just walked out of a church." Cope took a sip of coffee and spat it back into the cup. "This would expand your territory. Make you the biggest dealer in town."

Hermann grabbed Cope by the lapels, yanking him over the table, and rammed an index finger up his nostril. "She's your responsibility?"

Cope nodded, Hermann's finger still rammed up his nose. "And you handle Vic?"

Hermann agreed, pulled out his finger, and released Cope's lapels. By the time we had left, Hermann had taken all the credit for the idea. I had a job, and Vic never touched me again.

CHAPTER SEVEN

Taking two different buses across town to make sure I wasn't tailed, I would then circle the block three times to check out suspicious cars for undercover narcs. Once satisfied everything was safe, I jumped the neighbour's fence and walked across the yard. While other runners used cabs or personal cars, I flew across the city in subways, streetcars, and buses. That was my own personal touch. Narcs would never be looking for a sweet-faced girl in a blue and white sailor shirt riding the TTC.

The speeder house where Hermann had been crashing for the past month was a wreck. Two windows were broken, and an old sofa with the stuffing punched out was thrown on the back porch. Mom would have called the house a "civic embarrassment" and enlisted the United Church Women to engage in missionary work and clean it up.

Removing the key from its hiding spot in the drainpipe, I quietly opened the back door. The living room was full of beaten-up chairs and cushions. The kitchen table was in the dining room, covered with glasses of water, spoons with used filters, and the residue of dried-up speed. Climbing the stairs, I walked down the hall, past bedrooms with mattresses covered in twisted sheets. Milk-crate coffee tables covered in candle stubs cast wild light on the ceiling at night. One of the speeders had a guitar and used to jam till dawn, but Hermann didn't let him play anymore because he thought the music would tip off the cops. Hermann had never been what Dad would call stable, but things had gotten a whole lot worse since he'd turned paranoid.

Peeking in, I saw Hermann sitting in a chair by a second-floor window, staring through a slit of a heavy brown curtain. A suitcase rested by his feet. Charlene said she'd heard Hermann had a gun, but I never saw one. He looked like he could use some sleep. I'd been there every day, and he hadn't budged from that chair in over a week. When I rapped lightly on the door, Hermann jumped.

"Don't sneak up on me," he snapped, still staring out the window. He leaned down, pulled four ounces of speed out of the suitcase and told me to deliver it to an address on Main. His eyes never left the street.

"I've never been there before."

"You got a problem?" he asked, turning to glare at me with his rabies eyes. He'd been chewing on his lower lip hard enough to make it bleed.

"No."

"Then do what you're told," he said, turning back to the window.

When I got to Main Street, the buyer, a scrawny girl under twenty, answered the door. I couldn't get a good look at her because she kept the house dark. I followed her down the hall into the living room. The house smelled of weed and something else, something that reminded me of the root cellar in Granddad's house near the cistern. Roots, dirt, and the faint aroma of decay.

"Grab a chair," she said, going into the kitchen.

It took a while for my eyes to adjust to the gloom. The girl came out holding a glass of water and two spoons.

"Let's do a taste," she said.

"I've got to get back."

It was late. Hermann was waiting for me.

"I'm spending a lot of money."

True. Pulling an ounce out of the bottom of my purse, I dropped it on the table. Hands shaking, the girl tore open the bag and filled her spoon with white rocks. I prepared my fix, tied off, and hit up. As I closed my eyes, the good feeling rolled in, the feeling that washed everything else away. When I opened them, the girl was stabbing the needle into her arm, trying to find a vein. The syringe was full of blood and speed, and she was starting to cry.

"The vein's dead. The fucking vein's dead."

Kneeling, I reached for the syringe. "Let me help you."

She released the syringe but yanked her arm, hiding it away. "Use the other one," she said, sticking her right arm out.

Her arm was so skinny I could see the blue arteries pumping. Using my belt, I tied her off and hit her up. Once the speed hit, the girl stopped crying and she slumped back, eyes closing as she entered amphetamine orbit. I glanced at her arm. Green puss oozed out of a swollen hole in the centre. No wonder she couldn't find a vein in that mess. It was a furious abscess, and her body was revolting against all the crap she'd been pumping into it. A body that had simply had too much poison and was starting to rot away, piece by piece. I'd never seen real gangrene before, but I'd seen the photos in Dad's medical books and knew that if she didn't get antibiotics soon, she was going to lose her arm. When I told her what I thought, she didn't seem to care.

Dry heaving into the toilet bowl, I thought about the girl. That girl was so revolting, with no dignity at all. Stabbing a syringe into raw meat like that, over and over again. If I hadn't helped her, she would have shot up in the back of her knees or maybe tried the jugular vein. Cope told me he saw a guy do that once. I didn't believe him then, but now I did. That girl would have stuck a needle in her eye if it meant getting the speed.

There was nothing to vomit, so I pulled down my jeans and sat on the seat, trying to pee. Lately it had started to hurt, but I had to go.

Waiting for the urine, I examined my legs. They weren't much more than bone. Since the pee wouldn't come, I stood, stepping onto a beige scale. The needle bounced around and then settled, but it couldn't be right. When I left home, I weighed about 140 pounds, and now I was down to ninety. I did it again. Same result—ninety pounds. Who was I to judge the rotting girl? Mom would have called me a hypocrite. The girl and I were exactly the same. That was the smell in the house, the stink of rot and death. She was going to die, and so was I. It was just a matter of time before I flamed out in an overdose or got busted and thrown into prison, where a psycho would murder me. The weird thing was I didn't know if I cared. All I knew for sure was that I was on a train hurtling through darkness. I didn't know if I'd survive a jump and, if I did, where I would land? One thing was certain: there'd be nobody there to catch me. Those arms were long gone. Uncontrolled thoughts raced: What happened to you, Daddy? Why didn't you take care of me? I'm still your little girl, and I knew, thought, and believed with all my heart, for every minute of all of my life, that you loved me. You didn't. You don't. It was never real. Finally realizing that he was truly gone, even if it was weak and I wasn't a true Gillespie, I began to cry. After a long, long time, I stopped. There were no tears left. When I lifted the washroom blind, the sun was down.

Yanking up my jeans, I ran back into the living room. "It's dark out. Hermann's going to be pissed."

Pulling the rest of the speed out of my purse, I asked for the cash.

"I don't have it."

"Oh, shit," I said, stuffing the dope back into my purse.

"I'm good for it."

"Do you know what Hermann will do to me if I show up without his money?" I cried, snapping the purse shut. "I'm already going to be in so much trouble."

"Wait. Just wait!" she was already on the phone. The whirl of the dial.

"I don't front," I said, hand on the doorknob. "It's Cope," she said, passing me the receiver.

He told me to give her the speed and meet him back at the house.

"Are you sure?" I asked.

"Positive."

Cope had seniority, so I handed the girl four ounces of whiz and headed back to Hermann.

Slipping through the back door, I ran down the hall past a boy in the dining room, who glanced up from his spoon and told me that I'd better have a good story.

"He's been up there screaming your name."

Scared, I climbed the stairs and found Hermann still peering through the slit in the curtain, talking to himself.

"I see you out there. You think you're so smart, but I'm smarter."

When I cleared my throat, Hermann spun around.

"Where the fuck have you been?" he yelled.

"The buyer wanted a taste."

"Give me my money," he said, looking back out the window, sticking his hand out. His fingernails were filthy.

"I don't have it."

My heart pounded in my throat because I could see what was in his lap. Charlene was right. Hermann had a gun.

"It's coming," I sputtered.

Hermann pointed the gun at me. "Get your ass over here."

There wasn't a choice. He would have shot me in the back if I ran. Walking across the room, I stood before him. Hermann grabbed my wrist and yanked me down into his lap, ramming the cold metal barrel up against the side of my head. "How stupid do you think I am?" he yelled into my ear, so loud my brain clanged.

Taking a deep breath, I kept repeating quietly, using the voice Dad used with that lady who got up on the roof after her husband died, "Everything is fine, the money is coming."

But Hermann wasn't listening. The barrel of the gun, its icy metal, tight against my temple.

His breath quickened as he whispered, "You fucking bitch. I knew from the beginning that you were a narc."

Right then I realized I should have taken a chance with the bullet in the back because he was going to pull the trigger anyway.

So, this is it, I thought, staring at a single spot on the wall. My time to die.

Was Mom scared when her turn came? When the angel came into her room, was she ready to go and escape all the pain? Where was my angel? When I was little, she used to come and visit me, but now I was no good, and she'd gone away.

Hermann cracked me in the cheek with the butt of the gun and said crying was for weaklings. He kept looking through the slit in the curtain, rambling on about how there was a van across the street that had been there all day. Something was coming down. Hermann turned and looked at me, then cocked the hammer, hissing that he knew I was the one who turned them in.

"Please," I moaned, trying to get up and run away.

His free hand grabbed my hair harder, holding my head fast to the gun while his finger squeezed down. It was time. Closing my eyes, I thought of Mom, Dad, and the boys. Right then, I realized I didn't want to die.

There was a shout, running feet, and the metallic click of the trigger as the bullet was fired, its energy sweeping past like a falling star.

Cope had pushed the gun away from my head, the bullet ricocheting off the wall and into the ceiling. Hermann and I hadn't heard Cope, but we all heard the explosion of glass and wood rocketing up from downstairs as the front door crashed down.

Cope flew out the window and onto the roof. Hermann tore down the back stairs, and I hid in the back of the clothes closet as the narcs stormed up the stairs, through the bedrooms, and finally into Hermann's room. Clamping my hand over my mouth, I tried not to breathe. The bed crashed as it was flipped.

"Shit," a man's voice said. "He's gone."

Footsteps headed toward the hallway. They were leaving. Closing my eyes, I silently thanked God as the door handle turned over and light spilled in. Hands pushed back heavy coats on the railing, and there was Detective Read, the same cop who'd come to Dad's house to bust me for selling acid.

"Who do we have here?" he said, pulling me out.

I said nothing as the happy narcs started rifling through my purse and pockets. Their happiness didn't last long because there was nothing to find. The rotting girl had been my last stop, and she took everything I had.

"Give him up!" Read yelled, as his fist hit the desk. Files jumped.

I wouldn't. I couldn't. I was too scared. I sat in the metal chair beside Read's desk. We were in the police station. Speeders who were holding more than a quarter ounce were lined up on benches waiting to be booked. Everyone else had been let go. Cope was slumped up against the wall, his black leather coat wrapped around him like feathers, his beautiful glossy hair hanging down, shrouding his face. They picked Vic up at a pool hall with two pounds of meth in the trunk of the Mercury. There was still no sign of Hermann.

"Do you want me to call your parents?"

The threat didn't scare me. Nobody would come. "Go ahead."

"Do you know what Hermann'll do to you if he catches you?"

Yes, I did, and I stood a lot better chance if I didn't roll over.

"I don't know anything."

The cops didn't know about me. I'd been so good covering my tracks that the narcs had never fingered me as a runner. Too bad the same wasn't true for Cope. They'd been following him for nearly a year. Read slammed Hermann's priors down on his desk. I saw the list: arson, theft, drug dealing, assault with a deadly weapon, and rape. He'd never been successfully prosecuted, and I wasn't going to be their dead stool pigeon. The cops would have to get Hermann on their own.

"Get her out of here!" Detective Read shouted.

Charlene and I went to sentencing in Old City Hall. The courtroom, long and wide with wooden wainscoting and marble floors, was packed with nervous users shifting in their seats, waiting to see what happened to their dealers, their only source to the one thing they loved and needed. Tall oak doors at the back of the room swung open, and Cope, Vic, and the other guys who'd been charged shuffled out in shackles and handcuffs, surrounded by armed guards.

"He looks terrible," Charlene said.

She was right. Cope tried to smile, but I could tell he was scared. Someone had cut off his beautiful hair, and he was swimming in a suit that was way too big for him. Cope reminded me of Dad on his wedding day.

The judge, dressed in a long black robe, emerged from his chambers as the bailiff called, "All rise."

Out of habit and respect, I rose while the other speeders remained in their seats.

Detective Read recommended the judge deliver maximum sentences because of the severity of the crimes. The street dealers got two years each. Vic got five, and Cope would have, too, but since he didn't have a record, the judge handed down three. I thought Charlene would die, she was crying so hard, until a young woman with a baby in her arms shot to her feet.

"Please, your honour!" she cried. "I need my husband to provide for me and my baby."

"What?" Charlene shouted, as Cope shrank into the prisoner's box. "You bastard! You told me you loved me!" Then she went even crazier and took off her shoes, whipping them at Cope.

The judge slammed down the gavel, warning Charlene to settle down, as the court was adjourned, and Cope was dragged off to jail. Read picked up Charlene's shoes and brought them over.

"You should have given him life," Charlene said.

"If it was up to me, I would," he replied. Then he turned to me. "Have you seen Hermann?"

"No," Charlene replied. "And if we did, we'd run the other way."

Read handed me a card. "If you change your mind, call me."

I stuffed it in my pocket, but there was no way I'd ever call. Nobody screwed with Hermann. The best thing to do was drop out of sight and pray he forgot all about me.

Charlene and I walked out of the courtroom onto the steps of Old City Hall. Everything was different now. My best friend was in prison, Hermann was missing, and a long drought was on. The choice was simple. It was time to quit.

We had no access to downers or money for booze, so we spent that day tearing through the flat, pulling every pocket inside out, hunting through coats, turning drawers upside down, looking for the dregs of any old speed we could find. Slitting plastic baggies open with a razor blade, we scratched for any white film hidden in the corners or clinging to the sides, trying to coax out even a single hit. There wasn't enough to properly get us off, but it kept the monsters at bay for a day. After that, we stepped off the edge of an endless chemical run into the nightmare of a full out crash.

The next day, I was knocking at the door of the rotting girl. Maybe she had some left. Glancing around, terrified that Hermann was watching, I knocked again. Nobody answered. The rotting girl might already be dead, or Hermann might be in there with his gun. My whole body shook with need. I looked up and down the street, knocking even harder until I heard a rustle coming down the hall. The door opened a crack, and an eye peered out. The chain was on.

"Can I come in?" I asked.

The rotting girl weighed the idea. I could see her mind say no.

"Please."

The chain dropped, the door opened, and the girl pulled me into the foyer. Making sure the deadbolt was on, I followed her down the narrow hallway into the dark living room. A bag of speed sat on the coffee table. My heart jumped. She still had some left.

"I can give you a hit, but that's all. I don't have enough to sell."

The white rocks glistened as she squirted water into the spoon. Swallowing, I was already imagining the smell of green apples and feeling the rush, the Niagara Falls-speed rush that swept me away. Taking a seat, I watched her mash the meth and wondered how many hits I'd done over the last ten months and how I didn't remember most of it because everything had all been the same. Days of nothing but speed and needles, floating up and flying around in the clouds of drug heaven and then crashing down, punctuated by painful hours of desperate, screaming need.

Speed was all I wanted anytime, anyplace, anywhere. That's all there'd been. It wasn't heroic or death-defying, and it certainly wasn't cool. Dad would have said this was the behaviour of a parasite in suspended animation. The girl's hands trembled.

"You want me to hit you up?" I asked.

She nodded, handing me the syringe. I wouldn't look at her arm. The smell was worse. While tying her off, I asked a favour. She nodded, anxious for the syringe.

"You got any downers?"

"The shelf in the bathroom."

She stuck her arm out. Little abscesses bubbled, and the surrounding skin was scabby.

"You might want to try your wrists," I said.

"Blown out." She gave me a wry smile. "Hurry up." She'd been pretty once.

So I did. The intoxicating scent of green apples rushed out of her nose, and my heart skipped and my body begged me to stay, but I dropped the fit on the table, went into the bathroom and cleaned her out of every downer she had in the house, everything except a bottle of blue Valium. If the rotting girl ever decided to come back to earth, she'd need something to soften her re-entry. I closed the front door behind me. It was time to get normal.

The smell of eggs woke me up, and I really had to pee. Getting out of bed, I scratched my head. My hair was itchy, but the paranoia was gone. How much time had passed? Charlene was sitting cross-legged on the sofa, eating a huge helping of scrambled eggs.

"How long have I been asleep?"

"A day and a half," Charlene replied, taking another big bite of eggs. We were down.

My jeans struck the tiled floor as I sat on the toilet seat, but the moment I started to pee, I howled. The pain felt like rubbing alcohol poured on a burn. Doubling over, clutching my stomach, I tried to breathe through my nose. When my bladder emptied, the pain stopped, but I had no idea as to the cause. There was no blood on the toilet paper or in the urine. I scrubbed my face and hands. It had to be a stomach bug.

My stomach growled and I felt shaky. "Are there any eggs left?"

Charlene shook her head, shovelling the last forkful of food into her mouth. Poking my head in the fridge, I saw a loaf of bread and a pound of bacon in the keeper. I couldn't remember when I'd ever been that hungry, and by nightfall, Charlene and I had devoured every last morsel in the house.

Charlene sat in the window, chain-smoking, glaring out at the skyline.

"He has a wife," she said, flicking a butt out the window.

Sitting on the counter, I tried to figure out what to do. It was no minor bug. I was running a high fever.

Charlene turned to me. "I loved him, you know."

"Since when?" I asked.

"Since always."

"Me too," I replied, stroking the soft, red fabric of Cope's cowboy shirt.

Charlene began pacing the room. Clip clop, clip clop, her wooden wedges struck the hardwood floor. Her hair was greasy and stuck down on top and she had a funky smell. Charlene needed a bath. I probably did too. My jeans were filthy.

"I want more food," Charlene bitched. "I don't think I've had anything to eat in over two years."

We both laughed. I couldn't remember my last real meal either. In fact, I couldn't even remember how long I'd been stoned. All I knew was that I was going to be seventeen soon, and that meant I'd been out on the street for nearly a year.

"Now all I can think of is food," Charlene said, slapping her stomach. "And I'm going to get a big fat belly, and you know what? I don't give a shit because I'm never fucking another guy."

"I give you a week."

She sat down beside me and took my hand. "Can you be a virgin again?"

"I think once it's gone, it's gone."

"You're hot," she said.

I smiled at her.

"I'm serious, Maddy, your hand is hot."

There was a loud knock at the door. We stared at each other. "I know you're home," a woman called out.

My hand went up to signal quiet, but the landlady didn't go away. She opened the door with the master key, hair twisted into a sloppy beehive and an apron tied around her waist.

"I want you girls out."

Charlene reminded her that we were paid up for another week.

"There was a strange character asking for you last night."

"What did he look like?"

"Blond. Cowboy boots. Not the sort I want around my house."

Hermann.

"What did you tell him?"

"I told him you'd moved weeks ago."

"Did he believe you?"

"I don't know, but I want you out."

In less than five minutes, Charlene and I were on the street with everything that we owned stuffed into two green garbage bags.

Charlene's garbage bag landed on the sidewalk. "She should have given us back the rent."

Steady drizzle was threatening to turn into a full out, late summer storm. Lily and Gabe were nowhere around. The newspaper boy who always worked had just sold his last paper. He couldn't have been more than fourteen and I'd always wondered why he wasn't in school.

"See Lily around?" I asked.

The boy pointed up at the billboard for The Green Door. "She got a job."

Charlene glared at the sign. "Whore house? No way."

"I'm going to borrow some money," I said, stepping out into traffic.

A horn blared. Charlene flipped the car the finger and reluctantly followed, dragging the garbage bag behind her.

The lime neon sign at the top of a tall, rickety staircase read: "The Green Door." Faded pin-ups of topless girls covered the walls on either side. Inside the body-rub lounge, there were sofas, a couple of puffy chairs, and coffee tables with tin ashtrays and girlie magazines. A sign reading "Rules of the Management" hung over the manager's wicket.

The rules were: "No Extras. No Touching the Girls. Money Up Front." What were extras?

A pretty girl lay on the sofa. She lit a cigarette and asked me if I wanted a rub.

"No, thank you," I replied, trying not to sound judgmental.

The girl had green hair with green eyes, green fingernails, and wore ripped black pantyhose. She had fake black eyelashes and angry swipes of thick black eyeliner. She was stuffed into a bright-green bustier and mini skirt.

"Sit," she said, and I dropped down beside her, grateful to rest. My brain felt light, but my body was heavy.

Charlene remained on her feet, hands on her hips. "Who are you?"

"Helen," the girl replied, blowing a thick plume of smoke into Charlene's face.

She was about eighteen. Helen took my hand and held it. "You're hot, whoever you are."

"I'm Maddy," I said, smiling weakly.

"Your skin is hot, and I can tell you're scared," she added.

"No, I'm not," I lied, yanking my hand away.

"I don't believe you."

There was something kind in Helen's voice beneath the edge. A pudgy, middle-aged guy with mousy-brown hair appeared in the wicket. He was wearing a short-sleeved beige shirt with a white pocket protector. Leaning across the counter, he rubbed his hands, grinning at Charlene. He practically had no lips.

"I'm Ivan. Pleasure to meet such lovely young ladies such as yourselves."

Charlene glowered.

"We're friends of Lily," I said.

Ivan looked at the clock on the wall. "Should be out any minute. Unless, of course, things go over," he said, rubbing his hands even harder.

Helen started humming "Ziggy Stardust."

"David Bowie's a fag," Charlene said. "The Eagles are a real band that writes real music."

Helen turned to me. "Your friend's a no-taste fat cow." Charlene dropped her bag to the floor. "Listen, bitch."

I reached out, touching Helen's bare shoulder to stop her from getting up, as I had no strength to stop a fight. "We only need some money, and we'll go," I said. Helen's skin was soft.

While Charlene grumped around the lounge like a Presbyterian church lady, I tried to change the topic, asking Helen about David Bowie.

Obviously fascinated, Helen sat up straight, crossed her legs, and launched into a speech about glam.

"Everyone's either asexual or bisexual."

"What about you?" I asked.

A puff of smoke came out. "I used to be gay, but now I'm asexual. You'll see, working here will put you off sex for life."

Sure, Helen had green hair, but she was definitely pretty. Was she really gay? And what was the real colour of her hair?

"You'd be kind of cute if you cleaned yourself up," she said.

The downstairs bell jangled. Ivan poked his head out of the wicket. "Sit up straight. Somebody's coming." Footsteps thumped up the steps. "Hurry up," he whispered, scowling at Helen.

Helen repositioned her boobs in the bustier, leaned back, and posed. A couple of men arrived in the room, looking for a body rub. One smiled eagerly at Charlene.

"Pig," she hissed, snatching up her garbage bag and heading toward the stairs.

I didn't know what to do. I felt too sick to stand, but Lily was still with her customer. Grabbing my bag of clothes, I followed Charlene.

"Wait a minute," Ivan said. "If you need a job, come back. I can always use new talent, and the pay's good."

Helen was still reclining on the sofa as a man perched on either side, staring at her breasts. She gave me an easy smile while powering the room with her nuclear reactor boobs.

"I can't believe you'd talk to *that*," Charlene snapped, walking backwards up Yonge Street with her thumb out. "We'll go and see a friend of mine. She'll take us in."

But nobody stopped, so we had to walk all the way in the rain. When Charlene's friend saw us in the doorway, dirty, soaking wet, with garbage bags in our hands, she knew she'd never get rid of us. She knew we'd eat her food and drink her booze, and she would have been right.

"I'm sorry, Charlene, the old man's home," the girl said, nervously looking over her shoulder.

The door was open, and down the hall, a bunch of guys were drinking beer and playing cards. Occasionally, somebody shouted, "Get your ass back in here!"

When the girl closed the door in our faces, Charlene finally lost it. She stood out in the front yard, whipping the garbage bag in circles over her head, screaming about Cope breaking her heart and how everybody screwed her over, and she never ever got ahead. That was it. Even if her father beat the shit out of her, she was going home to see her mother. There was no way she was going to work in some body-rub parlour and whore herself out.

"No fucking way!" Charlene screamed, as I sat and waited for her to calm down.

While Charlene yelled, I checked my pulse. It was fast and jumpy, probably from coming off the speed. The irregularity would eventually pass. After about ten minutes, Charlene wore herself out and came up with another plan.

"We can stay with my cousin. She won't turn us away. Let's go."

It took nearly three hours. Past diners and late-night cab stands and wrecking yards full of snarling, white-fanged dogs crashing into chain-link fences. Charlene kept throwing away pieces of clothing to lighten her load. Every one she discarded was accompanied by some swearing about Cope. He must have given her everything she owned.

By the time we reached her cousin's apartment building, we were both ready to drop. She pressed the buzzer. Nobody answered. She pressed it again. Nothing. Charlene didn't have any angry tears left. We hung around waiting until a couple of kids came out, and then we snuck in behind them.

Charlene knocked and softly called out, "It's Charley. Let me in." But nobody opened the door. Charlene pulled what was left of her clothing out of the garbage bag and made a pillow for herself on the floor and told me to do the same ."We'll just rest our eyes for a bit," Charlene said, dropping onto the carpet. "And then I'm going home. I swear to God I'm going home," she mumbled.

Sitting beside her, I nearly lay down, but something inside me couldn't. If I did, I might not get back up. By now I knew I was running a dangerously high fever, and if I didn't take care of myself, I would be no better than the rotting girl. No. My life wasn't going to end with me dead on the floor of an apartment hall. Kissing Charlene on the forehead, I wished her luck and told her to take care of herself.

"Watch out for Hermann," was the last thing she said before she fell asleep.

The moment I walked out of the building, I passed out cold.

CHAPTER EIGHT

"We've got a girl here. A passerby found her unconscious and called an ambulance. Good thing, too. She's running a very high temperature," a female voice said. A fat nurse was taking my vitals. I was in an emergency room and felt safe. It reminded me of visiting patients with Dad.

"I'm okay," I said, trying to sit up. "Just hungry."

The big nurse put her hands on my shoulders, easily pinning me down.

"You're not going anywhere with a temperature of 104."

I passed out again.

I woke up in a private room, attached to a catheter, while a bag of electrolytes dangled from an IV pole, slowly dripping into a vein in my arm. The door opened. It was Aunt Bette and a doctor. Aunt Bette, Dad's sister, who I hadn't seen in a long, long time.

The only contrast to the blinding white was the shameful sight of the red track marks running up and down my arms like vicious bites. What was Aunt Bette doing there? Of course, she was an ER nurse. When she crossed the room, smiling kindly at me, I instantly crossed my arms as a deep blush flooded my entire body. Never in my life had I experienced this overwhelming sense of shame. Deep as an ocean, as distant as Pluto. I wanted to run, hide, or even jump off the building, but I was too sick to run.

Lying there in that horrible shame, self-recriminations harsher than anything even God would mete out, my mind lashing at my body and soul, I felt more shame than if I'd killed a child with a car. My mind, the car—my body, the child.

As Aunt Bette bent down to hug me, she quietly said, "I'll call your father," and I was up and off the bed, catheter dangling between my legs. "No! No! No!" I screamed, reaching for the catheter line to yank out the tube. Dad couldn't see this. Nobody in my family could ever know about this. Shame was blowing me apart.

The doctor was calling for a tranquilizer as Aunt Bette kept trying to settle me down.

"Okay sweetheart. It's okay," she said, brushing the hair away from my tear-drenched face. "I won't tell anybody. I promise."

My breathing slowed until a nurse arrived brandishing a syringe. What were they going to do to me now? Dope me up until Dad arrived and then put me in the psych ward for lez be friends? No! Aunt Bette put her arms around me, drawing me close. She had the same smell as Dad, and I'd always trusted her.

"Settle down, honey. Just settle down. This is a shot to calm your nerves. Nothing more than that. Trust me."

I looked at Aunt Bette. "Do you promise?"

She held me close. "On my heart, Maddy."

Sinking back onto the bed, the nurse administered the tranquilizer, and everything vanished.

When I woke up, Aunt Bette was hanging a new IV bag. The doctor stood beside her, giving me a sharp look.

"What's wrong with me?" I asked.

"Pyelonephritis," the doctor replied, giving me a quick abdominal exam. His fingers were stubby, not long and elegant like Dad's. And he wasn't very thorough.

Aunt Bette held my hand. That's why my back hurt and the urine burned. An untreated bladder infection had invaded my kidneys. Dad always said how important it was to nip things in the bud, but I'd let it fester. There hadn't been a lot of baths. I never wore a winter coat and sat on concrete stoops waiting for buyers, so the cold had passed into my bladder and traveled up to my kidneys. The doctor sat down on the other side of the bed, giving me a stern, mean look. His bedside manner was horrible. You were supposed to make the patient feel at ease, no matter who they were or how you felt about them.

"How long have you been sexually active?"

"I'm not," I cried.

Aunt Bette looked disgusted. Not with me, but with her colleague. She was getting all feisty faced.

"If you're going to have multiple partners, you'd better use birth control. The next time, it could be syphilis. Give me your arm."

Then he snatched it, pulling it out like a weed. And there it was. The bullet-ridden, stabbed-to-death-by-needles, ruined arm. Proof that everything he thought was true—the drug whore home to leech from her decent family.

"Sir, I do not mean to be rude to a man of your *considerable* reputation," Aunt Bette said. "However, this young woman is my niece, and quite frankly, it's not your place to judge her."

"Relative or not, this child is a street urchin."

Now Aunt Bette was all red in the face. "Doctor," Aunt Bette said, rising to her feet, hands on her hips. "You know nothing about my Maddy or her life circumstances."

My Maddy, I thought. Even if Dad didn't care about me, Aunt Bette still did.

"That's right, Nurse Barnes, and I don't care to."

Aunt Bette was working herself into one of her famous fits that might get her into trouble at work. It felt so good to have somebody finally defend me, but no matter how good it felt and how desperately I wanted to hear it, I had to save Aunt Bette from herself.

"Thank you for treating me, doctor," I said. "How long will I require hospitalization?"

"Two days of drip and then a round of antibiotics," he replied.

"Thank you," I said.

"I can take care of you at home," Aunt Bette said, turning to the doctor. "If that's acceptable with you, of course," she said, trying to stifle a tone.

The next morning, I was nestled into Aunt Bette's pickup truck, holding my own IV bag and using my garbage bag full of clothes as a footstool.

Rubbing my eyes, I looked around. I'd been asleep in the spare room for nearly two days.

"Good morning!" Aunt Bette said. "I'm going to remove the IV. All right with you?"

"Sure."

Aunt Bette's bedside manner was perfect. Her red hair was cut in a short crew cut, and she was wearing jeans, a plaid shirt, and a pair of work boots. Had Grandmother Barnes allowed Aunt Bette to wear boots in the house? That didn't seem like the grandmother I'd heard many stories about. She had died young, but Mom and Dad would never tell me what happened to her.

A plate of scrambled eggs and toast rested on the bedside table.

"Are you hungry?"

"Yes, I am."

While I was sitting up, Aunt Bette placed the plate on my lap. The eggs were delicious. How did I go for all that time without appreciating food?

"How are you feeling?"

"Better." I took another bite. "Thank you."

Aunt Bette gently removed the tape and quickly removed the needle, swiftly applying some cotton batten and a Band-Aid. When I pulled my arm up to hide the marks, she yanked it back down.

"What's this all about?"

My appetite left, as shame took its place. I set the plate back on the table. "I'll never do that again."

And it was true. I'd never touch speed again. But there was something else, a crucial error that needed correcting. "That doctor was wrong."

"About what?" she asked.

"I never had sex with a man. I would never do that."

Aunt Bette rolled up the tubing and put the IV bag away. "Why?" she asked.

"I'm not interested in them," I replied.

"In what way?" she gently prodded.

"In that way," I answered, still worried about the psych ward.

"You mean sexually?"

Not wanting to talk, I picked up the plate and continued eating.

"You know Maddy, there are more kinds of love than just between a man and a woman," she said. "We just live a little differently is all."

What did that mean? Was Aunt Bette a lez be friends too? She dressed like a man and certainly had a trucker haircut, but you never knew about women from the country. I remained still, taking everything in, but being ever so careful and marking every single word, since I could still be in danger.

"Your father and your mother, Laura, that is, knew all about me and Tina. Tina is my lover. We've been together for over twenty years."

"What did Mom and Dad do?"

"They loved us and accepted us from the very beginning."

"From when you were my age?" I asked, astonished.

"Yes. I just couldn't live in a box with a man. I never belonged there. It could never be a happy life for me. They understood and supported it."

Wow. So, Dad had a gay sister? Why didn't he help me when it looked like I might be that way too? "Why didn't they ever tell me?"

"Well, honey, a lot of gay people have to live secret lives. Women wear dresses and behave normally in public. I'm not big on secrets. I'm also not big on being normal. But over time, I wanted to live my life more openly. Yep, openly is the right word for it. I didn't want our love to be a dirty little secret. Teddy wasn't that troubled about it, but your mother was worried about ..."

"Her standing," I replied, instantly understanding why Aunt Bette didn't come around anymore. She had started wearing only men's clothing and drove a pickup truck. Mom was concerned about her position within the missionary group, Dad's career, what the neighbours would think, and how gossip would fly through the village.

If Mom was still alive, I don't think that she would much like having a gay daughter. It would have been like arguing about rock and roll music, only way worse. But I knew that I was a lez be friends, that I was gay. And that was simply me. That one upside about Mom being dead was that we would never have that argument.

That night, Aunt Bette brought Tina in, and they were even holding hands. Tina was so beautiful; no wonder Aunt Bette had fallen in love with her. She was blonde and had a wide, flashing smile. Tina reminded me of Ginnie. If Ginnie had loved me, I would have lived in secret with her, too.

"Do you mind if I sit down?" she asked.

"It's your house, T, you sit where you want," Aunt Bette said, pulling up a chair, but Tina waited until I said yes before sitting down.

"Did you take her temperature?" Tina asked.

"Of course I took her temperature, you goose," Aunt Bette replied, giving Tina a big smooch on the top of her blonde head.

Tina didn't dress like Aunt Bette. She wore a skirt, a freshly pressed white shirt, and looked more like Mom or other normal women.

"Hi Maddy, I'm Tina," she said, giving my leg a squeeze. "Bette tells me that you're ready to start walking, and maybe after a time, when you feel comfortable," she said, as she took Aunt Bette's hand, "maybe talking a bit, too."

"I would like to walk," I said, not sure about the talking part. "And thank you very much for having me," I added to Tina, swinging my legs off the bed.

"You're welcome here for your recovery," Tina replied. "It's nice to have a young dyke around the house."

I didn't really like being called a young dyke. I'd rather be a gay girl. As Tina tried to help me up, I instinctively pulled back.

"Just like you, Bette," Tina said. "No taking help when you're determined that you can do it yourself."

Aunt Bette replied, "It's a Barnes family trait. The women are stronger than the men, and we just keep going."

Slipping on my clothes, I followed them out the door.

Aunt Bette and Tina lived in a sturdy two-bedroom yellow brick bungalow on a long-treed street. My room was usually Tina's sewing room and Aunt Bette's study. Their house, like the others around them, had been built after the Second World War to house returning soldiers. I thought of Dad's best friend, Bill, who had been killed in the war, and I knew his death made a deep mark on my father. Aunt Bette, Tina, and I were out for a walk. It felt good to be outside. A couple of neighbours waved hello. We all waved back.

"Do they know about you two?" I asked.

"I think they suspect," Tina replied.

"But nobody's had the guts to ask," Aunt Bette added, offering me her arm. "How are you feeling on your pins?"

My legs were weak, but they were working, and I certainly didn't need anybody holding me up. "Pretty good," I replied. "So, tell me about what dykes are."

"That's something we're going to show you in person," Aunt Bette said. "When you're a bit stronger, we'll take you dancing."

"You're going to take me to a gay bar?" I asked, instantly excited.

"But first, you've got to get your strength back," Tina replied. "We've done about a half a mile," she added. "Time to get back to the house."

I didn't want to go back to the house. I wanted to go to the gay bar.

Aunt Bette's pickup pulled into the lot of a commercial building at the corner of Gerrard and Carlaw, a tough part of town near a railway overpass. My aunt was wearing a pale-blue tuxedo with a frilly white tuxedo shirt and wore her red hair slicked into a jelly roll. Tina was all dolled up in a matching blue dress. She looked much more feminine than Aunt Bette. What was that about? If we were our own tribe, then why did gay women have to dress like traditional men and women? It didn't make any sense, but it might be rude to ask, so I just got out of the truck.

The building was long and low, with grey brick walls and a Canadian flag draped over the door. Pickup trucks and a yellow Chevy Nova were parked to the side.

"This isn't a bar. It's a garage," I said, feeling disappointed.

"It's the Blue Jay. It's a hall," Tina said.

"Why don't you have a bar?" I asked. This wasn't what I expected at all.

"Good luck getting that," Aunt Bette said. "The police would always be trying to shut it down. Liquor licenses, underage drinkers. Anything to put us out of business."

We reached the entranceway.

"Plus, when the straight guys find out there's a dyke bar," Tina started, as Aunt Bette broke in with a laugh, "They come sauntering in claiming, 'a woman wouldn't want a man unless she was too ugly to get one' or," she added, as she slapped Tina's bum, 'They haven't met the right guy yet.'"

A couple of women wearing men's pastel polyester suits passed us by. Aunt Bette and Tina said hello. Aunt Bette yanked open the door. Country music twanged out.

"Come on in," she said. "Welcome to your new world."

A barrel-chested woman with a silver brush cut, wearing a three-piece men's suit, sat behind a green card table. Her hands rested on a steel cash box. She looked so much like a man that I'd never have known she was female if her hands weren't so small. The bartender greeted Aunt Bette and Tina, and a bunch of other women waved and shouted hello. Tina began acting way more feminine than she normally did and slipped her hand through the crook of Aunt Bette's arm, demurely kissing her cheek. Aunt Bette patted Tina on the bum. When I imagined Aunt Bette behaving like this at one of Mom's dinner parties, I laughed out loud.

"What's so funny?" Tina asked.

"Nothing," I replied, thinking about Dad likely asking Aunt Bette if he could take her gal for a spin around the dance floor. This time I snorted. Tina gave me a curious look.

"Hello, Ruthie," Aunt Bette said to the woman with the small hands. "This is my niece, Maddy."

"Hi, kid. Two bucks."

The woman didn't appear to have any breasts. What happened to them?

"Two bucks!" she repeated, as Aunt Bette gave me the Barnes woman stink eye.

"How do you do?" I asked, reaching out to shake Ruthie's hand.

Aunt Bette paid for all of us. Her black wallet was linked to a belt buckle with a long silver chain. The kind of wallets bikers used.

"What's the money for?" I asked, trying not to stare at Ruthie searching for any sign of boobs.

"Admission."

Maybe she wrapped them in tensor bandages to flatten them down.

"How many drink tickets?" Ruthie asked.

"Just give me a bunch," Aunt Bette said, pulling more bills out of her biker wallet.

While Ruthie made change, I looked around. Faded red-and-white bunting hung from the ceiling. Hurricane lamps threw up flickering candlelight and the tables were draped in red-and-white gingham. Stackable chairs lined the wall.

As we made our way to the bar and Aunt Bette talked to her friends, rude or not, I turned to Tina. "Why do you and Aunt Bette dress like that?"

"As far as I know, that's the way we've always done it. Butch and femme."

"Aunt Bette is the butch," I said, putting it together. "And that makes you the femme?" I asked.

"Yes," she said with a smile.

"Why?" I asked, still not understanding why any gay women would want to play magnified versions of the straight world.

"I don't really know, Maddy, but I do know that it's fun," she laughed, pulling me along.

It didn't look like fun to me. Plus, if I ended up a femme, it likely meant I would have to do all the dishes.

Dykes in men's pastel suits and rented tuxedos foxtrotted with fancy ladies dressed in frilly skirts, high heels, and puffy beehives. Others sat around the gingham-covered tabletops, drinking beer and pounding their fists. Some of the frilly ladies sat on the dykes' laps, playing with their ties, running manicured fingernails through brush cuts and oily ducktails. The candlelight was so low I ran into a chair. The women on stools, if you could call them that, turned, giving me suspicious looks. They knew I didn't belong, and so did I.

When we finally got to the front of the line, the bartender tossed a wet towel over her shoulder.

"How's tricks?" she asked Aunt Bette, while checking me out. The bartender's stiff jeans were hiked up under her breasts, held in place by a thick black leather belt, the kind Granddad wore.

"What'll it be, sunshine?" she asked me with a Kenneth kind of smile.

"A Blue please."

"Coming up."

Aren't there other kinds of gay women, I wondered. I would never fit in here. I just wanted a pretty girl to love and be with. While Aunt Bette and Tina visited with their friends, I looked around. The bartender placed the beer in front of me, a cigarette dangling suggestively between her lips.

"Dance?" she asked.

"You didn't need to be rude," Aunt Bette said, when we arrived home. My first gay bar had been a bust. The moment the bartender made her move, I ran out the door.

"She wasn't rude, Bette," Tina said. "It's just not her scene."

"I'm sorry, Aunt Bette. I didn't mean to embarrass you."

"Now you remind me of Laura, uppity miss," Aunt Bette snorted, as Tina made us all a cup of tea.

As much as I liked the idea of being compared to Mom, that wasn't the point. "I respect both of you … But I want something else. A different way of being gay," I replied.

"This is the only way we know," Aunt Bette replied, her temper was up.

"But it's not the only way," Tina said, gently placing her hand on Aunt Bette's arm.

Aunt Bette grunted and sipped some tea.

"You two sit and chat," Tina said. "I've got some sewing to do."

After she left, I reached out and took Aunt Bette's hand. "I'm really sorry," I said, knowing for certain that the way Tina and Aunt Bette lived wasn't for me. I respected them a lot, and to my mind, everyone had to follow their own ideas. But no. I wasn't going to be a butch or a femme.

"Can I call your father?" she asked. "He should know that you're safe."

I quickly shook my head, no.

"Why not?"

"Because he hates me and doesn't want me around."

Aunt Bette scratched her head. "Your father doesn't hate you, honey. Quite the opposite."

Funny way to show it.

"Your father nearly had a complete nervous collapse after your mother died."

"He wasn't the only one."

"He used to drive over here every night while your mo—"

"Was dying. Why didn't you ever tell me?"

"Because your mother didn't want anyone to know."

"Why?"

"I don't know. But I knew that it wasn't right."

"Was she ashamed?" I suddenly asked. Shame I knew all too well. Mom hadn't done anything to be ashamed of, but I certainly had.

"I don't know for sure, but I suspect you're right."

"Well, that's just stupid," I said, forgetting that I was talking about my perfect mother.

"You're right. It was stupid, and it damaged everyone around her. And oh, she was mad," Aunt Bette said, pausing. "Oh, Maddy, Laura was so angry with God. She'd lived her life following His rules. She said she had three little kids to raise. She tried so hard to be a good Christian, and then—"

The funeral we never got to attend.

"Teddy had no choice but to marry Isabel. Men, a lot of them anyway, need a woman to help them through life."

"I was there."

"You were a girl."

"But to get married to another woman …" I nearly yelled.

"Was better than leaving all three of you orphans," Aunt Bette quietly replied, taking a long, slow sip. So, she also knew what happened the night of the honeymoon.

"Teddy just couldn't handle it. He couldn't handle anything."

"How are the boys?" I finally asked.

"They're fine. Frank's on the debating team, and Tedder is playing a lot of hockey."

That was good. Nobody enjoyed arguing as much as Frank, and all Tedder lived for was hockey and wearing costumes.

I'd always felt bad about leaving them in the lurch. Another thing to feel shame over. That was me, a big walking bag of shame. At least my brothers were safe and happy. I didn't ask about Isabel.

"I'm better now, and I should get going," I said, suddenly keen to get on with my life. I knew that I wasn't old style gay, so that meant I had to find out where the girls like me were.

"No," Aunt Bette said. "You'll live here with us."

I shook my head. "You don't have the space."

"What about a job?"

"I'll find something."

Aunt Bette frowned. After a bit, her face cleared, and she opened her biker wallet, handing me a lot of money. "You're here for another week until I'm sure you're fine," Aunt Bette said. "You're to check in at least once a week. And I don't mean *maybe*."

While my aunt squeezed my hand, I was thinking about Mom. I wasn't the only one mad at God. Mom had been too.

CHAPTER NINE

"Follow me," the manager said, expertly navigating through the customers to a booth at the back. The clatter of dishes and loud conversation was deafening. Murray's was one of the busiest downtown eateries, crammed with hungry university students lured in by cheap but tasty food. Mom and Dad used to hang out there when they were at university, and the place was filled with so many happy memories. Maybe I could be happy there, too. There was a sign in the window advertising for a waitress, and I came in to apply for the job. The thought of washing dirty dishes was a drag, but I had to start somewhere.

"I don't have any experience, but I'm a quick learner."

The manager took a sip of coffee, thoughtfully stroking his beard as I quietly nudged the bag of clean clothes under the table. Had he noticed? I still had to find a place to stow my stuff.

The manager drummed his fingers on the table, taking another sip.

"And I'm a hard worker," I added.

"All right," he said, setting down the mug. "We'll start you bussing tomorrow morning and take it from there."

I thanked him and shook his hand.

"Without the garbage bag," he added.

The sidewalk on Bloor was busy with shoppers and students. Murray's was located on the main floor of the Park Plaza hotel, across the street from the museum—the same museum where Dad had found me begging. Now that I had a job, I needed a place to stay. Rooming houses were close by, but I remembered how lonely they were—another place I didn't fit. Rochdale was close. Maybe someone was looking for a roommate. At least I'd be with people I sort of knew.

Everything had changed. The dorks were gone, replaced with intimidating bikers who, like trolls under a bridge, demanded a toll to travel into the tower. The rest of the lobby was packed with people there to watch *Deep Throat*, a movie starring some girl called Linda Lovelace. Posters claimed she could perform erotic feats no one in the history of cinema had ever achieved before. The man's name was Harry Reems, and I overheard somebody say that his dick was a fake.

"How can it be a fake if he gets a hard-on?" somebody asked.

Rochdale felt so different than that first day with Mary. Back then, it was all about peace and love, but there was nothing peaceful about bikers and *Deep Throat*. A dog started humping another underneath the poster when someone threw hot coffee on them and laughed. The bitch howled. There was no way to see who burned the dogs because the crowd was so thick.

A short guy, who must have been one of the dog's owners, pushed his way through. "Why'd you do that?"

"Because I wanted to."

The voice was familiar. The movie crowd, spooked by the howl, began to mill and shift. A biker in Paradise Rider's colours stood by a coffee urn, holding a Styrofoam cup. At first, I didn't recognize him, but when he looked up, there he was, and he'd seen me, too. Hermann dropped the cup and started punching his way through the crowd. I dropped my garbage bag of clothing and ran.

Halfway across Bloor, dodging cars and trucks, I turned. Hermann was gaining. Pushing through people, leaping over piles of trash and splashing through puddles, I ran out onto University Avenue. A yellow cab idled in front of the museum. Hermann was still behind, but I'd made up a bit of ground.

"Yonge and Dundas!" I yelled, jumping into the cab, locking the door behind me.

"You got any money?" the cabby asked, casually slinging his arm over the front seat.

I slammed down the lock on the front passenger door just as Hermann pulled on the handle. Furious, he smashed his fist onto the windshield.

"You don't want that guy in here!" I yelled. "Go!"

The cabby squealed into traffic while Hermann thumped the trunk, waving for another cab, screaming and shaking his fist.

"Can you please roll up your window?" I asked. I didn't need to hear what Hermann was saying. I already knew what he'd do if he caught me.

The meter read one dollar and fifty-five cents. I handed the driver a tip. "Don't tell anyone where you dropped me."

Hiding in the doorway of a closed camera shop, I tried to breathe. Once I caught my breath, I peeked out. No Hermann. Head low, I walked down the street to The Green Door and ran up the stairs. Ivan wasn't there, only Helen and Lily sprawled out on sofas reading fashion magazines. Helen was wearing thigh-high rhinestone boots and a glittering silver lamé halter top, and this time her hair was blue.

Lily jumped up, searching my arms for needle marks. When she saw they were clean, she actually kissed me. Lily doled out affection like my family. Rare and spare.

"Hermann's after me."

Lily wasn't happy anymore. "Who's Hermann?" Helen asked.

"You don't want to know," Lily replied, snatching her purse. "I'm taking the rest of the night off."

"Ivan's not going to like it," Helen said, rubbing her hands back and forth, copying Ivan. "This is a serious job, ladies, with serious responsibilities."

Even though I was scared, Helen made me laugh.

"What goes up, must come down," she added.

I didn't get the joke, but Lily roared. "Tell him I'll see him tomorrow. Come on," she said, pulling me out the door. "We've got to get Gabe."

Hiding behind a rusted dumpster near the parkette where the alkies hung out, I tried not to think about rats. A Harley roared by. Gabe was surrounded by a cluster of his drinking buddies—rumpled, boisterous men with round, bright cheeks and noses red with exploded capillaries. A short guy known as Big Man opened a bottle of Aqua Velva, the blue aftershave lotion the winos drank when they didn't have money for real liquor.

Lily was trying to talk Gabe into coming home, but he kept yelling, "No!" trying to snatch the Aqua Velva. Big Man swatted him out of the way. Lily grabbed Gabe's arm, and he slapped her, not hard, but enough to attract unwanted attention.

I darted out. "Hey, buddy! How's it going?"

Gabe looked at me. At first, he wasn't sure who I was. "Cookie?"

A sedan slowed as familiar speeder faces stared through the cracked windshield. Somebody pointed, and I quickly turned to hide my face.

"Yeah, it's Cookie and I've got a bottle."

The other winos perked up. Gabe wrapped his arm around me. His breath smelled of rubbing alcohol. "Just for me, right?"

"That's right. But we gotta go."

Gabe roared, "I got women, and I gotta bottle!"

"Get outta here," Big Man said, spitting on the pavement. "I'm sick of your face."

Gabe started waving his fists, but Lily and I each seized an arm, pulling him away.

"I got women!" he crowed back as the three of us hurried up the street. "And I gotta bottle!"

Lily closed the bedroom door and walked into the living room. She'd saved enough to rent a large one-bedroom in a sprawling new apartment complex called St. Jamestown. St. Jamestown was built to attract young swinging singles, but the elevator had been full of immigrants and their children.

The unit had a panoramic view of Lake Ontario. Lights from bobbing oil tankers flashed against choppy whitecaps. Lily had decorated the apartment with modern furniture. Everything was as white as her hair: the sofa, chairs, walls, and broadloom. A large photograph of a sexy woman holding a vacuum cleaner hung over the sofa.

"General Idea," Lily said. "One of my customers sells modern art and said it would be a good investment."

Lily was buying art? What was General Idea?

"You should take Gabe to emergency."

He'd vomited blood nearly all the way home and had gone straight to bed.

Lily sat down, kicked off her shoes, and started massaging the balls of her feet. "I think you've got enough of your own shit to deal with."

Same old Lily. Nobody could take care of Gabe except her. "You look a lot better," she said, as I sat down beside her.

Thanks to Tina's cooking, I'd put some weight back on. Lily swung her feet into my lap while I rubbed between the toes, asking whether she'd seen Hermann at The Green Door.

"Never."

"Yonge and Dundas? Anywhere downtown?"

"Nope."

That was good news. Still, it was stupid dangerous for Hermann to be out in plain sight at Rochdale. Sane, careful Hermann would never have done that.

"You can stay with us. But you have to pay food and rent."

Aunt Bette and Tina's money wouldn't last long, and I couldn't go back to Murray's.

"And you'll have to share the pullout with Helen."

Helen was definitely pretty, and we'd be sharing a bed. She said she was asexual, but nobody really gave up on sex. That would be impossible.

"Maybe she can show me around the scene."

I didn't even know what a different gay bar might look like.

"Does that mean you're admitting you're a lezzie?" Lily asked.

"I'm *gay*," I replied, thinking of Aunt Bette and her butch friends. While I loved my aunt, I was a different kind of gay. Like plants, with many different varieties.

Lily wriggled her toes and stretched her arms. "I don't care about sex. I want to buy a house."

I stopped massaging her toes. "That's so weird."

Lily stopped wriggling her toes. "Why?"

"You're too young."

She snatched her feet out of my hands and sat up. "I want a home."

"Why?" I asked, looking around the apartment. "This is beautiful."

Mom would have approved.

"I want a real home. And a house is a home." Then her face clouded over, and she stopped talking. Lily did that sometimes. Just shut down, and there was no turning her back on.

"I'm going to bed," she said.

"Do you need a toothbrush?"

I nodded.

"There are extras in the linen cupboard and a couple of T-shirts."

"Okay, 'night."

Lily had extra toothbrushes? Things were certainly changing. Pulling out the sofa, I put on a borrowed T-shirt and turned out the light.

The lock tumbler clicked. Helen slipped into the room and began to quietly undress. Her shiny silver boots toppled. There were no blinds—only Helen's naked silhouette flickering against the lights of the city.

"Did you make a lot of money rubbing old pervs?"

Helen pulled a T-shirt over her head. "Were you staring at my boobs?"

"No." Yes, I was. I sat up, switched on the light and lit a cigarette. Helen brushed her hair. "I thought you might be Hermann," I said.

Helen set the brush on the glass coffee table. "Is he really that bad?"

"Worse."

She walked toward the bathroom. "Then why don't you turn him in?"

Water rushed as the bathroom taps turned on. Clearly, Helen had never had a gun held to her head. She walked back in, drying her face. Without any makeup Helen looked young, vulnerable, and sort of sweet.

"If you're too scared to go to the cops, why don't you just go home?"

She sat down beside me and lit a cigarette as I stubbed mine out.

Helen had curvy legs. I lay down, hoping she'd take the hint. "I don't want to talk about it."

"Why don't you just go home?" she repeated.

"Because I can't," I snipped. "And will you please put that out? I need to get some sleep."

Helen gave me a "you're so strange" look but put out the smoke and fell onto her back. I switched off the light and could smell her perfume, happy that she didn't shower.

"So, what are you going to do?" she asked.

"Sleep."

"You can't just lie around all day."

"I'll get something," I said, not much liking the hint that I was lazy.

"Do you have money?"

"Yes."

"I don't believe you. What kind of job are you going to get with Charles Manson after you?"

"Who asked you?"

"Don't get all bitchy," Helen replied, rolling onto her side and looking at me. "If you could get a job, what would your dream job be?"

"Is your dream rubbing pervs?"

"Fuck off," she replied, rolling away.

Now, I rolled toward her, jabbing her in the ribs. "I mean it. Why are you doing it?"

"I'm saving for a professional makeup kit. I want to work in the movies."

That made sense. Helen was obviously into transformation. Every time I saw her, she looked different. Moving closer, I thought about the time I cupped Charlene's boobs. "I bet you'll be good at it."

The room stilled as Helen's breath slowed.

"Were you really gay?" I asked, shifting my thigh near hers. "Before you went asexual."

She moved her thigh away. "I thought you were tired."

"How did you get rid of it?" My hand lightly brushed hers. "The gayness."

She pulled her hand back. "I have better things to do with my life."

Than love? Maybe somebody hurt her like Ginnie had hurt me. Or maybe it was rubbing the men.

"Have you ever been to a gay bar?" I asked.

"Of course."

"Will you take me?"

"No."

I touched her arm. "You asked me what my dream was. It's to go to a gay bar."

"What a stupid dream."

"Come on. I want to meet a girl."

"Maybe," she replied, sounding fuzzy, nearly asleep. "When it's safe …"

I fell asleep smiling. I knew Helen liked me—she never moved her arm.

Sitting on the Steps, disguised in Helen's blue-and-white polka dot dress and a bright red cardigan, I looked for Hermann. Three weeks had passed, but there had been no sign of him. When I'd called Aunt Bette to check in a few days ago, I'd lied and told her I was fine, but I was completely broke and couldn't stay there if I didn't kick in a bit for food.

Helen had done my makeup that morning and laughed the whole time while Lily giggled. Only Gabe understood the indignity. He sat beside me on the Steps rocking back and forth like an abandoned ship. He must have lost twenty pounds since I first met him and had taken to cocking his head the way dogs do when they're trying to understand. The doctor at the emergency room warned Lily that Gabe had suffered a lot of brain damage and advised treatment, but Gabe wouldn't go, and Lily didn't want to press the point.

"You got any money for old Gabe?" he asked, giving me his sweetest smile.

I shook my head as Gabe picked up a smouldering cigarette someone had just thrown away.

"Don't," I said, knocking it out of his hand. "You don't know where it's been."

Gabe simply picked it back up. His spiky white beard had yellowed, and milky clouds floated over his eyes.

"Can you see okay?" I asked.

"Better'n ever."

He probably had cataracts. Two girls dressed in McDonald's uniforms walked up the street. A new franchise had opened, and a HELP WANTED sign hung in the window. My job at Murray's would be gone by now, and besides, I couldn't work out in the open. Eventually, somebody would see me and tell Hermann. Dad always told me to keep my options open … and most of mine were closed.

"Looky looky!" Gabe chirped when the girls came near.

The girls glanced at each other and hurried past. Who were they to look down on us? Mom would have thought working at a fast-food restaurant was the same as being chained to a stove, cooking for hired hands. That's why getting an education was so important. A sigh slipped out.

"Why so blue?" Gabe asked.

"Money."

Gabe smiled and stuck his hand out, palm up.

I shook my head. "No more begging."

"Pogey?"

I shook my head again. No way I'd go on welfare.

"That's what it's there for."

"Never!" I said, snatching the butt out of Gabe's mouth and throwing it onto the street again.

"Jeez, you and Lily's got more pride than Queen Elizabeth." Gabe pointed at The Green Door. "The money's good, and it's respectable."

No, it wasn't, but there was no choice. At least I'd be tucked away at The Green Door—safe from sight. A truck rattled by. Lily said nobody from the street ever went up there. My gut knew it was shameful, but no one would ever find out. It would be my secret. And besides, all things being equal, wasn't it better to rub men for money than end up dead?

The dingy rub room was painted blood-red and dimly lit by a series of flickering red candles. Dad would have called the place a fire trap, but Ivan claimed it was all about ambience. Naked except for a towel wrapped around his waist, Ivan hopped up on the bed and lay face-down on a single mattress that stood on a tall platform with wobbly wooden legs. Briefly, I wondered what Dad would think and quickly stopped the thought.

"First, warm it up," Ivan said.

A line of slimy lotion shot into the palm of my hand. It smelled of coconuts and pine needles. I tried not to focus on what was happening and think about girls.

"Not too much. That stuff ain't cheap."

It sure felt cheap to me. Slapping the lotion across his back, some squirted on the fitted white sheet.

"You're not greasing a pig here," he said.

"Sorry."

"Rub the shoulders. Ah, that's nice. Now, take it down a bit. Trail your fingers over the skin, and it never hurts to talk. Guys like to hear a girl's voice when she rubs him."

"What should I say?" I asked.

"Not so loud. More like a purr, and just don't talk about yourself. Nobody cares about that."

Of course.

I looked around. It was like being in one of Dad's examining rooms, visiting with his patients. There were even red screens to change behind, but rather than slipping into a medical gown, I'd be taking off my top. Isabel never had to rub men to survive.

"Not so rough," Ivan complained.

"Sorry."

Ivan flipped over. I warmed more lotion in my hands and rubbed it onto his furry chest, pretending to work a stain out of a carpet.

"Most of the guys will want you to rub their stomachs so they can stare at your tits."

"And if they try and touch them?"

"Back up and tell 'em that you don't do extras."

"Okay," I said, rubbing Ivan while thinking about Dad. Was Aunt Bette right about him not hating me?

"Don't pull on the nipples. They're sensitive."

"Really?" I thought men only cared about their penises.

"You've got a way to go, but you've got good hands. Now let me rub those tits."

"No extras," I replied.

Ivan slapped his gut and sat up. "You've got the job."

Back in the lounge, a girl with a huge red afro and hooped earrings sat in a puffy chair, jotting something into a ledger. Helen looked up, flashing me one of her looks.

"My, my, my. Look who's here to rub old pervs."

"Shut up," I replied.

"Let's keep it ladylike," Ivan said, turning to the girl with the afro.

"I'm Cindy," she said, with a smile that revealed a golden tooth.

Cindy went back to her ledger while Helen and Lily explained the schedule. There were two shifts, noon to six and six to midnight.

"There's more guaranteed action at night, but the creep potential's higher," Helen said.

Lily advised me to get a steady roster of clients and service them during the day. Cindy looked up to make sure Ivan couldn't hear.

"Deal dope on the side," she whispered.

"What do you sell?"

"Downers and junk. You want some?"

"No, thank you." I'd given all that up.

The rules were simple. The john—that's what the customer was called—entered the lounge, looked at the ladies and selected one. The girl would slowly stand, smile seductively, and take the john's arm, walking him over to the manager's wicket. From there, Ivan would count the money and tell us what room was free.

"And you go behind the screen and strip down," Ivan added.

"It's all about the titillation factor," Helen said. "The longer it takes for you to take off your top, the more revved up they get."

Lily agreed. "It's like a mini striptease."

"But you can't hide back there. Remember, the clock is always ticking," Cindy said, looking over at Ivan. "'Cause if you do, he'll dock your pay."

The girls were responsible for changing the bed after each rub. There was a laundry hamper in every room, usually situated near a lone straight-backed chair. Helen thought that Ivan had stolen the chairs from some restaurant and made the bed frames himself because they swayed whenever a fat john hopped up.

"This is a topless rub. Don't take off your jeans," Ivan said.

"I don't want to take off my pants," I replied, already more than a bit nervous about the idea of taking off my shirt.

Ivan turned on the downstairs speaker so the guys could be lured upstairs by "Brown Sugar" or "Angie." He claimed that the Rolling Stones were an aphrodisiac.

"It's your job to show up clean and presentable," he said, leaning out of the wicket. "I don't want no whores working my place. I've got a reputation to think of. And wear something that shows off your titties."

We'd been working for four hours, and only Cindy and Lily had been busy. Lily was up at Ivan's wicket with another john.

"If the rub costs twenty and I get five, that means I do six rubs a day at five bucks a rub, and I'll bring home thirty dollars. I'll bank the money and retire after a couple of months," I said.

"I haven't retired yet," Helen said, looking into a compact and applying a thick layer of eyeliner. Her green eyes locked on mine. The red thunderbolts she'd hennaed onto the sides of her blue hair reminded me of Zeus. "The only way you do that is if you do extras," she added, glancing toward Lily.

Lily was pulling the john by his tie, leading him out the door and down the hall.

"What are extras?"

Helen looked at me through a veil of false eyelashes. "Are you serious?"

I hated it when Helen acted as if she had all the experience in the world.

"Yes."

She crossed her legs. Time for a lesson. "There's hand jobs. That's five bucks."

That's what I'd done to Kenneth.

Helen mimicked peeling a banana, opened her mouth and slowly brought her lips down over her thumb. "A blow job's ten."

"Gross."

"A full-out fuck is twenty, and around the world is forty."

"What's around the world?"

"That's the whole works. Plus," she said, pointing at her bum.

"No way!"

I opened a worn copy of *Hustler* to look at the centrefold. I'd never let anybody put anything up there. The *Playboy* girls reminded me of naked cheerleaders, but the *Hustler* women had boobs that looked as if they'd been pinched too often. I shifted towards Helen.

"When are we going to the gay bars?"

When she didn't answer, I moved even closer, fingers creeping across the back of the sofa until my arm settled around her shoulder. Helen looked at my hand, picked it up, and flicked it off.

"You said you'd take me out for my birthday, but you didn't," I complained.

I'd recently turned seventeen, and Helen had bought a yummy chocolate cake, and everyone sang. The downstairs door jangled, followed by a tentative shuffle of feet. Springing back from Helen, I held my breath as footsteps padded up the stairs. A very tall, bone-thin man wearing a beat-up black fedora poked his head around the door.

"Come on in," Ivan waved from the wicket. "We won't bite. Will we, girls?"

I sat up straight and tried to look welcoming, but my legs kept squeezing themselves shut. Helen stretched out like a lazy tabby. The man stood in the doorway, as if suspended in a magnetic field while Ivan ran out from behind the wicket.

"Why don't you meet the ladies?" Ivan asked, guiding the man in. Reluctantly, he allowed himself to be steered. "This is Mercedes," Ivan said, indicating Helen, "and this is …"

"Isabel," I replied, remembering that you needed a fake name to protect your true identity.

The tall, thin man suddenly realized he still had his hat on. Embarrassed, he snatched the fedora from his head and bowed. At least he had good manners.

"Who would you like?" Ivan asked.

"What?" he asked.

The man was as new to this as I was—a virgin customer.

"Which one of our lovely ladies would you like to give you a relaxing massage?"

Helen readjusted herself on the sofa to look appealing, which was easy because she was incredibly sexy. Smiling as sweetly as I could, I asked the man how he was. That's what Dad always did to break the ice. He smiled nervously at both of us and then took Ivan aside to wrangle over the price.

"How much?" the man mumbled.

"Twenty."

"What do I get?"

"You get a slow sensual rub from one of these lovely young ladies."

"Are they naked?"

"Topless," Ivan replied. "And as you can tell, they're both very well-endowed."

The tall, thin man snuck another peek. I grinned like an idiot, while Helen swung her boobs around. It reminded me of a song Aunt Anne used to sing: "How Much Is That Doggie in the Window?" The man pointed. "I'll take Isabel."

My breath shot out in short, anxious blasts when we reached the top of the stairs and walked down the long, narrow hallway. Cindy and Lily were rubbing in rooms down the hall. The red walls were covered with faded pin-ups, and some of the loose floor planks bounced when we stepped on them. The tall, thin man was close behind me, clutching his hat as if it was a bouquet of flowers. I pushed open the door and saw the screen, the lotion, and the bed.

"Take your clothes off, hop up on the bed. And cover yourself with a towel."

The tall, thin man sat down, his hat clenched tightly in both hands. "I don't want to get undressed."

We looked at one another for a moment.

"I don't do extras."

"I don't want you to."

"Then what do you want?"

Was he a creep? My heart thumped.

"There's nothing I appreciate more than a healthy young body." The hat bobbed up and down, shifting from hand to hand. "I want to watch you take your top off."

He stood up, removed a ten-dollar bill from his wallet and set it on top of the sheet. "And I want you to make it nice and slow."

He sat back down, waiting for my answer. How did this fit into hand job, blow job, straight screw, or around the world? Helen didn't say anything about this.

"You can't touch me," I said.

"I don't want to touch. I want to watch."

"But I'm supposed to rub you."

"Do you want to?"

"Not really."

"Then why not just take the money?"

Looking at the bill on the cot, I considered the deal. Since I really didn't want to touch him, this way I wouldn't have to. We'd already spent nearly five minutes, and that meant I only had fifteen to go. What was worse? Touching his body or showing him my boobs? If I rubbed him, he'd see my boobs anyway, so I was actually making ten dollars for free. Fifteen, when I counted in my commission.

"Okay." I snatched up the money and stuffed it into my pocket. "But you have to stay right there," I added, backing up a wee bit. "You can't move a muscle."

"Do you have any music?" he asked.

I turned on the speaker from downstairs, and "You Can't Always Get What You Want" rolled into the room. Slowly, I undid the white snaps on Cope's old red shirt while Mick Jagger growled. Thinking of Ginnie,

I leisurely slid the fabric down over my shoulders, remembering the times we kissed in her bedroom as the sun came up. The red cotton teased over my back, slipping down and sliding over my breasts as the man set his hat on the floor and grabbed his knees. Looking down, I lightly touched my nipple, and it sprang up. The tall, thin man was breathing like Kenneth in the trunk of the car.

As I swung my breasts, he began to submit to the spell. This was about power, and mine was absolute. Earlier I'd been really scared, wondering if I could take my top off in front of strange, horny men, worried that they might attack - but this was different. My body was the boss in this room, not the men, and as long as I didn't think about what was happening, everything would be fine. My body performed in this secret world, but my heart and soul were locked away like the tiny ballerina in my music box.

The music ended and my cowboy shirt lay around my ankles—a pond of red fabric on the floor. I stood there in the middle of the dimly lit room, my breasts exposed to a faint breeze from the open window, while the tall, thin man stared at me.

"Thank you," he said. He got up, crossed the room, and turned around at the door, fumbling in his pocket. He pulled out a card and handed it to me. "My name's Jack," he said, walking out, "and I hope to see you again very soon." The door closed.

"You're a whore," said Helen, queen of the universe.

"I am not. I'm trying to save some money, just like you."

I tugged at the neck of my new Ziggy Stardust T-shirt, looking for Hermann, which was now more a habit than anything else. Gabe had watched the streets for nearly two months and never saw him, so gradually I'd come out of hiding.

Lily, Cindy, Helen, and I were at the Zanzibar playing Pong and drinking Zombies while a gorgeous girl swung around a brass pole, her long, brown hair sweeping the stage floor. Lily twirled the little pink parasol while a white computerized ball bounced across the lime-green screen.

"What do you say, Lily?" I asked, wanting to prove Helen was wrong.

"I think as long as you get paid, it's good."

Lily took a furtive sip. "Tell me if you see Gabe."

If Gabe knew she'd been drinking, he'd start chirping, "What's good for the goose is good for the gander."

George arrived and set down another round of brightly coloured Zombies. He was the same waiter Vic and Cope had introduced me to.

"Hey, George, if you do hand jobs, are you a whore?" I asked.

"Do you like it? Does it turn you on?"

"No way."

He switched the ashtrays, placing a clean one in the centre of the table. "You're only a whore if you like it. There was a girl where I grew up who you could find out in the bushes by the Esso station any Saturday night with her toes in her ears. Now that's a whore."

"Does that mean I'm not a whore either?" Lily asked. "Even if I go a little bit further?"

"Same rules. If you enjoy it, you're a whore. If you're not, you're a businesswoman."

Lily slapped the table. "See?"

Helen was wrong. Cindy slapped the table.

George placed a Zombie and a napkin in front of each of us. "The drinks are from the gentleman by the stage."

It was Jack and he'd become one of my regulars. He was a tool and die maker from St. Catherine's who lived with his mother, and he came to see me once or twice a week. We slowly got to talking about everything.

He told me about his mother and what a sad life she'd had and how he did everything for her. When I told him all about Mom, I finally shared my first good, deep cry with somebody else. He wrapped his arms around me in the rub room, holding me close as I endlessly rocked and sobbed.

Fairly soon after I started doing sexy dances for Jack, he began asking for more. Since I'd already done it with Kenneth, I knew how to do a hand job. I'd made a secret promise to myself. If I never blew the guys or had sex with them, what was wrong with helping Mother Nature fulfill a man's natural urges? Sometimes when I was jerking a man off my head sent alarming thought bubbles, but my body said, "Stop worrying, think of the money." I chugged the Zombie and told my mind to shut up.

Lily waved to him. "That's the way to make good money."

"That's the way to become thoroughly fucked up," Helen said, taking a sip. "There are some things you just can't justify. No matter how hard you try."

"Is that why you went asexual?" I asked. "I don't get how you could just turn yourself off."

"I'm asexual because I can't sell my body for money and then go home to someone I love."

"Why not?"

"Because it will fuck up the love and fuck up your head."

"But love's supposed to be free," I said. "And if so, why not share it?"

"If you share your body, you're making love a commodity."

"You're sharing your precious tits," Lily said, javelining her pink parasol into the ashtray. "You're no better than the rest of us. You just think you are."

"I'm not sucking them off," Helen said, looking directly at Lily.

Lily stared back. "We're just trying to get ahead, Helen. Why do you always have to run us down?"

Now Lily's feelings were hurt, and Helen's back was up. Dropping a tip on the table for George, I walked over to Jack, thanking him for the drinks. It was Jack's turn to be rubbed.

"Let's go," I said.

Helen had to be wrong. I was just jerking the men off to save for a better life and Lily wanted to buy a house. How could that be bad?

Jack and I walked back to The Green Door and up the stairs to the rub room. With winter here, it was chilly and time for cheap Ivan to turn up the heat. Cindy said we could call the city and make a formal complaint. Who was going to listen to a bunch of rub girls? I'd thought when she mentioned it.

"How's your mother?" I asked, shutting the door.

"She's got arthritis in her toes."

"Make sure she elevates her feet."

"Have you ever worked in retail?" he asked, while shoving the rickety rub bed across the room.

What was he doing? "No," I replied.

"You might think about it," he said. "Is there anybody downstairs?"

Warning crawled across my stomach as he started jumping up and down on the floor.

"No."

Ivan was dragging trash to the dumpster and the other girls were busy with customers. If he tried to kill me nobody would hear.

"What are you doing?" I asked, trying to calm down.

Jack had always been nice to me. He took off his jacket, folded it, and set it on the floor, then off came his shoes, pants, shirt, socks, and underwear. One by one, they were neatly folded and added to the pile of clothing. Next, he removed a twenty-dollar bill from his wallet, placed it on the bed, and sat down in the chair, stark naked, staring at me while I stared at the money. A police siren screamed in the distance.

"What do you want?"

"I want you to do jumping jacks with no bra and no panties."

"That's all?"

And it was. Jack jerked off to twenty minutes of naked callisthenics while I jumped up and down to "Tumbling Dice."

Lily brought home pizza, but Gabe just stood in the window, watching the freighters out in the lake, hands thrust deeply into his pockets. He wanted to go to the Maple Leaf Tavern. The Maple was an alky bar where Gabe's buddies hung out.

Lily set the pizza box down on the glass coffee table. "You're not supposed to be drinking."

Gabe turned to me and Helen. "You want to take old Gabe out for a beer?"

"Sorry," Helen said. "Lily's house—Lily's rules."

He grunted, turning back to the window. Lily came up behind him and tried to hug him, but he walked away. Gabe wasn't the same happy guy anymore. I grabbed two slices of pizza, handing one to Helen. "Want to go out?"

"No," she replied.

Frustrated, I chewed on the crust. "You swore. You swore that when it was safe you'd take me to a gay bar."

"I didn't swear."

"You promised."

"I didn't promise. I said maybe."

"I guess your maybes aren't good for much."

Helen picked up another slice of pizza and took a bite.

I wasn't going to turn myself into a frilly woman like the ones in that Blue Jay place, and there was no way I was going to spend my life dressed like John Wayne. What was I going to do? I'd have to move to another city, but I didn't have any money. After rent, food, and clothes, there was never anything left. I always spent it all.

"Where did you meet girls? I mean before you went asexual."

Helen closed the top of the pizza box. "Get your coat," she said. "I'm taking you out."

Disco pounded down as Helen and I climbed the stairs to a club called Jo Jo's. Guys leaned against the railing and walls, drinking Labatt's 50 beers, playfully grabbing each other by the ass. Two boys tugged one another down the stairs out the door into the alley. One of them was tall and rangy with long, curly red hair. When he saw Helen, he immediately stopped. "Helen! Long time."

"Hey, Gerry. Been busy."

Gerry rolled his eyes at Helen and grinned at me. "Is this another Queen of the Dykes?"

"More like Queen of the Hand Job," Helen whispered in my ear.

I scowled at her. That was a secret.

"Come over for a visit sometime," Gerry replied, as the other guy grabbed his crotch.

"I'm Maddy," I said, instantly liking him. "Where are you going?"

"Sex in the bushes," Gerry replied.

"Don't you get cold and dirty?"

"That's the fun of it," he replied, and they ran down the stairs and out the door.

Helen and I entered the club. There were sofas, club chairs, and a long mahogany bar with a polished brass rail. The dance floor was raised and covered in brightly lit tiles flashing primary colours that pulsated with the music. Jo Jo's was nothing like the Blue Jay. Jo Jo's had style.

Most of the guys were dressed the same: skintight Levi 501s with folded cuffs and yellow construction boots, checkered work shirts with rolled-up sleeves to show off Popeye biceps, and multicoloured handkerchiefs dangling from their back pockets. They wore their hair short and moustaches long. Helen signaled for a couple of beers while I asked her why they all dressed the same.

"Clones. They want to look like sexy blue-collar guys."

More costumes. Was Tedder still wearing costumes?

"What's that?" I whispered, refocusing my mind to the handkerchiefs, not wanting to sound ignorant. It wasn't good to think about my brothers.

"Red means S. Black means M. Yellow means water sports and pink? Pink just means gay," Helen said, ordering two beers. "That way if a trick is cruising them, they know what the guy's into."

I looked at the yellow handkerchiefs. Water sports? Older men dressed in black leather motorcycle jackets and chaps leaned against the bar, eyes peering out from beneath black motorcycle caps, cruising coy boys who slithered by.

"When you're too old to be a clone, you become a leather man," Helen said.

"That's weird."

A leather man hissed, "then get the fuck out."

"We've got as much right to be here as you," Helen said loud enough so everyone at the bar could hear. She turned to the bartender. "Isn't that right?"

The bartender, a cute clone, nodded, setting down our drinks. New gay bars were opening, busy gay bars filled with younger patrons who refused to hide who they were. To bump up cash flow, the owners were integrating dykes and fags. The older homos didn't like it, but they didn't have a choice. Things were changing, and it excited Helen, who started talking about the power of being out and proud.

"I thought you were asexual," I said, not really wanting people to know about me. My sex life wasn't their business. It was private, between me and my girlfriend.

"Only while I'm working at The Green Door," Helen replied. "Then I'm proud to be gay again. You'll get into it, Maddy. I promise. It's infectious."

I knew all about infections and didn't want one. I didn't care about politics, and only wanted Jo Jo's for the girls. There were a couple of cute ones up on the dance floor, and sure, the rest of the women were young and fairly butchy, but at least they were dressed in jeans, tees, and motorcycle boots instead of polyester suits. There were hardly any frilly femmes. Thank God. The femmes freaked me out more than the butches did. The music was different, too, and when David Bowie screamed, "Wham Bam Thank You Ma'am!" Helen asked me to dance.

A golden rope around the dance floor held us in the ring. For once Helen didn't talk—we just danced song after song with other gays. None of us were pretending to be straight. We were who we were, and nothing ever felt so free.

Then the floor tiles began to vibrate in gold and the music slowed. My hair was slick with sweat and I felt like I was on the Yellow Brick Road. Helen and I stood—awkward because the song was now slow—but when I took a chance and put my arm out, Helen moved into me, settling the side of her head against my neck.

I noticed Gerry, back at the bar, twigs now twisted into his curly red hair, reminding me of Medusa. Only Gerry wasn't evil— he seemed more like a trickster. As if reading my mind, he gave me a knowing smile.

Halfway through the song, the beat picked up and the bass boomed. We seized each other by the hands and spun, heads thrown back, faces tilted up to the mirrored disco ball that flashed diamonds of dazzling white light. We whirled in endless laughter until something crashed, the record skipped and an enormous butch in a checkered shirt jumped up from her table, grasping a beer bottle by the neck.

Helen's grip tightened. "That's Easter. She's the meanest dyke in the city."

The bar went eye-of-the-tornado quiet as Easter glared across the room. Then, lightning-fast for a fat woman, she shot up onto the dance floor, pushing us aside, vaulting over the rope, nearly landing on top of a table where another butch held a girl's hand.

"You've been fucking my old lady!" Easter bellowed, smashing the beer bottle and lunging.

The other butch flipped the table to avoid getting a slice of glass in the face. Beer bottles started to fly. Glass shattered. One girl turned to run away. Another girl tripped her. Down she went. When she came up, she sprang, all claws and spit. Energy rippled through the bar. A couple of fags shrieked, "Dyke fight!" and dashed for the door, while one by one the women got caught up in the spirit of the brawl. I could see Gerry dodging the beer bottles being lobbed by rhino-charging dykes. It looked like he was having a good time.

Helen and I tried for the exit, but the stairwell was blocked with runaway fags, so we pushed through the crowd, heading toward the bathroom. A beer bottle bounced off my back and Helen nearly got punched in the face, but we made it. The bathroom was filling with scared dykes hiding in stalls, locking doors behind them. Easter staggered in, hand to her forehead, blood seeping between her fingers.

"Let me see," I said.

"Fuck off."

Grabbing Easter's hand, I pulled it back from the gash. The wound was deep and nasty. I told Helen to go tell the bartender to call an ambulance and get me a bunch of bar towels and a bucket of ice. While soaking paper towels in cold water, I told Easter to keep it tight against the wound. "You're going to need stitches."

"I don't want no stitches,"

"That's your face and you're going to take care of it."

Helen kept returning with ice, towels, and bandages, playing nurse while I tended to other wounded dykes. Most of them weren't really all that tough. A few cried. Easter even agreed to go to the hospital. A young woman in a denim jacket and a green checkered shirt asked me where I learned how to do this.

"My Dad's a doctor," I replied, looking carefully at her cut. "If you keep an eye on this you shouldn't need stitches. But make sure you change the dressing every morning and if it gets red or inflamed go to the hospital."

The living room was cold and there were no extra blankets. Helen shivered. The apartment was dark and quiet. Lily was out looking for Gabe. Harbour lights flashed in the distance.

"You were really good at that," she said.

Everything I'd learned from Dad just came back.

"Your father's a doctor?"

I grunted, knowing that she wanted to ask how a doctor's daughter ended up working at the body rub, but for once Helen had the good sense to keep her mouth shut.

"How about yours?" I asked.

"Baker."

I couldn't imagine Helen anywhere near a kitchen. All she ever did was order out.

"Where?"

"By the airport."

"What does your mom do?"

"I don't know."

How could she not know what her mother did? "Does she take care of the house?" I asked.

"She never took care of the house. Go to sleep."

Pillows were fluffed and adjusted.

"Does she work?"

Helen sat up, light blazing on. "I don't know! She left years ago, and my father is still waiting for her to come home."

"I'm sorry."

Helen shut the light off and flopped back down. "What are you sorry for? It's not your fault. Go to sleep."

We lay there for the longest time, but too much had happened for my mind to slow. I'd been to my first real gay bar, seen a dyke fight, and danced all night with Helen. Even a slow one. Especially a slow one. How could she dance with a girl all night if she was asexual?

"Helen?"

Nothing. I tried counting boats in the harbour. It didn't work. "Are you asleep?"

A rustle.

"Can I ask you something?"

Sigh. "As long as it's not about my mother."

Why didn't Helen want to talk about her mother? I guess a runaway mother was worse than a dead one. At least the dead one didn't have a choice. "How come you're asexual?'

"Because I am."

I rolled over to face her. "I mean it. How come?"

She rolled toward me, eyes only inches from mine. "I already told you."

"Tell me again."

Something in her was weakening; her wall was tumbling down. "Come on, explain it to me again," I softly asked.

"Because you can't have sex with men and love women at the same time."

"Why not?"

"Because it will fuck up the love."

"But we're not really having sex with them."

"If we were lovers, could you jump up and down for that pervert and then come home and get into bed with me?"

"Yeah, why not?"

"Because it's not right."

Helen was wrong. I was just jerking them off, trying to fill my empty nest egg. She wanted to buy a makeup kit. How could that be bad? Helen squeezed my hand and rolled onto her back.

"Let's go to sleep."

Helen's head rested on the pillow, eyes closed, pale skin glowing white in the night. She looked like Sleeping Beauty, who needed only one thing to be brought back to life, and I had to do it. I leaned over and kissed her, and then Helen's lips parted, and she kissed me back.

My heart flew around my chest as Helen took my face in her hands and kissed my lips, nose, and each of my cheeks. I could see her face. It wasn't in the dark like Ginnie. Then Helen pulled me close and her tongue touched mine. They danced and I made love to a girl that night, her fingers twisted into my hair, pulling my face deep inside her. It wasn't a perversion. It wasn't sick. It's who I was, and I knew in my heart that it was right.

We didn't leave the apartment for two days, only getting out of bed to eat or use the washroom. Lily said we were offending Gabe.

"You ain't offending me," Gabe replied, sitting down in the chair to watch as Helen quickly pulled the sheets up under her chin. "Reminds me of the time we got hookers on the ship."

"I'm taking you out for breakfast," Lily said, pulling Gabe to his feet. "And Ivan wants you both back today," she added, slamming the door behind them.

Rolling over, I rested my head on Helen's belly as she stroked my hair. We did need to get back to work, but I didn't want to leave. Her hand paused.

"You've got golden strands in your hair," she said.

Mom's golden strands. I leapt up and into the bathroom to look in the mirror. Helen came in behind me while I searched within the long black folds of my hair.

"Right here," she said, showing me one. "Aren't they beautiful?"

I nearly cried, because a bit of Mom was in my hair.

Helen started washing her face. "What are you going to tell Ivan?" she asked.

"It was a bug and now it's passed," I replied, still searching for strands of gold.

She kissed my cheek. "You know, we don't have to give notice. It's not like he would give us any." She touched my breast. "Let's just stay in bed."

"What are you talking about?" I asked.

"Quitting. My makeup kit is pretty much done. What do you think you'll do?"

Hold on. "I never said I was going to quit."

"You made me think that."

"No, I didn't. I don't have any money. What do you think I'm going to do?"

Helen stormed out and into the living room and started to power smoke.

"You knew how important this was to me, and you lied!"

"I didn't lie." But I sort of had. I knew Helen's guard was down after all the dancing, but I thought if we made love she'd give up on the silly asexual business. Boy, was I ever wrong. Helen took her gayness very seriously.

"I should have known," she said. "You lied to get me into bed," she said, clamping both hands on her hips. The long red burner on the cigarette looked set to fall off.

"I thought you'd changed your mind," I said.

"Because you're so hot? You're just like one of the johns."

Oh, that was low. I punched a pillow. "What am I supposed to do?"

"Something way better than this," Helen replied, still stark naked. "And you know that."

I loved her breasts. Only the love of Helen's breasts could ever make me do something else that filled me with such shame. Madeline Shame should be my name.

Helen and I ran up some stairs of a government building, ducking beneath the awning. She'd decked me out in some of Gabe's old clothes: a pair of ripped pants about three inches too short, a moth-eaten coat, and wrapped a tensor bandage around my wrist. Hard pellets of sleet began rocketing out of the sky, threatening a big snowstorm.

"Tell them your boyfriend beat you up and you're afraid for your life and you can't go home. Better yet, tell them that you've got a baby to think of."

"What if they want to see it?"

"Tell them that you and the baby are starving and have nowhere to live. They've got to give you money. That's their job. They're the government. Then we can figure out what you want to do. And make sure to tell them your boyfriend beats you up. That always gets extra money."

The sign over a desk read: INFORMATION.

The woman behind the desk handed me a form and pointed to a room on the left. "Take a ticket, fill this out, bring it back and wait. Someone will call you shortly."

The room was crowded. Young couples, broken men, disheveled women, and confused immigrants sat in a room full of grey chairs. The walls were plastered with ad posters for Manpower and other ads encouraging young people to seek careers in the trades. Two little kids bounced a red-and-white striped rubber ball back and forth.

The form asked for name, age, prior work experience, and current place of residence. I couldn't put down The Green Door and there was no way I was putting down my experience in Dad's office, so I checked off "None." "Married?" No way. "Willing to relocate?" Not really. Not with Helen and me being together. Doing the best I could, I returned the form to the lady, who brusquely told me to set it in the tray. I went back to the waiting room. The clock ticked. An hour passed. There were no magazines.

"Madeline Barnes?"

A thin woman in a tweed skirt, striped shirt, and sturdy shoes stood in the doorway holding a pile of folders.

"I'm Caroline Martin, your social worker. What did you do to your hand?"

Nervous, I'd forgotten about the tensor bandage. "Just a sprain. Nothing to worry about." I'd decided not to go with Helen's advice about being beaten up.

"Come this way," she said, ushering me into a large room filled with small brown cubicles. She sat at her desk and examined my file. I took a seat and stared at the carpet. It was industrial grey and spotted with deep coffee stains.

"You don't have any skills."

"No," I replied, wanting to scratch the bandaged hand. This was so humiliating.

"What would you like to do?"

A man in another cubicle looked up from his work. The fluorescent tubes made his skin look green.

"I'm not sure. I don't want to do just anything."

"It's hard to get anything other than menial work when you don't even have Grade Ten," she said, looking at what I'd written down about my education. "Why didn't you finish?"

It felt hot, as if the sun was burning down. "Stuff happened."

The social worker picked up a beige binder and began flipping through the pages.

"What's that?" I asked.

"Possible places for you to look for work. If we're going to give you welfare, we need to know that you're actively involved in a job search."

Welfare. My entire body took another dip in shame. Mom would die all over again. Nobody in our family had ever been on the dole. Not even in the Great Depression.

"Can't you get me a job I'd like?"

"Not without any education." She set the binder down. "Would you have any interest in getting your high school diploma?"

"I don't have any money."

"We'd pay for school, books, room and board. But you'd have to maintain a certain grade."

"Really?" I asked, recalling what Helen said about dreams.

"We're here to help people get back on their feet. And you're only seventeen. You're still a very young woman."

"Would it be high school?" It would be awful sitting in a classroom with fifteen-year-olds staring at me, but I'd do it if I had to.

"Adult education."

"What's that?" I asked.

"Woodsworth College is offering a program called Pre-U."

"Isn't that college associated with the University of Toronto?" I asked. Both Mom, Dad, and even the evil stepmother had gone there. Could I maybe go, too? "When could I start?"

"In order to get in, you need to get a grade point average of eighty."

"I can do that!" I replied, getting excited.

"Then we'll process your paperwork and give you some money to tide you over. But we're going to need your old high school transcripts."

I didn't have them. Dad did. Another door slammed shut.

Helen was busy with a client, Cindy was polishing her toenails, and Lily had gone home early to see Gabe. I pulled off my snow-covered sneakers, looking for something to read. Same old *Hustler*. I threw the magazine on the floor. Ivan leaned out of the wicket shouting for me to pick it up.

"Pick it up yourself. And while you're at it, why don't you buy something new. I've read these ten times."

"You're not getting paid to read. You're getting paid to rub. And since you're slow, go clean the rooms."

"I'm not the cleaning lady."

"I'll pay you!"

My arms were stuffed with used bedsheets and towels. Ivan was right. The rooms were filthy. The doorbell jingled, followed by footsteps. Helen was so mad that I wouldn't call Dad for my transcripts that she refused to speak to me. She didn't understand. Our family was expected to contribute to society, not leech. If you were a leech, you were a failure, should go away and be forgotten. I had no dream like Helen and no way to contribute. At least nothing that was possible.

Ivan shouted up from down below. "You've got a customer!"

Tossing the used linen behind the bed, I fluffed my hair and lit the candles. Maybe it was Jack. I wasn't in the mood, but I needed the money. Maybe Helen had saved hers, but I hadn't because I wasn't perfect like little Miss Helen. Heavy boots pounded down the hall. Luckily, I still had one fresh sheet left.

"I'm in the room at the end," I called.

The sheet billowed, slowly floating down. Through it all—Hermann, standing in the doorway, wearing the same thin smile, thumbs hooked into the top of a shiny PARADISE RIDERS belt buckle. When I tried to run, he kicked the door shut with his boot and grabbed me by the belt, tossing me backwards across the room. My head basket-balled off the glass as I hit the window, landing on the floor. Hermann stood over me, undoing his pants. The buckle dropped to the side.

"You scream and I'll kill you right now."

I cowered, hands over my head. "I never told them anything."

The teeth of the zipper chattered down. Hermann lifted me up by the hair. I held onto his wrist to keep it from tearing out. Then he threw me again, over the bed and into the opposite wall. My face smashed into the red screen, knocking it over as I flew by. Blood filled my mouth.

"I kept my word."

Then Hermann was on me, and I was trapped. He started booting me in the stomach and seized the back of my head. When I tried to pull away, he grabbed it right back. If I screamed, he'd snap my neck. He pulled his dick out of his pants. "Suck it!" He slapped me in the head again and again. "Suck it, you fuckin' dyke."

He drew his hand back, high in the air, fist clenched, about to drive it down, when flames shot up the wall.

The candles had fallen, landing in the pile of soiled bedding. The flames jumped from the cheap cotton sheets and licked up the plywood legs as the bed exploded into a ball of hot fury. It happened so fast, like a barn full of straw. Hermann stepped back as I rolled to my side and up on my feet. Open-armed, he lunged at me, but his loosened pants made him stagger. For a moment he lost his balance, just long enough for me to grab the chair and whack him across the head. Hermann roared but didn't go down, and he ran, head down like an enraged bull. Another wild swing of the chair, but this time Hermann caught it, tossing it into the fire that was quickly consuming the room. The walls and ceiling were aflame, but Hermann didn't care. He just stood with the inferno closing in all around us, laughing. We were going to die this time. There was no way out. The door was on fire and Hermann blocked the window. Sirens sounded and he charged, throwing me onto my back. The ceiling gave way, revealing a splinter of sky. Snow blew in as plaster and joists came crashing down. I rolled out of their way, but the main beam landed on Hermann, knocking him to the floor, pinning him like a butterfly. Jumping up, I instinctively began to tug on the beam, but it was too heavy. Then I heard Helen yell. She was still in one of the rooms. More sirens. The window, the only way out, was getting thick with falling snow.

Hermann reached out and gripped my ankle, trying to pull me into the fire with him. I heard Helen scream again as Hermann's fingers dug in so hard it felt as if the bones were going to break. With my free foot, I kicked him over and over again until he finally let go. Vaulting over the beam, I pushed open the window. As I jumped out, a raging fireball blew in, taking the whole room with it.

Fire trucks and police cars were arriving, their swirling red cherries sending beams of light through the snow. Ivan, the other girls, and their johns were out front, some of them naked, staring up. Helen wasn't with them. I ran across the fire escape toward the light of the last room. The whole building was on fire.

Helen and her john were trapped in a corner. Forcing open the window, I leapt in, snatching a sheet from the bed and another from the floor and soaked them in heavy, slushy snow from the windowsill. Running through the flames, I tossed the man a wet sheet. "Run!" I screamed.

Wrapping himself up, he took off toward the window as the wall behind us collapsed.

"Come on!" I yelled, bundling Helen in the other sheet.

"I can't!" she cried, frozen with fear.

Now the room was more fire than air. There was no time for fear. Grabbing Helen by the waist, I half pulled and carried her through the red-hot and out the window as the other walls disintegrated into flames.

The whole gang sat on the Steps as plumes of water from fire hoses shot into the sky. It was too late to save the building, but they'd stopped the fire from spreading. As an ambulance attendant applied salve and gauze to my arms, I heard a fireman talking to a policeman. They'd found a body inside. Hermann was dead.

"You'll be fine," the attendant said, securing the gauze with a piece of tape. "It's only a slight burn. Just keep it covered."

I already knew that.

He looked at me. "You were really lucky."

Spectators, the so-called good people, stood in the background staring at us. They were so naïve. They had no idea what went on in their city. People talked about Toronto the Good, but I can tell you now that if you had the money, Toronto was a sin city where you could buy almost any kind of kink.

CHAPTER TEN

Helen had gone to the only late-night drugstore for more gauze, but I just wanted to sleep. The cab pulled up at St. Jamestown. I paid the driver and got out. Cindy had just exited the building and was clipping down the sidewalk, lightning-fast for a girl on stilettos, especially when the concrete was slick. I stopped. She didn't slow. In fact, she looked upset.

"You okay?" I asked.

Cindy must have grabbed a cab to tell Lily about the fire.

"I'm late," she replied.

That was weird. Cindy usually chatted. The apartment door was locked. Lily had an open-door policy because Gabe always lost his keys. Digging mine out, I unlocked the door.

The living room was trashed. Lily's prized General Idea photograph lay shattered, face up on the floor. Somebody had taken a knife to it. The blue goo from Helen's lava lamp spattered the white walls and ceiling. Chunks of glass crunched beneath my feet like fallen broken stars.

Lily sat in the centre of the sofa, heating a spoonful of liquid over a candle. A syringe rested on the table beside a bag of white powder. Heroin. She must have gotten it from Cindy. It made no sense. Lily hated drugs. I sat down beside her as she rolled up her sleeve, hands shaking, crying like a little white kitten tossed out in the snow.

"What happened?" I asked, looking around, wondering who would do such a horrible thing.

"Gabe's dead," she sobbed. My body went cold.

"Big Man killed him." Lily set the needle in the spoon. The junk backed up into the syringe, as milky as Gabe's eyes.

"Don't, Lily. Don't do that."

"You understand."

I did.

As I tried to snatch the fit, she just twisted away, holding the syringe as tightly as if it were a dagger. And then she did it. Lily, who never even smoked a joint because she thought it was stupid. Lily shot up heroin. She'd learned how to do it from watching me.

The syringe missed the table and landed on the carpet as Lily fell back. Holding her close, I rocked her back and forth, feeling her body slacken and her breath slow. Getting stoned kills the pain and takes you somewhere else. I thought it was a place better than life, but that was wrong. When you're high, you're cushioned inside a syringe or bouncing around in pill bottles, separated by glass and plastic. Colours are muted, smells seem faint, and feelings don't burn as hot and bright. Drugs don't turn you on; they just turn you down until the lines that uniquely define you simply fade away.

Lily moaned. Kissing her head, I lied, telling her that everything was going to be fine. But that would be up to Lily, just as my choices had been up to me. So, there we sat, while Lily floated in a medicated wonderland, in the middle of the disaster that used to be her perfect home. The home that she'd just destroyed. Why did she do that? I was sick of these secrets and had to know why.

"How did you and Gabe meet?"

Lily lay down, burying her head in my lap. I couldn't see her face— only feel the soft whiteness of that halo of hair.

"He was a friend of my father's."

So, Gabe wasn't her dad.

"What about your mom?"

"I never knew her." Lily took a shallow breath and nodded off, but when she woke up, she started to cry again, and she told me a story that flowed out in jagged bits.

When she was a little girl, maybe three or four, she lived in an apartment somewhere near the ocean. She said she knew this because she remembered the sound of the sea. Gabe lived in the same building and knew her father, and Gabe used to come and visit. Gabe and her father drank and drank and drank, and when that happened, they roared and laughed, but then her father always got mad. He got mad if she spilled her milk. He got mad when she turned on the TV. And then he'd hit her. He hit Lily all the time.

One night, when she accidentally knocked over the ashtray, her father said he didn't want her anymore. Then he opened the window and threw her out. She went high into the sky and flew like a bird until she landed on the pavement and broke her legs. Her father never came down to see what happened, but Gabe did.

She looked up and told me that he picked her up in his arms and ran all the way to the hospital and told her the story of Humpty Dumpty while they braced her legs. Then Gabe took her away.

Lily cried and cried until the room went still. I held her tight. What did they do in that bedroom? What had they done together for all those years? Were they lovers? Friends? I chose to believe Gabe needed a child to call his own and Lily needed a father, because sometimes there's no explaining the unspeakable things we do for love.

The window on the rooming house door was so grimy I could barely make out the tall Victorian staircase that ran up the side. I cranked the bell. Its sound reminding me of the bell on that beautiful blue bicycle I won at the Sterling Fall Fair. What did I call it? I used to name all my favourite things. I cranked the bell again. The Bluebird of Happiness. That was the bike's name. Maybe the win came with a curse. The door handle rattled. Jack opened the door at the same time as the landlady poked her snoopy nose out. She should be cleaning the windows and not spying on her tenants. Jack shot her a look and she disappeared.

"Come on up," he said. I followed him up the rickety stairs, noticing that a step was missing.

After the body rub burned down, Jack rented a room so he could still be close to me. He claimed to love me, but he was just pretending to like me so I would jerk him off. But when I ran out of money, it was back to Jack. I never told Helen, and I never would. We were both supposed to be out of the business. Helen kept hammering at me to contact Dad to get my high school transcripts, but so far, I hadn't. I couldn't make myself. And if I didn't better myself, I knew that Helen would leave me. When I kept pushing the idea of school out of my mind, Helen, and the idea of losing her, kept pushing it back.

Jack lay on his back, one hand running through his hair, while the other stroked his belly, looking all full of himself. Men thought that their orgasms were something the world should take note of. Sitting at a chipped white Arborite table, I lit a cigarette. Jack opened his wallet, took out a red fifty-dollar bill and held it over his head. After a tempting money dance, he released the bill, and it slowly fluttered down onto the bed.

"What's that for?" I asked since Jack had already paid me.

"You know," he replied, patting the bill as I puffed away on the cigarette.

"I already told you that I won't do that," I said, turning away.

"Then open a bottle of Mateus and we'll have a drink."

You had to give Jack points for trying. I liked Mateus. Mostly because, once it was finished, you could turn the bottle into a cool candlestick holder. After popping the cork and filling the glasses, I walked over to the bed, still holding the bottle, and sat down beside him.

"You said that you knew a guy who might have a job in retail," I said, handing him the glass, running my fingers through his hair.

"Why don't you just live here with me?" Jack asked.

No no no no no! There was no way I was playing house with Jack. He'd probably bring his arthritic mother along and I'd have to rub her feet.

"That does sound great, but think of your poor dear mother," I said. "What would she do without you?" I poured more wine. "Besides, we see each other all the time." I kissed his forehead. He smelled of Brylcreem and sweat.

"You're right," he finally admitted and then opened his wallet again, pulling out another fifty-dollar bill. "But I want more." He set the bill on the bed beside the other one.

"No," I replied. "I'm still a virgin."

I thought of Helen and I rolling around on Lily's pull-out every moment we got. Yeah, right. Then again, I was still a virgin, as far as men were concerned.

"Get dressed," Jack said. "Rich should be working."

The bell rang when we opened the door to Slack Shack. The store was located on Bloor Street near Yonge, which meant a lot of foot traffic, and it was built completely out of yellow pine. Every style of jeans and cords were neatly stacked into shelving units, belts dangled from a display by the cash, and shirts and jackets hung on racks. I loved the smell of the place and the sight of all of those jeans. Could I get a discount? A bearded guy, a bit younger than Jack, was standing at the cash.

"Hey, Jack," the guy called out. "Haven't seen you bowling for a bit."

"Been busy," he replied, patting my bum as we walked in. Why did he always pat my butt, as if I were his dog? "This here's Maddy, that nice girl I was telling you about," he said. "This is Rich."

"Very nice to meet you, Rich," I said, wondering if Rich knew that Jack paid for sex. Probably not.

The bell rang again, and another guy wandered in, hanging close to the exit. He reminded me of Dad. Any time Mom got him into a store to shop, he wanted to get right out.

"Do you have any retail experience?" Rich asked.

"Not exactly, but I have worked in a doctor's office, so I'm good at talking to people."

Rich gestured to the reluctant shopper.

"Give it a go."

The man was nervously examining a pile of corduroys, working up his nerve to touch them.

"Hi," I said, walking up. "Time for some new pants?"

"Uh-huh," he replied.

"Would you like some help?" I asked, giving him my best, most helpful smile.

He nodded.

"You look about a size thirty," I said, knowing that he was way bigger than that. I'd watched my mother measure a lot of waists.

"Not with the Molson muscle," he replied with a slight laugh. "I'm a thirty-four."

"I wouldn't have pegged you for that," I answered, and by the time I'd finished, my first shopper went out the door with a pair of jeans, two pairs of cords, two new shirts, and a belt.

"I might be back for that coat," he replied. "You've got a good salesgirl," he added to Rich.

And I had my very first, *very* low-paying genuine job. Jack patted my ass in congratulations. When I patted his in return, both guys looked nearly shocked. Did ass-patting only go one way? That didn't seem right. So, I decided to pat Jack's ass again, adding, "Nice buns."

Gerry had invited Helen and me over to the house for dinner. It was a big brown brick house in the Annex with an enormous horse chestnut tree in the front yard that reminded me of Mom's annual battle with the fallen nuts. I brought along a twelve-pack of Labatt Blue.

"Why did you bring that?" she asked. "They invited us."

"It's a hostess gift," I replied, as a well-muscled, blond guy with a moustache opened the door. He was older than us. Likely mid to late twenties.

"Hi, Helen," he said, giving her a hug, then turning to me. "I'm Tom."

"I'm Maddy."

"And your full name?" he asked, as we walked across the hearth.

"Madeline," I replied. "Maddy is obviously the diminutive."

I rolled my eyes at Helen as we kicked off our shoes.

"I like having educated people in the house."

Now Helen's eyes rolled, topped with a grin. I handed Tom the beer. "Thank you for having us," I said, as we entered the living room, adding, "You have a lovely home."

It was a large room with a sofa, a couple of chairs, a coffee table, and a fireplace that looked like it was regularly used. The walls were all sandblasted red brick. A vase of fresh red tulips rested on the mantelpiece. The dining room stood at the back near a swinging kitchen door. There was even a real stereo system flanked by rows and rows of records. What a great house. A framed poster by an artist named Joan Miró hung on the wall.

"That's a nice piece," I said. "It's great to see female artists getting noticed."

Helen snorted.

"Actually Maddy, he's a Spanish painter and his name is pronounced Juan," Tom said.

Now Helen was laughing. She'd never let me live this down.

"Is that the joyful sound of dykes in the house?" Gerry shouted from the kitchen, walking in wearing an apron covered in red spaghetti sauce. Specks of sauce even dotted his face. Gerry waved a dripping spatula when he saw the beer. "Beer, too! Even better," he said.

"Did somebody say beer?" a deep voice called from upstairs.

"None for you!" Gerry called back. Rapid steps came banging down.

"You leave some for me!" the same voice shouted back.

"I'll grab a bottle opener," Gerry said, tugging two bottles out of the case.

Tom stopped him, disappearing behind the swinging kitchen door, to return with a tray carrying tumblers.

"Let's be civilized," Tom said.

Gerry lunged for the bottle opener and quickly cracked one open. The beer foamed down into a glass. Tom's open bottle sat on the table. Maybe he didn't drink?

Helen copied Gerry. I didn't know what to do.

"Madeline?" Tom asked, handing me a bottle.

"Aren't you having any?" I asked, remembering the Barnes family motto on alcohol.

"I don't drink a lot," Tom said, opening a beer and passing one to me. I hesitated, wondering if maybe flowers would have been a better gift. "But one can't hurt," he added, taking a small sip. "Especially since we might have cause for celebration."

What celebration?

Helen smiled. Gerry drained his bottle and was quickly cracking another when the handsomest man I'd ever seen came flying down the stairs.

"Don't you dare drink them all," said the guy. He had the blackest hair and bluest eyes.

Gerry made a point of draining the second bottle dry. "This is Bruce," he said. "The mentally challenged member of our collective. Bruce, say hello to Maddy."

"Hello. Hi, Helen. Give me a beer," he said to Gerry, who reluctantly tossed him the opener. "I am *not* mentally challenged," he said, sitting down beside Helen, dropping his head on her shoulder. His eyes were such an iridescent blue that they were nearly unnerving. "I'm undergoing primal scream therapy. Are you familiar with it?" he asked me.

After the Joan/Juan fiasco, I wasn't going to embarrass myself again, so I shook my head. Bruce was about to explain when Gerry interjected. "It's for drama queens," Gerry said, adding, "Essentially, Bruce locks himself in his closet and screams about his life. Which I really can't blame him for doing, since Bruce's life is such a mess."

"You're such an asshole," Bruce said. "You offer me no support. Which is what collective living is all about."

"In this instance, I must agree," Tom said.

"Am I not right?" Gerry asked Bruce.

"Primal scream therapy is about accessing memories that trigger intense emotion," Bruce said. "In some ways, it's like reliving the intense fear and horror we associate with our own birth."

"What a load," Gerry said.

Helen was quiet. Tom patted Bruce gently on his shoulder. "I'm very proud of you." Tom acted like a good father.

Was Bruce going to start to cry? Sure looked like it. I didn't remember my birth and wasn't particularly interested in reliving it. What was the point of that? Gerry put on a Moody Blue album while Bruce went out to finish making the salad. Dinner would be ready soon.

Soft classical music played in the background. I think it was Bach. Mom was partial to Bach and Beethoven. She was very proud when I played "Für Elise" for her bridge club and everyone clapped.

"What do you do, Madeline?" Tom asked.

I was chewing a delicious salad and didn't want to speak with my mouth open.

"Maddy works in retail," Helen said.

"Why aren't you in university?" Tom asked.

"That's what I say," Helen added.

"Fat good a degree will do you," Gerry replied, passing me a bowl of vegetarian pasta.

"Gerry's just bitter because even with a master's, he can't make a decent living," Bruce said.

"At least I'm not locked up screaming about it," Gerry replied.

Bruce opened a mouth full of food, flashing it at Gerry.

"You have a master's degree?" I asked, completely forgetting to check my teeth for food. "In what?"

"Social work," Tom replied. "We met at university. Gerry is extremely bright."

"Too bad he's wasting it," Bruce threw in.

"I'm not wasting anything," Gerry replied. "I'm simply following my life's work."

"What's that?" Helen asked.

"I was born to fuck and dance," Gerry said, looking at his watch. "Speaking of which, it's time for me to go out cruising. Shouldn't we get to the matter at hand?"

What was that?

"More pasta, Maddy?" Tom said, passing me the bowl. While the salad was very good, I would have preferred meat in the spaghetti.

"No, thank you, I'm full."

What was the matter at hand? I didn't like surprises anymore since they were never good.

"Helen told us that the two of you were looking for a new place to live," Tom said.

I took Helen's hand. What had she been up to now? When she squeezed my fingers, I squeezed hers back.

"We have one room on the third floor," Gerry said. "Across the hall from mine."

"But you can't make too much noise, and you can never, ever go into my room. I'm an intensely private person," Bruce added.

"Tell that to all the men you've slept with," Gerry said.

"You're just jealous that I trick more than you," Bruce replied.

"In your dreams," Gerry said. Tom broke up the growing argument, turning back to Helen and me.

"But it's only got a single bed."

"That's plenty of room," I blurted out. Helen and I always slept on top of one another anyway.

"What do you think, Maddy?" Helen asked.

"I'd love it," I replied, nearly bursting into tears. I wouldn't be living with a junkie or out on the streets or trying to avoid being bitten by bed bugs or covered in cockroaches in sleazy run-down hotels. I'd be living in a real house with gay men and my Helen.

"How much is the rent?" Helen asked.

"One hundred and fifty a month, and laundry is free."

They had a washing machine? Other than dodgy laundromats, I hadn't so much as seen one since I left home. But since Lily's place was practically free, now I had rent to consider as well. Another cloud, but I didn't care. "When can we move in?" I asked.

"As soon as you'd like," Tom replied.

Helen kissed me. "We can move in right away."

"Now that that's settled, I've got to go," Gerry said, rising to his feet.

"What about the dishes?" Bruce asked him.

"I made the pasta," Gerry replied, heading for the door.

"But I made the salad," Bruce practically bleated.

"And I think we should help with the dishes," Helen said.

"I've got somebody I need to see," I said, walking toward the foyer. "I'll bring our stuff back," I added.

Helen gave me a strange look, then followed Bruce and Tom through the swinging kitchen door as I went out the front.

Lily was walking the streets in Allan Gardens after sunset. Her good fur chubby was ripped, she was wearing a filthy skirt, and she'd dyed her white hair black. An angel in disgrace. Helen could never do this. As tough as she pretended to be, Helen had a soft heart. Mine was harder. While I didn't want to tell Lily either, it had to be done. You didn't just run away and leave messy people like my father had done to me, especially if you'd had a hand in messing them up.

"Lily?" I called.

She didn't hear me, as she'd paused to pick up a discarded butt on the path. After she'd blown off the dirt, Lily pulled a Zippo out of her purse.

"Do you want a fresh one?" I asked upon approach.

Lily turned and smiled. Her skin was sallow, and she was missing a tooth. Sweet Lily. Not even twenty years old and heading for heaven.

"You coloured your hair," I said, handing her the whole pack.

"Do you like it?"

"Sure," I lied, when I wanted to ask why.

"I'm heading home. Want to come with me?" she asked. "We can grab a pizza."

"Let's have a smoke first," I said, sitting on the same bench I had on the night I'd left home, when the cop had found me in the same park. Lily sat down, snuggling into me for warmth.

Lily made floaty O s as she smoked. Mine were long, steady contrails, white lines disappearing into the early twilight air. "I've got to tell you something," I said.

Lily smiled and I thought of all the time we'd spent together. Her, Gabe, and me and I felt sick.

"What is it?" she innocently asked.

"Helen and I are going to move."

She didn't understand. "What?"

"We're moving into a house with gay men," I said.

"Why?"

This was so hard. "Because I want to try to go back to school and the house is closer, that's all."

"But we've been friends for so long," she said, tears gathering.

No wonder Aunt Anne wouldn't allow them in her presence. Allowing them in really hurt. But sometimes you had to feel them, didn't you? "We'll still be friends, Lily. That's not going to change."

What was going to change was that Lily was going to die. I could see it in her face.

"Do you promise?" she asked.

Wrapping her arms around me, she quietly asked, "Why does everybody I love always leave? What am I doing wrong?"

"Nothing, Lily. You've done nothing wrong. I'm just so happy that you're my friend."

In silence, I walked her home and picked up our stuff. When I met Helen back at the collective with two garbage bags full of clothes, I felt it in my chest. Another pain. Another loss. The loss of Lily.

Since I'd left their house, Aunt Bette, myself, and sometimes Tina had been getting together weekly at the Mars Diner on College Street. When I'd first told Aunt Bette that I had a job at Slack Shack, she'd been proud of me, and it felt so good.

"I told your dad," Aunt Bette said, munching on some home fries. Little yellow chickens with happy faces were painted on the walls.

I knew that eventually, she'd tell him that she'd seen me. "Did you tell him about me being sick?" I asked anxiously, even more concerned about the needle marks.

"No. That's between us," Aunt Bette replied.

"What did he say?" I asked, squirting ketchup all over my eggs.

"He was happy to hear about the job." She took a bite of bloody omelette. "And he really wants to see you."

I shook my head. Things were finally going well, and I didn't want my father to mess things up. He might even get Isabel involved. Definite no to that.

"Say, Aunt Bette," I said. "I've moved into this great house. Helen and I have our own room and everything! The guys are all great and have real jobs with the government and selling books." I omitted Bruce. "Once we get settled, would you and Tina like to come over for dinner?"

She laughed. "Let's tie on the feedbag."

Nobody laughed like Aunt Bette. Well, Dad used to, but that was before "My roommates said you're welcome."

"Are they pansies?" she asked.

"You think I'd live with straight men?"

I sure hoped that Aunt Bette wouldn't call them pansies to their faces, but you never knew with Aunt Bette.

"Time and date?" she asked.

"I'll call you. There's only one thing."

"Does it involve money?"

Why did all the adults think I wanted their money? I paused. "My job doesn't pay very much. It'll get better. My boss is talking about making me assistant manager. But yes, it does."

"That's good news about the promotion, but sorry, honey, we just don't have anything to spare."

"I'm not asking you for money. You've already been very good to me."

"Then what?"

"Like I said, until I get a bump in pay, I need to make some extra cash."

Aunt Bette, working her way through the toast, nodded.

"I'm thinking about taking a job as a go-go girl."

"What?" Aunt Bette blurted, spitting out some toast.

"It's totally respectable," I said.

"You'd be naked in a cage?" she sputtered.

If she knew what I was really planning on doing, she'd be shooting the toast through her nose. I didn't really know why I felt the need to even tell Aunt Bette, but this was closer to being honest than I'd ever been about my life in the skin game. This was a roundabout way to get her permission, and it made me feel better about what I was thinking of maybe doing. "No, no, no. It's a very upscale club. I'll be like Goldie Hawn on *Laugh In*. I'll probably have to wear velvet hot pants." I hated hot pants.

"You are almost as pretty as Goldie," Aunt Bette said. "And Tina loves that show. It reminds her of being Queen of the Furrow."

"What?" I asked.

"Tina once won Queen of the Furrow in Rockton. It was a big deal. She was carted around town on a float in a pretty dress and even had a crown." Aunt Bette smiled at the memory. "My Tina even went all the way to Toronto to compete with all the other queens from all the farm fairs across the province. She didn't win, but it's one of her fondest memories."

Aunt Bette approved of that? To me, it was all the same. What was the difference between being Queen of the Furrow compared to being Queen of the Hand Job? It was all so that the farmers, who were men, could stand around and look at you, and the women could judge you. Sure, the Queen of the Furrow was supposed to support agriculture, but wasn't I supporting men's needs too?

"How much does it pay, this go-go dancing?" she asked.

"Three hundred dollars."

Aunt Bette's whistle was so loud that several diners spun on their stools. "That's a lot of money."

"So that means you approve?" I asked.

"Not big on women in cages, but that's good pay. More than I ever made." She resumed chewing toast. "I wouldn't make a career out of it," she added. "But sometimes the need outweighs the way you get there."

I had Aunt Bette's approval.

Then she set down her toast and looked at me. "Maddy, I would consider it a great act of personal kindness to me if you called your father."

I picked up the house phone in the collective's kitchen, trying to work up the nerve to dial. Everyone was seated around the table watching and waiting. Helen had been hounding me to get my transcripts, and now Tom, Gerry, and Bruce were pushing me too.

"Madeline, you're young. You're so bright," Tom said.

"I had the best time of life in school," Bruce added.

"Don't expect to make a lot of money, honey," Gerry said. "But it's time you broadened your mind. You don't want to stay stupid."

I frowned at Gerry. I wasn't stupid. It was life that was stupid. Stupid and unpredictable. The phone was bright red with a long, scrunchy cable that stretched so far that you could even talk in the living room. Not that any of my friends would let me out of earshot. Dialing the number, I began pacing around the kitchen with Helen close behind. A woman's voice answered the phone.

"Dr. Barnes's office." The nurse's voice reminded me of Ruth, and I nearly hung up. "Is anybody there?" she asked.

Helen gave me a sharp prod. She was right. No matter what, I had to get those transcripts. "May I please speak with Dr. Barnes?"

"He's with a patient."

Utter relief and total disappointment—double whammy. "I'll call back."

"Can I tell him who called?"

"It's his daughter."

"Please hold."

The phone struck the desk, followed by voices. A patient must have wandered in. There could be an emergency. You never knew what might happen in a doctor's office. The line clattered.

"Maddy?" Dad asked.

"Yes."

"Are you all right?"

His imagination probably went straight to jail. My voice tightened. Helen's ear was right up to the phone. I pivoted away. She followed, with the guys close behind.

"I'm fine," I replied. No thanks to you, I thought. "Do you have my high school transcripts?"

"They're likely down in the basement somewhere. I'll have to ask your mother."

The curly red cord twisted between my fingers. There was no point correcting him.

"Could you please mail them?" I asked.

"You could come by the house."

Now I was good enough? He didn't want me there before.

"The mail would be easier."

"Why do you want them?" he asked.

"I'm going to go back to school."

A long, slow intake of breath. "That's good news."

My friends watched as I gave him our address.

"I'll post them tonight," he said.

"Thanks, Dad."

I was about to hang up when he suddenly blurted out, "Why don't you meet me for dinner instead?"

No. No. No.

"We could go to the Inn on the Park."

Not there.

"I think the mail …"

"For dear old Dad?"

There it was—his sweet voice. And I just couldn't say no.

The bus roared through Leaside, past suburban backyards, snow-covered jungle gyms, shopping malls, kids dragging toboggans up distant hills, and parents waiting in cars, while I tried to keep the memories of Mom, Dad, Sterling, and the boys locked in the silo where I'd hidden them so long ago. I never planned to let them out, and now here I was with the key in my hand, hurtling back into the pain all over again.

The Inn appeared at the top of the hill in the distance, a large luxury hotel surrounded by acres of parkland. Mom said you could go for beautiful walks in the spring and summer, but I'd only been there once in the winter when the world was white. The bus driver called out, "Eglinton." I rang the bell, opened the door, and stepped into the snow, heading up the long, winding drive to the Inn.

Dad hadn't arrived. There was a bitter chill. I buttoned up the top collar on my coat and sat on a bench beneath the snow-covered awning. The bellhop kept giving me odd looks and I was worried he might ask me to leave. A little girl, dressed for a fancy evening, walked past me with her parents. She wore a red coat, matching hat, and gloves with black patent leather shoes, strutting proudly between them, holding onto their hands as if she were a princess.

"Swing me!" she cried. Her mother leaned down, telling her to hush, while her father gave her a tickle.

"Pick me up and swing me!" And so they did, and she laughed as the bellhop bowed and opened the glass doors as the family disappeared inside.

Mom and Dad had brought me here. It was New Year's Eve, and we were dressed in our best. I had a new maroon velvet dress, Mom wore a long black gown and a mink stole, and Dad looked dashing in his tux. The maître d' had ushered us in, past the other patrons. Nobody looked as handsome as my family. Heads turned as everyone wondered who that perfect family was. I was so proud—these two grown-ups were my mom and dad. We took our seats and the waiter handed me my own menu— not a kids' menu, but an adult menu.

"Thank you," I said, opening it.

Mom asked the waiter what he would recommend and smiled at Dad.

"I'd recommend the French onion soup," the waiter said.

A man coughed. "Well then, that's what I'll have," I replied, closing my menu. I was only eight and thought I was all grown up. I was so wrong.

"Madeline." Dad stood in front of me in his long overcoat with the fedora tilted back, hands thrust deeply into his pockets. We stared at each other for a second that felt like a million years. "I've booked us a reservation."

I rose. We didn't hug or kiss. It wasn't until we shook hands that I noticed he was trembling, too.

We followed the maître d' through the restaurant, past tables of well-dressed diners to a cozy table for two by the window. My heart pounded while I wiped palm sweat on my jeans. Dad left his coat and fedora at the coat check, but I hung mine on the back of my chair in case I had to run. Looking out the window, I noticed the frozen fountain standing in a wide, shallow pool covered in layers of ice and remembered.

"Teddy, we shouldn't be drinking champagne," Mom said, trying to snatch the flute from his hand.

"Nonsense." He moved it higher, out of her grasp. "A sip won't hurt."

Beaming up at the waiter, Dad handed me the flute. The champagne bubbles burst as they struck the side of the glass. The three of us were standing outside by the frozen fountain listening as the band inside played "Auld Lang Syne." Dad had insisted on the champagne, and he'd also insisted that we go outside to ring in the New Year. I could see Mom's breath. "Auld Lang Syne" suddenly came to a halt and the drum began to beat out the countdown as the bandleader called, "ten … nine … eight … seven …" Mom slipped her arm into Dad's, with me right in between them. She shivered, squeezing us tight. The bandleader kept going. "Three," he called. The flute felt cold in my hand. "Two … one …" Mom kissed Dad's cheek and smiled at him. "HAPPY NEW YEAR!" And horns honked, and streamers flew, and voices rang out in the night. Dad turned and kissed Mom right on the lips, in a deep way I'd never seen before.

Then they bent down and kissed me. Mom's cheeks were flushed, and she looked radiant. Dad raised his glass to the stars that were more plentiful than the bubbles in my glass and declared that our family was going to have a stellar year—no, he wanted to go further than that. He wanted to toast our future, certain that it would be bright and that we'd have the happiest and the very best of lives.

Dad set a manila envelope on the table beside him. They had to be my transcripts.

The maître d' handed us each a menu. "Can I have the waitress get you anything to start?"

"A coffee, please," Dad replied.

He didn't need the caffeine.

"Coke," I ordered, thinking we both needed hot milk.

Scanning the entrées, I was unsure of what to order. If it was too expensive, he might think I was greedy. Peeking up from the menu, I noticed that a lot of Dad's hair was gone, and he'd put on a fair bit of weight. But even with the extra weight he looked good. Toronto agreed with him. Toronto and Isabel. As if reading my mind, he pulled a comb out of his pocket and absentmindedly brushed at the remaining black strands. The waitress arrived, set down our drinks, and asked Dad if we were ready to order.

"French onion soup," Dad said, looking at me. "If that's all right with you."

My fingernails dug into the white linen. He'd remembered.

"Same for me."

"How are you keeping?" he asked.

"Fine."

I couldn't breathe. Please give me the transcripts. A table of diners near the front started to laugh. I thought of the last time we were here and how happy we had been. The difference between then and now was so stark, as if the world might tip and I'd fall off.

"Aunt Anne was asking about you."

"How is she?"

"Fine."

"That's good." I looked around the dining room. "Are those my transcripts?"

Dad nodded. My hand reached out, but his fingers dented the envelope. He wasn't letting it go. Not yet.

"Tell me about this school of yours."

Picking up my fork, I flicked it up and down to feel its weight. It was good silver. "It's adult education, to finish off my high school."

"How are you affording it?" he asked.

The napkin to the left of the silverware had INN embossed in raised black letters. Shaking it out, I watched the white linen drift down into my lap. Why did I owe him an explanation? Why should I feel so guilty when all I wanted was to go to school? Maybe I was a dirty little speed-freak dyke, and, yeah, I'd done a lot of incredibly stupid and dangerous things, but I started doing them because I wanted him to notice that I was still alive and needed him. He was the adult and should have done a better job. They all should have.

"I don't think it's really any of your concern," I replied, trying to sound as respectful as I could. "And I don't expect you to pay for it."

Dad looked at me over the cup of coffee. Waves of liquid rolled back and forth in the white china cup, tossing up splashes of black onto his tie.

"Is it legal?"

Of course, he'd ask that.

"Yes."

The waitress arrived and set down the soup. A hard crust of cheese floated on the top. I poked at it with my spoon as the cheese rocked back and forth. When my spoon broke through the crust, steam billowed.

"You look well," he said.

"You mean better than last time."

The waitress returned, asking if everything was to our liking. Dad smiled and said something funny. She laughed. He could still be so charming. After she left, Dad methodically unfolded his napkin and placed it on his lap. He looked up at me. "We had a conversation."

"Who?" I knew who.

"Isabel and I."

"About what?" I knew that, too, but I wanted him to say it. I dipped my spoon into the thick soup, quickly brought it up to my lips and swallowed. The liquid singed my tongue.

"About why you left home."

So, Isabel told Dad about the deal. Points for the wicked stepmother. I didn't know what to say, so I didn't say anything. Forgiveness was so far off I couldn't even see it on the horizon. Dad took a delicate sip of soup. He ate with great care, the same way he practiced medicine. Why didn't he treat me like that? I dipped my spoon into the soup again, more cautious this time.

"I wish you'd told me," he said.

I wanted to ask him what he would have done, but there was no point. He was too weak. Granddad was right. Stirring my soup and watching bits of onion swirling in the cheese, I thought about what a coward he was. He'd left me all alone to fend for myself. I took another sip.

No, that wasn't the truth. This was the man who drove through blizzards to deliver babies, who dragged car-accident victims out of flaming wrecks, who had run up onto a beam in the middle of the night to save me. My father wasn't weak. He didn't throw me away because of the drugs and the girls. It was something else.

I set the spoon down. "Why did you bring me here?"

He stared back at me. "I don't know."

Yes, he did, and suddenly, so did I. He brought me because he missed Mom just as much as I did and he missed me as much as I missed him, but every time he saw me all that pain came back. For both of us. It wasn't about lack of love. That was never the problem. There had always been love, maybe too much love, because there was too much pain. Pain that drove me into the dispensary and out onto the streets. Pain that made Dad tie his belt to the light fixture and step off the side of the tub.

He'd stopped talking. I wanted to ask about Frank and Tedder, but I couldn't. I'd finally crawled onto firmer ground, and I couldn't afford to lose my footing. Watching Lily get lost in junkie land, I saw how close I'd come to the edge and how it didn't take much to fall off. Finishing my soup, I set the sterling silver spoon into the white bowl. "Can I have my transcripts, please?"

Dad pushed the manila envelope across the white linen. Thanking him, I folded it and put it in my pocket. He wanted to stay for dessert, but I said it was time for me to leave.

Walking through the snow, back to the bus stop, I thought of him. Of the two of us. All the time we spent together making house calls, hanging out in his office helping with the patients, poring over new car magazines together while dreaming of Cadillacs, the time he fixed my painful ingrown toenail in a way that didn't hurt. Yes, my father had abandoned me, but I knew that he loved me. Even now. I could tell.

After cranking the bell, the landlady finally let me in.

"How may I help you?" she asked, a clean duster in hand. There was still plenty of dirt. The duster was all for show.

"I'm here to see Jack," I replied.

"I'm not sure he's home."

"His car is parked out front. Can I please go up? He's expecting me."

That was a lie. I'd come to see Jack because I was desperate to see him. Seeing Dad was really upsetting, and I was afraid to go home. Yes, I had the transcripts, but I was already behind a month in rent. Helen had covered my costs, but she wouldn't be able to do it again. And then I'd be out. Again.

"Well, I don't know ..." the landlady replied. "This is a respectable house."

"And I'm a respectable person," I said.

She crossed her arms. I crossed mine.

"Jack!" I called.

"No yelling in my establishment," she insisted.

I shouted, "Jack!"

He appeared at the top of the stairs. I almost turned and ran, but suddenly he stood right beside me, turning to the landlady. "Why don't you mind your own business?" he said, taking me by the arm.

In a huff, the landlady vanished into her room.

"I wasn't expecting to see you until later," Jack said, opening a bottle of Mateus. He must have bought a case of the stuff. When I gulped down a glass, he filled it up again.

"This is a nice surprise," he said. "What's up?"

When I quickly finished the second glass, he immediately topped it up. I knew he was curious.

"Nothing," I replied, trying to settle my nerves. The wine helped. Sitting down on the bed, I asked him to join me, and when I rested my hand on his thigh, the penis moved. Jack's wallet was resting behind him on the bed. How much was in there? How much was my virginity worth?

"I was just thinking," I said, my hand creeping up his leg toward his crotch and making the penis jump, while keeping my eye on the wallet.

He kissed me on the cheek, turning my chin, making us eye to eye. I could see his want. Pure desire. I had deep desires, too: Helen, a house with a new family, maybe even school—and the only way to get it was to sell my body.

"A few months back," I said, starting to falter already.

Jack tried to kiss my lips, but I turned my face. This wasn't about kissing. I had never kissed one of my johns and I wouldn't start now. That would always belong to Helen and only to her.

"What do you want, Maddy?" he softly asked.

Staring at the floor with my hand still resting on his thigh, I quietly said I needed money.

"What for?" he asked.

"To improve my life," I replied, briefly remembering Grandmother Barnes, my mother, and the importance of good standing.

Jack took my chin and gently turned my face back toward his. I only saw hope and desire and maybe even love. Maybe it looked the same in reverse. I had come to love Jack in my own way. He'd always held me whenever I'd cried. Jack wasn't as old as Dad, but he'd always given me unconditional love no matter what I'd done, and was always there whenever I needed him.

"How much?" he asked.

"Three hundred dollars."

He picked up the wallet, slowly opened it and counted out six red bills. "Is this enough?" he asked.

Trying to hide a deep sadness that no words could ever describe, I nodded and tried to smile. When Jack removed two more fifties and slowly began to undo the buttons of my shirt, I closed my eyes.

CHAPTER ELEVEN

The house was filling up with Christmas party guests. The table was set for twelve. Candles cast flickering light around the room. We'd borrowed chairs from the neighbours and cut small boughs of spruce from the tree in the backyard, wrapped them in red ribbon and covered the table and mantlepiece with them. Tom had bought a real Christmas tree that we'd all decorated together. Bruce was running around like the crazy man he was, making a huge salad.

"I said balsamic vinegar!" he barked, handing me back red wine vinegar. I had so much to learn about cooking and knew I never would.

Helen pulled a bottle down from a cupboard, handing it to Bruce.

"You'd better start learning, given that you're starting school next month," he said, as I put the vinegar back.

I wasn't sure where it really belonged. There were so many spices and sauces in our kitchen. Even Mom wouldn't have known what they all were, and she had a degree in home economics. School. School was starting in less than a month and I was counting the hours. Tom had given me a raft of books to read, and I'd devoured them all as quickly as they appeared. As a collective, we'd been discussing Hermann Hesse. One life, two Hermanns. Sipping a beer, I looked around the living room. The only smell missing was the scent of Mom's nuts and bolts toasting in the oven.

Somebody rang the front bell. I heard Gerry happily call out, "Old dykes in the house!"

I ran out to welcome Aunt Bette and Tina while Gerry kept singing out, "Old dykes!" They'd been regular visitors for a couple of months and every Sunday we had pot roast dinner like a good family should, and now I was part of another family. Finally, after so very long, I felt genuinely happy, safe, and full of hope. Both women were covered in snow. Aunt Bette kicked off her motorcycle boots. Gerry was putting his coat on, determined to pull a quick trick before dinner.

"Who are you calling old?" Aunt Bette asked, brushing snow from her hair.

"Let's say well-seasoned," Gerry said.

"Don't you ever worry about catching a venereal disease?" Tina asked, as she kissed him on the cheek, pulling a toque down tightly over his head. Uncontrollable red curls bounced out.

"I'm invincible," Gerry said, kissing Aunt Bette on the neck. As she shooed him out the door, Gerry called back, "Maddy, you've got mail."

A letter rested on the table inside the foyer. It was from a clinic I'd visited. I'd put on a bit of weight and wondered if my thyroid was overactive. Dad had always advised being proactive and I wasn't going to let anything interfere with school. Laughing voices rang out from inside the living room. Bing Crosby was singing "White Christmas." Tina sat down to pull off her boots as I tore open the letter. It was the result of the blood test. Aunt Bette, standing behind me, heard me gasping. I didn't have an overactive thyroid. No. My disease was called pregnancy.

Aunt Bette shut the foyer door. Jack had promised he'd pull out in time. I slid down the wall, head in my hands. He hadn't. Then I remembered I hadn't had my period for two months, but I hadn't even considered I might be pregnant. I'd never been regular, and I'd been so skinny with all the drugs, that I'd just never thought …

"It's all over," I said, breaking into tears. "Everything." I would lose Helen. I would lose my new family. They would all kick me out. More tears.

Aunt Bette and Tina had dropped down beside me and were trying to wrap their arms around me, but I pushed them away.

"It's over," I repeated, slapping my own head again, even harder this time. How had I let this happen?

"Maddy, settle down," Aunt Bette said, wrestling me into a hug. "It's not over," she said.

Tina was hugging me on the other side. "We'll figure something out," she said.

"Like what?" I asked through the tears. "I can't go to school now."

"Calm down," Tina said.

"It's true! Helen won't want me. Neither will my friends, and you'll leave, too," I sobbed, "and I'll deserve it."

I slapped my head again, hard, wanting to make it hurt. I was so stupid and careless and now a baby—a baby!

"You've never deserved any of this," Aunt Bette said, grabbing my hands. "And we won't leave you," she said, kissing my cheek. "I promise."

"There are ways around this Maddy," Tina said, softly kissing the other cheek.

"There's no way," I said miserably.

"Yes, there is," Aunt Bette said.

"How?"

"I don't know right now, but we'll fix it," Aunt Bette said.

"Really?" I asked, and when they both nodded, some of the sheer panic began to settle, and a part of me chose to sort of believe them. "Can I maybe still go to school?" I asked.

"Of course. Have some faith, girl," Aunt Bette said, squeezing me. "We're a family, and we'll see this through together."

Tom shouted in the background. "Dinner's ready!"

Other voices called for us to hurry. Inside the voices, I felt something bubble within me. Was it promise? When I looked at Aunt Bette and Tina, I saw hope—a way out.

Was I ready?

Prepared for this?

I thought of my father. My mother.

Placing my hands on my belly, I thought of Mom and Dad. I knew I was strong. I knew I was capable. And I guess that's about as ready for life as you can ever be.

Montreal Publishing Company publishes works of poetry, drama, fiction, and non-fiction. We seek writers that dare, and make us think—reconsider.

Relevance without fear.
Montreal Publishing Company
montrealpublishing.com

Thank you for reading, *Maddy.*
Should you wish to include it in your book club, get in touch, and let's see what we can help you with.

info@montrealpublishing.com

If you'd like to leave a review, that would be most appreciated, and you can do that here:

Goodreads

If you'd like to keep up with what's going on with Cathi Bond, she can be found at:

cathibond.com

www.ingramcontent.com/pod-product-compliance
Lightning Source LLC
Chambersburg PA
CBHW061115310726
48974CB00002B/548